Chasing After You

RECKLESS LOVE
BOOK ONE

LAUREA MATTHEWS

Bad At Love Duology

1. *Little Do You Know*

2. *Almost*

Reckless Love Series

1. *Chasing After You*

2. *Before You*

3. *Ruined By You*

Wilder Wolves Series

1. *Cold As Ice*

The Characters

The ages in this character list are accurate at the start of Chasing After You, but please keep in mind while reading that birthdays do take place, and the ages will change throughout this book.

<u>THE WALKERS</u>
Sebastian Walker (49) & Thalia Lewis (47)
Mirabelle ~ 20
JJ ~ 18
Hunter ~ 17
Bailey ~17

<u>THE LEWISES</u>
Owen Lewis (49) & Blake Morgan (48)

<u>THE PRICES</u>
Chris Price (49) & Penelope Baudelaire (47)
Henry ~ 25
Kaitlyn ~ 17
Henry's mother is Allison Moore from Chris's previous marriage

Prologue

MIRABELLE

I didn't mean to fall in love with Henry Price.

Does anyone ever choose to fall in love? Sometimes I wonder if that's why they call it *falling* in love. No one ever means to fall down—you trip, lose your balance, or maybe someone pushes you, but it's not something anyone chooses to do.

So . . . yeah. I fell in love with Henry, while quite literally falling, as I chased after my family's new puppy and busted my knee open on a rock hidden in the grass. My knee started bleeding immediately, and I freaked out as five-year-olds do when their leg has blood running down it, especially ones with a phobia of blood.

And then Henry appeared, offering me a hand like a white knight to help me up. He pulled his shorts up on one side, showing me the white indented scar on his knee that was nearly identical to the bloody mess on mine.

"Maybe we'll have matching ones," he said, and I forgot about the blood and how much it hurt, because Henry Price was smiling at me. One of his front teeth was missing after he knocked it out playing football with our dads.

That was the moment my fate with Henry was set in stone, and I prayed we would have matching scars on our knees. *Spoiler alert: we do.*

Honestly? Looking back, my feelings were inevitable.

Our parents were best friends, so Henry was everywhere all the time. My little heart thought it was a perfect fairytale. Despite being five years older than me, Henry never made me feel like I wasn't important. In my mind, there was never another option. Henry Price and Mirabelle Walker together forever, matching scars and all.

If I could do it all over again, I would, because that moment turned into me spending the next fifteen years chasing after *you*.

CHAPTER ONE

Mirabelle

"Bailey! You cut me off," I yell after my seventeen-year-old brother, wading through the water as I carry my surfboard under my arm.

He flips his shoulder length blond hair back, shooting me an infuriating grin over his shoulder. "Try paddling faster next time. I thought you were an Olympian."

"Gymnastics—not surfing." I throw my middle finger in the air at him as I feel the shells dig into the bottom of my feet. "*Imbécile,*"[1] I mumble under my breath. I can't believe we're related.

My dad is throwing passes for JJ, my eighteen-year-old brother, as he practices his footwork to get ready for his freshman year of college starting in a few weeks. "Dad, did you see what Bailey did?" I complain, catching his attention after he throws a perfect spiral for JJ.

He laughs deeply, glancing in my direction as I set my board in the sand, quickly undoing the leash from my ankle.

---

1. Idiot.

"I'm not getting in between the two of you—figure it out yourselves."

"He stole my wave," I continue, ignoring his answer.

"Mira, I can't do anything about it." He shrugs, shaking his head, the streaks of silver in his dark hair reflecting in the sunlight.

Is he kidding me? Dad could absolutely do something if he wanted to. "Well, you could ground him." *Okay, I might be taking this a bit far, but come on.* That's the second time today he pulled that shit, and it's annoying.

"Stop whining, Mirabelle. Dad's not going to ground me because you're butt hurt," Bailey taunts, taking off his own leash.

"Then stop dropping in on my waves if you're going to tag along with me. It's annoying."

He rolls his green eyes. "Explain to me how I'm tagging along when it's our beach?"

Hunter comes strolling down the stairs from the house, a water bottle in each hand. "What are you guys fighting about now?"

"How do you know we're fighting?" I ask, crossing my arms over my chest. Dad snorts as Hunter throws him a water.

"That's like asking if the sky is blue," Hunter replies, tossing me the other bottle.

Hunter and Bailey are identical twins, the only difference between them is Hunter's blond hair is cut short like JJ's dark hair. It's annoying how all three of my brothers inherited our mother's piercing green eyes, whereas I only got my blonde hair from her. Aside from Dad's height and build, the twins look exactly like Mom.

"*Dad.*"

Dad simply smiles at us, running a hand through his salt and pepper hair. "Sorry, figure it out."

JJ jogs over from where he was standing to join the conversation, the ball tucked into his arm as he towers over me. I'm a month shy of being two years older than him, and I know it might seem strange to other people, but he's my best friend. There's a light sheen of sweat on his forehead that he wipes off with the back of his hand, his green eyes twinkling. "What's happening with Mira's face?"

"Mira's face looks like that because she's complaining I stole her wave that wasn't even her wave. Hunt came out to give us water, then you walked over," Bailey recites like the smart-ass he is. *Is it considered violence if I kick him?*

"It *was* my wave."

"Was your name on it?"

I open my mouth to retaliate when Dad interrupts, "Guys, come on, don't make me be an adult. Mirabelle, Bailey's right —you can't put your name on the ocean because it's a living thing. Bailey, don't cut your sister off again. I don't believe for a second that you didn't know she was taking it. You could have both gotten hurt if you collided and then your mother would have murdered me, so maybe for the sake of my life, we don't repeat this."

"I'm going to shower. Maybe you won't be such a crybaby by the time I'm done," Bailey says, sticking his tongue out at me as Dad rolls his eyes.

I think I hate him. I love Bailey, but right now, I think I hate him.

JJ tosses the football to Hunter, who grins. Aside from JJ's freshman year of high school, this upcoming season will be the first time they won't be on the same team together. He's leaving for Beaumont University in California in a week, and I'm not ready for my best friend to be on the other side of the country.

Hunter waits for JJ to take off down the beach before throwing the ball for him, turning to face us. "Oh, by the way,

Mom wanted me to tell you guys Penelope and Chris are on their way over with Henry and Kaitlyn for dinner."

My annoyance with Bailey immediately fades at the prospect of seeing Henry. I didn't think I'd see him for at least another week. His best friend, Andrew, was traded to the Serpents for their wide receiver, and Henry went to help him move. "I didn't realize he was back from Seattle already," I say, trying to sound nonchalant, when in all actuality, my whole body feels like it's coming alive.

Henry is one of my favorite people in the entire world.

I've also had a teeny, tiny crush on him for about as long as I can remember. My crush is a small detail, though. Not important in the grand scheme at all.

He's simply a tall, dark-haired, ruggedly handsome quarterback with a sleeve of Greek mythology tattoos who somehow manages to get hotter every time I see him.

No big deal.

"He got back yesterday. Owen told me about the meeting he had with the front office and Henry this morning," Dad answers easily. It doesn't surprise me he knows this. It's only been five months since he retired from the NFL after a legendary career, setting the record for the oldest player to retire at forty-nine after winning eight of the twelve Super Bowls he took the Panthers to. Dad's been doing his best, alongside my Uncle Owen, the Panthers' head coach, to help get Henry ready for his first season as QB1.

My heart spazzes in my chest because I can't believe I'm arguing out here about this wave when I should be running inside to get ready before Henry arrives. "I'm going to shower too," I say nonchalantly, or about as nonchalant as I can get.

My hair is a complete tangled mess right now, despite the braid I have it pulled back into, from all the salt in the water and the North Carolina humidity. There is absolutely no way

I'm showing my face around Henry looking like I just crawled out of a swamp. *Maybe that's a bit of an exaggeration, but still.*

I carry my surfboard up the stairs, setting it on the wraparound porch of the beach house my parents now live in full-time since Dad's retirement. The twins didn't care about staying in Charlotte for their senior year since the school they're transferring to is the same one Kaitlyn goes to.

I start my sports public relations internship in Charlotte a few days after JJ moves, so the plan is for me to stay at the house there since my parents aren't ready to sell it. However, since graduation in May, I've spent every day on this beach. It's been great, but I'm ready to have a purpose again.

It's been almost four years since the Olympics, and I spent the last three years at Duke trying to figure out what the next step is. I won the all-around individual gold medal, and Team USA earned the all-around team gold. After winning gold medals from the highest-ranking sports competition, it makes everything else pale in comparison.

But who knows? Maybe I'll fall in love with this internship.

The fact it's with the Charlotte Blue Panthers—*coincidentally the same team Henry plays for*—had no impact on my decision to take it.

No impact at all.

~

I've taken way longer than necessary to get ready. I'm wearing a black sundress, my long blonde hair has naturally waved after towel drying it, and my moisturizer gives my tan skin a healthy glow.

I look in the mirror, giving myself a reassuring smile.

You can do this. Just don't let Bailey antagonize you into a petty fight in front of him, and maybe Henry will finally see that I'm twenty instead of ten. The key tonight is to not fight with my brothers. Kaitlyn and the twins are the same age, and have been best friends their entire lives, so hopefully that will keep Bailey distracted. JJ tries to have my back to keep me from acting like a fool in front of Henry, but there's only so much he can do.

The rest is up to me to keep my short temper in check. I think there's a better shot of aliens falling from the sky than that happening, but I'm going to try.

I know it's wishful thinking that Henry will finally see me the same way I've always seen him, but I'm not ready to give up.

Shit, does that make me pathetic?

I pull my hair over one shoulder, making my way downstairs. I'm definitely the last one down, but better late than never.

Don't fight with Bailey. That's my mantra for the night. I can't forget it.

Penelope beams at me when she spots me, her dark hair now cut short since the last time I saw her. "I swear you get prettier every time I see you."

Well, damn. If that doesn't do something for my ego. I hug her tightly. "You're the best."

Chris laughs, attracting my attention. "What? I don't get a hug too?" I smile at him, hugging him next before taking a seat on the other couch.

It's only been a couple of weeks since I've seen them, but they go to France a couple times a year to visit Penelope's family. She met my mom there during her year abroad in college, and they've been friends ever since.

Mom walks into the living room with two glasses and a bottle of white wine. "I was beginning to wonder if you were ever coming down," she teases, smiling as she sits down next to me.

"My hair was super knotted after surfing today. It took half a bottle of detangler to get it out," I say, groaning. *Just kidding, I was preparing myself to see Henry.*

"The boys are down by the water with Kaitlyn looking for shark teeth from that storm yesterday, but you're more than welcome to hang up here with us adults."

"Where's Dad?" I ask, looking around, noting that he and Henry are both absent from the room. It's less weird if I ask where Dad is, though.

She pours the wine into the glasses, passing one to Penelope. "Still in the kitchen. Henry wanted to talk to him about football. I'm sure they'll be out here in a couple of minutes."

"Gotcha," I say, curling my legs under me.

"Mira, are you ready for your internship with the Panthers? When do you start?" Chris asks, smiling proudly at me.

"Two weeks," I say. "I'm free a little bit longer, and then I'm a working woman with the rest of the population."

Penelope shakes her head, her face scrunching in mild disgust. "Work is overrated."

Mom laughs, her eyes sparkling with amusement. "Pen, we're literally in business together, you can't say that." Penelope helped Mom open her first gallery in Charlotte, and since then, they've opened locations in Paris and New York. When Mom isn't showcasing her own work, she rents out the gallery space to up-and-coming artists to give them an opportunity to get their work out there.

"And? Your daughter has already accomplished more than the three of us in this room combined, and she's only *twenty*. She got Bash's work ethic, and your stubbornness. Personally, I think Mira should travel the world, not be stuck in some office job," Penelope continues, taking a large sip of her wine. This is why Penelope is one of my favorite people in the world. She's like my own personal hype squad.

"I want to work," I insist. When I wasn't at the gym, I spent the rest of my childhood traveling with Mom to all the corners of the world. She's kind of a badass. Marrying my dad, she didn't have to work, but she wanted to have her own identity apart from him, and I've always respected her for it.

"How was surfing today?" Mom asks, redirecting the conversation.

"It was good, I caught some good waves. I think I'm going to go out early in the morning."

Dad picks that moment to walk in, his amber eyes full of laughter. "Just make sure you don't wake up Bailey. I'd hate for him to steal another one of your waves," he teases, sitting down on the other side of Mom, his hand falling to rest on her knee.

My rebuttal sticks in my throat as Henry walks in the room. His lips quirk upward into an amused smirk as he looks at me. "You two still fighting with each other all the time?" *He's smiling at you, don't make a fool of yourself.*

"No," I protest quickly, my cheeks flushing in embarrassment. "Not all the time—just when he's being an annoyance."

"So all the time," Henry says, laughing.

"Pretty much. Believe it or not, it is nice having all of them under the same roof again, at least for the next week," Dad says as Mom groans.

"Speak for yourself, we never have any hot water. I love my kids, but I'm excited to take a hot shower again. You didn't give Chris this much trouble, did you?" she asks, eyeing Henry.

"I never used all the hot water if that's what you're asking," he replies with an easy smile, crossing his arms over his chest. I don't think he intended for the movement to show off his muscles, but now I'm wondering what it would be like to have him hold me with them. My eyes go straight to his sleeve, an intricate collection of black artwork. I used to think I didn't like tattoos until Henry started getting them, but then again, Henry could do just about anything, and I'd probably end up liking it.

I'm hopeless.

"No, you just spent every waking minute eating, sleeping, and breathing football to attend Duke and get drafted," Chris says, but his proud smile says it all. "Bash, I think you hijacked my kid. Instead of following in my footsteps, he's a quarter-back like you."

The thing about Henry is that my parents adore him. They're his godparents, and they've always loved him like he was one of us. I remember when Henry was in high school, he went to a party and ended up wasted. His designated driver bailed, so he called my mom. She drove out to get him, leaving me in charge of my brothers, since Dad was out of town for an away game. After letting him stay in the guest room, Mom chewed him out but then hugged him, telling him she was glad he called her.

The day Henry was drafted to the Panthers, my dad was so proud I think he shed a few tears along with Chris.

Dad shrugs, putting his hands up in self-defense. "That's exactly how I felt when JJ decided he liked being the one to block or run the touchdown in more than being the one throwing it. Owen hyped up the glory of a tight end so much there was no way I could change his mind. Thank goodness I still have a chance with Hunter."

Mom jabs an elbow into his side. "Not all of our sons need to become professional football players, Sebastian. I think you're trying to give me a heart attack. Mirabelle gave us enough scares when she was on the uneven bars."

She's not wrong. The uneven bars were my favorite part of gymnastics because I felt like I was flying. Dad used to call me his little monkey because I hated being on the ground instead of up in the air somewhere.

The back door opens, and all three of my brothers spill in, with Kaitlyn right behind them, asking a chorus of questions fitting for three starving teenage boys.

JJ plops down on the other side of me, even though he's probably dying to ask Henry to throw the football with him. JJ idolizes Henry. Everyone in my family thinks Henry walks on water, including me.

"You look nice," Henry comments, and I shrug, trying to play it off.

"I always look good."

Chris hears me, snorting. "Jesus, how much time do you spend with your uncle? Next thing we know, you'll be talking to yourself in the mirror."

Oops. They don't need to know I already do that.

"Definitely too much time with Owen, but it's okay. We love her anyway." Mom smiles warmly at me as I return it. Dad grabs her hand, subtly threading their fingers together, not skipping a beat in his side conversation with Henry at all.

I want that.

I want a love like my parents have.

My gaze slides over to Henry as Hunter asks him a question about this upcoming season. Henry's hazel eyes are bright as he laughs, and the butterflies in my stomach go crazy at the sound. Almost as if he can feel me staring at him, his attention flits to me for a brief moment, and he offers me a slight smile before redirecting back to my brother.

JJ bumps my leg with his, breaking my concentration on Henry. I turn away from him completely to ask Kaitlyn if she's excited for her senior year of high school, hoping no one noticed that I was staring at Henry in the first place.

CHAPTER TWO

Mirabelle

THE WAVES LAP AT MY LEGS FROM WHERE I'M sitting on my surfboard, watching the sky turn pink from the rising of the sun. Surfing first thing in the morning is one of my favorite things to do. It's helped fill the hole in my heart that retiring from gymnastics left.

I successfully didn't wake Bailey up this morning, stepping lightly around all the known creaks in the floor. I spent the entire night tossing and turning as Kaitlyn crashed with me, and Henry slept in one guest bedroom while Chris and Penelope stayed in the other. It was probably the worst night of sleep I've had all summer, knowing he was just down the hall.

Dinner went better than I expected, but that was probably because Bailey and I were sitting on opposite ends of the table. I was pretty proud of myself for that accomplishment.

I rest my hands on top of the cool water as my board bobs upward with a gentle wave. I don't always get the best waves at this time, but even just sitting out here on the water helps me start the day on the right foot. Some days, I need all the help I can get.

"Mind if I join you?"

I jump half out of my skin, nearly falling off my board. Henry laughs behind me at my reaction, and I press a hand to my chest, trying to calm my heart rate from the jump scare. "You scared the shit out of me." I exhale as my heart starts returning to its normal rhythm—or as normal as it can get around him.

"I can see that. Sorry, didn't mean to scare you," he says, flashing me a stupid smile that doesn't slow my heartbeat at all.

"Well, you did. What are you even doing up this early?" I ask as he paddles to bring his board next to mine. His leg bumps mine as he sits up, looking out at the horizon.

"My brain didn't get the memo there's no early morning workouts today, but I remembered you saying last night you were going to be out here, so I thought I'd join you," he explains, as if this uninterrupted moment with him hasn't been the best thing to happen to me all summer. "Why are you out here so early? I thought the perks of living on the beach meant you could do this anytime you want."

I can't hide my smile as more of the sun begins to peak over the horizon, highlighting the sky with a pastel orange. "It's my favorite part of the day. Everything is . . . quieter. My world is very loud all the time, and I love it, but for a little bit each day, it can be quiet," I say slowly, looking over at Henry. He's watching me curiously, and my cheeks flush. He's a professional athlete, of course he understands how it all works. "Sorry, you probably understand better than anyone how loud it all can be."

"That makes sense. I'm sorry for disturbing your peace." He drags a hand through his hair, slicking back the dark strands. "I get my quiet from running," he adds.

"You're not disturbing my peace, but you are lucky JJ didn't wake up, or he'd be asking you to run with him. He's the same way."

Henry chuckles under his breath. "Yeah, you're probably right. I could use a few days off before everything picks up."

"Aren't you excited for this season?" I ask, eyeing him curiously. For once, I'm not checking him out, and I think that's an achievement considering his wetsuit clings to every crevice of his muscular body. *Yay me!*

"Of course I'm excited, but it's bittersweet at the same time. Your dad is a legend, and I'm glad I had the opportunity to learn from him, but now that he's retired . . . I imagined how the pressure would feel, but I didn't think it'd be like this. I had a meeting with Owen and the front office yesterday, and to say the least, there's a lot riding on this season for me," Henry admits, the tension practically rolling off his shoulders. *I bet that's what he was talking to Dad about in the kitchen last night.*

"For what it's worth, I think it will be fine—just show everyone what you can do."

"You make it sound so simple."

"You're overthinking it. It's only football. From what I hear, you've been throwing a ball since you could walk," I tease, lying down on my board to paddle further out as Henry follows my lead.

"How did you do it at seventeen? Perform with the whole world watching you?" he asks a few minutes later once we've settled again.

I play with the end of my braid, thinking back to the Olympics. "I don't know. I just kind of tuned everything else out. I know that's not much help, but I'm used to everyone watching me because of my last name. The only difference that time was the gold medal at the finish line," I say, but it's the truth.

I've lived my life under a magnifying glass and while I had my whole life to prepare for it, I still struggled some days. I'm able to tune everything out most of the time because I still keep my PR team on retainer for when anything pops up. Competing at that level brought a whole new level of scrutiny to me, and it wasn't healthy for me to see everything everyone said about me, my athleticism, and my body. Since my retirement from elite gymnastics after the Olympics, most have lost their interest in me as an athlete. I know there's some talk on discussion boards that I'll be training for the upcoming Olympics, but that couldn't be further from the truth.

"Have you tried talking to my dad about it?"

He falls silent, and I turn to look at him after a moment. "A little. It'll be weird without him there, but it's something everyone will have to adjust to. I don't want Bash to think I can't do it, but I feel different this season. I know I haven't taken things as seriously in past seasons, but I want to get it right this year. Football is my sole focus." Henry shakes his head, flashing me a quick smile. I recognize it for exactly what it is, but I don't want to push Henry too far in case he clams up. "I'm being ridiculous. I swear I didn't come out here to complain. Woe is me, right?"

"Dude, I complain all the fucking time. You're allowed to be nervous. It's stressful being an athlete, let alone a professional athlete. I can't even count the number of times I've come out here and screamed because everything got to be too stressful, or to exercise free will. Don't beat yourself up about it because I couldn't care less."

I'd listen to Henry talk about literally anything, but I'm selfishly glad he's talking to me about this.

Henry laughs, and this time it's genuine instead of self-deprecating. "Maybe it won't be so bad having you around this season. Congrats on your internship," he teases as we're pushed back by a stronger wave. "I feel like I should warn you that the guys on the team don't typically like anyone telling them what to do, but I have a feeling they'll end up making an exception for you."

"I'm pretty sure I won't be telling anyone to do anything, considering I'll be an intern," I correct, splashing him with water. "I suppose in the event I do have to tell someone what to do, I'm hoping they'll make an exception for me, being Sebastian Walker's daughter and all. I'm never one to play the name card, but maybe they'll take pity on me."

"Well, if they don't do it out of loyalty to your father, it probably helps your uncle is the head coach too. A lot of the guys are scared shitless of him," Henry says, and I grin, connecting the dots.

"Are you afraid of him?"

His cheeks grow pink, but it could also be the sun finally rising and hitting his face. "No comment."

"Seriously? He's like a giant teddy bear. I don't think I've ever even heard Uncle Owen raise his voice." I laugh, and it's Henry's turn to splash me back.

"Don't be mean. That's because you don't know him as a coach, just as family," he points out in defense as I continue laughing, holding onto my board so I don't fall off into the water.

"Fair, but your dad is a lot scarier than my uncle."

"I think I agree with you," Henry says. "So do you actually get any surfing done when you come out here? The water is pretty flat this morning."

"Depends on the day." I look at the surf suit he's wearing, curious if he had the foresight to bring it here. "Did you bring that?" I ask, motioning toward the black material clinging to his body.

"Thalia caught me on my way out. She said I'd be glad for it, and she's right. I think the water is warmer than the air."

"She's always right. You get used to it after a while, but it never stops being annoying," I say, not surprised my mom's awake. We're all early risers.

The conversation drops off for a bit as we watch the sun

rise completely, enjoying the quiet peace together. I don't feel the need to fill the silence with random words, but I'm keenly aware of Henry's presence. Honestly, I'm a little impressed I haven't said anything stupid, because I usually end up making a fool of myself in front of him.

We've always been friends, but the older we get, the further apart we've drifted. It doesn't help that I wear my heart on my sleeve, but I'm choosing to believe he's oblivious to the crush I've had on him for years.

I know Henry's older than me, but age is simply a number. I'm twenty, which only makes Henry five years older than me until he turns twenty-six in October. Besides, competing gymnastics at such a high level at a young age forced me to mature quickly.

I'm the first to admit I'm not perfect, though. My brothers tend to bring out the best and worst in me.

Everything would be so much easier if I were the same age as Henry.

Henry clears his throat, breaking the silence, my attention immediately shifting to him. His jaw has a shadow of dark stubble, and his hazel eyes find mine as my heart skips a beat. "I'm sorry we didn't get a chance to talk last night. JJ and Hunter did a good job of monopolizing all my attention," he apologizes, and my brain skips five steps to this being the moment he asks me out.

"Don't worry about it. You know they look up to you." I play it off with a shrug.

"I do, but I hoped to hear more about your summer other than the bits and pieces I caught last night," Henry continues, trailing his large hands lazily in the water. Is it bad that I find his hands attractive? Is that normal, or should I be concerned?

"It's not that interesting," I say, trying to not sound overeager. I need to chill out.

He raises his eyebrows at me in doubt. "Somehow I find

that hard to believe, but I'm asking because I want to hear about your life, and what you've been up to."

If only I could record this moment and play it back for JJ, to show him my crush is not entirely irrational. He can make fun of me all he wants, but he's the one who has been pining for some girl he spent twenty-four hours with in France this past spring. That's far more irrational than my feelings for Henry.

I hold my arms out, motioning at the ocean in front of us. "This is what I've been doing: surfing, reading, and overall, living life, while trying to have the best damn time."

He laughs, shaking his head as he smiles at me. "Sounds like a fun time."

"It's not too shabby. Of course, Penelope thinks I'm a fool to start this internship when I could be traveling, but I'm excited," I say, smiling at the thought of being back in Charlotte.

"Any boys in the picture?" he asks, and I can't help laughing. How ironic is it that Henry—*of all people*—is asking me about this?

"Nope."

"Really? I feel like I definitely heard your dad complaining about whatever ass you were dating not that long ago. Wasn't his name Reid or something?"

What the hell is going on right now? I chuckle, shaking my head. "You got it right—Reid. He broke up with me the day we got back from winter break. He was much more interested in my dad and my gold medal than he actually was in me. It sounds worse than it was," I add, as Henry grimaces in disgust. I definitely did the right thing leaving out the part where he thought having a girlfriend meant he could get *it* whenever he wanted, and I apparently told him *no* too often. I only know this because Reid made the mistake of running his mouth to some of the guys on the football team who knew me.

It definitely was as bad as it sounds.

"He sounds like an asshole."

Henry's not the only one who thinks so. My best friend from Duke, Emily, hated Reid with a burning passion. Too bad I didn't listen to her when she tried to tell me that before we started dating.

"Funny you call him that, because you're not the first to. Reid was an asshole."

An asshole who only ever cared about getting himself off, and would get annoyed when I didn't orgasm in five seconds. I have no problem when I'm by myself, but when I'm with a partner, I clam up, and it's nearly impossible for me. Maybe I didn't communicate well enough, but his attitude didn't help me relax. I know I can orgasm with a partner, but it's just harder for me to lose myself in the moment. That was actually one of the reasons he broke up with me. Reid said kissing me was like kissing a piece of cardboard, but he sure didn't have any problem *trying* to stick his dick in me. Emphasis on the word *try*. Once, he just thrusted up and down without actually penetrating me, and he never realized.

What the fuck was I thinking? Actually, I know what I was thinking. I was trying to give the cute guy from my business class a chance instead of holding out for Henry. All it turned out to be was a fucking mistake.

"What about you? Are you seeing anyone?" I ask, knowing full well his answer could crush me forever. I'm fairly certain the answer is no, but I guess if Henry is dating someone, I could fall off my surfboard and pretend to drown. He'd be forced to give me mouth to mouth and then Henry would see what he's been missing.

Sweet Jesus. I need some fucking help.

He shakes his head to my relief. "Nope," he mimics me before cracking a smile. "I've tried relationships, but it never seems to work out."

Well, duh. All the girls you've tried dating aren't me. Oh shit, I realize how conceited that sounds, but it's true. Our interaction right now is a perfect indication of what a relationship would be like. We're enjoying each other's company with periods of silence. I think that's a pretty good sign at least.

"I'm sorry to hear that," I finally say, when in all actuality, I feel like throwing my hands up in the air and cheering loudly. *Hallelujah.*

Our peace is interrupted by arguing behind us, and I swallow my groan when I turn to see Bailey's blond mop of hair. It's not the end of the world because JJ is with him.

"*Merde,*"[1] I swear under my breath.

I love my brothers—*I do, I swear*—but I don't want my bubble with Henry right now to be popped.

There's nothing I can do unfortunately, short of telling them to go away, but the odds of them listening to me are nonexistent.

"Here they come," Henry teases, and I splash him again, rewarded by the sound of his deep laughter.

"Where's Hunter?" I ask once they're in earshot.

JJ flashes me a knowing smile, paddling up next to me. "He'll be out in a couple minutes. He was grabbing a surf suit for Kaitlyn to change into."

"And you didn't wait for them?" I ask, causing Bailey to stick his tongue out at me.

"Pot calling kettle. You could have woken everyone up instead of just Henry, and then no one would have had to wait," Bailey retorts.

"That's literally not the same thing at all, so you can't call me a pot calling kettle."

Henry laughs quietly under his breath. "Mirabelle was out

---

1. Shit.

here by herself. I woke up early, so I joined without asking. She was staring off into space, and I scared the shit out of her."

"You don't have to ask if you can join. That's what Mom says, at least. The ocean belongs to no one." Bailey runs his hands through his hair, and I laugh at his choice of words.

"If you're talking about what Mom says, then you might want to say it the right way," I say, causing JJ to laugh.

"B, are you too cool to say the ocean belongs to mermaids?"

For as long as I can remember, Mom has always insisted mermaids exist. Once I was old enough to question it, I asked my dad about it, and he explained Mom always wanted to be a mermaid. He's not sure if she actually believes in them, but he asked us to go along with it because it makes her happy.

Sometimes I forget my parents have known each other their whole lives.

Kinda like me and Henry. Coincidence?

Bailey rolls his eyes. "Mermaids don't exist."

Excuse me? That's sacrilegious in our family. What the hell is he upset about this early in the morning he'd be throwing those words around? JJ speaks before me, and it's probably a good thing. I'll end up saying something that will probably end in another argument.

"Just don't say that in front of Mom. You'll hurt her feelings," JJ warns.

I shoot JJ a questioning look, and he shakes his head subtly.

Tell you later, JJ mouths to me.

I hate being out of the loop with them. I know I'm older, and not always around, but still.

I push the thought out of my head, slipping off the side of my board and into the water, dunking my head under to wet my hair. Henry's right, it is warmer under the water than above it, but the chill in the air feels good as I resurface, grabbing for my board. In the background, I spot Hunter and Kaitlyn walking across the beach, carrying their boards under their arms.

A part of me is sad we'll all only be here another week. I love this place, but I'm ready for this opportunity. I just hope it's ready for me.

CHAPTER THREE

Henry

"I DON'T NEED A BABYSITTER," I INSIST, CROSSING my arms over my chest as I lean back in my chair. I'm facing Owen, the head coach for the Panthers, along with some of the press team, my agent, the team manager, and a couple other bigwigs telling me another way I'm failing to live up to the great Sebastian Walker.

I promise, I'm not bitter about it. He's family to me, and I love him. I'm stressed because I've worked my ass off for this, and I'm afraid it won't be enough to please everyone. It's a lot of pressure.

"It's not a babysitter. It's just a PR specialist and an intern shadowing you around during practices, games, and team events to help the public get to know you better." *Awesome, so it's not just one babysitter, but two.*

"Why is this necessary? Walker rarely did press," I counter. I must be crazy because Owen's face softens for a brief moment at the mention of his brother-in-law.

I can't believe that he's in on this, and didn't give me a heads up. I know he has to keep the boundary clear since my father is one of his best friends from college, but as my coach, Owen could have given me a hint this was coming.

"Look, you're talented, but you're still unknown. Walker had a great career, but he still had to earn the public's respect. It's not just given, and Sebastian certainly didn't have privacy from the press, especially at the beginning of his career. During training camp, you refused interviews, and videos of you brushing off fans while they tried to get your attention are circulating on social media," Owen says, pulling no punches with his words.

"I paid all the fines for refusing interviews," I protest, but I don't really have an explanation for my interactions with the fans, or rather, the lack of them. In previous seasons, I tried so damn hard, but all anyone cared about was my personal life. I'm an introvert despite what everyone else might believe, and I like my privacy. The idea of everyone knowing everything about me makes my skin crawl.

It's the reason Andrew is the face of our nonprofit together, instead of both of us. He doesn't mind the attention, while I run in the opposite direction.

My agent, Calvin, gives me a glance to tell me to keep my shit together. "What happens if Henry doesn't comply with this request? Is there any room for negotiation on when and where they can follow him around?"

The team's general manager, Greg Ottaway, rests his hands on the table. "Honestly, if you deny this *request*, we'll either release your contract or trade you. Price, I've been looking forward to seeing you lead this team, but we need the public to support you, and they won't do that if you don't give them someone to root for. Sebastian retiring has everyone nervous for what this season will look like, and this request is a courtesy because we want to keep you here."

An acidic taste forms in my mouth that I swallow, but the

reality is sinking in. I don't have a choice unless I want to leave, and that's the last thing I want.

To pour salt on the wound, a magazine is slid across the table, landing in front of me. The cover is a picture of me sitting on a couch at a club with two scantily dressed girls on either side of me with a table in front of us littered with expensive alcohol. A couple more are laid out, each with an unfavorable headline, but none are as bad as the first.

It looks bad. It looks really fucking bad, but that picture is cropped and taken out of context. What the version—*the version that apparently ended up everywhere*—doesn't show is Quinn, our new wide receiver I was asked to welcome to the team, on the other side of the girl on the left of me, and the other girl's boyfriend standing to the side of her. I'm holding a bottle of water in my hand, but everything on the table counters the truth that I was stone cold sober and went home alone.

Sure, the last few seasons it probably would have been a different story. I would go out with some guys from the team, have a few too many drinks so I wouldn't act stiff as a board all night, before ultimately taking a beautiful woman home. Andrew and I always kept each other in line before anything too crazy could happen, but there were still more than a few headlines printed. When Sebastian confided in me about finally retiring last season, I knew I had to step up, especially with my upcoming contract renewal. I wasn't lying when I told Mirabelle my focus this season is football.

"Fuck," I swear under my breath, dragging a hand over my face. The headline only adds to the false narrative: *Henry Price, the Panthers' new golden boy or playboy?* "I wasn't drinking, and I spent most of the night with my ass planted on that couch, alone."

"No one cares what the truth is behind that photo—they care about what the photo shows. This is what people see you as, and it's not the first time you've been seen partying. If I were you, I'd agree with the plan we spent time and resources putting together to give everyone else something else to talk about besides this," Greg says, watching me closely to see what choice I'm going to make, but it's not like I have one. To put this conversation in simpler terms, *I have to get the fuck over it if I want to stay.*

I never should have agreed to go out that night. I've turned over a new leaf. I'm doing everything I can to get ready for this season because I refuse to let anyone down.

I nod slowly, trying to maintain my professionalism. "Okay. They can shadow me. Is that all?"

"No, it's not. We also scheduled some additional photo opportunities and press events for you to attend to help revamp and bolster your new image. You are not to attend any team functions, or anything additionally scheduled for you without one of your shadows," Greg continues, and I clamp my jaw shut so it doesn't fall on the floor. I can't fucking believe this is happening.

"Preseason starts next week. How am I going to have time for all of this with our schedule?" I ask, bouncing my leg under the table. I've apparently already fucked up enough to warrant babysitters, so the last thing I need is to lose my shit in front of half the front office.

"Nothing will conflict with the team's practice or game schedule," the team's public relations manager is quick to jump in. "Coach Lewis has agreed to be flexible with you if a conflict arises for any reason."

I look at Owen who is tight-lipped now, and if I didn't know better, I'd say he's not happy he has to be flexible for this PR bullshit.

"My priority is football. I'll do all this . . . stuff, but I'm not going to miss practice or workouts for it. That's nonnegotiable." The amount of self-control it takes to call this shit "stuff" is insane. It's probably not worth even trying to say my priority is football, because at the end of the day, I don't have a say in any of this.

Playboy is a new one, but it's not the only label I've earned in the media. I don't love talking to them, but apparently I can be described as broody, and if you add in my sleeve of tattoos to the equation, it ends up equating to me being a dark and mysterious bad boy.

The truth is, I've never done anything remotely close to deserving any of those labels. I'm a rule follower, obsessed with Greek mythology to the point that I have an entire sleeve dedicated to my favorite myths, and my little sister is my favorite person to hang out with.

The thing about labels, though, is you can't choose what you're given.

"Deal," Owen says, causing everyone at the table to turn to him.

"Coach Lewis, you're here as a courtesy. You don't have the authority to agree to that," Greg says, a warning in his voice.

"Respectfully, is Henry's job not to play football? If I'm remembering correctly from the meeting we had prior to training camp, you asked for back-to-back Super Bowls, and I cannot do my job and prepare my team for that if my quarterback isn't there. From my experience, winning games will also boost his reputation in the media just as well—*if not better*—than holding puppies in pictures."

I bite my lip to hide back my smile as Owen pretty much gets as close as he can to telling the general manager to fuck off. This whole thing is bullshit, but it's reassuring to know he's on my side.

None of them argue, too surprised he actually defended me.

"So when do I get to meet my shadows?" I ask, accepting

my fate, at least for a little while, hoping that if I bring the attention back to me, Owen won't find a way to lose his job in the next minute.

Greg clears his throat, a pleased gleam in his eyes as he focuses on me. "They're right outside," he answers, pulling out his phone to send off a short text. "I don't think I need to remind you this is the last year of your rookie contract. If I were you, I would take this all very seriously."

I'm still recovering from the whiplash of that when my babysitters step into the room.

I recognize the first figure walking through the door, although she's never acknowledged me before now. I don't know her name, but I can already tell she is going to make this as painful as possible. She's tall, wearing a pantsuit, and a pair of deathtrap heels that are intimidating as fuck. Her dark eyes narrow in on me, and I think I'm a little afraid. She seems like she'd have zero qualms about stabbing me with her pointy shoes.

Behind her, I spot a familiar short blonde that causes my mouth to tug upward automatically, despite the awfulness of the last twenty minutes. Mirabelle looks professional, wearing light grey dress pants and a white blousy top, and her wild mane of waves is pulled back into a bun with a few stray pieces hanging in her face. She looks . . . grown up. Mira's also wearing a similar pair of deathtrap heels that make her taller than normal, but I'm curious to know what they'd feel like hooked around my—I nearly jolt out of my seat at the intrusive thought that would normally be kept locked behind a stone wall in my mind, trying to slow the sudden racing in my chest. I cough lightly, trying to compose myself before anyone notices the heart attack I nearly gave myself.

I do everything I can to not let those thoughts pop into my brain when I'm around Mirabelle, because I have a feeling that once they start, I won't know how to make them stop.

Mirabelle's hovering behind her, but I stare, unable to look away. Her dark brown eyes are bright as she makes eye contact with me, offering me a hint of a smile. I'm not sure I know how to smile because I think my brain is glitching.

This has to be some weird dream. I'll wake up, laugh about this with Andrew, and forget all about needing babysitters and finding Mirabelle Walker attractive. Well, okay, that's partially a lie. I'm not blind—Mirabelle's a very pretty girl, but she's so off-limits, it's not even remotely funny to joke about, let alone allow my brain to consider the possibility.

"Henry, this is Stacey Arnold, but I'm sure you know who she is because she's been on the public relations team since you were drafted." Greg doesn't bother introducing Mirabelle. I'm not sure if it's because Mira's an intern, or because she's Sebastian Walker's daughter, and has been around the stadium since she was a kid.

Fuck, definitely not a dream.

I muster a pathetic smile in Stacey's direction. "I don't think we've met, but I've seen you around."

"Likewise." She smiles politely back, but all I can think is how long this season is going to be with her following me around.

And Mirabelle, a little voice in the back of my head reminds me. *Fuck.*

I take a drink of my beer, glancing at the baseball game Wilson put on the television in my living room. After the ass-kicking I got in that room today, I'm not sure when I'll be ready to go anywhere in public for a while.

Wilson and Quinn think it's hilarious I'm required to have a *shadow* this season. I thought Wilson was going to start crying from laughing so hard when I explained they brought out that stupid gossip magazine as evidence I can't be trusted without a babysitter. He knows nothing happened that night, and the photo was taken out of context, but I'm still the idiot in the photo.

I've decided that unless Stacey is talking to me, I'm going to ignore that she's there. Mirabelle on the other hand, I can't ignore unless I want the wrath of my family and hers for being a dick, but I'm trying to not think about her following me around.

"Man, I just can't believe they're actually having you followed by PR and an intern all season because of that cover photo," Wilson says, shaking his head. "That's messed up, even if the intern is Mirabelle Walker."

"I can't believe Coach is going along with it. You seem like the last person on the team who needs a babysitter," says Quinn before he resumes snacking on a bowl of chips, tossing them up in the air to catch them in his mouth. I'm tempted to tell him to knock it off, but Wilson beats me to it.

"You're dropping more of those on the ground than you're catching. Unless you plan on vacuuming before you leave, eat them like a normal person."

I chuckle quietly, but I do appreciate it. This house is mine, but Wilson's place is being remodeled so I told him he could crash here. That was a year ago, and there's been very little progress made on the remodel since, but I don't mind the company and I have the space.

Kaitlyn usually stays with me for a weekend or two a month so I have a bedroom set aside for her, but I'm guessing that her trips will drop off now that the Walkers moved to Wilmington full-time where my family lives.

"Coach pushed back as much as he could today, but maybe if I'm on my best behavior and we're winning, they'll decide I don't need shadows." It's wishful thinking that even if all that happens, Greg will get rid of my shadows, but I can have hope.

Wilson looks at me, shrugging. "Honestly, I think I'd switch places with you. I know it's weird and all since Mirabelle is Sebastian's daughter, and we played with him, but she's hot—in a non-creepy way. That was an internal thought that I probably shouldn't have said, but I'm not going to repeat it," he adds, probably due to the look on my face.

I remember Sebastian telling me what a prick his daughter was dating last winter, and how he was only putting up with the guy because Mirabelle seemed to like him. He was so relieved when they broke up, but I'm not sure there's anyone Sebastian thinks is good enough for Mirabelle.

"Super flexible too," Quinn chimes in, and I redirect my glare to him. We're not anywhere near close enough for him to say shit like that. I've spent enough time with him over the last few weeks I'd call him a friend, but I'd also have no problem decking him.

"What the hell is wrong with you, Quinn? She's a kid." I scoff, and he puts his hands up in defense.

"You're the one whose mind went straight to sex. I was just thinking she could show me some killer stretches to keep me limber on the field. My mom is a huge fan of hers. And for the record, she's twenty, which is only three years younger than me."

Wilson shoots him a look too.

I like Quinn, but the dude is a womanizer. He thinks with his dick, which is fine, but I don't want him anywhere near Mirabelle. Bash and Owen would kill me if I brought him near her. Hell, my dad would kill me. The only person more protective of Mirabelle than her father and uncle is my dad.

Thalia is his best friend, and Dad's always had a soft spot for Mirabelle, saying she reminds him a lot of Thalia at her age.

I still have to think of Mirabelle as a kid because the alternative has never been an option.

I happen to choose life, so Quinn will go nowhere near Mirabelle if I have anything to say about it.

Quinn smiles as he turns to look at me, the bowl of chips now balancing on his chest. "You know her pretty well, don't you? Can you introduce me?"

"No," I answer, confused on what part of this he doesn't get.

Wilson nods slowly in agreement. "Q, you gotta forget about it. She's Coach's niece."

I take a long drink, refocusing my attention on the game because if I keep talking about Mirabelle with my friends, my head might explode. My phone rings and it's my little sister. I answer it, pulling my ass off the couch to go out on the back deck.

"Hey, Kait," I greet, shutting the door behind me.

"Henry, I made the cheerleading team," she yells, nearly bursting my eardrum in the process. The pure happiness in her voice does make me smile.

"That's great. I knew you would." I was confused when she first asked what I thought about her trying out for the cheer team, but she wanted something new her senior year of high school. I'm glad she made it.

"Thanks. Maybe if I work hard enough, I could end up cheering for you at your games."

I nearly choke at the thought of my seventeen-year-old sister getting hit on by future Quinns. "Fuck no." It slips out, and I immediately regret it because the last thing I want is to hurt her feelings. I drag a hand through my hair tiredly as I sit by the edge of my pool, dipping my feet in the water. "I didn't mean it like that. It's just you're seventeen, and all the guys are . . . they're just . . . I don't know. If you want to be a cheerleader, then be a cheerleader."

Damn, I deserve a big brother of the year award for encouraging this.

"Henry, I won't be seventeen if I'm cheering for you," Kait says like it's supposed to make me feel better. Then I'll have to worry about her being too stubborn to listen to me.

"Just stay away from boys." *Great, now I sound like Dad.*

Kaitlyn laughs, finding my overprotectiveness endearing. "Yeah, 'cause you totally stayed away from girls when you were my age," she muses.

"You were eight, what exactly do you remember about it?" I tease. We have a nine-year age gap between us because Dad had her with Penelope a couple years after they got married, so Kaitlyn's actually my half sister.

"Ta gueule!" [1]

We both are fluent in French, which is helpful when all the families get together. Thalia started teaching me when I was little and then my stepmom, Penelope, helped fill some of the gaps after she married my dad. I think the only person who doesn't speak it is Owen. Everyone else learned. I don't use it all that often now that I don't live at home, but Kait switches back and forth frequently.

"Whatever. How is it having your boyfriends at school?" I taunt, knowing the right buttons to push with her.

"Henry, don't call them that. Hunter and Bailey are boys who are my best friends," Kaitlyn says, annoyed I've brought this up again. I love Hunter and Bailey, but they're teenage boys with raging hormones. I'm fairly certain that one, if not both, have a crush on Kaitlyn, but I don't want to touch that mess with a ten-foot pole. I'm not sure if she has a crush on one of them, but twins fighting over the same girl? *No thank you.*

---

1. Shut up!

"If you say so," I say, chuckling. "Is it nice having them there, though?"

Kaitlyn scoffs, mumbling under her breath too quietly for me to hear.

"Sorry, what was that?"

"Yeah . . . I guess it is nice. I don't think you have anything to worry about when it comes to me staying away from boys. Every guy is too busy obsessing over Hunter and Bailey because of their dad, I don't think any of them would notice if I walked into a room naked."

"Well, I'm personally on the team of *don't walk into a room naked* because I'd end up in prison for killing everyone who looked at you," I say, stalling because I don't know what to say. I'm out of my depth here, and I don't speak teenage girl. "I'm sure that's not true, Kait. It's only been a couple days."

"I know. I'm just annoyed."

"I know." I take a swig of my beer, looking out over my backyard.

"So have you seen Mirabelle around the stadium yet?" Kaitlyn asks, changing the subject.

"Yeah, I saw her today." I'll be seeing her every day for the next several months.

"She's so cool," Kaitlyn says in awe. I don't blame her, Mirabelle is pretty cool. She's easy to talk to, she's funny, and she's smart as a whip. "I wish she was my sister."

Okay, that's taking it a little far. "Excuse you, I think I'm a pretty awesome brother."

"You are, but she's an Olympian. Maybe you should hang out with her instead of your friends. She never would've let you get pictured with those girls," she suggests, and I'd completely forgotten about the possibility of my sister seeing that cover.

"You saw that?" I ask, wincing because the guy in that photo is not the type of role model I want to be.

Kaitlyn laughs on the other end of the phone. "Everyone has seen it. You're earning quite the reputation, but I sure hope you're wrapping it up. I'm not ready to be an aunt yet."

I choke on my beer, horrified my little sister just said that to me. I feel like this should be the other way around. "It's not what it looked like," I croak out, trying to clear my throat. "I was only there to babysit my friends. The only thing I had to drink that night was water."

"Wow, that's definitely not what it looked like. You might want to be more careful." She laughs again at my misery, and it's tempting to just drown myself in the pool. "Oh shit, Hunter is calling me. Can I call you back tomorrow?"

"That's fin—" I don't even have the chance to finish saying it before Kaitlyn's hung up on me.

Guess it's just me alone with my thoughts now, which is exactly where I don't want to be.

My phone rings again in my hand, and it honestly wouldn't surprise me if it was Kaitlyn calling back to tell me something quickly before hanging up again, but instead, it's an unknown number.

I click the answer button, but the voice on the other end makes my stomach turn more than that meeting did today.

"Henry? Baby, it's Mo—" I hang up immediately, acid filling my mouth.

My mother, Allison, disappeared from my life when I was four without a trace. I never received a birthday card, or a single phone call until the details of my rookie contract were released after the draft. I was the third overall draft pick, and a week later, I heard from my mother for the first time in eighteen years. I answered the first couple of calls out of curiosity, but it quickly became obvious she was only calling because she wanted money. I stopped answering and changed my number.

It doesn't matter, though. She always finds a way of getting my new one, and it's more of a hassle than it's worth.

I was tired of the questions from my parents every time I changed my number, so I started blocking her number, but occasionally, an unknown one slips through.

Everyone needs something from me, so why should my mother be any different?

CHAPTER FOUR

Mirabelle

When I took this internship, I assumed it would be a lot of grunt work: getting coffee, standing in the background to learn, and combing through the internet to find anything detrimental to a player's image before it can go viral. I certainly never dreamed I'd be part of the duo shadowing Henry to help repair his image, and help the public get to know him.

Stacey asked me to follow her and began briefing me on the way to a meeting, and to say it blindsided me would be an understatement.

I called my parents later that night to ask them if there were any favors called in regarding my position, and Dad swore there wasn't. It didn't do much to make me feel better about it.

I know I'm not like the other interns, but that doesn't mean I want to stack more bricks on the wall separating us.

Hence, I'm struggling to get out of my Audi while balancing two carriers of coffee after volunteering to make the coffee run today. Stacey only drinks coffee from a specific local coffee shop that conveniently isn't served at the stadium, but she's not wrong about it tasting better.

I make it all of two steps before one of the coffees tilts in my hands, spilling all over my cream-colored blouse. "Are you fucking kidding me?" I groan loudly, because my shirt is most likely ruined, and it's one of my favorites. *Stupid me, wanting to look nice for my first day shadowing Henry.* He looked horrified in that meeting to see I was one of the people assigned, and I want him to know I'm taking this seriously.

I adjust my grip on the coffee cups, eyeing them with pure disdain. At least the one that spilled on me was iced, so I didn't burn myself. I think I have an extra change of clothes in the back of my car, too. I turn around, trying to hold the other coffees steady because the only thing that would make this worse is if I spilled all of them on me.

Except when I turn, I crash into someone I hadn't even heard come up behind me. This time, it's not iced coffee, but a whole tray of hot coffee crushed against my chest. "Motherfucker!" I yelp, dropping the rest of the coffees to the ground as I swat the steamed liquid off me.

"Shit, I'm so sorry. Are you okay?" A deep voice asks, and I close my eyes, taking a deep breath to pause before reacting.

"It's fine." I force the words to come out of my mouth, but it's painful.

I look up, trying my best to keep a somewhat pleasant expression on my face, but I'm taken aback for a moment because it's a player. Quinn Mackie, the new wide receiver the Panthers received as part of the trade for Henry's best friend, Andrew, with the Serpents.

"Mirabelle, right?" he asks, a sheepish smile on his face.

Seriously? We're going to play this game?

"Yeah. Sorry, but now I'm late, and I have no coffee so my boss and coworkers are going to be pissed at me," I say, bending down to grab the now empty cups of coffee off the ground so I can throw them away. God, I couldn't even handle a simple coffee run. Not that juggling eight coffees is simple, but still, I didn't need to give them another reason to not like me.

"That's fine, I can walk with you," Quinn says, falling into step beside me.

Well, okay then. I *really* don't have time for this today. I clamp my jaw shut because I don't trust myself to be kind. I felt sick with nerves all last night because I don't want to say or do the wrong thing today, and everything has already gone wrong. I'm also annoyed he's pretending he doesn't know who I am, when he clearly does. I'm not trying to be conceited for once, but come on.

"How are you liking the stadium so far?" he asks, shoving his hands in the pockets of his jeans.

I cast him a sideways glance, my heels clicking against the pavement. "Considering I've been coming here since I was a newborn, I'd say it feels like home."

"What a coincidence, it feels like home for me now too. I can't say I've been coming here that long, that's impressive."

What does he want? "Makes sense, since you're from Seattle, unless you flew out here all the time to attend games."

He smiles widely as I swipe my badge at the door, dropping the coffee cups in the trash can behind it. "So, you know who I am?"

"It's kind of my job to know who you all are, at least I'm not pretending I don't know," I say shortly, turning a quick corner toward the offices.

Quinn keeps up easily, just as my phone rings in my pocket. It's probably Stacey, wondering where the hell the coffees are. "I'm also friends with Henry," he adds, not getting the hint.

"What exactly do you want from me?" I ask. Normally, I'd

be a lot nicer, but I'm late, and he *knows* this because I told him.

"Maybe I want to make a new friend." He smiles cheekily at me, but I don't buy it for a second. Quinn's in the tabloids more than Henry, and I'm honestly surprised he's not the one we're doing damage control for.

I laugh sarcastically, shaking my head. "Well, Quinn, I'll probably see you soon." I don't give him the chance to respond before I walk into Stacey's office.

Her piercing eyes drop immediately to my chest. *Oh, fuck me. I never grabbed the bag with my clothes.*

"The coffee spilled," I explain, my stomach churning.

"I can see that—the evidence is all over you," she says, the corners of her mouth turning downward. I wish I could smack my forehead against the wall. "Tell Ginger to go get more coffee," Stacey instructs.

"I can do it, it just all fell—" I protest, and she types quickly on her laptop.

"I'm aware you can fetch coffee successfully. I'm telling you to get Ginger to do it because we were due in the training room with Henry Price five minutes ago," she says, and I hate that immediate butterflies erupt in my stomach. I need to get my shit together. I can't be fangirling over him every day, but especially not today.

Wait—*today*—with coffee all over my fucking shirt.

I force a smile on my face when I feel like curling up into a hole and disappearing. *Awesome.* I grab my laptop and Stacey's off the desk to shove into my bag, double checking I have my phone to jot notes on. Stacey is already walking out the door, and I hold a sigh in. I definitely didn't plan to spend my first day shadowing Henry wearing a sopping wet, *stained* shirt, but apparently the world hates me.

As we walk toward the training room, Stacey has me keeping notes on my phone about the questions she plans to ask him. I type them all, despite knowing Henry isn't going to answer anything that isn't related to football.

I haven't told Stacey I know Henry because I don't want to abuse that connection. I also refuse to call him my friend because I don't want him to simply be my friend.

Henry is running on a treadmill when we walk into the training room, and my heart stutters at the sight of him. There's a thin sheen of sweat coating his body, making the impressive muscles on display glisten as he runs. My eyes drift to the dark hair that trails from his navel underneath his shorts.

My goodness, he's beautiful.

I blink quickly, reminding myself I'm working, and this is the last place I should be staring at Henry like a piece of meat. He makes eye contact with me, his mouth immediately turning downward as he slows the treadmill down, stopping it completely. "What the fuck happened to your shirt?" he asks, grabbing a towel to wipe his face off, and I can feel my cheeks flush bright red. I look like a slob. This is a nightmare.

"Coffee incident. I'm going to send your buddy Quinn my dry-cleaning bill."

Stacey shoots me a quick look of disapproval, and I take a half step back to stand behind her, allowing her to take the lead. I'm meant to be seen and not heard. "Good morning, Henry. After talking to your coaches and Greg, we decided today would be the perfect day to start gathering information for our first piece."

Henry runs a hand through his dark hair, his shoulders tensing. I feel bad how uncomfortable he looks. "Sure. Whatever, I guess."

"Great," Stacey says, smiling at him. I'm honestly impressed she hasn't let her eyes drift from his face because I can't say the same.

I pull my phone out, getting ready to record this conversation when out of my peripheral vision, I see Henry hang his towel over his neck. "Mira," he says, using my nickname, and I hate how quickly my head snaps up to look at him.

"*Oui?*"[1] I ask, responding in French because he's going to blow this for me before it even starts, if he hasn't already. Maybe I should have let him know I wanted him to pretend he doesn't know me.

"*Qu'est-ce-que Quinn a avoir avec ta chemise? Est-ce-qu'il t'embête?*"[2] Henry asks, an odd expression on his face, and I shrug.

"*Non. Je vais bien.*"[3]

"What language is that? French?" Stacey asks, guessing correctly.

Henry nods shortly, the look of unhappiness still not gone from his face. "My stepmother is from France. My godparents speak it as well, and taught me the language as a kid."

My parents and Penelope made sure all of us were bilingual from the start.

"And who are your godparents?" she asks, curiosity gleaming at the kernel she earned.

Henry's eyes drift back to me, thinking the same thing I am. It's not public knowledge my parents are his godparents. It's not a huge deal, but still probably not something that should be advertised if we can help it. He doesn't have a choice, though. I dip my head into a short nod, silently telling Henry the choice is his. "Some family friends," he answers.

Stacey purses her lips, shaking her head. "I was promised you would answer my questions honestly."

"I did answer honestly. My godparents *are* family friends. You didn't specify and ask for their names. If you had asked

---

1. Yes?
2. What did Quinn have to do with your shirt? Is he annoying you?
3. No. I'm fine.

the right question, maybe you'd get the right answer," Henry says, his face guarded, and I can't blame him. He digs into his bag, throwing a white bundle at me. *"Envoie-moi la facture de ta chemise. Je vais parler à Quinn."*[4]

I look at the fabric in my hands, my brain slow to catch up, realizing he threw me his shirt. *"Tu n'es pas obligé de faire ça,"*[5] I reply, resisting the urge to look at my boss.

Holy shit, I'll be lucky if I still have my job after this conversation. I guess if I get fired, then I can go to the house in France, and work at the gallery for a couple months. It's not what I want to do, but I'm fortunate to have options.

This isn't a version of Henry I'm used to. It's entirely different from that morning on the surfboards when it was just us, the mermaids, and the ocean.

"I know you're supposed to follow me around and all, but I'm going to shower without an audience if that's okay with you." He doesn't pose it as a question as he stares at Stacey, almost like he's expecting her to put up a fight. I have to give her credit, she doesn't react, whereas the thought of watching Henry shower has me nearly self-combusting inside.

"You need to stop thinking of this as a bad thing. It's not the end of the world for people to learn who you are."

He rubs his jaw, clearly disagreeing. "Really? Then why don't we switch places, and you can deal with everyone wanting to know every single fucking thing about you." Henry's hazel eyes have shadows underneath them, and he sighs tiredly. "I'm sorry. I don't mean to be a dick. I just . . . this isn't easy. I don't know how to do this."

This is more like the Henry I know. I smile faintly, because this is the guy I've been in love with for years. Stacey opens her mouth to say something, but I beat her to it. "You're in a posi-

---

4. Send me the bill for your shirt. I'll talk to Quinn.
5. You don't have to do that.

tion to be a role model and help people. You're a good person, Henry. So what if they get to know you a little bit? It doesn't mean they're going to shun you if they find out who you are."

Henry meets my eyes, but he doesn't say anything, staring at me for a moment before walking away. Walking away might be worse than the alternative of him getting upset with me.

Stacey turns to face me, her arms folded over her chest. "When were you planning on informing me that you know Henry Price personally?"

I wish I'd never opened my mouth in the first place. I look down at my hands still holding onto his shirt. Henry is literally the kind of guy who would give people the shirt off his back if they needed it. I don't know why he's so afraid of people learning who he is.

"He played with my father for a few years, and our dads played together at Duke. I didn't think it was important."

I don't think I like how she's looking at me, as if I'm suddenly more interesting. It makes my skin crawl.

"You might just be the key to getting him to open up."

Fuck me. I should have stayed home today.

CHAPTER FIVE

Mirabelle

THE DAY WAS RATHER UNPRODUCTIVE. HENRY didn't give me and Stacey much to work with, but it *was* only the first day. After he showered and cooled off, he was a little more forthcoming, but not by much.

I wanted to go home after getting off work, break into Mom's wine cellar in the basement, and lie in the hot tub for as long as I wanted—but that's not where I am.

I'm stuck at a bar with some of the other interns who have finally stopped treating me like a pariah who belongs at the circus. They reluctantly invited me along after talking about their plans tonight in front of me. It wouldn't have hurt my feelings if they hadn't invited me, but Ginger, the nicest one of the bunch, clearly felt bad.

I wore Henry's shirt until Stacey let me run out to my car to grab my spare. I haven't decided whether I'm going to give the shirt back to Henry or not.

That's what I've been pondering while answering mindless questions to get to know the people I work with. Except, for every question I ask them, they ask me three.

"Okay, I think I speak for everyone when I ask, is your

gold medal made with real gold?" Ginger asks, and I'd give anything to have a drink right now. Unfortunately, I'm not twenty-one until February.

"They're mostly silver, but they do have a certain percentage of gold in them." She didn't need to ask me that, she could have just looked it up on the internet like I did after winning them.

She smiles widely at my answer. "That's so cool."

"Yeah, it is." I force a short laugh, attempting to redirect the conversation back to them. "So where did you all go to school?"

There's a mixed range from West Coast to East Coast, but there is another girl who's from North Carolina. Miley went to North Carolina State University, but I'll try my best not to hold it against her. She seems nice enough, but she hasn't stopped *staring* at me. It's making me feel uncomfortable, and I'm trying not to stare back at her.

I take a sip of my water and nearly choke on it when Henry's name is brought up. "Dude, you're so lucky that you get to work with Stacey on that PR campaign for Henry Price."

"Yeah, I guess," I succeed at answering calmly, but my hand grips my water tightly.

Elias takes a drink of his beer. "Is it true you and Henry know each other?"

"Yeah, we grew up together."

Miley tilts her head, sizing me up. "So if you're an Olympian and your dad is one of the greatest quarterbacks of all time, why are you working as an intern?"

I wipe my sweaty palms on my jeans, trying to keep my thin patience in check before I snap. "I worked hard for my degree, and for my place here. I used my mother's maiden name while applying. I don't want any special treatment."

"Maybe I'd be more inclined to believe you if your mother's maiden name wasn't the same as the head coach's," she says, and I know she's not wrong. It's a deep blow, but I refuse to let them see it affect me.

The others have fallen quiet, avoiding looking at me.

Stand tall. Don't let them see they can hurt you.

"Well, I'm sorry you feel that way. I know you probably think this is all just handed to me, but my parents and family don't give handouts. I graduated Summa Cum Laude from Duke in *three* years while competing at a collegiate level of gymnastics because I work hard for *everything* I have. My parents didn't do fucking shit to get me this job, not that I should have to prove that to any of you. You don't see me asking what strings you pulled to get your jobs," I snap, standing to grab my things. I'd like to add a nice little *fuck you* in there, but I do have to work with them still.

"Mira, you don't have to go," Ginger says, offering me a small, embarrassed smile.

"No, I do. I know when I'm not wanted, and for the record, I make a great friend if any of you tried to look past my fucking last name." I leave on that note, walking quickly out of the bar, trying to keep my pride intact.

I miss my parents. I miss my brothers. I miss Emily. A part of me wants to say I miss Henry, but how can you miss something you've never had?

This has been the longest day ever.

I climb into my car and pull my phone out, immediately calling my brother. I sniffle loudly, trying to keep the tears at bay. Regardless, a few slip past, wetting my cheeks.

JJ answers after a few rings, and my leg is bouncing anxiously. "Hey Mira, I was just talking about you with Mom. She's on the line too."

I wipe my cheeks quickly, trying to dry them even though my family isn't here to see me cry. "Well, why wouldn't you be talking about me? I'm awesome," I joke, trying to mask any hint of how upset I am.

"Damn right. Don't let anyone tell you differently," Mom says, without knowing that's exactly what I needed to hear right now.

"Thanks, Mom," I say, trying to disguise the crack in my voice with a short cough. It's a pathetic attempt, and we all know it.

"You okay?" JJ asks.

"Been better. Just a bad day," I answer, wiping my cheeks again. I can't believe I'm crying over those idiots. I feel ridiculous letting them get to me like this. I'm freaking awesome, and if they can't see that, it's their loss.

"Who was it? I'll kick their asses," Mom says heatedly, and it does make me feel better to think of her beating them up. I wouldn't put it past her.

"No one I can't handle myself," I say, feeling a little bit better about sitting in my car crying because my coworkers don't like me. *Damn. This is a new low.*

"Does Henry know them? I'm sure he'd have no problem putting them in their place," JJ says, and I roll my eyes.

"I'm fine, I swear. I just miss you all. It's weird being at the house without everyone there."

"Henry isn't part of the reason you're upset, right?" Mom asks as I start my car.

"I'm sure you know about the campaign the organization put together to boost Henry's popularity. My boss is handling everything, so I'm helping with it, but I'm struggling to be professional with Henry. He's being a little difficult about . . . well, *everything.* Today was only our first day, but I don't want him to be upset with me, because it's not personal? I guess maybe it's a good thing I was assigned to this, since I'm not sure I could stand working closely with the other interns every day. They treat me like I'm a zoo animal, like I'm only there because of Dad and Uncle Owen, which is bullshit, but I can't make them believe it."

I am just so frustrated with everything.

JJ sighs, and I feel bad complaining about this to them. I'm twenty, and I should be able to handle this. I've only been dealing with it my whole life, growing up in the spotlight. JJ's felt it nearly as much as I have, but his life has been slightly more normal.

He chose to go to high school, whereas I was home-schooled to keep up with my gymnastics training schedule. JJ might not have competed in the Olympics, but he was listed as one of the top recruits of his graduating class, prior to committing to Beaumont University. There were a lot of eyes on him in the athletic world, being Sebastian Walker's eldest son and all.

Hunter and Bailey have had better luck hiding in plain sight, but they're still not normal teenagers by any means.

"Mira, I'm sure Henry knows it's your job. I don't think he'll be upset with you as long as you don't use anything personal from outside of work. It's a fine line you're going to have to walk, but you knew he was on the team when you took the job, and that this could be a potential conflict of interest." Mom is surprisingly the calm voice of reason. *This doesn't happen very often.* "However, fuck your coworkers because they don't even know you. Let them stare and see how far you go." *Yeah, that calmness didn't last long.*

I wipe my eyes, laughing. Some things just never change.

"Dude, you're awesome. They're just jealous. Mom's right, they don't even know you, so fuck them."

"*JJ*, language," Mom scolds.

I can only imagine how hard JJ is rolling his eyes. "Mom, that's *bullshit*. You and Dad swear more than anyone I know. Wait—Chris maybe swears more, but still. We should be focused on hearing Mira say *fuck them* because seriously, fuck them."

"Fuck them," I agree, smiling widely for the first time all night.

"That's my girl."

"All for fucking, but who are we fucking?" I hear Dad ask in the background, and Mom gives him a quick rundown. "I'm calling Owen," he announces, and I immediately regret calling them in the first place. I don't want my dad to be a stadium legacy and my mom to be the head coach's sister right now; I just want them to be my parents.

"Sebastian fucking Walker, if you pick up that goddamn phone to call my brother, you better just take your pillow right on outside with you, since that's where your ass will be sleeping tonight."

I mute myself before she can hear me laugh, but honestly, it's ironic how many curse words she just said after scolding JJ for saying "fuck". JJ doesn't mute his soon enough, but Mom is too busy threatening Dad to either notice or care.

"Love, you're overreacting—"

"Don't tell me when I'm overreacting, especially when you're the one overreacting. Just be glad I told you that you could take your pillow. We raised our daughter to be strong and capable of fighting her own battles. That doesn't mean having you step in the second things sound hard. Mirabelle will tell us if she needs us for more than our unconditional love and support," Mom says, and you can hear the daggers being thrown his way.

As odd as it might be, I miss hearing them fight. It's always over stupid stuff, but if they weren't fighting, I'd be worried.

"Thanks, Mom," I say, jumping in before Dad can dig himself a deeper hole. "Dad, I promise I'm fine. It's nothing I can't handle, I just miss you guys."

"You're your mother's daughter. Don't forget to let them swing first, and then hit 'em back twice as hard," he says.

He's been telling me that for as long as I can remember, it's the only way I survived growing up with three brothers. Personality wise, I'm very similar to my mom. She's been known for raising hell more than a few times, although some of the specifics have been hidden from me and my siblings.

"Of course. They won't know what hit them by the time I'm finished."

"Atta girl," he says, and I can hear the pride in his voice. "I promised Henry I'd come to the season opener, but I'm more excited to see you."

"I love you, Dad."

"I love you more, Mira."

"But not as much as I love you," Mom says, having to one-up Dad.

"Okay guys, we both love you, it's not a competition, but hang up, please. Go be gross somewhere else where we can't hear you," JJ interjects, and I turn my car on, letting it switch to Bluetooth as my parents remember to tell JJ they love him too before hanging up.

I pull out of the parking lot, feeling a million times better than when I got in the car. "It's just me now. Are you really okay?" JJ asks again, and I love him for it.

"Yeah, I'll be fine. I was upset, but it made me feel better listening to Mom and Dad fight. It felt normal."

"I get that, but I don't miss walking in on them making out. It's gross to even think of our parents like that, let alone seeing it with my own eyeballs." JJ makes a dramatic shuddering sound, but he's not wrong.

"Very gross," I agree.

"And Henry? How's that going, aside from being upset he needs help with his PR?"

What a perfect mood killer for the bit of joy I had

regained. "It couldn't be going worse. Every time I step into his line of sight, he stares at me like he's horrified. It's awful. In addition to now seeing me as the enemy, my boss figured out that we know each other, and she wants me to essentially exploit my relationship with him just like Mom told me not to do. But, on the bright side, Henry's friend spilled hot coffee on me today, so I'm now the lucky owner of a shirt that Henry so kindly offered me."

"But, you're not going to do that, right?"

"Fuck, if you even have to ask that, then you clearly don't know me very well. I know what this world is like, JJ. He doesn't want to do it, but if I don't do my job, I'll get fired."

JJ is quiet for a moment, pausing to think. "Would that be the worst thing in the world? It doesn't sound like you like it all that much."

"Besides the fact my coworkers suck, Henry hating me, and my boss being scary as hell, I do love it. Being at the stadium all day every day is incredible. It's a different perspective than we got being there with Dad, and I love having a purpose again."

"Well, I guess it's good you have a purpose, but maybe for the sake of your love life, you can make that a purpose, too. Anyway, your boss can't be anywhere near the level of scariness that Mom is," JJ says, and I think if he were next to me, I might smack him.

"First of all, maybe you should focus on your own love life instead of mine. I have this handled with Henry. I'm going to start dressing extra hot so instead of staring at me in horror, he realizes how hot I am. What's your plan for getting over your little girlfriend?" I tease, turning the conversation back on JJ.

"I have no plans to get over Marley, but she's not my girlfriend."

"JJ, we're hot, single athletes. I'm in love with someone who will probably never return my feelings, and you're pining for a girl whose last name you don't know, that you spent less than a day with. Why are we like this?"

For spring break last year, our family spent the week at our house in the countryside of France, and JJ met an American girl at the café in the village. He fell head over heels for her, but forgot to get some crucial details, like her full name or phone number. JJ's been looking for her ever since with no luck so far.

He snorts, clearly finding it as funny as I do. "Because we grew up watching our parents be sickeningly in love. We're hopeless romantics."

"Hopeless for sure," I agree, pulling into our neighborhood. "Hey, have you heard from Bailey? I sent him a text the other day and never heard back."

"No, he's been ignoring all my calls and texts, so I was going to ask you the same thing," JJ says, sighing. "Hunter said he's been a jerk the last two weeks, so if you have time, would you be willing to go to the beach house this weekend to check on him? I have a bad feeling, but my schedule is insane, and I'm not sure when I'll be able to get back."

"Yeah, it's no biggie. It's not like I have any friends to hang out with here, so at least I can force Bailey and Hunter to hang out with me," I say, poking fun at my sad social life. There's a distinct smell of smoke in the air, but it must be some teenager having a fire pit in their backyard. I'm glad they have someone to hang out with. "All seriousness, I'll head there after leaving work Friday."

"What do you think is going on with . . ." JJ's voice tunes out in my head as I go to turn onto our street. I see flashing lights everywhere, and I can't just smell the smoke, I can see it.

"JJ, shut up," I say quietly, parking my car up the street since all the spots in front of the house are filled with emergency vehicles.

"That's rude, I'm trying to tal—"

"JJ," I say his name sharply, and he stops immediately.

Oh shit. I climb out of the car, and I'm immediately met by a police officer. "Miss, please get back in your car," he says, holding up a hand to stop me.

"That's my house." I point, and his face immediately shifts to one of sympathy, silently telling me ours was the one on fire.

Mom and Dad are going to kill me. I've been here for two weeks, and the house is on fire.

"I'm going to bring someone over to speak with you. Just a moment," he says, backing away.

I didn't straighten my hair, so there's no way I accidentally left it on. I ate a granola bar for breakfast on the way to the coffee shop, so I didn't cook anything.

Was there something else I could have done to cause this?

I stare at the house in horror, smoke burning my eyes, and put the phone back to my ear. "JJ, I'll call you back. I have to call Mom . . . and hope she doesn't murder me for the house burning down."

CHAPTER SIX

Henry

My phone that I'm trying to ignore won't stop ringing and I don't feel like getting my ass chewed out for how today went with Mirabelle and Stacey. It wasn't a complete disaster, but I was still an asshole. I probably need to apologize to Mirabelle tomorrow, because she didn't deserve my shitty attitude. It's not her fault I put myself in a situation where I needed a PR boost.

"Fuck, if you aren't going to answer the phone, will you at least look and see who is calling you? I'm sick of listening to it ring," Wilson snaps exasperatedly, glaring from where he's sprawled out on the other end of the couch.

"It's on vibrate," I smart back. He's probably right, though. I should check it. Avoidance only works for so long.

"Just because it's on vibrate doesn't mean you can't still hear it, Price." He flips me off, turning to focus back on the game.

I roll my eyes, setting my book down to flip the phone over just as it stops vibrating.

Five missed calls from Sebastian Walker.

I sit up abruptly, running a hand through my hair. What the fuck did Mirabelle say to him about today?

I run through a quick list of every interaction I had with her. I wasn't mean to her in the weight room with Stacey, but I wasn't necessarily nice either. I even cracked a few jokes with her, but I know I was standoffish for the most part. I gave her my shirt after Quinn fucking soaked her other one, but I didn't feel the need to point out that her bra was showing through. She probably already knew, but I felt bad. I gave the shirt to Mirabelle for selfish reasons because I didn't want anyone staring at her.

I call him back, waiting to hear what my death sentence is going to be after being a dick to his only daughter.

Sebastian answers immediately, his words hurried. "Finally, I've been trying to get ahold of you for the last twenty minutes."

"I'm sorry, Bash. I know I was a dick to Mira today, but I'll call and apologize," I blurt out before he can say anything. The last thing I need is to have Thalia rip me a new one. She's terrifying when she's angry. Thankfully, it's only been directed at me a handful of times.

"*What?*"

Oh hell.

I just dug my own grave. Maybe I can figure out how to hit my head with the shovel, too.

I choke on air, scrambling to backtrack, but Sebastian continues. "For fuck's sake. Henry, if you hurt her, I'll . . . just never mind, that's not important right now. I need you to go to the house to check on Mira. Thalia and I are on our way to Charlotte now, but we're still a way out."

My stomach drops at the thought of something happening to her while I ignored Sebastian's calls. "What happened?"

"We don't know all the details yet, but there was a fire at the house."

"Was she there?" I choke out, grabbing my keys while slipping into my shoes by the door.

"No. *Thank god*," he says as I open the garage door, climbing into my car.

"I'm on my way now. I'll stay with her," I promise, pulling out of the driveway so fast I'm positive I left tire marks behind. *Fuck, I should have answered my phone sooner.*

Sebastian sighs. "Thanks, Henry. I appreciate it, but don't think we aren't going to fucking talk later about you being an ass to Mira."

"I'll text if there's any updates before you get there."

I hang up, and thankfully the Walker's house is less than ten minutes away since it's close to the stadium like mine.

I'm able to get to the house in record time, but I see and smell the smoke before I get to their street. I drive past the line of news vehicles on the other side of the street, taking advantage of filming this horrible moment. Parking behind Mira's Audi, I get out of the car, leaving the door to my Corvette open as I search for her among all the first responders.

I know Sebastian said she wasn't in the house, but I need her to be okay. I need to see for myself that Mirabelle isn't hurt. My chest feels tight, and I hate that I was caught up in my own shit instead of being here for her sooner.

I scan quickly over faces, finally spotting her next to a fire truck, a blanket wrapped around her shoulders as she stares blankly at their house.

"Mirabelle!" I call out, unsure if she can hear me over all the commotion, but her head snaps immediately toward my direction. Mirabelle stands shakily, the blanket falling from her shoulders as she bolts straight toward me. She slams into my chest, and I fold my arms around her immediately, holding

Mira tightly as some of the tension escapes my body because she's okay.

The smell of ash is thick in the air, hanging like a cloud.

Her face is tucked into my chest as she clutches my shirt like a lifeline. She's trembling, and I don't know how to make this better, but I need to try. "Hey, you're okay. The house can be replaced, but you can't be."

She doesn't say anything, simply melting into my body. She's clinging tightly to me, and despite this absolutely being the wrong moment, I don't think I've ever held her this way. We've always been friends, but she's five years younger than me. Mirabelle's always acted mature for her age, but at some point, I started distancing myself because I never wanted to cross any boundaries that couldn't be taken back. It's hard not to notice she molds perfectly against me.

"*Tu vas bien*,"[1] I whisper, because I don't know what else to say. "You're okay."

We stand there for a long time, while I run my hand up and down her back, repeating my words in both French and English. Mirabelle's not crying, but she won't stop shaking.

"Mirabelle," I say gently, and she untangles herself from me but that's the last thing I want. I didn't say her name so she'd back away.

"I'm sorry. I shouldn't have thrown myself at you," she says, running her hands over her face, exhaling a short breath. *Is she seriously apologizing right now?* "I just—I was happy to see a familiar face. Well, not happy necessarily. Ah, fuck, you know what I mean," Mirabelle mumbles, and guilt hits me at full force because if I had answered Sebastian's first call, I would have been here sooner.

"Don't worry about it. Are you okay?" I resist the urge to ask what happened because I'm sure she'll tell me when she's

---

1. You're okay.

ready. She seems overwhelmed. I'm an idiot. Of course, she's overwhelmed. Her house was on fire.

"I promise, I didn't fucking set my house on fire accidentally," she tries to joke, but it falls flat. Mirabelle closes her eyes, pinching the bridge of her nose. "The police think they found a broken window around the back. The alarms didn't go off because I think I forgot to set it this morning when I left in a rush. I guess they think someone broke in and could have started the fire, but we won't know until the official report is back. Until then, the house and everything in it is part of a crime scene."

"*Shit.*" I wish I could stuff the words back into my mouth after I say them because she opens her big brown eyes, staring at me. Then, to my relief, she relaxes into a smile.

"Yeah. *Shit* is kind of all you can say to that." Then her smile fades. "You know, I keep running all the *What ifs?* through my mind. I didn't think those twits from work did me a favor by inviting me for drinks tonight, but what if I were home when . . ." Mirabelle trails off, stepping back to wrap her arms around herself. "I'm sorry. I don't mean to get all depressing. I'm fine, I promise. You don't need to worry."

"You don't need to apologize, and you certainly don't need to pretend to be fine." The thought of Mirabelle being home when this happened nearly brings me to my knees. I look at Mirabelle, seeing this determined, kind, and stubborn person who is always willing to help others. Her family are some of the best people I've met so I'm not sure why anyone would want to light their house on fire.

She pulls her phone out of her pocket, staring at it for a moment. "It's Bailey."

I take it from her hand before she can answer it because Mirabelle's all over the place. I'm not sure she'd make it through a conversation with her little brother without bursting into tears again. "Hey, B," I answer, trying to keep my tone light.

"Henry?" he questions, and I watch Mirabelle's face as she stares at me.

"Yeah. You okay?"

"Is Mira okay?"

"She's okay. A little rattled, but I'm with her while we wait for your parents to get here," I say, trying to ease him.

And then I hear the kid sniffle, and my heart nearly cracks in half. I figured out a while ago that Bailey lashes out at people because he feels things so deeply, and he doesn't always know how to deal with his emotions.

"Bailey, I promise she's okay. The house is still there, it's just a little crispy in some spots." More like charred, and lucky to still be standing, but I don't want to worry him more than he already is.

"Can I talk to her, please?"

I offer the phone to Mirabelle, who hesitantly holds it up to her ear. She walks a couple feet away for privacy as she talks to him, and I take the time to send her parents a quick update like I said I would. I leave out the part about it potentially being arson because they're driving. They'll find out when they get here.

When she returns, Mirabelle's eyes are red and swollen.

A police officer finds his way toward us, repeating the same information Mirabelle already shared with me. It still doesn't make it any easier to hear, but I can only hope this was the result of a tragic accident, instead of the unthinkable.

"Your parents will be here soon," I say, leaning against the front of her car. "I'm sorry I was an asshole to you and Stacey today. You didn't deserve it."

She smiles at me, but it doesn't meet her eyes. "You weren't *that* bad."

Mirabelle sucks at lying.

"Except I was." I snort, shaking my head. I appreciate her trying to make me feel better, but I was an ass. "Where are you going to stay tonight?"

Mirabelle shrugs, looking away. "I'll probably end up staying in a hotel or at Uncle Owen's. Aunt Blake has an event for her firm tonight, or they'd be here instead of you. I'm sorry my parents called you—"

"I'm not sorry they called me," I interrupt her. "Stay with me at my house. I've got plenty of room," I offer without thinking it through. I probably should ask Wilson if he's okay with it, but I'd rather she stay with us than in a hotel by herself if there's a potential arsonist on the loose.

Her eyebrows skyrocket upward in surprise. "Are you sure? You don't have to offe—"

"I know I don't have to, but I wouldn't offer if I wasn't serious, Mira. I have a spare bedroom Kaitlyn uses when she visits, I'm sure she won't mind."

"Henry . . ." Mirabelle looks unsure, twisting her hands.

"You're welcome to stay as long as you need."

Her eyes are searching my face for something before she nods slowly. "It'll only be until I find a place. Thank you," Mirabelle says, and her parents pull into the cul-de-sac, barely having time to park the car before Thalia is climbing out to hug Mirabelle tightly.

I hang back, letting them have their moment as a family, and take the opportunity to call Wilson. It's not like he pays rent or anything, so I shouldn't feel bad for extending the offer without checking with him.

Wilson sends me to voicemail, and I roll my eyes, calling him again. I'm sure his ass is still glued to the couch, and this will be easier to say over the phone than to explain in a text. He finally answers, irritation seeping into his voice. "What could you possibly need right this second? The game just went into extra innings," he grumbles.

"I need you to put fresh towels and an extra set of my clothes on the bed in Kait's room. I told Mirabelle she could stay with us until . . . well, I guess my offer doesn't have an expiration date. Is that okay with you?"

"Why does she need to stay here?"

"Because someone tried to burn the Walkers' house down tonight." The words almost stick in my throat. It's hard to say. I mean, what the hell would possess someone to do this?

"Oh shit. Yeah, of course. I'm cool with her staying here as long as she needs."

Thalia and Mirabelle approach me as Sebastian heads toward a cluster of police officers. "Thanks, man. I appreciate it. I gotta go, I just wanted to check with you quick."

Wilson mumbles something about grabbing towels and clothes after the inning ends, but I hang up. "Thanks for being here, Henry," Thalia says, hugging me briefly. She's always been there for me and I'm thankful to be able to return the favor.

"Of course. I'm sorry about the house."

"*C'est juste une maison. Je suis content que personne n'ait été blessé,*"[2] she replies, looking at the house, but I can't look away from Mirabelle. The thought of her getting hurt is worse than a knife to the heart.

"Me too."

"Sweetie, I know you want to stay, but Dad and I have this handled. You need to get some rest," Thalia says to Mirabelle.

"But, Mom, I want to stay with you," Mirabelle protests, and Lia smiles, patting her cheek.

"I know, but you had a long day. You don't need to be here."

Shit, I was the reason she had a long day. "Wilson's setting

---

2. It's just a house. I'm glad no one was hurt.

out clean towels and clothes on the guest bed," I add, and Thalia shoots me a grateful smile.

Mirabelle's gaze bounces between us. "Okay, but call me if you find out anything please?"

"I will, now follow Henry back to his house. We've got this covered here."

I'm not sure Mira should be driving.

"We can go back in my car. We'll come back for yours tomorrow?" I suggest, and Mirabelle looks a little relieved at the idea, hugging her mom again. Thalia says something to her that I can't hear, but it makes Mirabelle smile.

She slips into the passenger seat of my car, sitting in silence as she stares at the house until I pull out into the street. It makes me sick to see all the people standing nearby watching. "I didn't mean to give you a hard time today. I promise it won't happen again," I say, needing to apologize again for making her day harder than it needed to be. I only thought about how it affected me, and not any of the potential repercussions Mirabelle could face due to my lack of cooperation.

She looks at me in surprise. "Henry, I said it's fine. That's not a promise I'm sure you can keep anyway."

I'm not sure it is either, but I'm willing to try a lot harder to keep it.

"I feel bad, okay? I could have been fucking nicer today. I wasn't thinking."

"Is this about what my mom said?" Mirabelle asks, shifting in her seat to face me.

I tap my fingers on the steering wheel, trying to keep my eyes on the road. "It was my fault you had a long day."

"She wasn't talking about you. Mom was talking about the drinks I got with some of my coworkers. They don't like me very much because everyone assumes my parents pulled strings instead of considering I'm actually qualified for the internship." She exhales, shaking her head. "It's whatever, though. I can't make them like me."

"They're jealous. Mira, everyone in your life knows how hard you work for everything you have." I mean, for fuck's sake, she's an Olympian. They don't just hand out gold medals based on last names.

"I know, it's just frustrating, but I don't want you to think it was your fault I had a bad day. Despite how awesome I am, I'm allowed to have bad days," she says, chuckling quietly. It takes a special kind of person to be able to laugh after the kind of day she had.

Tomorrow will be a better day, I'll make sure of it.

CHAPTER SEVEN

Henry

"Where are you going?" I ask Mirabelle, walking into the entryway with my protein shake as she slips into her towering heels. How the hell does she walk in those?

She looks at me like I'm an idiot. "Um, work?"

"I thought you were taking the day off."

Mirabelle raises her eyebrows in surprise. "One hundred percent sure I never said that, so I don't know why you think that's happening."

"I don't know? Maybe because your house was on fire last night, and there's an arsonist who probably hoped you were in it?" I say, because I'm not sure she understands the gravity of the situation. Mirabelle could have been seriously injured last night.

"*Alleged arsonist.* We won't know until the investigation is completed," Mirabelle corrects.

"Right, which is why you should take a day off."

"Well, lucky for me, I wasn't in the house, so I don't see any reason why I can't go to work," she says, crossing her arms over her chest in defiance.

"Mira, just take the day," I say, not wanting to argue with

her about this. I want her to stay here where I know she'll be safe. Unfortunately, that's assuming Mirabelle cooperates with me right now, and I see a low probability of that happening.

"I thought you of all people would get it, Henry. All the interns are just waiting for me to fail. We've been in the office for two—nearly three—weeks. I can't take time off if I want to have a job," she says, and while it makes sense after what Mira told me last night, I still think she should stay here.

"I do get it, and I still think you should take the day off. I'm not going to be there to keep an eye on you."

Mirabelle takes a step back, her mouth falling ajar in shock. Perfect, now I've fucked up again.

"Well, I'm sorry I'm such a big fucking inconvenience for you. No one is making you keep an eye on me. If anything, it's *my job* to keep an eye on you, since you can't seem to get your shit together in front of the cameras," Mirabelle snaps, and it's my turn to be shocked.

We've never argued before, but I have witnessed plenty of arguments with her brothers. I'm the one she comes to after fighting with them when our families are together, which realistically was all the time growing up.

"Mira—"

She grabs her bag, glaring at me fiercely. "You are being an ass. A fucking asshole, Henry. You're not my dad or my brother, so you don't get to tell me what to do."

"I'm not being an asshole. I'm looking out for you," I argue, my shortened temper getting the better of me after a late night, and Mirabelle flips me off, grabbing my keys off the hook.

"What the hell are you guys yelling about at seven in the fucking morning?" Wilson asks, his massive frame filling the entire doorway from the kitchen.

"She's being unreasonable," I say, looking to him for backup.

Mirabelle scoffs, swinging the door to the garage open. "Oh, I'm the one being unreasonable? You're the one with a giant stick up your ass, because you're being an ass!"

"Will you both just shut up? It's too early for this," Wilson says, shooting a look at me as if I'm the one to blame. *So much for backing me up.*

Mirabelle takes the opportunity to walk into the garage, slamming the door behind her.

"She's right. You are being an ass," he mutters under his breath, turning around. "You should never tell a woman what to do. I thought you were smarter than that."

The sound of my car's horn echoes through the house as she leaves in a very clear *fuck you* manner.

Apparently, I'm *not* smarter than that.

~

"How did you decide you wanted to be a quarterback? Wasn't your father a lineman at Duke?" Stacey asks, and it takes everything in me to not ignore her. The click of Mira's heels is driving me crazy—actually, she is driving me crazy because she shouldn't be here today.

If I weren't busy trying to figure out how to apologize to her, I'd probably be mad she took my car this morning. While I still believe I'm right, I probably shouldn't have picked a fight with Mirabelle this morning. I'm just worried about her.

Last night was a lot for anyone to handle, and I get wanting to act like nothing happened, but something did happen. I've had this pit in my stomach I haven't been able to shake since getting Sebastian's call last night, because the idea of someone hurting Mirabelle wrecks me. I know it's easier for her not to acknowledge that possibility until the investigation is completed, but I haven't been able to stop thinking about what could have happened.

I've always tried my best to keep an eye out for her. I can vividly recall my dad pulling me aside when I was eight, asking me to promise I'd always be there for Mirabelle to help keep her safe. That promise always lingers in the back of my mind.

"Henry?" Stacey asks, and I stop walking to turn back at her.

"What was the question again?"

"What made you want to be a quarterback?" she repeats evenly, clearly not pleased to be repeating herself. I glance at Mirabelle a half step behind Stacey, taking notes on her phone.

"I wanted to be like Sebastian Walker when I was a kid. He's a huge influence in my life."

Mirabelle's chocolate eyes blink at me in surprise. I'm not sure what else she thought my answer would be. I practically worship the ground he walks on, regardless of how long I've known him.

Stacey's phone begins ringing in her hand, pulling her attention away from me. *Thank god.* "I'll be back in a moment, I have to take this call. Mirabelle, why don't you ask Henry some of the other questions we discussed this morning?"

"Yes, ma'am," Mirabelle says, and I wait for her to walk next to me, because that's where she belongs. Not five feet behind me.

"What do you like to do outside of football?" she asks, and I'd actually prefer she tell me what an ass I am again over the politeness.

"Surfing, reading, swimming. You know the answer to that question already," I point out, and Mirabelle doesn't look at me as she writes it down.

"What are your weaknesses as a person?"

I chew the inside of my cheek as I think of how I want to word my apology, now that I actually have the chance to give it without Stacey listening in. "I worry too much about people

I'm close to, and I can come across as an asshole, instead of trying to show how much I care about them. I'm sorry about this morning, Mirabelle."

Mira sighs, crossing her arms over her chest. "I shouldn't have called you an ass. I don't exactly like being told what to do."

"You forget I've known you since you were in diapers," I tease, trying to lighten the mood.

"I'm aware," she mumbles quietly, her cheeks flushing pink as she clears her throat. "So you were worried about me?" Mirabelle asks, sounding more like herself as she looks up at me.

"I was." My voice unintentionally deepens, and I shift back, putting distance between us. "Are we okay?"

She smiles hesitantly, the corners of her eyes crinkling. "Yeah, we're cool, Henry, but I did book a suite at a hotel nearby. I don't want us to have any more problems, so I think it's best if I stay somewhere else."

"No," I blurt out, causing Mirabelle to jump at the abruptness. "I just mean . . . I'd rather you stay at my house until the police figure out what's going on."

"I don't think it's a good idea. We've never fought, and not even twelve hours into me staying with you, we're fighting. Plus, I don't want to cramp your style or Wilson's," she says, but I think those reasons are bullshit.

"We were fighting because I stupidly tried to tell you what to do. That's a bad excuse, too. Season is about to start, and our 'style' is usually just us going somewhere to hang out where we have cameras shoved in our faces the entire time, which isn't exactly my definition of a good time. Besides, I'm not supposed to be going out anywhere like that, remember?" I point out, trying to reason with her, but Mirabelle proved earlier how easily she could tell me to fuck off. Her mouth turns downward, and I definitely need to start thinking before speaking. I didn't get much further than my initial apology. "Not that I'm complaining or anything. I don't want to go out to those places anyway, I'm much happier with a book at home, but the media portrays it to be worse than it actually is."

Mirabelle hums a response, unfolding her arms as she scrutinizes me.

"Please stay. I can't promise I'll be less protective of you, but I'll work on being less of an ass."

She laughs briefly, a smile cracking through, and a warm feeling flutters in my chest. "If you insist, then I'll cancel my suite. But you need to promise that you'll tell me if you want me to go."

Yeah, fat chance of that happening. I take a half step forward to pull Mira into a hug when Stacey approaches, looking like she's on a fucking mission. *Awesome, I'm sure this means I'm getting roped into something else I want nothing to do with.*

"Did your family's house burn down last night?" Stacey asks, looking to Mirabelle for answers. I can't say I'm not relieved for the reprieve in questions being directed my way.

Mirabelle freezes like a deer in the headlights, and for that sole reason, I wish the question was for me.

"I wouldn't say it burned down, but it was on fire. Why are you asking?" Mirabelle recovers quickly, straightening her shoulders back.

"Are the two of you involved in a romantic relationship?" Stacey asks curtly as my brain struggles to process the question.

"No, we're not," Mirabelle answers quickly, her face pale.

Stacey looks at me for further confirmation, and I shake my head. "I'm not dating anyone. We're just friends," I repeat, trying to piece together where Stacey is going with this line of questioning.

"Well, fortunately for you, Henry, someone took pictures of you hugging and leaving the scene together last night. Gossip magazines are reporting that you have been in a secret relationship for months, and it's trending across all social media outlets."

"I'm sorry, what?" I blurt out, waiting for either one of them to begin laughing and admit this is a bad joke.

Stacey's gaze bounces between the two of us as my head spins. "It could work. I'll be damned." She chuckles under her breath.

"What could work?" I ask, glancing at Mirabelle who is frozen.

"It's already having a positive effect on your socials. Mirabelle is a decorated Olympian who already has the support of the public in multiple demographics, including football because of her father."

"But we're *not* together," Mirabelle says, dragging out each word.

"Mirabelle, your press team just called me, and they mentioned that you asked them for suggestions to help Henry," Stacey explains, and Mirabelle looks worried.

She did that?

"I was only tr—"

Stacey waves her hand, silencing Mirabelle. "You're not in trouble. I applaud you for using your resources because I believe they gave us the solution. Can you tell me why you weren't aware our client is trending online right now?"

Mirabelle glances up at me briefly, but I can't get a read on her anymore. "If Henry's name is trending with mine, I wouldn't have received any notifications because I have all alerts involving my name blocked."

"I see," Stacey says. "Your team has suggested the two of you enter into a fake relationship to boost Henry's PR in a way that these interviews won't. The only thing I'm mad about is that I didn't think of it first."

My mind goes blank.

Stacey stares expectantly at us. "Can one of you say something?"

"I . . ." I trail off because after how the rest of the day has gone, I don't trust myself to not say the wrong thing. My mind immediately goes to the initial meeting where I found out about my shadows, and the way I'm trying not to look at her again, despite every intrusive thought that pops into my brain telling me otherwise.

I'm not supposed to see Mira as anything other than a friend. I mean, how exactly does this fit into my promise to protect her? Won't our age gap be concerning to the fans and media?

"Are you serious?" Mirabelle asks in disbelief.

Stacey clasps her hands together. "Obviously, there are some finer details that need to be hashed out, and I can't make you do this, because it's not under your initial job description, but I think the circumstances warrant something like this based on the positive effect it's already having from the specu-lation alone."

"The circumstances warrant me dating Mirabelle? I'm sorry, but I think there's a disconnect here. I know I haven't been the most forthcoming with the media and fans, but is it actually that bad we're considering doing this?" I ask, laughing at the absurdity of it all. I've heard of shit like this happening, but it never dawned on me that it could happen to me.

"You *need* this, because during the offseason this year, the public perception of you was poor and over half the front office wanted us to trade you despite Coach Lewis fighting against them. No one knows who you are, and as of this moment, they don't care to. Your actions during training camp made sure of that, so congratulations, Henry. They're doing what you want by leaving you alone because you're seen as the guy who doesn't care about the fans—fans who make all of this possible. The fans, whose hard-earned money pays your salary, think their quarterback cares more about partying than about football. This whole PR plan that you hate was created to keep you from getting traded when your rookie contract is up," she says. I can feel my face drain of all its color. I knew there was talk of trading me and bringing in fresh meat after Bash retired, but they decided to keep me. I didn't realize it was *that* bad.

"This girl right here?" Stacey motions to Mirabelle as I swallow the lump in my throat. "She's football royalty in everyone's eyes. Dating the daughter of your mentor who happens to be Sebastian Walker is a huge step in the right direction. People are excited and talking about you right now in a positive way. If I were you, I'd stop laughing and say *thank you*."

I'm speechless.

I had . . . I had no idea about any of that.

Dragging my hand over my jaw, I turn to look at Mirabelle, but she won't meet my eyes.

"I'll do it," she says, making the choice for us.

Stacey doesn't wait for me to protest, which at this point, I'm not even fucking sure I would do. "Great. I need to go handle the logistics so we can release something this afternoon to the press. Figure out some details between the two of you like how long you've been together, when you started liking each other, and some other details to make it more believable. I'll come find you in an hour. You're a trooper, Mirabelle."

"No problem." Mirabelle smiles, but it doesn't meet her eyes. When it's a genuine one, her eyes crinkle at the corners, and her smile is brighter than the goddamn sun.

Stacey walks away quickly, typing at the speed of lightning on her phone.

What the fuck just happened?

"Mirabelle—" I begin to say, and she shakes her head.

"If you actually meant your apology, don't tell me I'm not allowed to do this. You need this, and I'm doing it, so let's not fight about it."

God, Mirabelle's . . . incredible. I look at her in amazement, wondering how I could ever deserve this kindness she's offering. There's no denying Mirabelle's beautiful, and if I'm being honest, she's exactly my type, which is why I've fought so hard to keep my mental block in place to only see her the way I'm supposed to.

Mirabelle's long blonde hair is pulled back into a ponytail with pieces framing her face, the unruly waves flowing down her back. Her eyes reflect how tired she is, and the splash of freckles over her nose are prominent from a summer spent in the sun. She carries herself with confidence and grace, and she's smart.

She's the total package, but she's *untouchable*.

I can't forget that during this charade.

"Thank you," I finally say. What else can I say? She's right, I can't tell her what to do. I might not be a fan of the idea, but Mirabelle's not wrong. I think I do need this.

Fuck.

I didn't know things were this bad with my contract. My agent never said anything about how close I was to being traded, so clearly I need to have a conversation with Calvin.

It's no secret that the Panthers planned to play Sebastian until he retired. I knew that I wouldn't get much playing time, and I could have put feelers out with other teams, but I wanted to learn from Sebastian. I wanted to stay close to my family. I want to be a Panther, but I was too stupid to consider the effect my actions would have on my career. I guess I thought the fans would give me more of a chance to prove that

I'm still the guy who led Duke to back-to-back championship titles.

"Well, I guess we should figure this all out, right?" she asks, looking at me for confirmation.

"Probably," I agree, trying to push the thoughts of how thoroughly I've fucked myself to the back of my mind.

We start to walk silently around the stadium, the tension in the air thick. *I need to say something, literally anything.*

"We've been together for a couple months. It's still new, which is why we haven't told anyone?" I suggest, scratching the back of my neck. "I'm sorry, I don't know how to plan a fake relationship when I'm not very good at legitimate ones under the best circumstances," I admit, racking my brain for a better cover story.

It's not that I haven't tried to make relationships work, but I have a hard time trusting that people want to be around me for the right reasons. I know my birth mother is to blame for this, reinforcing my belief love isn't worth the pain it can cause, but I don't know how to fix it. Being alone doesn't bother me either; I'm an introvert, despite the reputation I've earned.

I'd be lying if I said the media didn't play a role in my hesitancy to get over my fears. It's easier to take a girl home for the night and never see her again than to fall in love, only to find out she's interested in my money or the fame that she'll undoubtedly earn by tying herself to me.

In the past, it's made me nervous to think about the invasion of privacy I would face in a relationship, along with my partner's, but I guess I don't have to worry with Mirabelle. She understands it better than anyone else would, and since these interviews are ensuring my lack of privacy, a fake relationship might not be the worst idea in the world.

"Me either, but we have to figure something out. We can say I've had a crush on you for years—I'll finally be living out my childhood fantasy. That'll be a good headline for Stacey," Mirabelle jokes, and I shake my head immediately. She's doing this to help me, I'm not throwing her under the bus.

"You're already agreeing to fake date me for the sake of my reputation. The least I can do is say that I've been interested in you for a while, and I pursued you. We could tell everyone that something sparked after the Super Bowl, and we've kept it under wraps until now."

I can see Mirabelle's brain processing it over, and the more I think about it, I think it's the first smart idea I've had in a while.

"That might actually work," she says, an impressed note in her voice. Mirabelle hits my arm with the back of her hand. "Henry, this could work."

"Thank you. Hopefully it's not for too long. I don't want you to have to do this any longer than necessary." If people simply speculating that we're dating has already helped my image, this might be enough to fix everything if I make more of an effort with the fans and the media.

Mirabelle pulls her ponytail over her shoulder, playing with the ends. "I don't mind. You heard Stacey: I'm football royalty."

"What if you meet someone you're actually interested in?" I ask, lowering my voice as a few maintenance workers walk past us.

"What if you do?" she counters, twirling her hair around her finger.

"The chance of that happening is slim enough it doesn't even justify an answer." I snort when Mirabelle rolls her eyes at my response. "You were right this morning, Mira. I've done a brilliant job of fucking this up for myself."

She smiles, but it's more sympathetic than anything. "Well, if the shoe fits . . ."

"It does," I agree as another potential problem pops into my brain. "What the hell are we going to tell our parents?"

"Oh shit. I forgot about them."

I don't particularly want to tell my parents or hers how close the team was to trading me. I've worked so hard to be ready for this season, and it's already a steep climb to get everyone's approval without them knowing I was almost traded.

"I think it'd be fun not telling them the truth," Mirabelle says, a slow, mischievous smile curving her lips upward, her dimples peeking through.

I'm not sure "fun" is how I would describe the way I'm predicting they'll react, but I'm so damn relieved I don't have to tell them the truth.

"Then we need to be pretty damn convincing if they're going to believe us. Maybe it's a good thing you have this fascination with my ass after pointing it out so many times this morning," I joke, attempting to lighten the mood as she gapes at me.

"There's a difference between discussing your ass and calling you an ass, Henry."

I chuckle under my breath, considering the possibility that maybe everything will be okay. Aside from this morning, we've always gotten along.

Perhaps a fake relationship isn't much different from a friendship.

CHAPTER EIGHT

Mirabelle

See, when Stacey said she was releasing an article this afternoon about our "relationship," I didn't think she actually meant *by* three o'clock. Instead of today being all about interviewing Henry, it ended up turning into *let's make sure Mirabelle and Henry know what the fuck their backstory is.*

How fun.

The best lies have threads of the truth woven into them, but in this case, the only lie is that my feelings for Henry are real. Of course, he has no idea they actually exist because the one area of my life where I can't be brutally honest is when it comes to my feelings for Henry.

Stacey asked when I knew I had feelings for him. I instantly thought back to the day I got the small scar on my knee—the one identical to Henry's. I thought about how I lived for the days when Chris and Penelope were coming over because I knew I'd get to see Henry.

Instead of saying all that, I go along with Henry's suggestion that it started when he comforted me after my boyfriend broke up with me after the holidays.

When she asked when we started dating, Henry answered

that he kissed me at a Super Bowl after-party, and we've been secretly dating since.

If only that were true.

We take a break while Henry runs through drills on the field with Quinn and Tyler, as my uncle and the offensive coordinator work on routes. I'm sitting in the stands next to Stacey, going through some of the emails she got today. I'm putting the ones regarding me and Henry into one folder, the ones about Henry into another, and finally, the ones involving the team into a different one.

It's mindless and boring, but it's helping me work through my nerves about everything transpiring today with Henry and the awfulness of last night.

Part of the reason I was so upset with him this morning for telling me to stay home—well, stay at his house—instead of coming into work is that I knew if I did, I'd sit around all day doing absolutely nothing but think about someone trying to hurt me and my family. Just like Mom said last night, a house is just a house, but family is irreplaceable.

I need things to be normal.

Too bad nothing about today is normal.

Who knew I was the answer to Henry Price's problems? Well, I always knew we were supposed to be together, no matter how many times JJ and Emily told me I needed to move on. Maybe it's irrational to keep hoping after all this time, but I'd say I'm one step closer than I was before. Now, I just need him to see how great it would be to fake date me, and maybe Henry will actually want to date me for real.

Stacey called my PR team, to get them on board before she released a quick statement less than an hour ago, confirming the relationship along with a few minor details about when we got together. JJ, Kaitlyn, and Hunter have been blowing up my phone since, in addition to my best friend, Emily, who has been trying to reach me since this morning. I've been screening calls all day because I don't know what to say to anyone.

The only person in my family who currently knows Henry and I aren't together is my Uncle Owen. He warned us our parents won't take it well, but I'm not sure I agree with him. My parents love Henry, and his parents love me, so why wouldn't they like us together?

I don't think I can hide this from JJ, but I'll cross that bridge when I get to it.

This new development has made me even more of a social pariah with the interns. None of them have bothered even looking in my direction. I'm surprisingly okay with it. I don't want to beg people to be my friends if they don't want to be.

I'm fucking awesome, even if I don't feel like it at the moment.

Stacey straightens next to me, causing me to look up from the screen to see what's attracted her attention.

Oh shit.

Shit, motherfucker, goddammit.

Fuck.

Dad is walking across the field right in Henry's direction like he owns the goddamn place—I guess he did for years—and Mom is right behind him. "Stacey, are you okay if—"

"You might want to go handle that," she agrees. I move quickly down the stairs to get onto the field, kicking off my heels after nearly breaking my ankle on the first stair.

Uncle Owen looks up from where he's talking with the offensive coordinator at the sound of my mom's voice calling after my dad. "Sebastian, you know your legs are longer than mine, just wait a second," she shouts, and he stops as Henry turns around. I move faster, cutting in front of them to block their path to Henry.

"What are you guys doing here?" I ask, slightly out of

breath and I can feel Henry's looming presence right behind me.

"Bash? I didn't know you were coming today . . ." Uncle Owen trails off, and the look of anger on Dad's face is downright terrifying.

"Are you fucking kidding me? My daughter?" he asks, his voice shaking in anger as he looks directly over my shoulder at Henry.

When I told Henry earlier that we shouldn't tell our parents this is fake, I was sorely mistaken in predicting how my dad would take it. Uncle Owen was definitely right, they're not taking this well. "Wait, Dad—"

"Not now, Mirabelle."

My jaw hits the fucking floor. My dad has never, *ever* used that tone with me. Mom's eyes widen in surprise, clearly not expecting that either. *"Je sais que tu es en colère, mais tu ferais mieux de te souvenir à qui tu t'adresses."* [1]

"Sebastian—" Henry tries to speak, but Dad talks right over him.

"After everything I've done for you, this is how you repay me? Sneaking around behind my back with my daughter who is five fucking years younger than you," he thunders, and I can honestly say, I don't think I've ever seen my father this angry before.

"Look, I know you're upset, but you need to walk it off. This is not the kind of scene you want to be making, and not the place to be making it," Uncle Owen warns.

"Owen, he's—"

"It wasn't supposed to happen," Henry says calmly, and I'm not sure if I think he's an idiot, or if I should be impressed he hasn't blurted out it's fake.

"Please, will you just listen to us? We were going to tell you

---

1. I know you're angry, but you better remember who you're talking to.

tonight," I say, and his face turns downright murderous at the use of Henry and me as an us. We're an *us* now.

"Is he taking advantage of you?" Dad asks, staring directly at me, and I don't miss the sharp intake of Henry's breath at the question. "Mirabelle?"

"Oh my god, *no*. Dad, it's Henry. He'd never do anything to hurt anyone, especially me."

"*Tu peux nous le dire, tu sais?*"[2] Mom asks, watching me closely.

"You really think that of me?" Henry asks, his voice thick, and I look over my shoulder at him. He looks hurt, and I don't blame him. If I ever thought my parents would react like this, I never would have suggested keeping it a secret. "I would *never* hurt Mirabelle. I'd sooner hurt myself than hurt her."

"You were supposed to be looking out for her! What part of that included screwing her behind our backs? We've treated you like you were our own, and this is how you repay us?" Dad lunges forward, bumping into Uncle Owen who quickly steps in front of him, blocking his path. "Owen, get the hell out of my way."

"So you can what? Beat the shit out of him in front of Mirabelle? Great parenting move—beating up your daughter's boyfriend, who also is your best friends' kid. I don't think so. Walk away, Bash."

"He's right. I'm not happy about this either, but this isn't the time or place." Mom shakes her head, trying to get Dad's attention to calm him.

"Sebastian, Thalia, I'm sorry. We were going to tell you. You weren't supposed to find out this way." Henry makes a dangerous move and entwines our hands together. His calluses are rough against my own, and his hand dwarfs mine. I think he has a death wish.

---

2. You can tell us, you know?

My mom has unshed tears shining in her eyes. "Mira, why didn't you tell us?"

Dad steps back, running his hand through his graying hair. "How long, Henry? How long have you been interested in her? Mira's twenty, and if you got together at the Super Bowl, she would have been nineteen. You're twenty-five, about to be twenty-six. Were you just counting the days until she wasn't a minor anymore so you wouldn't go to jail for statutory rape?"

"Sebastian," Mom scolds sharply as my jaw falls open.

Did he actually say that?

"It wasn't like that. It's only been a couple months. I swear, I never even saw her like that until recently, and certainly not when she was a minor."

"She is a kid still. *My kid*, and you're taking advantage—"

Oh my god. I can't listen to this anymore. "That's enough, Dad! Henry isn't taking advantage of me, and if you'd stop your rampage long enough to hear what we have to say, you would know that," I shout, cutting him off. *This is a nuclear disaster.*

"I'm sorry. Is that what you want to hear? We didn't mean to hurt you, but Mirabelle isn't a kid anymore, and realistically, she hasn't been for a while. I know you're upset and if you need to hit me to feel better about us being together, then please do. But I like Mirabelle. She's an incredible, strong, beautiful person that I enjoy spending time with. I wouldn't risk *everything* good in my life, including your trust, if I didn't see something with her. I don't love that I'm nearly six years older than her, but I am not taking advantage," Henry says strongly, his voice never wavering. His hand is tightly gripping mine like an anchor I don't dare pull away from.

I stare at Henry in awe. I have to hand it to him, he's pretty damn convincing at selling this fake relationship. That's all I think I've ever wanted to hear him say about me. Granted, when I imagined it, I didn't think it would be because we're in a fake relationship, but he just stood up to my parents, who were accusing him of grooming me, and offered to let my dad hit him if it would make things better.

Honestly, I don't think I've ever been more in love with Henry Price than I am in this moment, even if the pretty words he's saying aren't real.

"I'm sorry," I whisper, a few tears slipping down my cheeks as I look at my dad. He looks at Henry, then at me, closing his eyes as he walks away without another word. The silence packs more of a punch for me than anything he's said.

Mom steps forward to hug me tightly. I'm slow to return it, not expecting her to hug me. She pulls away, tucking a stray hair behind my ear. *"Nous t'aimons quoi qu'il arrive. Donne-nous un peu de temps."*[3]

She steps away to follow Dad but pauses to look over her shoulder at Henry. Her mouth opens as if she wants to say something, and I hold my breath. If my father's words were vicious, I don't know if either of us can stomach what will come out of her mouth. Instead, she simply shuts her mouth, shaking her head as the look on her face hardens before walking away.

Owen turns to face us, running a hand over his jaw as he grimaces. "I don't want to say *I told you so*, but I fucking told you so. Price, your balls must be bigger than your will to live, because I don't know if I would have kept the secret after that. You must have a death wish. Are you two okay?" he asks, concern filling his features so similar to Mom's.

I muster a smile, but I don't know how to say I'm okay, because none of that was okay. I nod, pulling my hand out of Henry's. I don't hear his response because I'm walking

---

3. We love you no matter what. Give us a little time.

through the plush grass toward where Stacey is pretending like she wasn't listening to everything that happened.

~

There's a knock at the door of my temporary bedroom that I barely register as I devour the romance book I've been carrying around in my purse all week. "Come in," I call out, not bothering to look up from the page I'm on.

I hear the door open, and I glance up to see Henry hovering in the doorway. *I guess for Henry I can put the book down.* Reaching for my bookmark, I gently set it in the folds of the pages and let the book close as I sit up.

"You settling in okay?" he asks, fidgeting with his hands before shoving them in the pockets of his sweatpants.

"I unpacked hours ago, can't you tell?" I ask as he glances around the space. "There wasn't much. I did some online shopping earlier to make up for it, though," I try to joke, but after the day we've had, it falls flat. It's tempting to smother myself with one of the pillows.

Henry's mouth tilts upward into a faint smile, at least he's trying to make me feel like it was funny. We haven't spoken much since everything with my parents this afternoon. I haven't known what to say. I feel awful because it was my idea to let my parents think we're actually together.

"I hate it when people interrupt me when I'm reading so I'm sorry to interrupt you, but someone is here to see you," he says, his eyes lingering on me. "Where did you find that sweatshirt?" Henry asks, and I look down at the faded Duke sweatshirt that I'm swimming in.

"It was in the closet underneath a sheet?"

He chuckles to himself. "I knew Kaitlyn hid it. She told me she had no idea where it was, and it was here the whole goddamn time. That's my lucky sweatshirt from when I was at Duke. I wore it every time I had a test."

I pull the sleeves of the sweatshirt over my hands, unsure of what he wants me to do. "Is it okay I'm borrowing it? I got a little cold an—"

"It's fine, Mira. I just wasn't expecting to see you wearing it. I haven't seen it in months, thanks to my sister."

"Are you sure?" I ask, hating how weird it is between us now. I've always been weird and awkward, but Henry has never tiptoed around me.

He nods, his bright eyes meeting mine as they sparkle with amusement. "It looks better on you than it ever did on me. Hopefully it still has a little luck left in it, I think we could both use some."

I sigh in relief, sliding off the bed, but I falter in front of Henry. "Hey, Henry?"

Henry looks down at me as I swallow the lump in my throat. "Thank you for earlier. I know how much you look up to my dad, and I'm sorry for everything he said to you. You didn't deserve any of it, and I hope you don't believe any of it was true," I clarify awkwardly. I cross my arms over my chest as if that could protect my heart from how he's about to splinter it into a million tiny pieces when he says it was all pretend.

"I meant every word, Mira. You're not a kid anymore— you're an incredible, strong, and beautiful person. You're also selfless. I don't think anyone else would help me the way you are. You had my back today, so of course I had yours." Henry drags a hand through his hair, the sleeve of twisting ink catching my eye as his arm flexes during the movement. I wonder what it would be like to trace them with my fingertips. "Thank you," he says, pulling my attention from his tattoos. He leans down to brush his lips over my cheek, sending a spark through my body. I flinch in surprise, causing Henry's chest to rumble with quiet laughter. "Relax, Mira. No one's going to believe us if I can't even kiss you on the cheek without you flinching."

My cheeks flush because he's right. "I wasn't expecting it since we're at home." *Do it again*, I'm tempted to say. I'll be ready this time.

"Have you changed your mind yet?" he asks, concern marring his handsome face. "That was a lot with your parents earlier."

Forcing my mouth into a smile at the reminder of that shit show, I shake my head, willing myself to not look as miserable as I feel. "I haven't changed my mind. We're doing this. It'll get easier. You heard my mom—they need some time." I also heard Dad say a lot of horrible things to Henry that I'm hoping he apologizes for at some point.

I pat his arm reassuringly, internally groaning as Henry raises his eyebrows at me, before slipping past him to see who's waiting for me. I know it's not my parents, considering Henry didn't have a black eye when he opened the door.

My uncle is chatting with Wilson about something related to the team when he notices me. "Hey, Mira, got a couple of minutes to chat?"

"Are you going to tell me *I told you so* again?" I ask, crossing my arms over my chest.

"I don't think that's what you need to hear right now, so it wasn't my plan," Uncle Owen says, cracking a smile that helps me relax. I'm not sure I can take another lecture today, it's been the longest day ever.

"Perfect, then it looks like my schedule has cleared up." I smile back at him as I hear Henry walk down the stairs behind me.

Uncle Owen steps forward to ruffle my hair like I'm five years old again. "Atta girl, let's get some ice cream."

Ice cream sounds like the perfect Band-Aid to soothe the injuries inflicted during the last twenty-four hours. "I think that's the best idea you've ever had," I say, slipping into my flip-flops next to the garage door.

"Have fun," Henry calls after us, and I look at him over my shoulder, waving slightly.

"Thanks, Henry. I'll be back in a little bit," I say, hesitating to follow Uncle Owen. I let my impulsiveness get the better of me, closing the distance between us to lean in and press a short kiss to Henry's cheek before I lose my nerve.

He doesn't flinch like I did, but I don't miss the sharp intake of breath as my lips kiss the stubble on his cheek.

Would Henry be opposed to me asking if we should practice anything prior to making our first appearance together? The last thing we need after the disaster with my parents is for someone to guess that this relationship is fabricated to make Henry more likable.

Actually, practicing is not a bad idea.

My uncle clears his throat from where he holds the door open for me, and my bravado immediately disappears. *Holy shit, I kissed Henry Price's cheek, and I did it in front of my uncle.*

I back away, taking care not to trip over my own feet as I follow Uncle Owen out the door, praying my face isn't as cherry red as it feels. Thankfully, he cuts me some slack and doesn't say anything about it.

"What kind are we feeling? Soft-serve or scooped?"

"Either works, but we don't actually have to get ice cream. I'm okay, so there's no need to take me out for a treat after a bad day," I offer, smoothing my hair back down from when he mussed it.

"Honestly, I'd rather take you for a drink, but as your dad so graciously pointed out earlier, you aren't twenty-one. Ice cream is probably better for you anyway, and I want ice cream. So if it makes you feel better, it's mainly for me," he says as I do my best not to backslide into a puddle of guilt and sadness at the mention of earlier.

"If you insist," I agree, sliding into the passenger side of his BMW.

He pulls out of the driveway, staying unusually quiet. I don't like it. It's abnormal for Uncle Owen to be quiet, and I know he has something to say about all this. He can't fool me. "Just say it," I say, and he rolls his eyes.

"I hope you know how much you take after your mom. She's done the same damn thing since we were kids." Uncle Owen chuckles, tapping his hand on the steering wheel, but I'm waiting for him to get to the real reason we're going for ice cream. "Okay, fine. I know you care about Henry, but you don't have to go through with this fake relationship if you don't want to."

"I know I don't have to, but I want to help Henry. If this is what he needs, then I guess the fake relationship needs to happen. I never thought my parents would hate the idea so much."

"Your parents love you. God, Mira, you have no idea how much they love you," Uncle Owen says. "They're not perfect. Sometimes they are so far from perfect, the only thing they resemble is a walking disaster."

I look down at my hands, cringing at the sight of the chipped pink polish on my fingernails from picking anxiously at them today. "I know they love me, and I don't expect them to be perfect. I expected them to at least hear us out."

"Not their strong suit I'm afraid."

I turn to him, wondering what exactly he means by that. I'm not sure if I asked him, though, whether he would tell me. "Why were they so mad at Henry? I thought they loved him."

"They do, but they love you more," he says, glancing over at me after stopping at the red light. "I can't pretend I understand all their decisions. What makes the most sense to me and

Blake, is it caught them off guard. Henry has always played the role of a big brother in your life, and they trusted him with you. Five years doesn't seem like that big of a deal to you, but I guarantee you that Bash is replaying every time they've left you alone with Henry. At some point, you were thirteen and he was eighteen, or fifteen and twenty."

"But it's never been that way between us," I defend Henry, and Uncle Owen's hands go up in defense.

"You asked why they were mad, and that picture Stacey painted today was pretty damn believable, even if it's not the truth. Just because you know Henry didn't groom you, it doesn't mean your parents are wrong for considering it could have happened. Sometimes the people closest to you are the ones that can do the most damage," Uncle Owen says wisely, and I'm dumbfounded by how much that makes sense. "They're worried. The fire last night has them both on edge, and I'm not speaking for your dad because I've always thought he was an idiot, but they're good people, Mirabelle. They'll come around."

I never thought about it from their perspective.

"Oh."

"It's a bit more complicated than you realize, but it's their job to look out for you. Yeah, they reacted poorly, but if you look on the bright side, no one was hit," he jokes, trying to lighten the mood in the car.

It's so incredibly not funny, the only thing to do is laugh. "Yeah, only because you body blocked my dad."

"Take the win where you can get it, missy."

CHAPTER NINE

Mirabelle

I TAKE OUT MY HEADPHONES AS I JOG UP THE FRONT porch of Henry's house. My skin is covered in sticky sweat, and I'm out of breath from the three miles I decided to run at the ass crack of dawn. Even at this hour, the Carolina humidity is killer. I miss the ocean, and unfortunately, running doesn't give me the same high as it does for my brothers.

Quinn's motorcycle is parked in front of the garage door. I didn't see it earlier when I left, but I also wasn't looking for it. I think I remember Henry or Wilson saying something about how he crashes here sometimes.

I walk in the front door, making a beeline toward the kitchen to throw back a few glasses of water. Is this what dying feels like? I didn't think I was this out of shape, but maybe I am.

Quinn glances over his shoulder to look at me, clearly having heard me come in.

"Good morning," he greets, setting his protein shake on the counter as I do my best to muster a tired smile. Why is he shirtless? Doesn't he know it's rude to walk around half naked in other people's houses?

"Morning," I reply.

"If I'd known you were going for a run, I might have gotten up even earlier to join you." And then, before I can get my own, Quinn grabs a glass from the cupboard and fills it up with water. He sets it on the counter for me as I freeze, staring at it for a moment.

He cracks a charming smile at me. "Don't worry. I'm not going to spill that all over you."

I move to sit at one of the barstools, my legs feeling like jelly. "As much as I appreciate that, it honestly might feel pretty good right now. It's so humid outside."

"I feel bad about the coffee disaster," he says, flipping what looks like an omelet in the pan. "It wasn't exactly how I wanted to meet you."

"Well, you also pretended you didn't know my name, so how am I supposed to believe that you wanted to meet me?" I taunt, taking a long drink of my water. It tastes so unbelievably refreshing I almost can't believe it.

Quinn chuckles, taking my jest in stride. "I thought I was being cool by pretending I didn't know who you were. Henry talks about you, plus my mom is a huge fan of yours. She actually saw you compete a few years ago when you were touring with the US team. She would kill me if she knew I pretended not to know who you are."

Okay, that's sweet of his mom, but my mind immediately fixates on the first part about Henry. He talks about me?

I can feel my heart leap in excitement, but that can also be blamed on post-run recovery.

I smile at Quinn's admission, trying not to swoon at what Henry might have said about me to his friends. "And what do you think now that you've met me? Am I everything Henry and your mom said?"

"I think you would do anything for the people you care

about. You're doing a good thing for Henry. I don't know many people who would selflessly agree to something like that." I nod because it makes sense that he would bring that up. Quinn is one of a handful of people in on the relationship ruse, but I wouldn't say I'm doing it selflessly. However, I don't think that's a statement I need to refute. "I think you have a big heart to go with your sassy personality, and I think you have an incredible work ethic. You're also beautiful, but that's my personal opinion, not Henry or my mom's."

Oh.

I stare at him, taken aback by Quinn's answer. *What . . . what am I supposed to say to that? I was half-kidding when I asked what he thought, but I didn't actually expect him to answer.*

He turns around to grab his protein shake, opening up a cupboard to look for something. "Did I say too much?"

I clear my throat, stalling to find the right words. "No, just surprised," I reply, taking another drink of my water to get rid of the chalky feeling coating my mouth.

With Quinn's back to me, I take the opportunity to check him out. Maybe it's not a bad thing that he's shirtless, and damn, do I have a thing for muscles. His back is well-defined, but his arms . . . fuck, they look nice. I don't see any tattoos, which is only a little disappointing because I love Henry's—

I choke on fucking air, causing Quinn to quickly turn around to look at me. *Holy shit, am I checking out Henry's friend? Henry, as in the guy I've been in love with for forever?*

"Are you okay?" he asks, scanning over me as I cough, trying to catch my breath.

"Perfect," I gasp out, thumping my chest as if that will do anything. How does one recover from choking on the literal air I breathe perfectly fine all the time?

"Are you sure about that?" he asks, raising a skeptical eyebrow as he crosses his arms over his chest. Okay, seriously, now that I've started looking at his muscles, I don't know how to stop. What is wrong with me? I'd be chewing his ass if I caught him checking me out, and I have to give him credit, Quinn's eyes haven't strayed from my face during this entire conversation.

I nod quickly, feeling my face grow hot. "I'm . . . um . . . going to get ready for work," I say, reaching for the glass of water to put it away, but instead, I accidentally push it straight off the edge of the counter.

It shatters on the hardwood floor with a crash, and I gasp, immediately hopping off the barstool as Quinn sets his drink down to help me.

"Shit," I mumble under my breath, gingerly scooping the larger pieces into my hand. I can't believe I did that. I'm a fucking fool.

"Careful, don't cut yourself on the glass, Mirabelle," Quinn warns, kneeling down as I lift my head with every intention of telling him he's not the boss of me. Unfortunately, the crown of my head collides with his chin, and my hand tightens in a knee-jerk reaction around the glass.

I feel the sharp pain immediately, cursing through my teeth as Quinn groans, rubbing his chin. The glass in my hand falls to the floor, already stained with my blood. "Ouch," I hiss, immediately feeling queasy at the sight of the red streaking the glass. I don't even want to know what my hand looks like, but if the way it feels is any indication, I'm sure I cut it good.

I close my eyes, trying to inhale through my nose and exhale through my mouth. I *really* don't like blood. My phobia of blood is so extreme that my gynecologist put me on an IUD with a higher hormone level to prevent my period from coming. It took one time of me passing out at the sight of my period at the gym as a teenager, and being woken up by paramedics, for that to happen.

His hand wraps around my wrist to steady me from falling into the pile of glass as I keep my eyes tightly shut. It dawns on me that I thought about how rude it was that Quinn wasn't wearing clothes in Henry's house, but I'm also wearing a minimal amount since I ran in a sports bra and running shorts. I still have more on top than he does, but that's because I don't have a choice.

"Let me see," he instructs, taking my hand in his, and I feel light-headed. This sucks, but I definitely need help because if I see the blood again, I might actually pass out.

He's too quiet. Oh god. I must have cut it deep. *I can't believe I did this.* At the very least, I can blame Quinn; if he hadn't been here shirtless, I wouldn't have gotten distracted and knocked the glass off the counter. Then, if he hadn't crouched next to me to tell me the obvious, I wouldn't have hit my head on his chin, thus preventing me from slicing my hand open.

"Is it bad?" I ask after a moment of silence as he touches my hand.

"You might need to go to the hospital to have it amputated. It looks pretty deep."

Did he say *amputate*?

My eyes flash open to look at him, doing my best to avoid seeing my hand. "Are you fucking serious?"

Quinn's mouth curls into an amused smile. "Sweetheart, I'm fucking with you. I don't think you even need stitches, you should be fine with a little gauze and tape. It's long, but not deep."

I shake my head, accidentally looking at my hand, and I fall backward slightly to rest my back against the cabinets. "I'm not a sweetheart, and that is so not funny. How do you know?"

"I've spent enough time with athletic trainers over the years, I know what a superficial cut looks like. And I think you are a sweetheart—I bet if they cracked your chest open, they'd find a candy heart inside," he says, and I chuckle awkwardly. It's harmless flirting.

"Mira? Where are you?" I hear Henry call out, and my head immediately turns to look in the direction of his voice like a moth to a flame. Henry steps into my line of sight as he finishes pulling a shirt over his head, much to my dismay. His eyes are wide as he searches for me, halting at the sight of us. "Quinn?" he questions, dragging a hand through his dark hair, still sticking up in every direction from how he slept. I'd give anything to run my fingers through his hair. I wonder if it's as soft as it looks.

"Can you grab the first aid kit out from under the sink?" Quinn asks Henry, who is staring at us.

Henry blinks, his gaze shifting from whatever Quinn is doing to my hand, following directions immediately after seeing it. "What happened?" he asks, his voice low from sleep. I keep my eyes on Henry, enjoying his disheveled appearance perhaps a little too much, but it's a nice distraction from the nausea I feel. "I thought someth—you know, it doesn't matter," he trails off, handing the kit to Quinn.

"I knocked a glass of water over. I'm sorry," I apologize, and he crouches down next to me, thankfully in the opposite direction of my hand.

"What the hell are you apologizing for? I don't care about a glass, I care about you. You're not looking so good," he says, tilting my chin up to examine my face as Quinn presses something against the cut, causing me to wince.

"Just what every girl wants to be told," I joke, and Henry's eyes crinkle. "I'm fine, it's the—"

"The blood, I know. Try not to faint, Walker. Keep your eyes on me," Henry interrupts, and I'm distracted by the fullness of his bottom lip. It's tempting to drag my good hand through his hair to smooth it out.

As if I could look anywhere else when he's in the same room as me. Is it stupid for me to be excited that he remembers I hate blood? Actually, yeah, that is stupid. He definitely remembers the time our families were on vacation in the Bahamas when Hunter slipped on a rock, slicing his foot open. I fainted at the sight of all the blood, and poor Henry was stuck lugging us back to where our parents were lounging on the beach with JJ, Bailey, and Kaitlyn.

"What about blood?" Quinn asks, and Henry briefly looks at him, as if remembering he's still in the room.

"Why are you shirtless?" Henry asks pointedly, and I force a short laugh, suddenly very nervous to be in the kitchen with Quinn and Henry. *Fuck, if you count me in the mix, the level of hotness in this room is combustible.*

"I have an extremely bad reaction to seeing blood that usually ends up with me fainting," I explain quickly, as Henry's hand falls from where it still lingered on my chin.

Henry's jaw is covered in dark scruff, and since he told me to keep looking at him, I have free rein to note all the imperfect details on his perfect face. There's a small bump on the bridge of his nose from where he broke it in college, his lips are slightly chapped and in need of lip balm, and his lashes are dark and stupidly long. *I could give him some of my lip balm if he doesn't have a problem with me applying it with my mouth.*

We're both trying to adjust to our new dynamic. I have yet to ask if he'll practice making out with me, mainly because I'm not sure what I would do if Henry said no.

"What did you think happened when you came down? You look like you just got out of bed," I point out, trying to distract myself from Quinn wrapping my hand up. At least this is almost over, and I can go drown myself in the shower.

Henry shakes his head quickly, averting his eyes from mine. "It doesn't matter what I thought."

It does matter because I want to know. "Do I need to tell

Quinn about the time you were caught—" Henry moves quickly to cover my mouth to shut me up. I laugh maniacally against his hand, tempted to lick it so he'll take it off. I know plenty of shit about Henry that I could use to blackmail him into doing whatever I want.

"Whatever the fuck you were about to say, *don't*. I heard the glass break, and I thought someone had broken in. You weren't in your room when I checked, and I needed to know you were okay," he answers, pulling his hand away.

Henry's admission sobers the mood in the room, and it dawns on me the investigation into my family's house is still ongoing. I received a call from a detective a few days ago asking if I had seen anyone new around the neighborhood. The case was officially declared arson, but I've been doing everything possible to keep my mind occupied.

"Nobody broke in. I was being a klutz."

"All better," Quinn says, and I feel guilty for directing all my focus on Henry.

"No blood?" I ask, still keeping my head angled upward to prevent my hand from being in my line of sight.

"No blood," Quinn confirms, and I carefully lift my hand to examine my palm now covered in a light layer of gauze and tape. Flexing my hand, I'm impressed the tape doesn't pull, but it still doesn't feel great with the freshness of the cut.

"Thank you, Quinn. I appreciate it," I say, smiling at him. He even brushed aside all the glass so I don't have to see the shattered pieces anymore. I didn't hear him do that.

"I know exactly how you can make it up to me," Quinn says, and my smile grows. I'll take the bait.

"And how is that?"

Henry clears his throat as if to subtly remind us he's still here. It's not possible for me to forget he's in the room, but I do accept the hand Quinn offers after standing up. "You can make it up to me by telling me what you were about to black-mail Henry with."

It *does* seem like a fair trade.

I turn to smile mischievously at Henry, gauging on a scale from one to ten how upset he would be. "Quinn *did* help bandage my hand."

"*No,*" Henry immediately protests, a wary expression on his handsome face.

Meh, I'm not very good at doing what I'm told.

"Henry got caught by his dad jerking off to a Wonder Woman comic after forgetting to lock the door," I blurt out before Henry can put his hand over my mouth again.

His glare is murderous, and maybe I should be a little afraid of him being upset. Quinn howls with laughter as the sound of footsteps gets louder down the stairs.

"How the fuck do you even know that?" Henry gapes, his face tomato red. I laugh easily as Wilson walks into the kitchen with a gym bag over his shoulder.

He stares at Henry for a moment, cocking his head to the side. "What am I walking into?"

Quinn is too busy laughing to form words, leaning over the counter hysterically.

Henry shakes his head in disbelief, dragging a hand over his face. "I was thirteen, okay? It was all I had."

It doesn't help. In fact, all of us end up laughing harder.

The only reason I know is because Chris and Penelope told my parents while I was eavesdropping. Of course I had no idea what jerking off meant at the time, but I sure wrote about it in my diary that I reread before I went to college. I'm not even embarrassed to say I went as Wonder Woman for Halloween my freshman year at Duke.

I start to back out of the kitchen, my side aching from laughing so hard. "On that note, I think I'm going to go get ready for work. Don't leave without me."

"You can drive your own car today," Henry grumbles under his breath.

Quinn flashes me a confident smile. "I'll take you if he leaves. There's an extra helmet on my bike. Gotta save the planet one carpool at a time, sweetheart."

I laugh off the endearment because Henry's entire body stiffens. "You know, Quinn, I think you might have yourself a new friend after all."

"Fuck no, your dad is already prepared to throw me in a wood chipper. I'm not letting him find out I let you ride on a motorcycle. I'll wait until you're ready, and you'll ride with me," Henry says, but I'm not sure I love the way he says he'll "let" me do something. I thought we'd already covered this.

I roll my eyes, crossing my arms over my chest. "You don't let me do anything, Henry. I think that stick is lodged up your ass again. Want me to send you a clip of Wonder Woman so you can relax a little?"

Henry's eyes flash dangerously, and the guys burst into laughter again as I retreat up the stairs, praying he doesn't kill me in my sleep tonight.

CHAPTER TEN

Henry

It's been a shit day from the start.

I was slow getting out of bed until I heard the sound of breaking glass, and my mind immediately leapt to the possibility of someone breaking in to hurt Mirabelle. She wasn't in her room when I checked, but it might have been better if someone had broken in than to find her and Quinn in the kitchen together after I specifically asked him to stay away from her. How does that translate to walking around the kitchen shirtless, calling her sweetheart, and offering her rides on his motorcycle? *Quick math: it fucking doesn't.*

I think she deserves better than Quinn. In the short time I've known him, he's been a good friend, but I don't love that the first thing he said about Mira when this shit started was how she's flexible. He justified it afterward, but it's still bothering me. Maybe that makes me a possessive asshole, but she's more than that.

Then my day got worse because I missed a call from my sister while I was in a meeting with Stacey, which Mirabelle wasn't present for. We haven't spoken much since the news of our relationship broke, and I hate that. Our parents are probably grilling her, and I don't want to put her in a position where she has to lie to them.

The real icing on the cake today is I received another call from my birth mother. I declined it, but it's ignorant of me to assume she'll get the message to stop calling. I need to come up with something better to call her in my head because she's not my mother—Penelope is. Penelope has loved and raised me for as long as I can remember.

It feels like I'm discrediting everything Penelope has done for me by calling Allison my mother.

I rack the bar I'm using for bench presses while Wilson spots me. He and Quinn have been cracking Wonder Woman jokes all fucking day since Mirabelle told them that mortifying story this morning.

How the fuck did she even know that? Dad wouldn't have told her . . . at least, I don't think he would have. That happened so long ago, I'd forgotten about it.

I pull myself up, and Wilson smirks. "I would have offered to give you a hand, but I'm not Wonder Woman, so I didn't think you'd want it."

"Very funny. Your turn, buddy. I hope you don't need a hand yourself," I remark back, taking it in stride.

Wilson holds his arm up, flexing to make his pectoral muscle pop out dramatically. "With these guns? No thanks, man," he replies, laughing quietly. He looks over my shoulder, and I turn to see what he's looking at, but it only further sours my mood.

Mirabelle and Quinn are chatting, and whatever he said has her head tipped back as she laughs. Mira's smile is wide, and she looks . . . beautiful. Beautiful is the only word that comes to mind when I look at her.

I haven't let myself linger too much on this morning.

When Quinn was bandaging her hand, I told her to look at me to distract her from the blood. It felt like she was looking into the inner depths of my soul, but I think I liked it?

I certainly like it more when she looks at me instead of Quinn.

Shaking my head, I turn back to Wilson, who is eyeing me knowingly. "You cool with that? I think he's actually interested in her."

No, it makes my blood boil, but I can't explain why. "They're both adults. As long as they aren't photographed together, I don't care." It feels like a lie, but what else am I supposed to say?

"Whatever you say." Wilson snorts, clearly not buying my bullshit.

As Mirabelle's melodic laughter echoes through the room, I can't keep my eyes from drifting back toward them. Is Quinn actually interested in her, or is he interested in finding out how flexible she is?

As if she can tell I'm watching, Mirabelle looks over at us, smiling at me. Her cheeks are flush with happiness, and I instinctively smile back, pushing Quinn's motives to the back of my mind.

She turns back to him, saying something quickly before beginning to walk toward us. Selfishly, I take the opportunity to check her out, lingering on those heels she loves to wear, drifting upward to her long, tanned legs to the pencil skirt and blouse she's wearing. Her light blonde hair is pulled back into a high ponytail on her head, swishing behind her as she walks.

Goddamn.

I didn't notice earlier what she wore to work today because I was annoyed she told my friends about my love for Wonder Woman, but I think those heels are starting to grow on me. I shouldn't care what she wears or what shoes she's wearing, regardless of how amazing they make her legs look. I shouldn't be wondering what it would be like to wrap my fingers around her ponytail to pull it back so I can see the look on her face—*fuck, what is wrong with me?*

Mirabelle pulls her ponytail over her shoulder, twisting the strands between her fingers, and I'm jealous. I'm fucking jealous, especially since I have no business thinking about her in that way in the first place. "Hey, can I talk to you for a moment?" she asks, and I look at Wilson to see if he needs me to spot for him. I was lifting light with our first game coming up this weekend, so he should be fine.

"I told you I didn't need a hand. This is easy, go talk to your girlfriend," he says, and I roll my eyes.

"I hope that bar falls on you."

Mirabelle hits my arm with the back of her hand, shooting me a look. "That's mean."

"So was telling my friends this morning about an embarrassing moment, but you said it anyway," I grumble under my breath as she laughs at my misery, leaving me to follow after her. Not that I mind, because it gives me the perfect opportunity to look at her ass.

Mirabelle leads us to a quiet corner of the gym, and I quickly wipe away the sweat running down my face using the bottom of my shirt. When I drop it, her face is a flaming shade of red. What the hell is her deal?

"You good?" I question, and she makes a weird, high-pitched sound that I think was supposed to be a laugh.

"Yeah. Perfect, I—uhm—I wanted to ask you about something quick?" she stammers, and it feels like I've been kicked in the stomach. It was foolish of me to think that she actually wanted to talk to me about something; instead, Quinn asked her out, and she wants to go out with him. Except, everyone already thinks we're together. I fucking knew this fake dating thing wasn't going to work.

"If you want to date Quinn, it's fine. All I ask is that you guys are careful so no one sees you," I say, not interested in hearing her gush about how charming my friend is. I don't want to hear her talk about anyone that way, but especially not Quinn.

Her eyes widen in shock, staring at me in disbelief. "Wait —I'm sorry. What the hell are you talking about?"

After everything today, I'm not sure I have it in me to even pretend to be kind about this.

"It's obvious that you like him, and vice versa. I'm cool with it, but maybe try not to make it so obvious to other people since, you know, *we're supposed to be dating*." I cross my arms over my chest, leaning against the wall.

"*Obvious*?" her voice rises in pitch, and I look around to see if anyone is paying attention to us. "Oh my god, Henry. You're an ass," Mirabelle hisses at me, in a quieter tone, frowning. "I was going to ask if you were cool with my best friend, Emily, staying a couple nights at the house."

Huh?

"So this isn't about Quinn?" I ask, starting to feel like the ass she keeps calling me.

The murderous look she gives me reminds me so much of the one I see her mother give Sebastian sometimes. "No. It's not about Quinn. Fuck, men are idiots." Mirabelle scoffs, walking away, but she immediately turns right back around to stand in front of me. She opens her mouth but hesitates before closing it. She frowns again, and I'm staying absolutely silent because clearly, I keep saying the wrong things. I'm a little afraid that the next time I say something, she'll kick me in the balls instead of telling me what an ass I am. I wouldn't put it past her.

"Would it really not bother you if I were interested in Quinn?" she asks, and immediately red lights start flashing in my head. She's told me she doesn't like it when I give her permission to do things, so I feel like this is a trap she's trying to catch me in.

I swallow the lump in my throat as she stares at me for my answer. With the added height from her heels, the top of her head is even with my shoulders. It's the perfect height for me to lean down and brush a kiss over her lips opposed to her cheek.

I don't want to see Mirabelle with Quinn. This isn't up to me, though. Our relationship isn't real, and she's free to see whoever she wants. Why wouldn't she want to be with Quinn? He's closer to her age, they clearly get along, and her parents would be ecstatic because the idea of her dating me is apparently a nightmare.

Still, picturing them together makes me want to put my fist through a wall.

"No, it wouldn't," I say calmly, deciding that's the safe answer instead of telling her how pissed it makes me.

Mirabelle shakes her head, her eyes narrowing as she laughs. *Oh shit. That was the wrong answer.* "Obvious, my ass. Fuck you, Henry."

This time when she walks away, she doesn't turn back.

I roll my shoulders, exhaling sharply as I watch her for a moment, noting the subtle sway of her hips before forcing my gaze to the ground. How can I be angry with Quinn for questioning how flexible she is, when I can't stop staring at her, thinking thoughts I shouldn't be.

Wilson laughs when I return, clearly having seen the whole interaction. "For someone who is supposed to be in the honeymoon phase of a relationship, you two don't look very lovey."

"We're going on a date tonight."

He raises an eyebrow in surprise. "Since when? She did not look very happy with you as she stomped away."

Since now.

We didn't fuck everything up with her parents for us not to follow through with the plan.

"Shut up," I grumble, grabbing my phone from the floor. I send a quick text to my assistant who handles my calendar, asking her to get a table at one of the best restaurants in town this evening.

It's going to be a night we won't forget.

CHAPTER ELEVEN

Mirabelle

I can't believe Henry. He thinks I obviously like Quinn? What about all the years I've *obviously* been in love with him?

I hate that word.

Obvious.

Fuck me. Except no one's doing that, because I'm so fucking obvious about who I have feelings for!

The only saving grace is Emily getting into town tomorrow afternoon. Then, I'm out of my boy bubble and back with a girlfriend my own age, since none of my coworkers want anything to do with me. Joke's on them; I don't want anything to do with them either.

I stomp into the house, still irritated from my conversation with Henry in the weight room. He's an idiot. I'm aware I haven't exactly come out and said *Hey, Henry. I have had the biggest crush on you since I was like five years old. Will you just marry me already?* So granted, how is he supposed to know that I like him?

Maybe because I'm so *obvious* about who I supposedly like.

Idiots.

Men are idiots.

"Hey, Mirabelle?" Henry calls after me before I can disappear up the stairs and into my room. I ignored Henry the entire drive back, having shoved my headphones into my ears to make it apparent that I wanted nothing to do with him at the moment.

"What?" I ask, trying to keep the frustration out of my tone. *At least I'm trying? Not very well, but I think I deserve an A for effort.*

"We're going out tonight. Dinner plans are at eight thirty, in case you want to get ready."

Excuse me? "Were you even going to ask me, or are you assuming that I don't have plans with say . . . maybe Quinn?" I turn around, resting my hands on my hips.

I'm highly aware I'm being a bitch, but Henry will survive. *Obvious.*

His jaw tightens and he tilts his head. "Do you?" he asks, and I can read his body language like it's another foreign language I'm fluent in. Oh, it *so* bothers him that Quinn might be interested in me, but not enough for him to tell me it doesn't.

I smile playfully at Henry, enjoying the rise I'm getting out of him. I miss fighting with Bailey, believe it or not. It's hard to fight when he doesn't answer any of my texts or calls, and I haven't gone home because I feel like I'm a huge disappointment to my parents right now. Everything is *awesome* at the moment.

"No, but I could have since you don't care if I see him. Next time you want to plan a date, you might want to ask me first to make sure I can go."

"You're right, I should have," he admits, at least having the decency to look guilty. "I'm sorry. Will you please go out with me tonight?"

I purse my lips, half tempted to say no to prove that I can. Alas, that wouldn't mean following the agreement to fake date him, and the other part of me that is hopelessly in love with Henry—despite whatever dumb thing comes out of his mouth—is desperate to say yes. "Yes, I'll go out with you."

I wish he was actually asking me out.

"We'll have fun, I promise," Henry says, smiling as if he's relieved, but all I hear is him saying earlier that he's okay with me dating Quinn. It might bother him, but not enough to the point he'll tell me not to do it. Whereas if the roles were flipped, it might actually break my heart to see him with someone else.

But . . . if I can show him how great it would be to date me, then maybe Henry will realize he cares enough to tell me not to date Quinn.

"We definitely will," I muse, eager to dart up to my room with renewed energy that I could wow the socks—*or the pants, I wouldn't complain*—off Henry.

"Thanks Mirabelle, I appreciate it."

Oh, you shouldn't be thanking me yet.

~

"So I asked Dad if they were going to the season opener, and he wouldn't give me a definitive answer. I think you should talk to him," JJ suggests through the iPad screen as I straighten my hair, trying to be careful of my finger.

"Yeah, not sure if that's the best way to get an answer. That's assuming he picks up the phone in the first place," I reply, feeling my stomach twist at the thought of Dad declining a call from me. I've been too much of a chicken to call out of fear that they won't answer and of what they might say if they do.

"Mira, you should call. I know it was awful, but Hunter

said it's weird at the house," he says, munching on some potato chips. I can tell from the background noise that he's in his dorm room.

I put the straightener down, the pit of anxiety growing in my stomach. "You weren't there, JJ. You didn't see how upset they were with us."

"You know how they are, they probably need some time to cool off," he tries to defend them, but I shake my head. I don't want to talk about this right now. I miss them so much it hurts, but I'm not making the first move this time. I took what Uncle Owen said into consideration, but I'm not the one that owes them an apology. I need to save all my energy right now for my date with Henry.

"How's football going?" I ask, changing the subject entirely.

JJ looks disappointed, but thankfully, he doesn't push the topic any further. I pick up my straightener again to finish the front section of my long hair.

"Good. I'm learning a lot, but I sure am glad Uncle Owen is the one who put my training schedule together this summer. His drills were a fuck ton harder than the ones we do here. Everyone else is suffering after practices, but I feel fine."

"You could stay after practice with some of your teammates to run those drills and help strengthen your team? It could get you some playing time if your coaches notice?" I suggest, running my brush through my hair, satisfied to see the bright blonde strands looking extra smooth and silky. All my time in the sun this summer helped brighten my natural color.

I grab my mascara wand, touching up my lashes to get all the clumps out.

"Actually, that might be a good idea. Who knew you had them," JJ teases, and I flip him off with a smile.

"Screw you. I have plenty of good ideas."

"Oh yeah? How is fake dating the love of your life going

for you?" he muses, and I feel my cheeks flush. It's not going how I imagined it would.

"Shut up, JJ. He's not the love of my life." *Unless he is.* "It's going fine. We're arguing a bit more than I thought we would, but other than that it's going well." I step out of the camera frame to get dressed. I smooth my dress down, looking in the mirror. It's a black satin halter top dress that makes me look like I'm definitely not twenty. The open back is dramatic and is one of the reasons I bought it during my shopping spree after the fire. I thought Henry's head was going to explode when the packages started arriving, but I don't think he'll complain after he sees what I'm wearing tonight.

"Goddamn, Mira, you're pulling out the big guns tonight. What have you been arguing about?"

"Hair up or down?" I ask, my nerves finally starting to hit me. What if I look like I'm playing dress up? If Henry laughs at me, I might simply never recover.

"Leave it down. You ignored my question. What are you arguing about with Henry?" JJ repeats his question, and I roll my eyes, slipping on the tennis bracelet Dad gave me for my sixteenth birthday. It survived the fire since I wore it to work that day, but I'll eventually need to go to the beach house to get more of my things. The bracelet sparkles on my wrist and is the perfect addition to my outfit, distracting from the bandage on my finger.

"He's an idiot." JJ tries to stifle a laugh, and I sigh, brushing my hair one more time. I have to look perfect. "Henry thinks I'm interested in his friend, Quinn. Said it was obvious I have feelings for him, and all I want to do is smack Henry upside the head while telling him how obviously in love with him I am. Instead, I asked him if it bothered him, and he said no. Maybe I'm the idiot for asking a question, knowing the answer wouldn't be the one I wanted to hear."

"You're not an idiot, Mira. *Are* you interested in Quinn?" JJ asks, popping more chips into his mouth, crunching loudly.

"Would you stop eating so loud? It's annoying," I grumble, avoiding this question. I'm not interested in Quinn, but I don't know what the fuck I'm doing letting him flirt with me.

"Dude, you will never believe what just happened outside with this girl," a different voice says in the background, causing JJ to turn.

"Hey, I'm actually on the phone with my sister, can you tell me in a minute?" JJ asks as the phone is yanked from him as a guy with light brown hair fills the screen.

"Your sister is hot," he says, his eyes growing wide in surprise. This must be JJ's roommate, Asher.

"Give me the phone back," JJ complains, but it's a nice boost for my ego.

"Are you single?"

I laugh shortly, shaking my head. "I'm afraid not."

"She's dating Henry Price, which I know you know because you asked me if he was going to come to one of our games this season since he's dating my sister."

Asher winks at me playfully. "If you ever decide to dump him, will you promise me I'll be your first call?"

"Asher."

"Dude, shut up, I'm hitting on your sister," Asher says, talking to JJ.

"As amusing as this is, I do have to go. Love you, JJ. I'll call you later," I say, hanging up because if I don't finish getting ready, Henry and I will be late for our reservation.

I slip into my new black stilettos, grabbing the small black purse I bought for the sole reason of matching this dress. I do a little spin, satisfied with how I look, even if I'm overdressed for the occasion.

I feel like I'm going to throw up. Is it too late to cancel?

Henry has his back to me, but he turns at the sound of my

heels on the hardwood as I finish descending the stairs. His hazel eyes widen, slowly trailing down my figure, and I clutch my bag to hide the shaking of my hands. Henry's mouth parts, and he sucks in a sharp breath.

Meanwhile, I'm rendered just as speechless.

He looks good—dangerously good, in fact. Henry's white button down has a few open buttons at the collar, and his black sports coat fits perfectly, hugging him in all the right places. His chocolate hair is somewhat styled, but it still looks like he's been running his fingers through it.

I laugh nervously, adjusting my bag as he continues to stare at me. At least I can tell by his attire that I'm not over-dressed. "Are you ready to go?" I ask, since I'm not sure if he's going to say anything.

My question seems to jolt him out of whatever is going on in his head, and I think I'd give anything to know what he's thinking right now.

"Yes," he answers, his voice low as he twirls his keys in his hand.

With the way he just eye-fucked me, I would have thought I'd at least be told *you look nice, Mirabelle,* but I guess not.

We're walking toward the door as Quinn lets himself in, his jaw falling immediately open. "Holy hell, you look amazing."

Okay, that's a much better reaction.

I smooth the dress down, smiling brightly at Quinn. "Thanks."

"Are you two going out tonight?" he asks, glancing at Henry before refocusing on me.

"Yeah," Henry says, sticking with one-word replies.

"I can go change quick, and I'll join you," Quinn says, but now I'm confused. I thought with both of us dressed up, it was fairly obvious we're going out on a date. I look to Henry, trying to figure out what the right thing to say is, but Henry shakes his head, taking the lead.

"Sorry, Q. You'll have to try the restaurant another time. It's only me and Mira tonight," Henry says. His next move pretty much stops my heart when he grabs my hand, lacing our fingers together to pull me past Quinn before he can say anything else.

He's holding my hand.

Henry fucking Price is holding my hand because he's jealous.

He opens the passenger door of his car for me, and I slide into the seat, careful not to flash him as I get in. I drag my fingertips over the smooth leather interior after he shuts the door. "Where are we going?" I ask Henry, trying to distract him from the fact Quinn tried to crash our date. I'm not mad about how Henry responded, but I do feel slightly bad that Quinn walked in at that exact moment.

"It's a surprise," he says, directing a slanted smile my way.

"Apparently, you're full of surprises. Makes you pretty mysterious," I tease, hinting at how the media has wrongfully stereotyped him as this mysterious bad boy. However, our previous plan—with the addition of the relationship— seems to be having a better effect on his image than we anticipated.

Henry chuckles, and I hope that means he picks up on my reference. I know he's under a lot of pressure, but he never gets to . . . *be*. Part of my plan is to make our PR stunts environments Henry can just exist in. "I thought you were supposed to help make me less mysterious?" he questions, and I roll my eyes.

"That's the goal, but I'm excited for what we have planned on Saturday. I think you'll actually have a good time."

He raises an eyebrow, appearing skeptical. "You sound awfully sure of that."

"Well, you get to play with puppies, so who wouldn't be happy about that?"

"I thought Owen promised there would be no holding puppies?" he asks, his eyes glimmering with amusement. Did he not read the schedule Stacey sent him a few weeks ago?

"No, he said holding puppies wouldn't interfere with football. We're simply combining the two," I say. "To celebrate the first game of the season and what not, we're hosting a Puppy Bowl Saturday with a local animal shelter to help with adoptions, and for every touchdown you throw Sunday, Uncle Owen has offered to donate five thousand dollars."

"Really?"

"Yeah. Uncle Owen's a huge animal lover. But the real kicker is that if you throw any interceptions, you're donating seven grand per interception." That was my idea. He shouldn't have pissed me off earlier. It was only supposed to be five thousand per interception, but I suggested to Stacey that seven might make the public be more forgiving toward him if he does throw an interception.

"So they get more money if I suck? How the fuck is that fair?" Henry shakes his head like it doesn't make any sense to him.

"Just let me finish," I interject, laughing at his reaction. "If we win the game, the stadium has agreed to donate a percentage of every ticket sold to the animal shelter." Which is a lot of fucking money—that was my idea, too. Actually, the entire thing was my idea, but that's not important. It's a tax write-off for them, and good press, so it's a win for everyone involved.

Henry's face softens for a moment, redirecting his attention back to the road. His hands are loosely gripping the steering wheel, a picture of assuredness as he drives a car that costs more than some people make in a year. *I wonder what his hands would feel like if he put them on me? What would the calluses on his hand feel like scraping over my skin? Does he like to be gentle or rough?*

"How much of this was your idea?" he asks, connecting the dots together, pulling me from my explicit thoughts about his hands. *God, I'm a mess.*

My cheeks flush and I glance down at my hands. Is it dumb that it gives me butterflies knowing he can tell I helped with it? "I submitted it with my application for the internship, but I never thought they'd actually use it."

"It's a great idea. They'd be dumb not to use it. I'll have to make sure I'm on the top of my game so it's Owen's wallet that's hurting and not mine."

"Either way, I get to play with puppies so I'm happy, but if I were you, I'd try not sucking on Sunday," I tease, smiling as I'm rewarded with a smile in return. That's exactly how it feels when he smiles—*like a reward*. As much as I like his slanted half-smiles, it's the ones that transform his whole face that make my heart skip a beat. I wish Henry would smile like this more, but if he did, I don't think it would feel as special when he does.

"Shit, maybe we should have gone to play with puppies tonight instead of going to dinner." He shakes his head as if scolding himself.

"I'm excited for dinner. I like food," I say, but honestly, I think I'd like anything as long as Henry is the one next to me.

"I like food too, so we must be a perfect match."

I don't know if Henry is aware of what his words do to me, but they make my heart soar. Even if he's joking, we are a perfect match.

I play with the edge of my dress as I try to think of a response, rolling the satin fabric between my fingertips.

Lately, I think we've spent too much forced time together, and it's had a negative impact on our friendship. It's nice to willingly spend time together tonight—well, I guess we're only going on a date because we're fake dating, but still. Actually, that sounds wrong. It was nice of him to ask to spend time together . . . not that he asked, of course, but he eventually did so after the fact.

Henry breaks the silence in the car as we're stopped at a red light, halting the racing thoughts inside my head. "You look great, Mirabelle," Henry says, and I turn in surprise.

"Thank you," I say, smiling at him as my heart does flips in my chest. "You look nice too."

The music playing faintly in the background fills the comfortable silence in the car, but my nerves from earlier reappear in full force as Henry pulls up to the valet at one of my favorite restaurants. The front of the building is swarmed with paparazzi, all beginning to take pictures of Henry's car, the bright flashing of the cameras dimmed by the tint of the windows.

"I'm sorry. Stacey must have called them. I told her earlier we were going out tonight so she didn't keep you late at the stadium. We can go somewhere else if you want?"

"It's nothing I'm not used to," I reassure Henry who is starting to look pale. It makes me feel slightly better that he's nervous too. "The whole point of this is to be photographed together, so Stacey did the right thing. We might as well put on a good show for the cameras, right?" I ask, resisting the urge to reach over and grab his hand.

"You're the best," he says appreciatively, but the tension in his body remains coiled as he looks at the restaurant.

I flip a small piece of hair dramatically, hoping it's enough to distract him. "I know."

Thankfully, he laughs, and pulls up to the valet, climbing out of the car smoothly. I have enough time to take a deep breath and exhale as Henry opens my door, offering me his hand. I smooth my dress, climbing out in a manner that ensures I'm not flashing my goods at anyone, focusing entirely on Henry as the flashes in the background begin at a rapid rate.

If I hadn't been in the car with him a minute ago, I would think he does this all the time with how calm he looks now. It'll probably be in our best interest if we start traveling everywhere with sunglasses on us at all times to help with the bright lights. This reminds me of how I couldn't go anywhere after the London games without someone shoving a camera in my face.

A hint of anxiety threatens to surface, but I can't let it. Part of this world is faking it until you make it.

My heel catches in a crack in the pavement, sending me tumbling straight into Henry, who catches me easily and helps me straighten up. Believe it or not, it wasn't intentional, but it is the perfect photo opportunity. I lift my head to look at him, grateful he didn't let me fall on my ass.

His bright eyes drop to my lips, and my breathing hitches at the potential lying in our position. After all these years of pining for Henry Price, he might finally kiss me.

I tilt my head up in anticipation as his chin dips, holding my breath.

Please kiss me.

Please please please.

And then my heart sinks at the flicker of hesitation in his eyes, and I know he isn't going to kiss me.

So I kiss him.

I curl my hand on the back of his neck to make it easier to meet his full lips as I rise up on my tiptoes, pressing my mouth softly against Henry's. It only takes half a second for Henry to react, but his arm resting on my lower back tightens to pull me closer to him.

Fireworks explode in my chest as I lose track of everything around us, reveling at how right this feels. Henry's hand slides into my hair, holding me in place as his mouth moves firmly against mine. It might not be real, but it sure as hell feels like he's enjoying kissing me. It definitely doesn't feel like he thinks he's kissing a piece of cardboard.

A low rumble sounds from his throat as Henry *devours* me, and instead of stealing all the air from my lungs, it feels like Henry has brought me to life.

I fight against every instinct in me that wants to part my mouth and deepen the kiss, but instead, no matter how difficult it is, I pull away. The sense of wrongness is immediate, but I can't give Henry everything the first time we kiss, I have to leave him wanting more.

If that wasn't everything, then I'm a little nervous to find out what everything will feel like. My heart feels like it's about to beat out of my chest.

Henry looks . . . well, I'm not quite sure what his expression means, but his hand falls slowly from my hair as he stares at me, his devastatingly handsome face illuminated by the flashing of the cameras. This isn't the time or place to ask Henry about it either.

I compose myself, patting his chest playfully as I look over my shoulder at the photographers, winking at some of them. I wonder if they can tell how quickly my heart is hammering inside my chest, or how that kiss just changed my entire perspective of what a kiss is supposed to feel like. "Now that you all got your money shot, do you mind leaving us be to enjoy the rest of our night in peace?"

CHAPTER TWELVE

Mirabelle

I KISSED HENRY. THAT REALLY JUST HAPPENED.

If only fifteen-year-old me could see me now. She might go into cardiac shock.

I'm having a fun time with Henry, and I think he is too. He seems to have relaxed from all the stress he carries on a day-to-day basis, and I think the stick he has permanently lodged up his ass has shifted. We're in an isolated area that has an amazing view of the night sky through the glass windows surrounding us. Only a couple of other small, clustered groups of people are up here, but they're on the other side of the room, giving us some semblance of privacy.

Henry doesn't seem freaked by the idea that we kissed, or at least he isn't acting like it. Meanwhile, I'm trying to keep myself from having a major freakout. It's taking everything in me not to run to the bathroom to call JJ or Emily.

Is it weird I want to talk to my brother about kissing Henry?

His lips were so soft, and he reacted quickly to kiss me back. And the way his hand tangled in my hair? It's a good thing I have some serious willpower, because I'm not sure if I could pull away again. It's almost like he needed me to take the first step, but once I did, it seemed like Henry wanted to keep kissing me—

"Mirabelle?" Henry asks, redirecting my attention back to the conversation. I blink rapidly and notice that the waiter is waiting patiently to hear my answer to whatever he just asked me.

Oh god. I smile at the waiter as my cheeks burn with embarrassment. "I'm sorry, I wasn't paying attention. Would you mind repeating that?"

"Would you like dessert?" he repeats.

Henry chuckles, not even bothering to hide his amusement at this. The worst part is that Henry easily could have answered this question for me, considering I've never turned down dessert anywhere.

"Absolutely. Surprise me with your favorite," I say, smiling at the waiter as Henry asks for the same.

I consider kicking him under the table, but that wouldn't be very loving of a fake girlfriend to do to her fake boyfriend, who she's trying to seduce into being her real boyfriend.

"You were in la-la land," he teases, and I roll my eyes.

"You could have answered for me. You knew what my answer was going to be."

He laughs, shaking his head. "I know, but I've also heard it's rude to order for your date," Henry says, but there's something weird about how he says it. I study him for a moment, and under my scrutiny, Henry shifts his eyes away to look out the window. I gasp, clapping my hands over my mouth as surprised laughter bubbles from my chest.

"What are you laughing at me for?"

"You've totally ordered for someone on a date before, and she bit your head off, didn't she?" I grin at him, finding this funnier than I probably should. Normally, the idea of Henry with another girl makes my stomach hurt, but he's not here with her, he's here with me. I could be totally delusional, but it doesn't feel entirely fake.

Henry's ears immediately turn pink, and he pushes his sleeves up his forearms, my attention immediately drawn to the ink that was previously hidden. All that's visible is the rolling ocean in shades of grey and black, with the scaly tail of a hippocampus, while the rest is hidden from view.

"I wouldn't say she bit my head off, but I did listen to her go on about how controlling men are and how misogynistic they can be after I ordered an ice cream sundae for us to split. I didn't mean it that way, but who doesn't like ice cream and chocolate sauce?" he says, defending himself. Henry clears his throat, meeting my eyes as his widen. "Oh shit, I didn't mean I think you would react like that if I ordered for you, but I'm trying to listen more so I stop pissing you off. I didn't want to say or do the wrong thing, so I thought it'd be better if you ordered for yourself," he rambles, and I try not to melt into a puddle.

There is nothing sexier than a man hearing your words and caring enough to value them.

"Did you go on another date with her after that lecture?" I ask, forcing my brain to move past that before I say something dumb like *I love you* or *can I have your babies?* Both are acceptable options, but not for this moment.

Henry cringes, his gaze shifting away momentarily. "No, that was the end of that," he answers, tapping his fingers on the tablecloth. "Probably for the best."

"Probably, it doesn't sound like she was the right person for you," I say, taking a sip of what is technically Henry's wine, since I can't order my own legally for another five months. If only we were in France.

"Who do you think is the right person for me, if you don't mind me asking?" he asks, probing for an answer to my statement. A lock of Henry's dark, unruly waves has fallen in his face as he tilts his head to look at me.

A lump immediately forms in my throat, and I take another long drink of the wine, trying to wash it away. "You know, I think I'm going to go to the restroom. I'll be back in a minute," I squeak out, pushing my chair back as I snag my phone off the table. I'm totally calling Emily in the bathroom, and if she doesn't answer, I'm calling JJ.

His face shifts in confusion, and I hear his deep voice say something, but I've already walked too far away to hear what he said.

That might be the worst way I could have reacted to that question, but honestly, I've done rather well with everything else tonight. I was bound to crack at some point. I'm not sure how Henry is single, because while he might say dumb shit, he's pretty good at playing the role of a boyfriend.

A quick scan underneath the doors of the stalls reveals I'm in here by myself. I hit Emily's number, dragging a hand over my face in agony.

She answers immediately, catching me by surprise. Normally it's harder to get ahold of her. "Aren't you supposed to be on your date with your boyfriend?"

"I'm hiding in the bathroom," I blurt out, smoothing down my dress. Why can I be bold in every other aspect of my life, except with Henry?

"Um, why?"

"Henry asked me a question I didn't know how to answer after we had the most life changing kiss ever, and he's so fucking sweet, and I'm acting like a child by cowering in the bathroom," I ramble, pacing back and forth.

"Woah, slow down. Give me a second to catch up," Emily says. "What did he ask you?"

"We were joking around about one of his previous dates,

and he said it was for the best it didn't work out. So I obviously opened my mouth and agreed with him that she wasn't the right girl for him, cause, duh, hello, she's not me. And then it opened the door for him to ask who I fucking thought was right for him? So I ran, and I'm hiding in the bathroom like an idiot."

"Would it be so bad if you finally told him that you like him?"

That is absolutely the worst possible thing I could do. I think the only thing worse would be if I asked to have his babies. "Yeah, and get rejected? That'd be amazing for my self-esteem, Em."

"Bullshit. He could like you too, Mira. You're the most confident person I know. Get your ass back out there, and tell Henry you like him instead of hiding."

I roll my eyes, shaking my head. "You don't get it. I can't do that, it would change everything." That kiss might have changed my entire perspective on what kissing should be like, but Henry wouldn't have even kissed me if I hadn't made the first move.

Why couldn't I say, *Oh, I don't know who the right person is for you, Henry?*

"Okay, but you still have to leave the fucking bathroom," my best friend reminds me, and I groan as the door opens. An older woman walks in, giving me an odd look.

"Fine, I'm going," I whisper, checking my hair in the mirror first.

"Proud of you."

"You should be. I feel like I'm walking to my funeral," I say, stepping onto the restaurant floor.

"At least you'll die looking good. Love you, babe."

"I love you too," I echo automatically, realizing I messed up leaving Henry alone, especially when he looks as good as he does tonight. There's some woman standing over him, and the man I'm assuming is her date has taken my seat. He seems more interested in the fact that Henry is well . . . *Henry*, to even appear upset his date is fawning all over my fake boyfriend.

I note how stiff Henry is, and anyone with half a brain can tell he's uncomfortable.

"So what is it like working out all the time?" she asks, following it up with a fake high-pitched giggle, dragging her hand down his arm as Henry tries to shift away. I want to gag and shove a steak knife through her hand for touching him. Too aggressive?

"I'm sorry, I'm having a private meal. Do you min—"

"Yeah, do you take steroids? I think I read somewhere that you do. There's no way those muscles are real without extra help," the guy adds in, cutting Henry off. He did *not* just speak over Henry *politely* trying to ask them to leave—*which is honestly a huge step for him*—to ask if he juices.

My temper flares because I've been accused of that shit, and it's not cool. His muscles are *definitely* real. I saw the article after its publication the other day, and Stacey had me issue a release denying it with recent drug tests results. The site posted a retraction, curing most of the backlash.

"Excuse me, that's my seat, and that's my boyfriend so get your hands off him. Pretty sure I heard him trying to tell you he's having a private meal, and I'm guessing Henry didn't ask you to touch him, or give you permission to. If I were you, I'd back the hell off," I snap, ensuring I follow it up with a polite smile as she stares at me like a deer caught in headlights. I know I'm letting my own experiences after the Olympics bleed into my reaction right now, but it doesn't mean I'm wrong to tell them off. Relief floods Henry's face, and I'm happy I didn't actually grab the knife on the table to stab her with it.

Any other man, I'd probably be irritated, but for Henry, I'm ready to cut a bitch.

The man sitting in my seat gapes at me, his jaw ajar, clearly recognizing me, but my patience wavers further when his eyes drop straight to my chest.

Seriously?

I swear, men have a one-track mind.

"My eyes are up here," I say, crossing my arms over my chest. Henry's chair screeches on the flooring as he stands up.

"You're Mirabelle Walker," he stammers, jerking his eyes back up to my face, and then over to Henry.

"Show some respect," Henry warns, and I give him a look telling him silently to back off. He doesn't get to pull the penis card and be all macho right now. I can handle this myself.

"Yes, I am Mirabelle Walker, and I'm sorry, but not actually, because you're interrupting a private dinner," I say evenly. "I understand it might be cool and all to see us at the same restaurant as you, and we happily would have had a conversation with you or taken a picture had you asked, but instead, you accused him of taking steroids and put your hands on him. You shouldn't believe everything you read, and you definitely shouldn't touch anyone without their consent."

All three of them are speechless as the waiter happens to appear with two plates of dessert.

The woman's face is flaming with embarrassment—*as it should be*—and she looks at Henry as if asking him whether I can speak to her like that.

The waiter looks at the couple, narrowing his eyes. "Excuse me, but I believe your seats were in the main dining area. Please return to them before I call my manager to have you removed," he says, and they immediately make their exit. The waiter huffs, smiling apologetically at us. "I'm so sorry that they were able to disturb your evening. If you'd like this to be boxed up, I would be more than happy to get that done for you right away."

Henry looks at me, raising an eyebrow to ask what I'd like to do. Honestly, I'm upset, but I don't want to ruin the evening any more than I already have. Perhaps I should have bit my tongue, but I couldn't help myself.

"No, it's okay. We'll stay. Thank you for the apology, it's appreciated," I say, mustering a smile as I take my seat. Henry follows my lead, and the waiter sets the plates in front of us.

"Let me go speak with my manager to see what we can do to make up for the interruption," he says, but Henry shakes his head.

"Please don't worry about it," Henry interjects, smiling at the waiter.

The chocolate cake in front of me looks incredible, but unfortunately, I've lost my appetite. I was dangerously close to losing my temper on that couple, and that would have reflected poorly on us instead of them. Maybe I was more awful than deserved, but I don't understand why people think it's okay to touch us and accuse us of shit like taking steroids because we're public figures.

I'm sure they'll still sell the interaction to the tabloids, but hopefully it backlashes on me more than Henry. My reputation can take it, but his can't.

I mean, come on. They were treating Henry like he wasn't a real fucking person.

I push the chocolate chips around my plate, wondering how crazy Henry now thinks I am. This night was going so great. And then I had to ruin it. If I hadn't left Henry alone to go freak out in the bathroom then whoever the fuck that was wouldn't have had the opportunity to approach Henry. I was ready to go full psycho on that woman.

"Mirabelle, you haven't taken a single bite of your cake," Henry points out, watching me closely as I look up at him.

"I lost my appetite." I shrug, setting down my fork as I glance to the side out at the Charlotte skyline.

"I'm sorry about that. I'd hoped they'd be gone before you got back," he apologizes.

"It was my fault for leaving you alone. They might have approached regardless, but I can't stand that she felt like she could touch you." I shudder dramatically, but it makes me sick to my stomach. "You have nothing to apologize for. I'm the one that should be apologizing. I'm sorry. I could have held my tongue better, but it makes me so damn mad. It's no excuse, though. I'll call my PR team later to give them a heads-up in case those two say anything to anyone."

"Well, I don't think you have anything to apologize for either, so why don't we agree that they should be the ones apologizing, and enjoy the rest of our night." Henry takes a bite of the cake, a groan of satisfaction sounding from his mouth. I watch as his tongue flicks to get the stray dab of frosting from his lip, and all I can think about is how badly I want to kiss him again. "You should try it. It's delicious," he says, his lips quirking upward, and I almost wish he didn't know me so well.

I relax a little in my seat, picking up my fork again. "I'm shocked you're actually eating it. Your diet is pretty strict."

"I won't tell if you won't." Henry laughs, and I can't help joining him. I'm still feeling slightly defeated, despite how nice tonight's dinner was. I didn't exactly wow Henry and prove to him why I should be his real girlfriend instead of his fake girlfriend.

Right before we exit the building, Henry grabs my hand, looping his fingers through mine. I look around but there's no paparazzi to be seen, which means he *wants* to hold my hand.

Hell yeah.

Maybe tonight wasn't such a disaster after all.

CHAPTER THIRTEEN

Henry

I KNOW IT'S NOT COMMON KNOWLEDGE TODAY WAS Mirabelle's idea, but if the other interns knew she was behind today's success, maybe they'd stop fucking with her and making snide remarks in her direction. She's smarter and more capable than all of them combined, but Mira's so determined to prove she belongs here that she isn't going to breathe a word to anyone who has the power to put a stop to it.

I only know because I overheard her talking to Emily in the pool last night, but I guess they've been piling this extra responsibility on her which explains all the multi-tasking when she's helping Stacey shadow me at the stadium and with the PR responsibilities that I have.

If Mirabelle ever wanted to quit her job for the team, I'd hire her in a heartbeat to run my PR team full-time.

I feel like I've barely seen her this week since our date last weekend, but a best friend trumps a fake boyfriend, regardless of how real that kiss felt.

The kiss I can't stop replaying in my mind as I try to come up with an excuse to selfishly do it again. Until that happens,

I'm stuck grasping to the memory, trying to place the flavor of her lip balm.

That kiss was unlike any I've had before. I don't know how to explain it, but it's embarrassing how many times thinking about it has given me a reason to rub one out in the shower.

Is it wrong I'm hoping I'll have an opportunity to kiss Mirabelle today? With both of our families here, it's probably not the smartest choice, but I have to know if it was a fluke.

So far, everything has been a hit. In addition to the animal shelter here, Mirabelle also reached out to one of her old classmates who works with a youth special needs organization to spend the afternoon at the stadium.

Between all the children and puppies, I'll come out of this weekend looking like a saint, unless I throw an interception. My relationship with Mirabelle has been trending all week, and the photo of us kissing has vastly overshadowed the single gossip article posted about the couple from dinner.

Everyone has been all smiles today, but no one's shining brighter than Mirabelle. Her energy is infectious.

Despite Mirabelle not being on speaking terms with her family, they showed up today. It's how the Walkers roll.

Her parents and the twins came into town this morning with my parents and Kaitlyn, but I've been avoiding my parents after the lecture I got from my dad when he finally called after news of our relationship broke. I'd been holding out hope he'd react better than Sebastian and Thalia, and that him waiting to call was a good sign, but I was wrong.

Mirabelle is standing with her best friend, Emily, holding a fluffy puppy in her arms as they pose for a picture with Tyler, an offensive lineman and a friend of mine. She's wearing a pair of denim overalls that show off her legs, and her hair is pulled back into a long braid down her back. Mirabelle looks happy, but I can tell it's taking a toll on her to have her parents so close, yet so far at the same time.

"You guys are doing a good job of selling the relationship," Stacey says, pulling me back to reality. I blink rapidly, tearing my gaze away from Mirabelle.

"Thanks," I mumble, dragging my hand through my hair.

"If I didn't know better, I'd think you actually had feelings for her. You've been staring at her every chance you get," Stacey says, turning off her phone to slide it into her pocket. *Have I been staring at Mirabelle today?*

Stacey's in a surprisingly good mood today, giving me more leeway with her questions than usual, even without Mirabelle with her. "Make sure you get a good picture together," she instructs. I must be hallucinating because I think she might be smiling at me? What the hell is going on today?

"Do you have enough for the interview?"

"Take the opportunity to flee while I'm offering it. I could always find more questions I've been meaning to ask."

The dots connect in my brain, and I think I smile in Stacey's direction for the first time ever. "Nope. I think I'll get that picture with Mirabelle instead."

"Maybe you do have a brain in that head of yours," I hear her say as I walk away, but I couldn't care less. Instinctively, I head in Mirabelle's direction as she kneels down to chat with a child holding a speech tablet. It makes my heart flop funny when she beams at this child, and I wish I knew the right things to say to make her smile like that all the time.

My stepmom darts in front of me, forcing me to stop, and my stomach drops. I knew it was too good to be true I'd managed to avoid my parents so far. "Do you have a moment?" she asks, smiling at me.

Hearing what my dad thought of me the other day was awful, but I'm not sure I could stomach hearing how disappointed she is in me. She didn't have to love me after falling for my dad, but she chose to, and finding out what she thinks of me might break me.

"Are you planning on yelling what a horrible person and predator you think I am for dating Mirabelle?" I ask, crossing my arms over my chest.

She snorts, shaking her head as her smile grows. "Hell no. If you marry Mirabelle, it'd be my dream come true. I've been waiting for this to happen, but maybe don't tell your father I said that."

Excuse me, did she really just bring up marriage? *Marriage?* I know she doesn't know this is a fake relationship, but even if it weren't, it would be far too early to bring that up. I cough abruptly, choking on the breath caught in my throat. "Then, yeah. I have a moment," I croak out, my voice rough as some of the tension seeps from my shoulders. It feels nice to finally have someone on my side, even if she doesn't know the truth.

Mom hooks her arm with mine, leading me away from the main area of the event to a quieter part of the field where only a couple of volunteers are lingering, but thankfully, none of them are in earshot.

The few inches of height I have on her don't feel like much at the moment, and I know she said she wasn't going to yell, but I think I have good reason for being a little doubtful. "Are you ready for the game tomorrow?" Mom asks, a proud glimmer in her pale blue eyes.

What is she up to? I say stupid things, but I'm not dumb. I know she wants to talk about Mirabelle, so why is she asking about football? Normally, if Mom has something to say, she just says it.

"I've never been more ready for a game," I answer honestly. I'm in the best shape of my life, having worked harder than I ever have. I never imagined I would come so close to losing it before it was ever mine.

"I bet Mirabelle is excited to see her boyfriend in action," she hums, and I feel my cheeks flush.

"Mom," I complain, and her smile grows wider. I guess I don't call her "Mom" as much as I should these days. Penelope married my dad when I was eight, so I was old enough to understand that my biological mother didn't want me. I loved Penelope, but when I found out they were getting married, I fought against it because the only thing worse than one mother rejecting me, would be two mothers rejecting me.

I had Thalia as a maternal figure, and I knew she would never go anywhere. Her love wasn't conditional on my dad's love, so why did I need someone else who was only going to leave?

But then Thalia helped me see that Penelope didn't love me because of her relationship with my dad. She wanted me, and it was safe for me to let her be my mom in every way that counted.

"J'ai toujours espéré, qu'un jour, vous finissiez ensemble."[1]

I feel slightly guilty for lying to her, but as much as I'd like to tell her it's not real between us, I'd only be putting her in a bad spot with everyone else.

I don't know what to say.

I muster a smile, but her eyes narrow, analyzing my face quickly. "What's wrong, Henry?"

Everything.

My dad is disappointed in me.

Sebastian and Thalia think I'm forcing myself on their daughter and won't even look in my direction.

I can't talk to my sister about what's going on because she's a teenage girl and I'm afraid she'd spill the beans accidentally, leaving me in a worse position than before.

Andrew is in Seattle.

---

1. I always hoped that, one day, you would end up together.

My career is in jeopardy because I'll never live up to the legacy Sebastian left behind in the organization.

All the pressure I feel is constantly threatening to crush me into a speck of dust, and the only time I feel like I can breathe, is when I'm with Mirabelle. She makes me feel like all of this is going to be okay, even without knowing how deep my anxiety runs.

"Je vais bien."[2]

It's not very believable, though. I'm not selling it well, but I only have so many lies in me.

Mom's mouth turns downward into a frown, and she shakes her head, refusing to accept my answer. *"Tu peux me parler, tu le sais, n'est-ce pas?"*[3]

I scope out the field, looking to see if there's anyone who might overhear us. Fortunately, Sebastian and Thalia are with the Panthers' General Manager and a few other veterans on the team that Bash played with. My dad is with Owen and his wife, Blake.

"Ils sont tous tellement en colère contre moi. Qu'est-ce que je peux faire pour arranger ça?"[4] I ask, trying not to let her see how badly hurt I am by all of this.

She taps my chest comfortingly above my heart. "The heart wants what it wants, Henry. Everyone else will understand that eventually. Bash and Lia are more hurt than angry. They wished you would have gone to them first about the relationship rather than letting them find out through a press release, but that doesn't mean you deserve the things they said."

I note how she doesn't say anything about the fight I had with my dad. I don't doubt she knows about it.

---

2. I'm fine.
3. You can talk to me, you know that right?
4. They're all so angry with me. What can I do to sort it out?

"And Dad?"

Her bright eyes sharpen and she musters a smile. "You let me handle him. He's hardheaded, but he'll come around."

"I need you to believe me when I say nothing ever happened between Mirabelle and me until the Super Bowl after-party. What Sebastian and Dad accused me of? It makes me sick to my stomach because all I can think is how I would murder someone with my bare hands if Kaitlyn were dating someone while she was a minor and they weren't." I exhale, shaking my head as my stomach rolls at the thought of anything happening between us when Mira was a minor. "If that's what they want to think of me, then they clearly don't know who I am, and maybe they don't deserve to. I would never force myself on anyone, especially if they were under-age," I insist, miserable that I even have to say this. I love my dad, but this hurts.

"Je sais. Il sait. Je suis désolée, Henry."[5]

"You're not the one who needs to be apologizing," I say, stepping out of reach. I hate the pained look that appears on her face, but I don't want an apology from my stepmom. "I probably need to find Mirabelle. She did an incredible job planning today."

"She did," Mom agrees, her bright eyes shining. "If you'll let me, I'd love to take the two of you to dinner soon. You make a beautiful couple."

A lump grows in my throat, and I press my tongue to the roof of my mouth to try to keep tears from forming in my eyes. Mom has no idea it's fake, but she's willing to go against everyone else to support me and the relationship she believes I'm in.

"I'd like that, Mom."

"I love you, have fun with your girlfriend." She winks,

---

5. I know. He knows. I'm sorry, Henry.

absolutely beaming. It dawns on me that maybe I don't call her as much as I should.

"I love you too," I say, making my way back to Mirabelle who is now speaking with a reporter. His eyes meet mine over her shoulder, and I wink quickly at him, holding a finger to my lips to tell him to be quiet. I've probably stunned him into silence more than anything, because I normally don't act this way with the media.

"—nd it's wonderful that the Panthers Organization is working with both of these incredible causes," Mirabelle says, the smell of vanilla invading my senses as I hover behind her. It crosses my mind as I'm sliding my arms around her waist to wrap them around her torso that she could easily react in a manner that results in me getting seriously injured.

She yelps, jamming an elbow into my side, causing me to grunt in pain at the well-placed jab. I'm not even mad about it because I'm impressed that was her first reaction. Mirabelle's head turns quickly, her whiskey-colored eyes wide with shock. "Henry!"

"What?"

"You can't sneak up on me like that," she protests, and I chuckle quietly.

"Sorry," I say, fighting a grin, but I'm in fact, not sorry at all. She's cute when she's mad.

Mirabelle purses her lips at me, turning around to look at the reporter again, who is smiling after watching the whole exchange. My hand is still slung around her waist, and I tug her back against my chest, sliding my hand into the front pocket of her overalls. I can feel the heat of her body radiating through the fabric, but I'm more focused on how stiff her whole body goes as she's pressed against me.

"Relax," I murmur next to her ear, the intoxicating aroma of vanilla threatening to overwhelm me. How am I supposed to think straight around her? *"Mon cœur,"*[6] I say loud enough for the reporter to hear, brushing my lips teasingly over her cheek, playing the part we've agreed to.

Mirabelle softens underneath my touch, relaxing into me. "Henry, this is Dave. He's a reporter with the Charlotte Observer."

"It's nice to meet you. Thanks for coming out today." I offer my free hand to Dave, refusing to remove the one from inside Mirabelle's pocket. I don't care what he thinks. I've been waiting all day to be near her.

"I wouldn't miss it. I was asking Mirabelle a few questions, but do you mind if I ask you some as well?" he asks, and if it means I get to be by Mirabelle, he can ask me anything he wants. Just because he's asking doesn't mean I have to answer, but I do get to stand here holding her.

"That's fine," I agree. Whatever he asks me surely can't be more invasive than Stacey's lines of questioning.

"Are you ready for tomorrow?" he asks, diving right in, quickly pressing a button on his phone to no doubt record the conversation. I can't blame him, I'm not known for my patience with interviews. I'm trying to be better about it for a couple of reasons: I don't want to get traded, and I don't want to make Mirabelle's job more difficult than it needs to be, especially after seeing how hard she's working to help me. The only reason we're in this fake relationship is because of my shitty reputation.

"More than ready. We've got a great group of guys on the team this season, and our coaching staff has been going above and beyond to make sure we're ready. I'm excited for everyone to see our hard work pay off tomorrow."

Dave nods in agreement. "Head coach, Owen Lewis, has been speaking rather highly of your performance in recent

---

6. My heart.

practices and preseason games during the press conferences. Will you be able to rise to the occasion now that Sebastian Walker has retired?"

It's my turn to stiffen, and I know Mirabelle can feel the change in my demeanor. Honestly, I can't blame the guy for asking the question. It seems to be the same question everyone has been asking.

"Coach Lewis has done a great job in helping me prepare for my new role on the team. Sebastian is a legend, and I've learned a lot from him. I can only hope to be half the player he was during his career, and that starts by taking it game by game."

Wow, Stacey should be proud of me. I'm proud of me. That was a very professional response to an uncomfortable question, but I also didn't have a choice. Everything is on the line.

"This next question is for both of you," he says, looking at Mirabelle momentarily, and something resembling guilt flickers on his face. "Is it true that Sebastian and Thalia Walker aren't supportive of the relationship?"

Mirabelle sucks in a short, audible breath, and I try to remember what Stacey coached me to say if this question were asked. She suspected it was only a matter of time, given how many eyes and ears were on the field at practice when Mirabelle's parents barged in. *Oh shit, what did Stacey say again? I probably need to pay more attention to the important things, but how am I supposed to do that when she says every-thing is important.*

"My parents aren't happy about the idea of me dating anyone. I am their only daughter, after all," she answers, evading the truth far better than I would have been able to.

"Will you be wearing a jersey with your father's number on it or your boyfriend's?" Dave continues, and I'm curious to hear her answer. It's not something we've talked about, but now I'm wondering what she'd look like with my name and number on her back. If she doesn't have one, I'm sure as hell going to buy one today for her to wear tomorrow.

I think I'd like that a little too much, if the way my pants are fitting tighter than they were a minute ago is any indication. Fucking hell, I need to calm down.

"You can find out tomorrow with everyone else." She laughs, causing Dave to smile.

I crack a smile, taking my hand from her pocket to twist the end of her braid between my fingertips. It's perfect to wrap around my hand. "Let's stop trying to keep it a secret. We all know it'll be my jersey."

Mirabelle laughs and leans further into me, pressing against me perfectly. I don't stand a goddamn chance right now. "You sound awfully sure, baby," she says sweetly, but the glint in her sparkling eyes is anything but.

The only thing I'm awfully sure of is that since we kissed, Mirabelle has the ability to turn me back into a raging hormonal teenager, and I'm not sure how to feel about it.

"*Mon cœur*, I'm awfully sure I'd like to see you try out my name," I say, knowing that Dave is eating up every bit of this. I tug Mirabelle's hair enough to cause her smug mouth to part in shock, and if we weren't having this conversation with Dave, I think I'd kiss her.

Dave clears his throat, redirecting our attention back to him. Mira's cheeks are a rosy red, and I should feel bad, but I don't. "Mirabelle, has there been any new information regarding the fire at your family's house? The last update was that the fire had been ruled arson, and the police were looking for any potential leads."

My entire body goes cold at the reminder. Mirabelle doesn't talk about the fire much, or that it was ruled arson. I don't like to think about how someone could be following her, and that I might not always be there to help Mira.

"The detectives are doing their best, but any details

regarding the case are confidential," I interrupt, taking the lead on this one. The edge in my voice is a firm warning he needs to change the line of questioning, or we're done here.

"I've heard rumors you're considering competing in the Olympic Qualifiers coming up in order to compete in the games next year. Is this true?" Dave asks, getting the hint as Mirabelle threads her hand with mine.

People were surprised when Mirabelle bowed out of the international circuit to compete on Duke's team, but I wasn't. I'd seen firsthand how hard she worked to train her body and her mind. That type of dedication isn't easy, and it's perfectly okay for her to want as normal of a life as possible outside of the sport. She didn't stop competing entirely, but I think she was happier at Duke than she would have been if she continued training for the next Olympics.

Mirabelle seems to find her voice, and her hand squeezes mine, silently asking for reassurance that I immediately give, being the supportive boyfr—*fake boyfriend*—I am.

"I retired from elite gymnastics after the games in France, and while I love the sport, my focus is on my career. I do plan to attend the Qualifiers, but only to support my old team-mates," she answers, but now I've hit my limit. This should have been over the second he asked about the arson case.

"Dave, it was great speaking with you, but you'll have to excuse us. I'd like a moment with my girlfriend, if you know what I mean."

Mirabelle looks up at me, raising her eyebrows.

Dave nods quickly, clearly understanding exactly what I'm getting at. "Of course. Thanks for answering some of my questions. Good luck tomorrow," he says, walking away, and in case he looks back, I let go of Mirabelle's hand and turn her to face me, resting my hands on her hips.

Mirabelle's breath hitches as she looks up at me. "What are you doing?" she whispers, resting her hand tentatively on my chest. I wonder if she can feel how fast my heart is beating in my chest.

"I didn't like the questions he was asking you," I say honestly. "None of this was supposed to involve you having to talk about shit you don't want to."

"That's . . ." she trails off, ducking her head as if needing a moment to gather her thoughts. "That's sweet of you. Thank you."

"Of course," I say, acting like it's nothing. It's honestly the least I could do.

"I'm impressed. You did well answering his questions."

It feels good to know Mirabelle thinks that. I shrug, playing it off. "It helps I had my babysitter next to me, ready to jump in if I needed it."

Mirabelle rolls her eyes, but her smile grows. "Just accept the compliment."

"Thank you, Mira," I say, smiling.

"I think I prefer *mon cœur*," she teases, using a perfect French accent.

I feel my cheeks flush because I'm not sure why that was the name that came out of my mouth. There are a thousand different pet names I could have gone with, but it felt like an accurate way to describe her. *My heart.*

"I don't want people questioning the validity of this. It seemed like the right thing to say."

The sparkle in her eyes dims as she blinks, as if she's surprised, and immediately, I regret saying that's the only reason. Rationally, I know it has to be the right reason, but there are a million reasons why I shouldn't like her. Fuck, maybe there are more than a million.

Would it be such a bad thing if this weren't fake?

The thought seems like a joke to even consider, but I'm starting to lose the internal battle against my attraction toward Mirabelle.

"Of course," she says, painting on a smile that might be the saddest one I've ever fucking seen. *I hate that I put it there.* "I know that. You're getting better at faking it—you were pretty believable, and Dave ate it up."

It was believable because I'm not sure I'm faking it.

"Mirabelle . . ." I say her name, trailing off because I don't know what to say next. I want to take the opportunity to kiss her, and see if I'm imagining the connection between us, but over the top of her head, I can feel the weight of her parents' stare. If looks could kill, I'd be buried six feet under.

It's enough to snap my brain back into reality.

I need to keep my focus on football, not on a girl—no matter how she might make me feel when I'm around her.

She parts her lips, drawing my attention to them before I flit my gaze back up to meet hers. "What, Henry?"

My phone rings in my pocket, breaking the moment. I pull it out, but immediately decline it at the sight of the name, sliding it back into my pocket. I'm not letting her ruin today.

"Who was that?"

I shake my head, my mind racing a mile a minute. "No one," I lie, taking a step back from her, my hands slow to let go of Mira's waist. I run a hand through my hair, offering her a half-smile. "You've done an incredible job with all of this. Thank you for what you're doing." My mouth feels sour, but it's the right thing to do.

I only wish it didn't make me feel so shitty in the process.

CHAPTER FOURTEEN

Mirabelle

I'VE SPENT A GOOD PORTION OF TODAY STEALING glances at Henry when I knew he wasn't looking at me. On the flip side, I've also felt my parents' eyes on me, but not once have they approached.

Do I want them to?

Absolutely. I miss them. But I'm not in the wrong here, so stubbornly, I refuse to make the first move. Maybe that's a mistake, but I'm hurt by how they reacted, and they owe Henry and me an apology.

Professionally, I know it's great that they're here today. Their presence is great publicity for the charities, in addition to everything else the team is doing for the event.

Personally, though? I feel like crawling into a hole and never coming out.

Hunter already suggested I go talk to at least one of our parents. I guess things have not been going well with Bailey over the last few weeks, and with JJ at college and me in Charlotte, he's feeling lonely.

I considered it, but after Henry walked away from me, I

saw the look they gave him. They're not over it. They're punishing him for no fucking reason.

I never thought they'd treat Henry this way. I thought they'd be happy to see us together. I imagined Mom saying age is only a number, and Dad welcoming him to the family.

Apparently, that's another fantasy I had to go with the one where Henry actually liked me instead of pretending to be in a fake fucking relationship. It's the delusional part of my brain that thought maybe Henry wasn't faking earlier while Dave was interviewing us.

It felt almost real, if that makes sense? It doesn't at all, but I'm pretty sure he was smelling me too. Holy shit, when he pulled my hair, I'm glad I didn't moan, especially when Henry told me he'd like to see me try out his name. *Jokes on him, I've been doodling Mirabelle Price in notebooks for years.*

I just keep replaying the part where he essentially dismissed Dave because he didn't like the questions he was asking me? It's a shame Henry didn't take that moment alone with me. I would have happily let him do whatever he wanted to me if he called me *mon cœur* again.

Since that interaction, I've been distracting myself with puppies so I don't overanalyze everything about it.

I'd love to keep one, but I'll be traveling with Stacey and the team, so it's not a good time. Luckily, we've been able to find homes for so many of the dogs today.

The puppy in my arms is sleeping, and I noticed a family nearby that's been eyeing him, but they haven't approached. Sometimes people need a little shove in the right direction. As I get closer to them, out of the corner of my eye, I note the flashes coming from a nearby camera, making sure my smile is in place.

"Hi, I'm Mirabelle. Are you interested in adopting a dog today?" I ask warmly, trying to keep their focus on me, and not on the cameras behind me.

"Yes." The little boy smiles brightly at me, and my heart melts at his missing front tooth. It adds to his cuteness factor.

I look to the mother for permission before crouching down next to him. "This little guy is looking for a home if you'd like to meet him?" I offer, and he reaches out, but immediately freezes before he can touch the fur.

"Can I pet him? Mommy said I have to ask first," he asks, his face full of hope.

"She's right, but you can absolutely pet him. I think you will get along very well. He likes for his ears to be scratched," I whisper the last part, causing the little boy to giggle. Maybe I should have become a teacher; kids are a blast.

I set the slumbering puppy on the warm turf, as the little boy starts petting him gently.

I explain a little more about the adoption process to the parents before giving them a chance to make their decision, but I have a feeling the puppy has found its forever home.

On my way back to where Emily is chatting with another potential adopter, I spot Bailey sitting in the stands by himself. Looking around, I see my parents are with Henry's, like they have been all day. Hunter is with Kaitlyn, and Henry is with Wilson and Quinn, playing with a group of kids.

At least in person, I know he can't decline me like he's been declining my phone calls. I don't understand why he's up there by himself, though?

I climb the stairs, half-expecting Bailey to bolt in the other direction as he immediately frowns after noticing me. "Hey, B," I greet cheerily, trying to start the conversation off on a good note. Bailey stays silent, and I lean back in the stadium seat, opting for a different direction. "How's soccer going?"

He scoffs quietly, crossing his arms over his chest. "Fine," Bailey answers shortly.

"Do you know when you're going to visit Duke? I could ask for the day off if it's during the week." Their head soccer coach offered Bailey a spot on their roster after watching one of his exhibition games in June. Bailey wanted to wait to commit until the team was in season so he could get a feel for the dynamics, but a few of his old teammates who have already graduated play there, so I'd be surprised if he chose to go somewhere else.

"No."

Bailey's temper is shorter than Mom's, which is pretty damn short to begin with. I chew my lip hesitantly, wondering if maybe I should have gone home for a weekend regardless of where my relationship with my parents currently stands. "So—"

"Go back to your boyfriend and your perfect life here so you can continue forgetting about the rest of us. We don't need you," he snaps, his entire face marred with anger. My jaw unhinges in shock, completely taken aback by the harshness of his words. Is JJ getting the same treatment for moving out of the house, or is it just me?

"Bailey—"

My brother stands up, shoving his hands into his pockets. "I didn't even want to fucking come today. Mom and Dad made me because that's what Walkers do: we're there for each other always," Bailey says bitterly, and I barely recognize him. "When have you been there for me lately?"

What the hell did Hunter leave out when he said things aren't going well with Bailey?

"I'm sorry I'm not living at home anymore. I'm sorry I haven't visited, but I'm always here for you, Bailey. I love you," I say, hoping the message gets through to him. "I've been calling and texting, but I can't be there for you if you won't pick up the phone."

I stand up slowly, trying to take a step in his direction, but Bailey shies away. "Just leave me the fuck alone. You've gotten pretty good at it."

"B, that's not true," I try to protest, and he flees. I don't know what's going on, but this isn't the same kid I spent the summer fighting over waves with. I could go after him, but I think that'd only make things worse. Hunter definitely has some explaining to do, though.

I sit down again, racking my brain to piece together when Bailey decided he hated me so much. No one on the field is looking for someone in the bleachers, so it's a safe bet that I can hide up here until I'm ready to rejoin everyone on the field. I understand now that's exactly what Bailey was doing.

Tears blur my vision, and I sniffle, wiping my nose on the back of my hand as I spot Quinn walking up the stairs. I want to be alone, but maybe that's the same thing Bailey wanted when he was up here. Clearly, it's the last thing Bailey needs. His smile drops, and I can only assume my fucking feelings are plain as day all over my face.

"Are you okay?" he asks, taking the seat next to me, angling himself to face me. It looks awkward with his long legs, and I can't help laughing, despite how broken it sounds coming out.

"I'm fine, Quinn. I need a moment." I might need more than a moment, though.

His eyes scan my face, and I want to shrink under the attention. I should be getting my ass up and putting my big girl pants on to talk to my parents so we can get to the bottom of what's wrong with Bailey.

"Is it Henry?" he asks, and I shake my head. The only thing wrong with Henry is he'll never see me the same way I see him.

"No. My brother, Bailey," I admit as Quinn reaches forward to wipe a tear I didn't know had fallen. I shrink back from his touch, remembering where we are and why anything affectionate can't happen. Quinn frowns, clearly not thinking about it, but that's not a luxury I have. "There's photographers here," I murmur under my breath, and realization dawns on his face.

"Fuck, I forgot. Follow me," he says, standing up.

But I stay where I'm at.

This whole event has been designed to help Henry. Yes, it's great for the charities and the organization as a whole, but the entire thing happened with Henry at the helm to try and give people a reason to support him.

"Mirabelle?" he asks, his face twisting into an expression of confused disappointment.

"I can't, Quinn. If anyone sees me leave with you, it'll put everyone in an awful position," I say, hoping he can understand where I'm coming from. I think Quinn is nice, and could some of our conversations be perceived as flirting? Maybe. But it doesn't change the way I feel about Henry, or mean I'm going to follow him to a private area at a team event with the press everywhere.

How exactly would that look if I'm supposed to be Henry's girlfriend, but I'm pictured walking off with his friend?

Quinn doesn't take his seat again, which is probably a good thing. "Are you doing anything for yourself right now?" he asks, and I'm not sure why he's even asking me this in the first place.

Does fake dating the guy I want to be dating count?

"Not really." I decide upon, and he shakes his head. "I promise, I'm not some damsel in distress. I'll get my shit together." I need to get my shit figured out with my parents first, and then I'll tackle everything with Bailey.

"Mirabelle, we're all messes so I don't care about that. What I care about is that you're not doing anything for yourself. Every day not spent living is a wasted opportunity, especially when we're only given one life to live. Maybe I'm wrong, but it seems like you're so focused on everyone else that you're not making any time for yourself in the process," Quinn says, as if we're talking about different types of cheese instead of this philosophical idea I should be doing more for myself, but I already feel like I'm too selfish to begin with. "You're going to wear yourself thin. Tomorrow is only the first game of the season, and the higher ups haven't said when they want you and Henry to break up."

Which means I'm in this for a while still.

I force a smile on my face that I hope is fucking convincing because I am so emotionally drained right now. "That's a nice way of looking at it, but I've already lived more in my life than most people live in a hundred years. I can sacrifice a little to help the people I love."

Quinn's dark eyes are swirling with emotion as he looks at me, dragging a hand over his jaw as if realizing something he didn't see before. "You love Henry?" he asks after a moment, and I freeze, but that's not necessarily what I said. I have time to deny it. It would make sense to deny it, considering how quickly my plan to seduce Henry is crashing and burning.

I actually thought Henry was going to kiss me again earlier. He was looking at me so intensely, and his lips parted, but then he backed away, just like last time.

"Yes," I say, surprising myself that I admit it.

"I appreciate the honesty," he says, before smiling faintly. "You couldn't pick a better guy than Henry. I know there's probably nothing I can say to change your mind, but if you do, I'd love a chance to let you see what a great guy I can be too."

"Quinn, I—I don't know what to say. I'm supposed to be dating your friend, and this can't happen," I stammer, but the only thing playing on repeat in my head is how Henry said he wouldn't care if I dated Quinn.

He shakes his head. "I'm not asking you to say anything, Mirabelle. You're supposed to be *fake* dating my friend, there's a difference. I know how I look in the media—I like women, and I like sex. I'm not ashamed of it, and I'm not going to deny it. I like you because I think you're funny, beautiful, and you have no problem telling me what you think. You know what this world is like and how rare it can be to find someone who honestly wants to be with you instead of wanting all the things that come from being with you. If you tell me to back off, I will, but I like what I've seen so far, and I hope you don't."

Is this real?

I look down momentarily at the pink polish on my fingernails, trying to gather my thoughts to say literally anything in response, but I don't know how to. It's chaos in my brain.

The sound of Quinn's footsteps walking away causes me to look up, and a part of me wishes that he never said anything about having feelings for me. The other part of me wonders if I'm a fool for still holding out for Henry.

Nope, this is not the place or time to be making big decisions. I roll my shoulders, feeling how tight they are from stress. I've hidden up here long enough.

I make my way back down to the field, moving in the opposite direction from where my parents are, which also happens to lead me right back to Henry. His eyes immediately find mine, and I can't look away, even if I wanted to.

"Hey," I greet as I walk up to him, trying my best to act as normal as possible. Kaitlyn is grinning like a fool at the sight of us. It's crazy how despite only biologically sharing a father, they look similar enough they could be full siblings. They share the same dark hair and hazel eyes, and Kaitlyn's tall, her head reaching Henry's shoulders.

I've never seen a picture of Henry's biological mother, but sometimes I wonder what parts of him are from her. I don't know why she's not in the picture, but you'd never know Penelope wasn't his biological mother by looking at him. I don't know much about Chris's divorce from Henry's mom, but from the little comments made over the years, I've gathered enough to know it didn't end amicably.

He doesn't talk about her, but I've noticed he seems to get a lot of calls like the one he got this morning that he declined. I saw the screen last week while he was lifting, and the caller ID said, *Maybe: Allison Price.* I connected the dots, realizing it was his birth mother after watching closely as he grabbed it. I could practically see the tension rolling off his shoulders as he clenched his jaw like earlier. I wonder if she's the one who called him today, but Henry hasn't brought it up, so I've been nervous to ask.

"Hey," Henry says, taking an intentional step to close the gap between us. My heart skips a beat when he wraps an arm around my lower back, pulling me into his side. *Relax, Mirabelle.* It would be weird if he didn't do this.

I'm tempted to ask Kaitlyn what she knows about Bailey, but I don't want to ruin her day.

"Are you having fun?" I ask Kaitlyn, relaxing my head against Henry's side. I feel like I could melt into a puddle against him, and I wish I knew what it was about Henry that made me feel this way. At the end of the day, I know that even if it were a choice to love Henry Price, I'm sure it's still a choice I'd make.

"It'd be more fun if Dad would let me bring a puppy home, but his excuse is that we don't have anywhere for this hypothetical puppy to stay when we go to France to visit Mom's family," she says, rolling her eyes.

"Being responsible sucks," I agree.

"It does. I've been meaning to text and ask, but I'm trying to find a weekend to visit. Would you be okay with that?" she asks, staring at me with wide eyes.

"Oh my goodness, it's your room. You don't have to ask.

I'll get a hotel room or something to let you guys have some time together," I say without thinking, and her head tilts.

"Why would you get a hotel? Wouldn't you stay in Henry's room with him?" she asks, and my entire body freezes as I realize she's right.

"Mira's trying to preserve your innocence," Henry interjects smoothly. "That's fine, Kait. You know you're always welcome."

God, that was close. For once, Henry's brain is the one working.

Kaitlyn relaxes some, but she shrugs. "Sorry, I'm not trying to kick you out or anything—"

"Not at all how I took it," I say, trying to force myself to relax, but there's been too many things thrown at me today. I'm not sure I know how to relax anymore. "I know how busy things are going to get, and how much Henry values his time with you. I wouldn't want to intrude or anything, so I'll probably still get a hotel room, and pamper myself with a massage. Just let me know when you plan on coming."

Kaitlyn fidgets with the charm on her necklace. "I was actually kind of hoping you would be there too, if that's okay? We usually play board games and hang out, but you don't have to if you don't want to."

Henry runs his fingers back and forth over my hip, distracting me. I know Kaitlyn because she's best friends with the twins, but I can't say I've spent too much time with her when they aren't around. It'd be nice to get to know her better.

"That sounds perfect, Kaitlyn. Thanks," I say, smiling reassuringly at her while trying not to focus on the fact Henry is touching me.

"Great, I'll start looking at my weekends," she says, and I wish I had half the energy she does right now. Kaitlyn pulls out her phone, groaning at whoever's name is on the screen.

"What, Hunter?" she asks, giving me a look as if to say, *Can you believe this?*

She's funny.

"Fine, I'm coming. Just so you know, I'm officially picking your sister as my new best friend. You've been replaced," Kaitlyn says, huffing.

I turn my head into Henry's chest to hide my laughter, but I can feel him silently laugh, clearly finding her amusing as well. I smile, breathing in the crisp scent of laundry detergent and sandalwood. It's fucking intoxicating.

"You guys are so sickeningly cute, I could vomit," Kaitlyn says, gagging dramatically behind me.

I reluctantly move back, but Henry doesn't let go of me, keeping me at his side.

"If you're going to vomit, at least do it somewhere I don't have to see it," Henry teases, pressing a gentle kiss to the top of my head. "Besides, she can't be your best friend because Mira's mine. I don't share."

My heart stutters in my chest, and I'm not sure if I'm breathing. He's full of shit, but damn, if that isn't confusing as hell for my poor, smitten heart.

Kaitlyn's eyes widen in surprise, clearly not expecting that either.

What the fuck is going on today?

I think I've ended up in some alternate reality, because yes, Henry and I are fake dating, but that seemed . . . I don't know. I think I need to sit down.

"Okay, caveman. She's yours. Please don't forget our conversation: wrap it before you tap it," she says, putting her hands up in self-defense, and my face feels like it's literally on fire.

"For fuck's sake, Kaitlyn." Henry groans, and I cover my face with my hands. I don't have words.

"What? I'm not ready to be the cool aunt, but—okay,

okay, I'm going. Don't kill me," Kaitlyn says, her laughter growing softer the further away she gets.

Oh my god.

I can't look at him. My hands are literally never leaving my face ever again. This has been the absolute worst day. What might be the worst part is that I think I liked it too much to be told I was his. *Just kidding—it was pretty awful hearing what Bailey said to me.*

Too many things have happened today. It might be better for me to drown myself in Henry's pool later.

"Mirabelle," Henry says, the proximity of his voice sending shivers through my entire body. It's not fair.

"No."

He has the nerve to fucking laugh. "No, what?"

"Just . . . no," I say, absolutely mortified by this.

"Look at me," he instructs, but I shake my head. "Mirabelle, look at me please."

"Why?"

"Because I want you to see how serious I am when I say this."

It's enough to get me to reluctantly spread my fingers to peek at Henry through them.

"All the way," he says, gently curling his fingers around mine, to pull them down. "I wasn't lying when I told Kaitlyn I don't share, but I did lie when I said I was okay with you going out with Quinn. I'm a selfish motherfucker when I'm in a relationship, even if ours is fake."

I think I'm going to have a heart attack before this day is over. My throat grows dry, and I force myself not to look away under the scrutiny of his stare. "Why are you telling me this?"

His gaze drops to my mouth, then makes its way back up to meet mine. "Because I don't share what's mine, and right now, you fall under that category."

Well, shit. I guess I can't drown myself after that declaration. I'd hate to miss when things get interesting.

CHAPTER FIFTEEN

Mirabelle

I PULL UP OUTSIDE MY UNCLE'S HOUSE FEELING MY insides twisting with nerves telling me to run in the opposite direction. I would have done this last night after the Puppy Bowl, but it lined up with JJ's first game, so I stayed in to watch the game with Emily, Wilson, and Henry. The last thing I want to do this morning is have this conversation, but I have to talk to my brothers. Uncle Owen invited me to breakfast, but I declined that invitation for everyone's sake.

My family is staying at Uncle Owen's for the weekend since our house is still considered a crime scene, and he loves to show off his home. I don't blame him, it's beautiful, but I'm ready for construction to start on our house.

I'm pushing the fire out of my head to focus on the problem at hand. I haven't thought it through too much, but my plan for the moment is to pull Hunter outside and call JJ so we can get to the bottom of this. I think if I try to bring Bailey into the conversation, he'll lash out worse than he did yesterday.

This is *so not* going to be fun, but I also know Bailey is

more important than the fight going on between our parents and me.

I use my code on the door handle to open it, walking in hesitantly. I push away every thought telling me it would be easier to leave before anyone sees me because I'm certain everyone already knows I'm here. My uncle probably received a notification when I entered the neighborhood.

Uncle Owen is wearing an apron with "Mr. Good Lookin' is Cookin'"written across the front, which would normally make me die of laughter if I weren't already on the verge of a fucking anxiety attack. The quiet chatter in the room stops as everyone sees me, and Mom's eyes widen in shock. "Mira?"

"Sorry, I didn't mean to interrupt."

Uncle Owen walks over and ruffles my hair. "You're not interrupting. I invited you, but I am highly offended you didn't compliment my apron."

I crack a smile, pushing his hand away. "You know, maybe you're not as good looking as you think you are if you have to remind everyone all the time."

"She has a point, Owen," Blake chimes in, her laughter the only one filling the room.

Yeah, this is awkward. Normally, a poke at Uncle Owen's vanity is the quickest way to lighten the mood. Apparently not today.

"Can I make you a plate?" he asks, motioning to the spread on the counter.

"No, thank you. I had a protein shake earlier," I say. I feel so anxious right now, I'm not sure I'd even be able to finish a single bite.

"Wait, Mirabelle—" Mom stands from her seat at the bar, and Dad looks . . . well, I'm not sure how he looks. I'm afraid to look too closely because I think the disappointment I'll find there might send me over the edge.

"I'm only here to talk to Hunter," I say, hating that her

face falls. It's not my fault. They have all the power in the world to take back what they said.

Hunter chooses that exact moment to make his presence known, walking up the stairs from the basement with Kaitlyn. I hold my breath to see if Bailey walks up behind them, but he doesn't. I'm not sure if that's a good or bad sign.

Hunter looks at me, probably wondering what I'm doing here since I told him I wasn't coming. "What's wrong with everyone's faces?" he asks, and Kaitlyn's face lights up when she sees me.

"Mira! Is Henry with you?" she asks, looking around, but her smile fades. "Never mind, I hope he's not," she mumbles under her breath, crossing her arms over her chest.

"Kaitlyn, will you please come eat breakfast with us?" Chris asks, and I'm honestly a little impressed by the look she gives him.

"Did you invite Henry for breakfast?" she asks defiantly, and I bite my lip to hold back a laugh.

"Kaitlyn, we talked about thi—"

"No. *You* talked about this. If Henry's not here, then I'm not hungry."

As amazing as this is, I would prefer to not stay here all day. "Hunt, can we go talk?"

"Anything sounds better than staying in here," he says, dragging a hand through his blond hair. I'm glad we're both in agreement on that. I hope Hunter has answers to the questions I have. I follow my little brother as he walks outside, keeping my eyes trained on his back.

Stepping out of the house, I breathe a long exhale of relief. "Thank fuck, I can breathe again," I say, rubbing my chest, but I still can't get rid of the anxiety plaguing my body.

"Yeah, maybe a heads-up next time you change your mind about coming over. I would have eaten first," he says, frowning as his stomach grumbles. "What's going on?"

I look back at the house, pulling my phone out of my pocket. "Where's Bailey?" I ask, and Hunter's entire body stiffens. Okay, well, now I know for sure he knows something is going on.

"He said he was hanging out with some of his old friends," Hunter says, fidgeting with the chain around his neck.

I press JJ's contact, and he's quick to answer since I gave him a heads-up. "I have never been more grateful to be an early riser with how often you forget the time difference between us. How is *Operation Get Bailey To Talk* going?" he asks, and if he were next to me, I'd probably punch his arm.

"JJ, you texted me before I was awake this morning. That's your own damn fault," I say, shaking my head.

"Whatever. How's it going?"

I look at Hunter who is literally looking anywhere but at me. "Well, Bailey's not here, but I'm with Hunter, and you're on speaker."

"Hey, dude, I meant to text you yesterday, but I streamed your game on Friday, and it looked like you got some good snaps in," JJ says, and Hunter shrugs, shifting his weight. It's crazy how he got all his height from Dad, whereas I'm short like Mom.

"It was okay. Weird playing without you, but I'll get used to it," Hunter says.

"Yeah, I feel the same way," JJ says, and I clear my throat impatiently. "Sorry, we can talk about Bailey now. I don't have anything new. He's been declining my calls and texts since the fire, but I still try every day."

I give Hunter the opportunity to chime in, but he says nothing. *Fine, I'll talk.* "I talked to Bailey yesterday at the stadium for a couple minutes, and I'm worried. He wasn't himself. He basically told me to go back to my perfect life and fuck off because he doesn't need me anymore."

"Woah, that's . . . awful." JJ exhales, and I watch Hunter

who is still finding the ground more interesting. "Hunt, have you noticed anything?"

Hunter shrugs, kicking at the ground. "I mean, he's been a little off lately, but he'll be fine."

"Off how?" I ask, and Hunter shakes his head, a pained expression filling his face.

"He's my twin. I'm not going to rat him out."

Yes, you fucking are.

"Is it soccer?" JJ guesses before I can.

He drags a hand over his face, groaning. Clearly, he isn't happy with whatever is going on, so I don't understand why he's keeping quiet. "He quit soccer," he finally admits, and my stomach drops.

"What do you mean he quit soccer?" I ask, now a lot more fucking worried than I was at the beginning of this conversation. Bailey loves soccer. He would never just quit. Bailey was right—I haven't been there for him.

"He asked me not to say," Hunter explains, and I take a seat in one of the patio chairs, my mind spinning.

"Say anything about what? I can't believe you knew he quit soccer and you didn't tell us, Hunter," JJ exclaims, and I tap my foot anxiously. *This is bad.*

"Look, if he wanted to talk to you guys about it, he would have picked up the phone when either of you called. This isn't my fault," Hunter defends himself, and I shake my head.

"No one is saying this is your fault, but you need to tell us what's going on. He wouldn't quit soccer," I reason, trying to stay calm, but that pit of anxiety is growing again, and now isn't the time to explode.

"It's not any of your business."

JJ scoffs. "It absolutely is our business. We look out for each other. That's what we do, so since you're the only one with any information, feel free to share it."

"JJ, take a breath," I warn, looking at Hunter who looks

like he'd rather be anywhere but here. I bet if I turned around, our entire family will be hovered in the windows trying to figure out what's going on. "If you won't tell us, then maybe we need to get Mom and Dad involved."

"No, you can't." Hunter's head finally snaps up to look at me, his eyes wide. "You're not even talking to them right now, but you're going to walk in there and blurt out that Bailey quit soccer? That sounds like a great idea, Mirabelle," he replies sarcastically.

Honestly, it's not the worst thing that's been said to me the last few weeks. I let it roll off my shoulders, even if it stings. Bailey is my focus right now, not everything else.

"Hunter, that was a low blow," JJ snaps.

"It doesn't matter. Please tell us what's going on so we can help," I say calmly, hoping he'll tell us before things get worse. I know they have a special bond being twins that I can't relate to, but I don't understand why he isn't more worried about Bailey.

I can see Hunter considering it, and I hold my breath as JJ thankfully stays quiet on the line. I think we finally got through to him.

But my stomach falls when he shakes his head. "I can't. You don't get it, Mira. Just let it go. This is something he needs to figure out on his own," he says, walking back into the house before I can stop him. I was right, though. Kaitlyn, Penelope, Aunt Blake, and Uncle Owen are hovering in the window, but scatter quickly now that I've seen them.

"Hunter, we're not going to le—"

"He walked away," I interrupt, sighing softly.

"How did I not know Bailey quit soccer?" JJ asks, and I'm asking myself the same damn thing.

"Because the Bailey we know, would never quit soccer," I say, pressing my fingers to my temple. I didn't get much sleep last night, agonizing over yesterday and how this was going to go, and I'm definitely paying for it with a monster-sized headache.

"What else did he say to you yesterday?"

"It doesn't matter. It wasn't about what he said—it was the look in his eyes and the anger in his voice when Bailey spoke to me. He didn't look like our little brother in that moment, and it scared me."

JJ doesn't say anything, because there's not anything to say.

Behind me, I hear the creak of the back door swinging open, and I turn to see Chris approaching. *Awesome*.

"JJ, I'm so sorry, but I gotta go. We'll talk more later, okay?" I say, hanging up before Chris can hear our conversation.

"Can we talk?" Chris asks, and I motion to the seat next to me. "Hi, Mirabelle."

"Hi."

Fuck, this is awkward as hell, and all we've said is hi. I can tell Chris isn't comfortable either, but it doesn't make me feel any better. "How've you been?"

Am I supposed to answer this honestly? "I've been better. Did my parents send you out here?" I ask, and he chuckles, but I'm not sure what I said warrants laughing?

"No. They didn't send me out here, but I know your dad wanted to come talk to you."

I know he didn't say it to hurt me, but it still feels like a knife to the heart. At least Mom got up to talk to me earlier, but Dad sat there staring at me. "Then why didn't he?"

Chris smiles sadly, spinning the wedding ring on his finger. "Because he's not proud of how he reacted, and he's afraid of saying the wrong thing that will push you further away. It's a scary thing having kids, Mira, especially when they're old enough to make their own decisions."

I wonder if by telling me this, it's Chris's way of trying to explain how he's been treating Henry.

"They've never had a problem with me making my own decisions before. They're not listening to me." Which I'm sure he already knows as my mom's best friend. "It was my decision, Chris."

Chris exhales, the chair creaking with his shifting weight. "It's more complicated than that. It's that he's five years older than you, six after his birthday next month. Henry *knows* better."

And it dawns on me there might be another reason why Henry won't kiss me—*other than him not being attracted to me, but come on, how could he not be attracted to me?* It's all the role models in his life telling him that it's wrong, including his own father. I can't believe I didn't think of this sooner.

"I'm sorry, but it doesn't matter what his age is because I'm not a minor. I'm a consenting adult, as is Henry. There's no reason for you and my parents to be treating Henry like he's some kind of criminal when he's not," I insist stubbornly. Chris stares at me for a minute, contemplating my words before a small smile breaks the hard line his mouth had previously been set in.

"You sound so much like your mother right now."

It makes my heart bloom with happiness more than I'd like to admit. My mom is amazing when she's not looking at me and my boyfriend like we're huge disappointments to her.

"He's not a criminal, kiddo, but that still doesn't make it right. Don't you want to date someone your own age? He is in a completely different point of his life than you are. How is that fair to either of you?" he asks me, and I cross my arms over my chest stubbornly.

"You're still not getting it. When have I ever been able to relate to people my own age? I've been treated like an adult since the day I started competing globally. How many times did my parents leave me alone in different countries with my coach because they trusted that I would make the right decisions without them there because of Dad's schedule?" I ask, trying to keep my voice even. "The answer is more times than we can count on our hands together. I like Henry, and he makes me happy. I hope I make him happy too, but that's what you should care about. I want to see where the relationship can go, but it's difficult when we're being lectured by the people who are supposed to love both of us unconditionally."

"Mirabelle—"

I stand up abruptly. We're going around in circles, and I have places to be today. "I love you, Chris, and I love my parents, but you're all so fucking wrong about this. Dad's right. He shouldn't be proud of how he reacted. And you? You have no idea what your son is going through right now. He doesn't need this on top of it."

His face shifts to a look of concern, and I know I immediately took things too far. *Shit. Henry is going to kill me.* "What is that supposed to mean?"

I can't mention the team wanting to trade Henry. I'm not sure what Uncle Owen has and hasn't told them. Fuck, why did I open my mouth? "He carries the weight of the world on his shoulders from the amount of pressure he puts on himself. And, for the record, before criticizing us about our relationship, you might want to have a conversation with your ex-wife."

Chris's mouth falls open in disbelief. "Allison's calling Henry?"

Yeah, it's time to go. I absolutely shouldn't have said that. I grab my phone off the table and briskly walk toward the house, realizing now that I probably should have gotten confirmation from Henry that the Allison Price whose calls he's been declining are actually from his mother, but now I definitely know they are. I hate seeing Henry upset every time it happens, and after, he usually disappears to go to the gym, hides in a book, or sulks in the pool.

Fuck, I'm going to have to tell Henry about this. Maybe if I ask Uncle Owen nicely, he'll slam my head between the front door and the frame around it to put me out of my misery.

Penelope is packing a container of food as Uncle Owen and Aunt Blake stare at me. *I can't believe I came here this morning.* "Wait, will you take this to Henry please? It's some of his favorites," she says, pushing the container into my hands.

"Yes, sorry, I have to go. I'll talk to you guys later. Love you," I blurt out, securing the food in my hands as I make my break before Chris can catch up to me, especially after I hear the door open behind me.

"Mirabelle, you can't say that and run away!"

Oh shit. He sounds pissed, but I'm hopeful it's not directed at me. Why did I open my mouth?

My dad unfortunately chooses that exact moment to step into the doorway, effectively blocking my escape path as I bounce off him. I bobble the container, quickly securing it against me before it can hit the floor and break. He stares at me for a moment, and I see all the physical similarities we share. This might be the closest we've been in terms of proximity since that day at the field, but I've never felt further away from him. He looks above me where Chris has narrowed the gap between us.

"Jesus fucking Christ, you really are your parents' kid," Chris swears under his breath, despite the fact we can both hear him. "How long?" he asks behind me, and Dad's silent gaze shifts back to me.

"How long what?" Dad asks, and I gauge the gap between him and the doorway to see if I can slip through it.

I bite down, choosing silence which is what I should have done in the first place.

"Allison's been calling Henry, and I want to know what else Mirabelle knows about it, but she ran off after dropping that bomb. Fucking spitting image of her mother at this age," Chris says, and I can confidently say, I never want to be on the receiving end of that tone again. God, my head is pounding.

Dad blinks in surprise, clearly not expecting Chris to say that. "What? Why wouldn't he say anything if she was?"

"I don't know. Maybe because you accused him of statutory rape," I reply without thinking, causing my father to visibly flinch.

Good. He should know how awful that is.

"Mirabelle, you don't know the situation. How long has Allison been contacting Henry?" Chris presses, and my temper flares.

How dare he say I don't know the situation? Up until a minute ago, nobody even knew there was a fucking situation to begin with.

"*Monkey, je sais que les choses sont difficile entre nous en ce moment. C'est vraiment important,*"[1] Dad says, and I feel tears burn in my eyes at the use of my childhood nickname. He hasn't called me that in years. I used to climb anything I saw, and after giving my parents enough heart attacks, they enrolled me in gymnastics.

I blink rapidly as my insides feel like they're being ripped in two. The logical part of me insists that he's wrong and owes an apology to me and Henry, but the emotional part longs for my dad to hug me and tell me everything is going to be okay.

I look closely at him, noting the sadness lingering in his eyes and in the aging lines of his face. It's the type of sadness that appears after talking about his family.

---

1. Monkey, I know that things are hard between us right now. This is really important.

"Je ne sais pas."[2] The truth slips quietly out of me, and he tenses, clearly not believing me.

I use this as my chance to escape, because if I don't, then I'm going to throw myself at Dad for a long hug and I'll probably tell him everything.

I make a beeline for the doorway, not sparing a second look toward my mother walking into the kitchen because I know that if I do, I'm going to break down.

---

2. I don't know.

CHAPTER SIXTEEN

Henry

"ARE YOU SURE YOU'RE FINE?" I ASK MIRABELLE, leaning to speak in her ear so she can hear me over the pounding bass echoing through the club.

She rests her hand on my chest, staying close to me, and I'll be damned if that touch doesn't feel electric. "If I wasn't, I would have said something." Mirabelle angles her head back to let me see her reassuring smile, but there's something missing. I noticed it earlier, but between the game and press conferences afterward, I was a little distracted.

Her hair is pulled back into a high ponytail, and for a second, I consider pulling on it to either make her smile or to finally kiss the hell out of her. *For practice, of course.*

Stacey pulled us aside earlier to tell me how people are starting to notice we're never seen together outside of the stadium and team functions. Honestly, I'm pretty sure that's all I was allowed to do, but she heard some of the guys on the team were going out to celebrate our first win of the season, so we were told to go out and make it look like we're a couple.

I wish we weren't here.

I wish we were at the beach house, sitting on our surf-boards at sunrise talking about anything and everything.

But that's not where we are.

"I'm fine, Henry." Mirabelle leans up to press a short kiss to my cheek, flashing me a quick smile as she slips out the VIP section and into the crowd. Her best friend, Emily, makes her way over to me a minute later, her mouth turned downward in a frown.

"Where did Mira go?" Emily asks, standing close enough for me to hear.

"I think to get a drink," I say, craning my neck to find Mira in the masses. I had a strong drink shortly after arriving to help numb some of my anxiety over the number of people in this place, but it spikes again at the thought of Mirabelle being by herself.

"Dude, you kind of suck as a fake boyfriend. Are you trying to give other guys an opening to hit on her?"

I raise my eyebrows in surprise because I definitely don't know Emily well enough after for her to say this. "No, I'm not," I say, but I really hate the fucking idea of other guys going up to Mirabelle.

"Then maybe you should show Mira your caveman decla-ration wasn't bullshit," she says, staring at me with her dark eyes as she pats my arm. I'm not even embarrassed Mirabelle told Emily what I said, because I meant it. Now, I need to prove it.

Quinn is sitting on a couch, making out heavily with a girl who I'm surprised still has clothes on with the way they're groping each other. Wilson is chatting with a few of his friends from defense, and I make a split-second decision to chase after Mirabelle.

One thing I learned from Thalia and have never forgotten is when a girl says she's fine, it usually means she isn't.

I'm careful not to shove anyone over as I make my way to

Mirabelle, catching sight of her hot pink strappy top that shows off her cleavage perfectly. I'm not stupid enough to let her get to the bar where she'll no doubt be hit on like Emily suggested. I catch her wrist loosely, and she turns in surprise.

"You followed me?" she asks, or at least that's what I think she asks, considering the music is all I can hear.

"You're hard to resist," I say, leaning in so I know she can hear me. Her eyes flicker with happiness for the first time all night, and it's a relief to finally say the right thing.

"If that's the case, then I'll let you buy me a drink," she says, and I grin, leading her to the bar.

Mirabelle orders a vodka cranberry with a splash of lime juice, flashing the bartender a pretty smile before tilting her head my direction. "It's on his tab," she says, stirring the drink with the tiny straw before wrapping her lips around it to take a sip. *I'd like to know what it feels like having her lips wrapped around something else.* Goddamn, I'm a fucking fool for resisting seeing Mirabelle this way for so long.

"It's under Price," I add, and the guy nods, ringing it in quickly before moving on to the next customer.

"You don't want a drink?" she asks.

"I shouldn't since we're officially in season," I say, offering her my arm so we can find a table away from the bustle of the bar. I'm even kind of getting used to the loudness of the music, but it could be that being by Mirabelle makes everything better.

Mirabelle nods, understanding better than anyone. "That's probably a good idea. You had a great game today."

"No interceptions," I say, smiling in relief. My bank account is thanking me, and I hope Owen's is crying. *Suck it, Coach.* I threw four touchdowns today, and we won by a thirteen-point lead.

"Not bad for your first game as a starter. Way to go, Price," she says, smiling happily at me.

"I had to show up and prove you made the right decision agreeing to help me. Maybe next time, I'll get lucky, and you'll wear my jersey," I tease, but I'm not kidding in the slightest. I have the jersey sitting in a bag in my room for her, but I chickened out on giving it to Mirabelle last night. There wasn't a moment to catch her alone because immediately after JJ's game finished, Emily and Mirabelle disappeared to the pool with a bottle of wine. The sounds of Mirabelle's laughter through my window taunted me until they went to her room.

"Maybe," Mirabelle agrees, taking a drink, and I take the opportunity to check her out. She has these sparkly boots on her feet that she keeps smiling at, and a pair of jeans that are hugging her ass irresistibly. Maybe we should have gone back to the VIP section. There are too many people down here getting to look at her.

Temptation gets the better of me, and I can't keep my hands to myself. "I don't think I'd be mad if you showed up to the next game wearing one of these," I say, slipping my finger under the strap to snap it against her tanned skin.

Her chest hitches in surprise and her lips part as she looks up at me. "A corset?"

"I can't take my eyes off you," I say, and if I didn't know better, I'd say I'm drunk. *Drunk words equal sober thoughts, but the only thing I'm drunk on, is Mirabelle.*

There's a tap on my arm interrupting the moment before Mirabelle can respond, and I twist to see a girl from the next table over, gaping at me in awe. "Oh my god. You're him. You're Henry Price."

I blink in surprise, not expecting this when I absolutely should have been. Mirabelle laughs on the other side of me, and I'm glad she's enjoying this. "Hi, it's nice to meet you," I say, finally finding my words.

"I'm so sorry, I promise I never do this, but my boyfriend is obsessed with you. You're on his fantasy team and everything. He would literally never forgive me if I didn't ask to take a picture with you. Can you please take a selfie with me?" she asks, looking up at me. Her friends are noticing she's turned away, and I feel my face flush as they point at me. *This is my hell, but I'm willing to try for Mirabelle.*

"Sure," I agree, leaning in as she holds out her phone to take the picture.

"Thank you so much. Seriously, you have no idea how excited he'll be," she says, clutching the phone to her chest. I'm just relieved she didn't ask any questions. This is the kind of stuff I don't mind, but the shit like my date with Mirabelle, where people feel entitled to put their hands on me while asking if I use steroids, are the reason I normally avoid everyone altogether. You never know what type of person will approach.

"No problem, but I did promise my girlfriend a dance," I fib, and that's when she sees Mirabelle behind me.

"No fucking way," she shrieks, and then all her friends approach.

"Oh my god."

"I can't believe I'm in the same bar as Mirabelle Walker. I'm really sorry if we're bothering you, but holy shit!"

"You're my idol! I love your outfit."

Mirabelle looks at me as if asking whether this is okay, but I don't mind at all. I don't like the attention, but they've been nice.

"I can take a picture of all of you?" I offer, and the amount of screams is an overwhelming response.

Mirabelle poses with them for nearly a dozen pictures as I practice my new career as her personal photographer before she politely tells them we have to go.

Maybe I've been looking at all this the wrong way.

I realize after we excuse ourselves that I've reached for her hand without realizing it. It feels so natural—everything with her does. "Are you okay? I'm sorry, that was a lot," she asks, peering up at me, but it wasn't.

"I didn't mind, but I do want to dance with you."

Her eyebrows raise in surprise. "I thought you only said that so she'd go away?"

She's not wrong, that might be the reason I said it, but I actually want to. "Let's dance," I say, pulling her in the direction of the thick crowd of grinding bodies. I stand there awkwardly for a moment, staring at her because I don't know what to do with my hands, and Mirabelle's head tips backward as she laughs. She covers her mouth immediately to stifle it, but fails. Her eyes are crinkled, and she looks so damn happy that I'd make a fool of myself any day if it makes Mirabelle laugh.

"What are you laughing at?"

She stands on her tiptoes, her hand resting on my chest for balance. "I'm sorry. I shouldn't be laughing, but I can't imagine you dancing. You're just . . . you're not a dancer, Henry."

Mirabelle absolutely has me there. I'm not a dancer. In fact, I can't even remember the last time I danced. I smile at her, feeling more like myself than I have in a while. Today feels like a day where anything can happen.

"I'm not a dancer, but I'd like to try anyway with you."

She grabs my hands, entwining them with hers. "Please don't step on my feet," Mirabelle requests, moving my hands to trail down her sides, leaving them on her hips as she moves them in a way that short-circuits my brain.

I pull her against me, touching her as her hands drift up my abdomen, and my restraint threatens to snap as my heart beats quickly in my chest.

We're dancing.

Grinding, actually, but still technically dancing.

Her cheeks are flushed, and then we're kissing.

I'm not sure who kisses who, and I don't care, but I give Mirabelle everything I have in me to give. Her mouth moves hungrily against mine, and my only regret is not doing this sooner.

The music pulses in my ears, but the only thing I'm aware of is her. We're in a room filled with people, but somehow, we're in our own little world.

My hand slides to grip her ass, squeezing firmly, and the way Mirabelle moans into my mouth only spurs me to kiss her with more intensity. I can taste the cranberry from her drink on her tongue as we devour each other. My lungs are screaming at me to breathe, but I don't fucking care. I'd sooner die than stop kissing Mirabelle.

Mirabelle turns her head away, breathing heavily, and I move to press my lips against the soft skin of her neck, inhaling the smoky vanilla scent that is as addictive as kissing her. Her hand twists through my hair, pulling on the short strands as she presses her hips up against the bulge in my pants. My entire body reacts, and I nip at her neck before soothing the spot with a gentle kiss.

For the first time since high school, I'm worried I'm going to make a mess in my pants just from making out with a girl.

"*Henry,*" Mirabelle moans my name into my ear, and I reluctantly pull away to see if she's okay. Her lips are swollen, and damn, if it doesn't make me feel good knowing I made them that way.

"Do you want to stop?" I ask, trying to catch my breath. I'll do whatever she tells me to do.

Her whiskey eyes are intense as she looks at me. "No. The opposite, actually."

"Stacey did say we should practice . . ." I trail off, twisting her ponytail between my fingers. "Think we're convincing anyone yet?"

Mirabelle bites her bottom lip shyly—*which is fucking*

ironic because shy is the last thing I'd ever describe her as—and shakes her head, her ponytail swishing behind her. "No. In fact, I think we need to try harder to convince them," she says, tilting her head at me.

Challenge fucking accepted.

I kiss her again, making sure to take my time to fully commit this to memory. "You taste like cranberry," I mumble against Mirabelle's lips, feeling her smile. I don't even like cranberry, but if you asked me right now what my favorite thing in the world is, I'd say cranberry.

Sliding my hand up her side, Mirabelle arches into me again, holding onto my bicep firmly.

I'm not sure if it's a good thing or a bad thing that it feels as good as the first time, because when this fake relationship is over . . . how are we supposed to go back to normal?

Do I want to?

I shove the thoughts to the back of my head as Mirabelle's other hand drifts over the front of my pants that are poorly concealing how turned on I am. She freezes, and I turn my head, breaking our kiss to talk in her ear so she can hear me over the music. "Convincing enough?" I ask, trying to keep my voice from shaking. Hell, I want to know what it feels like to have her actually touch me. I want to know what Mirabelle looks like when I'm touching her. I want to know everything that makes her tick. What part of her do I have to touch to make her moan, what part to make her gasp, and how can I worship her to make Mira fall apart because of me?

Mirabelle pulls her hand back and I can see how bright red her face is, even in the dim lighting. "I'm sorry. I wasn't thinking. I should have aske—"

"Don't apologize. You don't have to ask. You can touch me—feel what you do to me," I say, biting my tongue to keep from begging Mirabelle to touch me. *I'd get on my knees for her, right here, right now.* Instead, I stay still, waiting for her to make the next move because I'm not going to ask her to do anything she doesn't want to.

She says stop, and we stop. There's nothing more to it.

Mirabelle palms me through the material, and I couldn't stop the moan from the back of my throat if I wanted to. Her lips curve into a wicked smile, and she leans up to kiss me again. "Pretty convincing."

I cup her face gently, kissing her like the precious gem she is.

"Henry," Mirabelle says my name softly, and I press another to the corner of her sweet mouth. She says my name again, but I can't hear it because the music has somehow been turned up another level. However, I do know what my name looks like coming from her lips.

"Your phone," she says louder, and I realize my phone is vibrating. I don't know how I didn't feel it before, but I hate that she takes a half step back.

I reluctantly reach into my pocket, pulling out my phone to see my mother's name flashing on the screen. *I fucking hate caller ID.* I hesitate, knowing that Mirabelle can see the screen from the angle I'm holding it. The smile on Mirabelle's face has disappeared, and now she won't meet my eyes. "I think you should take that." And in a blink, she's faded into the crowd before I can stop her.

The phone stops ringing before I can decline it. Why does she keep calling?

I shove my phone back in my pocket, making my way toward the VIP section where I'm hoping Mirabelle went. Shit, I never asked her what was wrong. Instead, I made out with her and told her she could touch me. I'm an ass.

I drag a hand through my hair, taking a seat at the table Quinn is at, surprisingly by himself. I thought he would have been long gone by now.

"You're still here?" I ask, scanning the area for any hint of Mirabelle, but she's nowhere to be found. *Great.*

He grunts a short greeting, taking a long drink from his glass while ignoring my question.

What's his deal?

"You good?" I ask, making sure to keep an eye out for Mirabelle.

He runs a hand over his face, clearly bothered by something. "I don't know, man. I think I fucked up."

I sit up straighter, immediately jumping to the worst conclusion. "What the hell did you do to that girl?" I ask, lowering my voice. *Have I read Quinn all wrong?*

"What? No, it's not about the girl from earlier. The only thing I didn't do was leave with her when she asked." Quinn scratches the back of his neck and avoids making eye contact with me. "I told Mirabelle I have feelings for her at the event yesterday," he admits.

It feels like a bucket of ice water has been dumped over my head, snapping me back into a reality where Mirabelle and I don't work. "What?" I ask, hoping I heard him wrong.

"She's fucking incredible. It's not like you like her, it's all fake for you," he says, taking another drink, shaking his head. "I know she's young, and you asked me to stay away, but I can't get her out of my head. She asked me to give her time to think, and it's driving me crazy not knowing where her head is at."

My mind is blank. How the hell am I supposed to respond to that? That it might not all be fake between us? I'm finally admitting to myself I have feelings toward Mirabelle, but I'm nowhere near figuring them out.

"See, you think I fucked up too." Quinn groans, downing the rest of his drink.

I blink, quickly trying to think of anything to say. One thing I do know is that I don't speak for Mirabelle. "I don't know if you fucked up or not. Mirabelle's a wild card and always has been," I choke out, wishing I had my own drink in front of me.

I don't know if what happened on the dance floor meant anything to Mirabelle. She makes me feel alive compared to what I can now recognize as sleepwalking through the last few years. I know I don't trust people, and I struggle to let them close to me, but I don't have to worry about that with Mirabelle. When I'm around her I feel like myself—not the version everyone expects me to be.

I know it's complicated because of who we are, and our goddamn age difference that everyone else is fixated on, but I'm almost past the point of giving a shit.

"Are you cool that I made a move?" Quinn asks, now eyeing me.

No. I'm not fucking cool with it, but I also can't blame him. She's been in front of me all along, and it's my own damn fault for trying to suppress any attraction toward her because of how wrong or right it would have been.

"It's Mirabelle's decision. I hope you keep in mind that if you hurt her, she has a lot of men in her life that will be coming for your head," I say, deciding that is the best answer because I don't have a claim on her. Mirabelle's her own person. Regardless of how it makes me feel, this is about how she feels.

That doesn't mean I'm happy about the situation, but if she needs to think about it, then I'm not going to stand in Quinn's way.

Fake.

Mirabelle and I are fake, even if tonight didn't feel fake.

I finally catch sight of her chatting with Wilson and his friends, using her hands animatedly to get her point across as Emily laughs next to her. The sense of relief I feel at knowing she's safe is overwhelming. I smile at the sight of her fitting into my world when she looks over at me, making eye contact. She smiles in return, winking at me from across the area, not missing a beat in the conversation.

That's my girl.

Quinn regains my attention when he speaks again. "I know, but that doesn't scare me. She's worth it."

He's right.

She *is* worth it.

CHAPTER SEVENTEEN

Mirabelle

"So what do you think?" I ask, sitting on my bed as I work on a proposal to help boost sales of Henry's jersey that's due in the morning while Emily looks through my recently acquired clothes from my online shopping to replace everything thrown out after the fire. It's a good thing my credit card has no limit.

"Dude, if you were pretty much having sex with your clothes on, I'd say there's a pretty good chance he likes you as well." She grins over her shoulder, and even though it's Emily, I'm still flustered. "Don't even try to deny it, I saw how he watched you afterward and the pictures are everywhere online."

My entire body ignites at the memory of Henry's body pressed up against mine. It was incredible, and his mouth? It should be illegal for Henry to say things like *"you can touch me —feel what you do to me"* because I thought I might combust right there on the spot. And then I followed instructions, feeling what he was hiding in his pants, and I'd be lying if I said it didn't cross my mind that if Henry and I ever got to that point . . . it might not fit. He's certainly bigger than Reid was, and I'm feeling way out of my depth. Even kissing Henry is better than anything I imagined.

It was enough to make me forget fighting with my parents, everything with Bailey, the conversation I had with Chris, and whatever that was with Quinn at the stadium. Well, I guess I forgot until Henry's mother called. Then reality came rushing back, and I ran.

"I know, but I keep asking myself how much of it was real, and how much was for the cameras?" I groan, fidgeting with my hands in my lap. As much as I wanted to kiss him in the club, I was there when Stacey warned us that people were starting to get skeptical about us dating. I know why he kissed me.

I checked online earlier to see if anyone had taken any pictures of us, and based on the comment sections, no one was questioning anything after seeing them.

My old teammates from the Olympics texted me to ask if Henry knocking me up was the real reason I wasn't competing in the next Games, and I laughed before quickly denying it.

Stacey gave me a pat on the back at work today, which is as good of a compliment as I can expect from her.

"Shut up." Emily scoffs, throwing a shirt at my face.

"What was that for?" I ask, laughing.

"Because you're questioning something that is so obvious."

Obvious. I still hate that word.

"It's complicated," I say, throwing the shirt back to her.

Emily crosses her arms over her chest, her long dark hair flowing over her shoulders. "Mirabelle, this pity party is not cute. You have Henry right where you want him. I've seen how he looks at you when he thinks no one is watching. Why don't you ask him if this little fake arrangement you're in can turn into a real, permanent one?"

"Em, I love you, but I think you're imagining things." I

pull my phone out, checking to see if Bailey responded to the text I sent earlier, but there's nothing there. I shoot JJ a quick message, asking if he's had better luck hearing back from Bailey.

A different phone is shoved in my face, and I blink quickly, focusing on the screen. It's a picture from last night, capturing the moment Henry snapped the strap of my corset against my skin. It was taken behind me, so my face isn't visible, but the way Henry is staring at me in it sends shivers up my spine.

"Does this look like a man that is faking things? I've met Henry. He's not this good at acting," she exclaims, and Emily has a point, but it's so much more complicated than she's making it out to be.

If he says no, how am I supposed to face him after that? And with everything going on in my life with my parents and Bailey, should I even be focused on a guy right now?

Henry's not some guy, though. He's *the* guy.

"I'll think about it," I say, glancing at my computer screen before shutting it. I'm not getting any work done right now, but I should have enough time after my morning run to finish it then.

"You're Mirabelle fucking Walker. I know Reid fucked with your self-confidence when it comes to dating, which is only one of the reasons I still think you should have let me take a baseball bat to his windshield, but you're a catch. You're smart, absolutely hilarious, and you have a heart of gold," Emily says, sitting next to me on the bed.

"I'm all that, but not pretty?" I tease, and she rolls her dark eyes.

"You and I both know you stare at yourself enough in the mirror to know how beautiful you are, but if you need to hear me say it, you're so freaking pretty that a picture of you should be hanging in the Louvre."

"I love you," I say, laughing quietly as I reach to squeeze her hand.

"Damn right you do," Emily says, smiling. "You deserve a man who would hang the moon and the stars for you, and the way Henry's looking at you in all of these photos, tells me that he would do that and more."

My eyes begin to water, and I press my tongue to the roof of my mouth to stop it.

"Besides, Mira, worst case scenario, if Henry doesn't like you, it's his loss, and then you should go out with Quinn."

Oh god. I can't even imagine that.

"Let's not even speak that into existence," I say, dragging my hands over my face. I feel bad, but I've definitely been avoiding Quinn since he told me he had feelings for me. It didn't seem like he was too bummed about it last night at the club based on how far his tongue was stuck down that girl's throat.

"So are you going to go talk to Henry?" she asks, and it sounds like a truly awful idea.

"Do I have a choice?" I ask, despite already knowing what Emily's answer is going to be.

She grins and shakes her head. "Nope, but if you want your ego stroked, you should take off that sweatshirt and let him see how good your boobs look in what you're wearing underneath."

I look at her like she's dumb. "Em, I'm literally not wearing anything underneath."

"Exactly," she says, awfully pleased with herself, and I shake my head in disbelief.

"I can't believe you."

"Go get the man of your dreams while I help myself to the closet of my dreams. Do you think your insurance will notice if you purchase some clothes in my size?" Emily asks, making her way back to my closet. She studied business at Duke to help her run her online boutique that she wants to eventually bring to a physical space.

"You have fun with that. My goal is to not pass out while confessing my feelings," I grumble, exhaling a shaky breath. The short walk to Henry's room feels like a death march. My stomach actually hurts right now. *This is a terrible idea.*

I knock softly on the door, forcing myself not to run back to my room for shelter. *What is taking him so long? Should I have taken off the sweatshirt? Actually, no—that's an awful idea. I absolutely need to keep my clothes on. Why would Emily even suggest that? That is some truly horrible advice.* I tap my foot anxiously as I wait for it to open so I can ruin my entire life, and I'll never be able to show my face again. At least there's a pool in the backyard I can drown myself in after he rejects me. I go to knock again so I can tell Emily I did try to talk to him, he just didn't answer, but right before I can, the door opens, and my knuckles make contact with Henry's dripping, tattooed muscular chest.

"Fuck me," I whisper as my jaw hits the fucking floor. This actually is from one of my dreams.

Henry's standing in the doorway with a towel wrapped around his waist, rivulets of water still making their way down his body. My brain nearly explodes at the sight of his ink in all its glory, twisting up his arm onto his shoulder and left pec where my knuckles are currently resting happily.

"What?" he asks, tilting his head, causing droplets of water to fall from his wet hair in the process.

I snatch my hand back quickly, forcing an awkward laugh. "What?"

"I didn't hear what you said?" Henry questions, and I'm having a very hard time looking him in the eye. "Mira?"

I clear my throat, tearing my eyes away from all his spectacular muscles to look at the fan rotating in the background above Henry's shoulder. It's like right by his face, so there's no way he'll know I'm not actually looking at him. "Hi," I try to say, but my voice squeaks instead.

Yeah, my next move is to go in the pool.

"Hi," he says, adjusting his grip on the towel around his waist.

Don't look down. Remember your words. Fuck, what were my words? I blink and do my best to maintain my focus on the fan, but I definitely should have picked something over the other shoulder because that damn tattoo . . . *I want to touch it.* Henry told me last night I didn't have to ask if I could touch him, but I still feel like I need to hear explicit consent before touching him again. Yes. That seems more important than why I came here—*oh fuck! I'm here for a reason.*

"Hi," I say quickly, sounding at least a little more like a human than a mouse this time.

Henry's eyebrow is raised. "You already said that."

"Did I? I don't think I did," I ramble, and this is absolutely when I should be making my retreat. I've fucked this up enough, and it's all because he answered the door shirtless.

"Is everything okay?" Henry asks, and I nod.

"Yep, totally perfect," I say, shifting my weight.

"So did you need something?" he asks, and I blink in surprise.

"Yes."

Henry looks at me expectantly, and I'm not sure what to say.

"Yes, what?" he prods, and it dawns on me that maybe Emily and I should have role-played this scenario before I showed up here without a damn clue about what I'm supposed to say. The only thing coming to mind is, *Can I have your babies please and thank you?*

I'm setting back the feminist movement decades right now.

"Um . . . I just came to thank you for last night. Yep, that's why I'm here. I came to thank you for last night, the kissing, and yeah. It made me feel pretty good about myself, and I'm sorry if I wasn't any good—"

"You don't need to thank me. I should be thanking you." Henry steps closer, and his amused expression fades into one of suspicion as he narrows his hazel eyes. "Why would you think you weren't any good?"

Reid.

"No reason," I say quickly, taking a step back, but Henry anticipates this, caging me against the wall with both arms on either side of me. I can smell his body wash, and I think he should have his team look into making some kind of deal with them, because if people knew this is what he smelled like, I'm sure it would fly off the shelves.

"Mirabelle, tell me."

I open my mouth to tell him to back up, but instead my eyes drift down to his impressive abdomen and the goddamn white towel that's slipped a little to show the V lines on his pelvis.

"*Mon cœur*, tell me why the hell you would think you weren't any good at kissing?"

I am so out of my depth here. I make the fatal mistake of finally looking Henry in the eyes, and instead of whatever I thought I'd see, he only looks worried.

"You're only wearing a towel," I whisper.

"Then I guess you better talk faster before I flash you."

Yes, please.

I chew my lip, tucking my hands into the sleeves of Henry's sweatshirt so I don't reach out and do anything I'll regret. You'd think I've never been around him shirtless before based on the way I'm acting. I have, and it gets better and better each time.

"My ex-boyfriend. He . . . I haven't dated a whole lot. I spent too much time focused on gymnastics to care much about it. I've kissed people, but relationships . . ." I swallow the lump in my throat. It's the truth, but only half the story. None of the guys I was around ever measured up to Henry, so it didn't feel worth it to try with any of them. Reid was my first attempt at giving someone a real chance without comparing them to Henry the entire time, and it blew up in my face. I was nervous about my lack of experience prior to dating Reid, but after him, I'm fucking terrified of saying or doing the wrong thing with Henry. I know I shouldn't let a guy I dated for a few months get in my head like this, but I haven't been able to brush off the shit Reid said to me, leaving me worse off than I was before him. The last thing I want to do is blow my chance with Henry because I have no idea what I'm doing. "One of the reasons he said he broke up with me was because kissing me was like kissing a piece of cardboard and—" I shut my mouth quickly because I'm definitely not going to say the next part.

Henry's entire body has coiled with tension, and it takes him a moment to gather his thoughts before speaking. "And what?" he asks, his voice hoarse as if the little restraint he has is about to snap.

"I made him feel like less of a man because he couldn't make me orgasm." *Holy shit. I didn't actually admit that, right?*

"You're joking," Henry says, and a low chuckle sounds from his chest. "He's not a man, Mirabelle. He's a fucking *boy*. No man worth anything would ever make a woman feel like it was her fault she couldn't come from five seconds of foreplay, which is giving him the benefit of the doubt that he even attempted foreplay. Never in a million years would I compare kissing you to kissing a piece of fucking cardboard. *Never*."

"Okay," I say softly, overwhelmed by all of this right now. Henry's lack of clothing, the topic of conversation, and Henry's lack of clothing.

His gaze falls slowly to my mouth, and then he looks

further down as if noticing the sweatshirt he told me to keep. "You look better in that than I ever did."

My brain is melting.

"In case I wasn't clear last night, I really enjoyed kissing you. Thank you for helping me." Henry presses a sweet kiss to the top of my head.

My heart is still racing when I walk into my room, and Emily is holding a red blouse up to her body. "Did you tell him?" she asks, and I shake my head slowly.

"No, but I think I'm ready to drown myself in the pool."

"Not an option, but continue."

I groan, flopping onto the bed. "He was only wearing a towel, and I forgot how to use my words with him standing there looking like some Greek god."

Emily rubs my back reassuringly. "It couldn't have been that bad."

"It was."

By the time I explain the conversation to her, we're on the same page agreeing, it actually *was* that bad.

CHAPTER EIGHTEEN

Henry

Normally, PR staff wouldn't travel with the team to away games, so when Stacey and Mirabelle board the team plane to travel with us to our first away game, it causes quite a stir.

I hear someone a few rows behind me grumble about wishing their girlfriend could travel with the team.

"Here, let me help with that," Quinn says, standing up to help Mirabelle put her carry-on in the above compartment before I can move. She smiles at him, saying something I can't hear, and I pull my phone out to see if I missed a message from Mira about traveling with the team, but I have nothing.

"Did you know she was coming?" Wilson asks, and I look away from Quinn trying to show off he can lift her bag with one arm. Doesn't he know she has enough upper body strength to do that herself without showboating?

"She didn't say anything to me."

Mirabelle would have to be talking to me to say something, and she's been avoiding me ever since our conversation outside my door earlier this week.

Stacey makes eye contact with me and shakes her head,

disappointed. My phone buzzes half a second later with a message from her, followed by another one a second later.

STACEY

Why is Mackie acting like a better boyfriend than you?

Is there something I need to know?

Wilson snickers, having read the text before I could shut it off. "I know you say you don't like Stacey, but she's kind of funny."

"That's because she's not hovering over your shoulder twenty-four seven," I say, grumbling. She's growing on me, but I'd prefer to keep that to myself.

"Do you think if I asked Coach, he'd let my girlfriend travel with us?" Tyler asks, leaning over the back of my seat.

I snort, the theoretical scenario playing out in my head. "Why don't you go ask him?" I ask sarcastically, and Tyler actually seems to consider it.

"Don't be fucking stupid. Price is kidding," Wilson says, and this causes a few heads to turn our way.

"Price made a joke?" Crosby asks, and I flip him off, pulling my headphones out.

"It wasn't very funny," Tyler says, sitting back in his seat as I look for where Mirabelle is on the plane. I feel a little better seeing her sitting between her uncle and Stacey, instead of next to Quinn.

"The funny part would have been seeing you go up to Coach and ask him," I say, putting my headphones on.

I can't let the fact that Mirabelle is here fuck with my head, even if she's the only thing I've been able to think about for the last week while she ices me out.

The only thing keeping my self-control in check is that I'm in season, and I have no business getting wrapped up in a girl.

Especially one that I could find myself consumed by very easily.

I start the audiobook I've been listening to in the gym, trying to focus on the profile the main character is giving on the serial killer they're hunting.

Most people listen to music to get in the zone, but there's nothing that calms my brain more than a book.

Correction: usually there's nothing that calms my brain more than a book.

I guess it only works when a certain blonde isn't on the same plane as me.

I chew anxiously on my mouthguard, itching to get back on the field.

This game isn't the blowout the last one was, but somehow that makes it feel more real.

I'm impressed by the level head Owen has been able to keep, especially when he has more reason than anyone to be high-strung in this stadium. We're playing the Lions, our division rivals, but this rivalry is more personal for Owen than for anyone else.

Twenty years ago, Owen was on track to become one of the best tight ends in the league when he helped score the winning touchdown in an intense rivalry game against the Lions. He and Thalia were walking through the parking lot when a drunk fan struck Owen with his car, nearly killing him. The injuries he sustained ended his career, leading him down the path of climbing through the coaching ranks to become the head coach of the Panthers.

I remember as a kid, during one of the first years with Owen on the coaching staff, there was a sideline-clearing brawl between the teams that ended in a record number of players facing suspensions and fines amounting to millions. It's hard to forget when it resurfaces every year during recaps of unforgettable moments in sports.

Owen pulled me aside earlier and made a point to make sure I knew there were no scores to be settled other than those on the scoreboard.

"I don't know where your head is at, but going into this game, I'm going to say to you what I always said to Walker. There's no debt to be paid that's worth risking an injury today. Lead by example, and show everyone you have the character and the talent to lead this team."

I refuse to let Owen down after all he's done to fight for me to stay with the Panthers. I need him to know that I'm not taking this chance for granted.

I didn't understand why he said it at first, but once we got on the field, the shit people were yelling at Owen was awful. It was enough to make me want to abandon all common sense, but if I launched myself into the stands to fight the fans, I would only end up getting myself suspended.

The Lions have gotten away with a lot of hits in this game, and I have a feeling a lot of us will be spending time with the athletic trainers this week.

"Settle down, there's still time," Owen says quietly, stopping next to me on the sidelines.

It doesn't feel like there's time. "I'd feel better if they weren't at the twenty-yard line."

"They're not scoring," he says, a tone of finality in his voice before he covers his mouth with the playbook in front of him. "They'd be stupid to score when all it would do is put them less than a field goal ahead of us with three minutes to go. They're going to stall, and hope it psychs you out, so if they do score with enough time for us to respond, you're in your head."

I know that's the plan, but it doesn't make it easier to breathe right now.

"I've got this," I say confidently, even if I feel my insides starting to shrivel under the pressure.

Owen looks at me, his face unreadable. "Good, then maybe you can stop chewing your mouthguard like a fucking rodent. It won't keep your teeth pretty for my niece if you mangle it. You won't be such a pretty accessory for her if you look like Toothless."

"I'd hate for her to be associated with someone that looks like a cartoon dragon," I agree, snapping my mouth shut. I look back at the field, just in time for the play to be stopped by the Lions calling a timeout. I cross my arms over my chest, trying not to let my irritation get the better of me.

"You're a good player, Price. Maybe you'll be great one day, but don't fuck it up by letting their mind games get to you," Owen warns, clapping me on the shoulder. He steps away to talk with our defensive coordinator, and I let the words sink in.

I want to be great. I want this more than anything.

I grab the collar of my jersey, looking out around me. The stadium is packed, and I can feel the roar of the crowd in my bones.

Let them play their games. It's not going to change the outcome, we *are* going home with a win.

The play clock resumes, and the sound of the stadium somehow grows louder when the Lions' quarterback drops back, scanning for an open receiver, just as our left defensive tackle breaks through the offensive line. The quarterback sees him, darting out of the way at the last moment to avoid being sacked, causing his pass to end up out of bounds.

Hell yeah.

My excitement is short-lived when on the next play, their quarterback finds his mark in the end zone—a wide receiver left open as our cornerback is a second too slow. Owen swears, turning to find me as they score the extra point on the kick, followed by the kickoff, before nodding at me.

Adrenaline is pumping through my veins, but my head has never felt clearer. Everything else falls silent as I jog out onto the field, taking my place as everyone else falls into formation around me.

I focus on breathing as I hear Owen's voice through the microphone in my helmet. The clock is running out, and I need to get us close enough for our kicker to have a shot at making a field goal.

"Set, hut," I call, the ball landing in my hands. I find Tyler as he darts to my side, handing off the ball as he tries to find a gap in their line. He dodges, making it far enough to get a first down before he's hit by a defender, and there are immediate flags thrown. Yelling erupts from all around as Tyler rolls onto his back, the ball still clutched in his hands.

I don't hear what Crosby says to the guy who hit Tyler, but Wilson yanks him back as I reach Tyler, who is slow to get up.

"Are you good?" I ask, offering him a hand as whistles are blown.

"Knocked the wind out of me, but I didn't drop the ball." He grimaces as the flags are explained over the stadium's speakers.

"Targeting number fifty-five. Fifteen-yard penalty."

Are you fucking kidding me? I'm ready to shut them up once and for all.

"Took it like a champ," I say, tipping my head as I turn back to my guys. "I don't care what they say, or what they do. We keep our shit together and let the score at the end do the talking," I say, making sure every single one of them hears me.

Crosby's mouth is set in a hard line, and if we had more time, I'd probably try to say something else.

We're fifteen yards closer than we were before, and I'm going to use every bit of it to my advantage.

Two more first downs later and thirty seconds on the clock, our kicker sends a perfectly placed kick through the middle of the goalposts.

I breathe a sigh of relief as the sidelines around me erupt into chaos, and I barely had enough time to shower and get dressed before the media was let into the locker room.

I did a good job of not letting myself think about Mirabelle during the game, but I'm having a hard time keeping my eyes off her as she hovers in the back with Stacey, taking notes of our answers. She looks beautiful, but she'd look even better wearing my jersey.

Actually, she'd look better wearing nothing, but I shouldn't be thinking that, especially right now while she's working.

I'm not able to fully relax until I'm on the plane. As I pull my headphones out of my bag, I see Mirabelle appear. I stand up, causing everyone's eyes to turn to me.

"Price, what are you doing?" Wilson asks and I grab my bag from below the seat in front of me.

"I'm going to sit with my girlfriend," I say, stepping into the aisle, closing the gap between us. Mirabelle is staring at me in surprise, and she looks at Stacey who is already seated.

Stacey shoos her away. "Go sit with him before I change my mind," she says, rolling her eyes in annoyance as she taps quickly on her phone.

I've been dying to catch her alone to ask why she didn't tell me she was coming on this trip. I tried texting Mirabelle last night to ask her, but when she didn't respond, I knocked on her hotel door before curfew. It didn't matter, though. Mirabelle still didn't answer. It's irritating how good she is at avoiding me actually, and I'll be damned if I let another minute go by without talking to her.

I smile because if she refuses in front of everyone, Stacey will lose her shit. Did I trap her into talking to me? Maybe, but I regret nothing.

Mirabelle adjusts the strap on her shoulder, and I take that as my sign to walk to the empty row at the back of the plane. I don't care if it means forfeiting my first-class seat for the ride back. I'd rather sit next to her.

She takes the window seat, immediately continuing her streak of trying to avoid me by looking out the window.

"I think I deserve to know why you're avoiding me," I whisper, and Mirabelle answers with a scoff.

"I'm not avoiding you."

That's hilarious. "You could at least look at me while you try to lie," I muse, buckling my seatbelt per the flight attendant's instructions. I have a pretty good feeling I know why Mirabelle's avoiding me, but I'd like to hear it from her. I thought I said all the right things in the moment, but clearly, I did something I'm not aware of.

Mirabelle turns to look at me, her cheeks flaming red. "Are you happy now? I'm not avoiding you."

"I tried to talk to you last night, but you didn't answer your door," I say quietly, doing my best not to say the wrong thing. I want her to tell me what I did, because I can't stand the silence.

Mirabelle turns back to the window again. "Huh, that's weird. Maybe I was in the shower."

I'm not great at this whole passive aggressive shit. I can barely say the right thing when she's speaking normal English, and not whatever this is. "Mirabelle, please."

She fidgets with the strap of her seatbelt as the plane smoothly lifts into the air, but she doesn't react.

"It's not a big deal that you haven't dated a lot."

Her entire body tenses up, and I'm glad we're stuck on a

plane together because she can't run from me. "Stop," she whispers.

"No, I'm not going to stop until you talk to me."

"There's nothing to talk about. I want you to forget I ever said anything about it," Mirabelle whispers, looking around to see if anyone is paying attention to us, but no one sits at the back of the plane if they can help it. We played an entire game and are now on a plane back to North Carolina. Half the team is either asleep or about to be, and the other half definitely has headphones on.

"Sorry, it's hard for me to forget that you think kissing you is the same as kissing a piece of cardboard. I like to recycle, but not that much." I try to lighten the mood, but her face falls nonetheless. It fucking kills me to see her sad.

"It's not only that. I'm embarrassed, Henry. I'm embarrassed because when Reid broke up with me, he made me feel like I'm not good enough." Her eyes are sparkling with unshed tears, and I open my mouth to talk, but Mirabelle shakes her head quickly. "I know you're going to say he wasn't man enough to try to make me orgasm, but what if I'm the problem? I said no too much, I'm a bad kisser, and I'm so . . ." She falls quiet, and I think I'm ready to kill this asshole. She sniffles quietly, wiping her nose on the back of her hand. "I'm afraid I'm so inexperienced that when I'm finally with the right guy, I'll mess it up. I hate that I'm insecure about that. I'm Mirabelle Walker, for fuck's sake. I shouldn't care about this because I know the right guy won't care, but I do."

Her ex better start counting his days because he doesn't deserve to breathe anymore. I'll make it as painful as he deserves if she never looks this sad again about the bullshit he said to her.

Did I hear her right? She said no too much? That's not even a real fucking thing. You can say no as much as you like because if it isn't consensual, it shouldn't be fucking happening.

Mirabelle's mouth falls open, and she looks at me in horror. "Did I say all that out loud?"

"Would it make you feel better if I told you no?" I ask, and she inhales sharply, wiping her cheeks.

"I'm sorry. None of that is your problem, so seriously ignore I said any of that."

I don't think there's a single damn thing I can say right now to make her feel better, so I take her hand, softly pressing my lips to the back of it. "When I need to clear my head, I listen to audiobooks. It helps calm my brain to escape somewhere else for a bit, and I'll be honest, I'm terrified to say the wrong thing that will make you more upset. I'm glad you told me, though. Thank you."

She unbuckles her seatbelt, sliding into the middle seat I left open to give her space. "Can I listen to your book with you?" Mirabelle asks, squeezing my hand as she rests our intertwined ones in her lap.

"We can find a new one so you're not jumping in halfway."

"That's okay. I want to listen to yours."

No one has ever asked to do that with me.

I open my headphones case, passing her one before inserting my own, trying to focus on the case that's about to be cracked wide open.

Mirabelle rests her head gently on my shoulder, and the intoxicating vanilla scent that clings to her is the only thing I can focus on.

CHAPTER NINETEEN

Mirabelle

"I'm sorry. I think I need you to repeat that," I say, staring at Henry in disbelief.

Did he actually offer what I think he offered?

"Can I come in?" he asks, and I rub my tired eyes, but I doubt I'll be getting much sleep tonight after this. I open the door wider, letting him into my room. I shouldn't have slept on the plane, but avoiding Henry was a lot of work the past week. I was exhausted, and now I'm paying the price for falling asleep on his shoulder.

"Am I still sleeping?" I ask, crossing my arms over my chest as Henry drags a hand through his damp hair. Thankfully, his water heater is large enough that both of us were able to jump in the shower immediately after getting back to his house, despite it being two in the morning. I don't mind flying, but it always makes me feel so gross.

"I did a lot of thinking after our conversation on the plane while you were sleeping, and I keep coming back to one thing. I want to help you feel more comfortable and confident with sex. You're doing me this huge favor by helping me, an—" I cut Henry off by laughing. *Yeah. That's what I thought he said. This is amazing.* "Why are you laughing?" he asks, but I'm not laughing because I think it's funny. I'm laughing because I feel like I'm dying inside.

"You know, I can understand where you're coming from, but I think this might be more embarrassing than anything with Reid. I don't need you to fuck me out of pity because you think your magical dick can fix whatever is wrong with me," I exclaim, trying not to crumble into a puddle on the bed.

I should have tried harder to continue avoiding Henry. This is awful. *Don't cry.* Crying isn't going to make this situation any better.

Henry shakes his head, putting his hands up in self-defense. "Mira, that's not at all what I'm doing."

"Then what do you call it?"

I can hear my heart beating in my ears and Henry steps closer to me. I swallow the lump in my throat, matching it to take a step back. The air feels stifling, and I pull the collar of my shirt uncomfortably. I want to look away—*I should look away*—but I can't.

"There's *nothing* wrong with you. Not once did that thought cross my mind, and I promise I'm not offering out of pity," Henry says, his eyes cataloging every move I make as he continues to get closer. I don't have anywhere I can hide physically, but emotionally? I feel like the only piece of me he doesn't see is the one that's madly in love with him. "When you told Stacey you would help me with my PR by pretending to be my fake girlfriend, was it out of pity?"

I agreed because I wanted Henry to see how amazing fake dating me would be, so he wouldn't be able to resist falling for me. It wasn't out of pity.

"No," I say.

Henry nods, satisfied with my answer. "I was embarrassed. I almost fucked everything up before I even had the opportunity to step on the field as a starter. *That's embarrassing.* I can't tell you how to feel, but I can say that I don't think you should be embarrassed. I'm offering to help you because everyone deserves to be comfortable during intimacy. Everyone deserves to know what it's like to have a partner that gives a damn about making them feel good. You said you were afraid to mess things up with the right guy, and I *loathe* the idea of you thinking you're not good enough. I don't want you to miss out on the happiness you deserve with the right man when he comes along, so use me to practice. Use me however you want, but please let me help you."

My lower back hits the dresser behind me, but Henry doesn't stop advancing closer to me. I'm not even sure I'm breathing when he slows right in front of me. My brain short-circuits when Henry brushes a damp strand of hair behind my ear, his knuckles grazing down the length of my cheek and the curve of my jaw. He tilts my head upward by applying gentle pressure under my chin, his eyes reading me like I'm a goddamn book written in a language only he understands.

Oh my god.

I'm not breathing, but I think he'll catch me if I faint.

"If I'm pitying anyone, it's your stupid fucking ex-boyfriend for not knowing what he had in front of him," he says.

I swallow the lump in my throat, wetting my lips. "And what's that?"

His hazel eyes soften, and I hate seeing the bags underneath them.

"You. He had you." Henry takes a shuddering breath, looking at me in a way that makes my heart do somersaults in my chest. "You're . . . *incandescent*. You're a beacon of light in a world that has seen too many tragedies. You're the sun in the middle of a fucking hurricane. You're everything good that a person could possibly be, all wrapped into one, and that's exactly what you deserve. You deserve *everything*, Mirabelle."

My heart can't take this. How can he say all of that and not have feelings for me?

Except, he didn't offer to make this real. Henry is offering to let me use him to practice if it means I'll be happy later down the line with another man. I can practically feel my heart grow as I fall more in love with him. Too bad I don't plan on there being another man, especially after that little speech.

"How would it work?" I ask, and his gaze drops to my mouth. God, even the way he looks at me turns me on.

"However you want. I'll be honest with you every step of the way. I know what I like, and I can't say it's the same for everyone, but I have an extremely hard time believing you could do anything wrong. Use me any way you want to give yourself the freedom and safety to learn what *you* like, without some undeserving asshole making you feel like you're doing it wrong."

Oh fuck. My entire body is screaming that I should just agree because nothing sounds better than that, especially with Henry. Logically, however, my brain is throwing up warning signs about how quickly this can go wrong.

But, if I'm going to be ruined by anyone, I'd rather it be Henry.

I nod slowly, the craving I have for Henry overpowering whatever logic is trying to keep me from giving in. The logic entirely disappears when Henry smiles, and he leans down, kissing me gently. Angling my head to kiss him back, it's like the restraint in him snaps, and Henry cups my face in his hands.

This isn't for show.

I'm unsure if knowing that makes this kiss better than all

our other ones, but I don't hold back. I fist the front of Henry's thin T-shirt, pulling him closer to me because now that I know what this feels like, a week was too long to be avoiding him.

I can feel how soaked I am already, and if Henry's words can cause my body to react in a manner it never has with another person before, I'm a goner.

Henry coaxes my mouth open, and I moan softly at the feeling of his tongue brushing against mine. Somehow, without breaking our mouths apart, Henry bends to lift me up, setting me down on top of the dresser. He steps between my legs, his hand slipping underneath the edge of my shirt to skim my lower back. *Yes, yes, yes.* I'm nearly vibrating under his touch, and I'm not sure why I thought this would be a bad idea in the first place.

I can feel how aroused Henry is, and I hook a leg around his waist, pulling him closer, feeling the smallest bit of satisfaction when the thick ridge of his erection rubs deliciously against my clit through the clothes separating us. Henry groans as I grind my hips against his, tipping my head back to gasp his name. "Henry."

The rough calluses on his palm only make the moment more real as his hand slides up my back, his touch confident and sure as I hold him close. I want more—*I need more.* I reach between us, kneading my breast, causing more pleasure to spark through my body as Henry kisses my neck.

Fuck. This is unreal, except it is real. *This is happening.*

"That's it, *mon cœur.* Make yourself feel good," he murmurs against the sensitive skin of my throat. I love that he could call me anything in the world, and he chooses to call me *my heart.*

"Henry, more. *Please.*" The words fall out of my mouth without a second thought, followed by another breathy moan as Henry scrapes his teeth teasingly over a spot that causes my hips to jerk reactively.

"What do you need?" he asks, his voice husky as he kisses the same spot soothingly. "Tell me, and it's yours."

I need you. I've always needed you.

"Do that again . . . with your m-mouth. Touch me, please," I struggle to say, my head spinning in delirium.

He chuckles, his hand still underneath my shirt, trailing down my side. "Here?" he asks, gripping my side, and I bite my lip, shaking my head.

My body arches when Henry scrapes his teeth again, biting gently this time before kissing the sting away. *Fuck, I really like that.*

"Hand h-higher," I stutter, trying to focus on the other part I asked for, and Henry brings his hand to the front, sliding it underneath my hand still playing with myself. Through the fabric of the shirt, I can feel the warmth of his skin as he pinches my nipple. "Oh my god, yes," I manage to say before I'm silenced as Henry threads his other hand through my hair to kiss me with so much desperation, my body sings.

I used to think gymnastics was the only thing that could make my body feel so alive, but Henry has proven me wrong.

"Need to kiss you, sorry," he mumbles in between kisses, and I couldn't care less what he does, as long as he doesn't stop.

I hold onto Henry's hand touching me for dear life through my shirt as he rolls my nipple between his fingers, and I frantically chase the high of my impending orgasm, the dresser rocking to hit the wall with the force of our bodies colliding. It's almost too much for me to handle, but my tipping point comes when Henry wraps my hair in his fist, yanking it back, and the spark of pain mixed with the intoxicating feeling of Henry kissing me causes my body to explode into a million tiny stars as his mouth hungrily swallows my cry.

Henry shudders against me, taking everything I have to give. I sag in relief, exhaustion finally catching up to me as Henry drops his head to the crook of my neck. My chest heaves, trying to catch up on the oxygen my brain was deprived of.

Did . . . *what the hell just happened?*

Henry exhales shakily, pressing a sweet kiss to my collarbone. "Do you still think I'm offering out of pity?"

"I'm not sure I care," I admit, causing both of us to laugh. He can pity me any day if it means *that* happens again. "That was . . ." I trail off, unsure how to put into words how good that was.

"Yeah. It was." He lifts his head, an easy smile forming on his swollen lips, and I love knowing they're swollen from kissing me. Henry looks like something out of a wet dream with his flushed cheeks and messy hair. "Did you like anything specific?" he asks, and I feel my cheeks flush.

"I liked all of it, but I think I liked when you pulled my hair?" I say, forcing myself to maintain eye contact when the idea of telling Henry exactly what I enjoyed about that entire life-altering experience makes me want to hide in my shirt.

"You think, or you know?" he asks, clearly picking up on my hesitancy, and I exhale. If I can come with all my clothes still on after dry humping Henry, I can definitely tell him what I liked about it. Holy shit, that's a sentence I never thought would be true.

"I know I did—a lot, actually," I correct myself, and his eyes gleam with satisfaction. I have never seen this side of Henry, and I don't know how I'm supposed to ever forget it exists. "I liked when you used your teeth on my neck."

"Noted. Was there anything you didn't like?" he asks, brushing my hair out of my face.

"Nope. I liked all of it, honestly." I smile at him, and suddenly, I feel a little silly for getting upset with him at first for offering. "I'm sorry I snapped at you. I hate that Reid put this doubt in my head, and I think I took some of my frustration out on you. I appreciate that you offered to help in the first place. I don't want you to think I only agreed to be your fake girlfriend because I thought I'd get something in return."

"Don't get in your head about it, Mira. I meant everything I said." Henry leans forward, pressing another soft kiss to my forehead.

"Would it be weird if I thanked you?" The last time I thanked him for something like this, I wound up spilling my guts about Reid. I suppose that wasn't entirely a bad thing because it led to tonight, but it feels wrong not to thank him?

"Thank you, Mirabelle. I'm not sure why you feel like you're inexperienced, I'm not sure I've ever come in my pants before," Henry admits, finally untangling our bodies. My mouth parts in shock, and I'm a little sad I missed getting to see Henry come undone. I look down at his pants as if needing to see proof he isn't telling me that to make me feel better, but there's definitely a stain on the front of his grey sweats. They're still tented, and my mouth waters at the idea of trying to take him in my mouth.

"Do you want help?" I ask, and Henry shakes his head.

"I'll take care of it in the shower like I have been, but maybe next time. There's no rush."

Like I have been.

I slide off the dresser, and I should be pissed I have to jump into the shower again, but I'm not mad in the slightest. Does that mean Henry has been thinking about me while jerking off? What does that mean?

"Henry, wait?"

He stops immediately, looking back at me.

I can't ask him about that. "What happens next?" I blurt

out instead, and he tilts his head, a playful smirk quirking the corner of his mouth up.

"Make a list of things you want to try, and things you think you need to get better at. We'll go from there," he says.

Despite how exhausted I am, I know I won't be sleeping at all.

CHAPTER TWENTY

Mirabelle

"Oh, he's good," JJ says, laughing at the dilemma I've found myself in. I roll my eyes, looking out at the stadium from where I'm camped out in our family's suite for my lunch. The world is quiet up here, especially in the middle of chaotic days trying to juggle everything for Stacey and prove that I'm still pulling my weight with the other interns.

"Yeah, I'm aware." I groan, covering my face. I've spent the better part of the last few days trying to make this list, but so far I haven't been able to write anything down.

"Like, I might need to write some of that shit down. Why the hell am I studying mathematics when I could be studying English and learning to put my degree to use by wooing girls? I mean, Henry's a good-looking dude, and I already have a hard time looking away from him on the football field because of how he plays. But he also says shit like, 'You're the sun in the middle of a fucking hurricane.' No wonder you've been holding out for him," JJ says.

"Shut up, JJ. Does that mean you're done trying to find Marley?" I ask, taking a sip of my latte.

"No, it doesn't. She's out there, and I'll find her when I'm supposed to. In the meantime, can I ask that you don't call me from the bathroom immediately after checking things off the list like you did with Emily?"

I snort, twisting the necklace I'm wearing today between my fingers. "It was an emergency, but I can promise you that I won't call you from the bathroom if anything happens." Nothing can happen until I make the goddamn list, but when Henry said to make a list, how many did he mean? Five? Ten? How many is too many?

"If? It sounds like he's willing to do anything you want. What do you have so far?" JJ asks, and I can't help laughing.

"Not a single fucking thing so you have no reason to worry about me calling you afterward."

My brother sputters on the other end of the line. "I'm sorry. What?"

I know. I'm awful. "Henry hasn't brought it up, but we've been swamped at work so it's not like there's been an opportunity to have a conversation about it. Hence why I'm calling you for help."

"Sorry to pop your bubble, but I'm a virgin so I'm probably not the best person to help you fill out your golden ticket to sex."

I wrinkle my nose in disgust at the analogy. "Don't call it that. You're making it sound like Henry's dick is a trip to Willy Wonka's factory."

"Maybe it is." JJ laughs, clearly finding this amusing. "There's seriously nothing you want to do?"

That's definitely not the issue. Reading romance books has given me a very active imagination as to what sex is supposed to be like, but I've found the real thing to be rather lackluster to say the least.

"There's plenty I want to do, but how many is too many?"

If the whole point of this was to get me out of my head, then I'm failing miserably already.

"Mira, I love you, but as your brother, I cannot help you make this list, and if you love me, you won't ask me to."

"I know, I know. This is something I need to do myself," I say, letting out a long sigh. I swirl the latte in my hand, the melting ice cubes clinking together. "I've been thinking about calling Mom."

"Really?" JJ asks, and the phone beeps, interrupting.

"Hang on, I'm getting another call," I say, pulling the phone away to see an unknown number. I quickly decline it, because if I don't have the number saved, I don't need to be answering it. "Sorry, wrong number or something."

"Stupid scammers, they call me all the time."

"Sam—" The phone begins to vibrate again. Seriously? "Sorry, I'll call you right back. They're calling again."

I end the call with JJ to the sound of him laughing, before answering. "Hello?"

"Hi, this is Principal Rogers from Shoreline Preparatory Academy. I'm calling for Bailey Walker's mother, Thalia Walker?"

My jaw hits the floor, and I quickly clear my throat. The principal? Why the fuck is the principal calling me, thinking I'm our mother? "Yes, this is she. May I ask what this is regarding?" I answer, trying to sound older.

"Ma'am, I apologize for interrupting your day, but I'm afraid that Bailey will need to be picked up as soon as possible. His teacher smelled alcohol on him, and I was immediately notified. Upon further discovery, we found that his water bottle contained alcohol. We believe that he is . . . well, that he is drunk, to put it bluntly. As this is a first-time offense, he will only be facing a five-day suspension."

"Oh my god," I say, gasping in horror. *What the fuck?*

"We have not notified the police, but if this happens again, I'm afraid it will be out of our hands per our handbook, and we will be forced to notify the authorities. Will you be picking Bailey up, or should I call your husband?"

I drag my hand down my face, choking back a laugh of disbelief. "Would it be okay if his brother, Hunter, were to take him home?"

"*Um,* I guess that should be fine. Are you sure you don't want to pick him up yourself?"

"Thank you. I apologize, but I am out of town on business, and my husband has a meeting today, but I assure you, we are going to take this very seriously," I say, trying to sound calm without making my parents seem like absentee parents. God, what the hell is going on?

"These things happen unfortunately. If you'd like, I can send some pamphlets home with your sons about alcoholism and—"

"That'd be lovely. Thank you again for calling," I interrupt, hanging up to silently scream in my hands. *That'd be lovely? Who am I?*

I gather my things into my bag quickly, trying not to spill my coffee, while juggling my phone and bag in the other. What the hell is going on with Bailey? I should absolutely be calling Mom and letting her deal with this, but I'm a little afraid that if I tell her, I'm only going to have two brothers instead of three.

I dart out of the suite, making my way toward the stairs to figure out how the fuck I'm going to convince my boss to let me leave in the middle of the day to save my idiotic brother. I have no words. I seriously think I'm going to kill Bailey.

Pressing Hunter's contact, he answers immediately, his tone a hushed whisper. "How did I get excused from class?"

"The principal called me, thinking my number belonged to Mom. I'm on my way to beg my boss to let me leave, but is there somewhere you can take him until I can get home to keep our parents from killing him?"

"I can ask Kaitlyn to check where her parents are today. It could buy a little bit of time for you to get here."

"That's perfect, but what the fuck is going on?" I ask, trying to keep myself from taking my frustration out on the wrong twin. "Never mind, we'll talk about it when I get there. I'll see you soon."

Hunter mumbles goodbye, and I hang up, continuing toward Stacey's office where I find Henry walking out of her office instead, holding my jacket.

"What are you doing? I thought you were scheduled to meet with the coaches?" I ask, trying to keep my voice level.

"Coach excused it after I got a call from my sister. Told him I needed to drive you home for a family emergency, and he cleared the rest of my day. I also talked to Stacey and promised her I'd make some post about us online if she let you work remote for the day," Henry explains, offering me my jacket.

He did that?

I take the jacket, my hand shaking, and it's tempting to blurt out, *I love you*, but instead all I do is smile. "Thank you. You didn't have to do that."

Henry holds my bag and latte as I put my jacket on, passing back only the latte when I'm done. "I did, and it's already done."

"Can I have my bag back?" I ask, taking a quick sip of my drink.

He slides it up over his shoulder, shaking his head. "I've got it. I think I'll make this my professional side gig. Mirabelle Walker's accessory holder has a nice ring to it, don't you think?" he teases, succeeding in the impossible task of getting me to smile in this chaotic moment.

"I think it does," I agree, relaxing for a moment. "Are you sure I shouldn't talk to Stacey myself? We've been swamped the last few days, and I think I need to make sure she's fine—"

"Mirabelle, she said if she needs anything, she'll call. Family first, okay?"

"Okay," I agree, but I don't feel much better.

It's almost as if Henry can feel the anxiety radiating from me, so without saying anything, he turns on the audiobook we listened to together on the plane. Turns out it's a great way to distract my brain from the disaster we're heading toward, but we're halfway through the drive back to Wilmington when my phone dings with a message from JJ asking if I'm going to call him back, and I groan. "Fuck," I mutter under my breath, typing back that I'll call him later.

Henry's watching me closely, concern knitting his face, even though his sunglasses are hiding his beautiful eyes. "You okay?"

I chew my thumb anxiously. "No. What did Kait tell you?" I ask, turning off my phone.

"That Bailey was caught drinking in class and will probably be suspended. She sounded upset and asked me to tell you, but based on the way you were racing to Stacey's office, you already know," he says.

"I don't know what to do, Henry. Hunter told JJ and me that he quit soccer, and I don't know what I did to make him so upset, but he won't talk to me."

Henry reaches over to pull my hand away from my mouth, entwining my fingers with his. "Teenagers are hard. You're doing the best you can," he says, pressing his lips to the back of my hand.

"You think so?" I ask, turning to watch Henry drive. I don't need his validation, but I really want to hear it. Henry's fucking awesome with Kaitlyn, and I feel like I'm letting the twins down, and JJ's on the other side of the country.

"I do."

"The principal called me thinking I was my mother. How

does that happen?" I ask, and Henry tries to cover up his laugh by coughing, but I see right through him.

"Do you want my opinion as an adult, or as someone who once was a teenage boy?" he asks, and I'm honestly curious how the answer would change between the two of them.

"I think as someone who once was a teenage boy?"

Am I going to regret this?

A part of me expects Henry to pull his hand away, but instead, he rests it comfortably on top of my thigh like this is a normal thing to do. "Well, as someone who once was a teenage boy, I'm wishing I was smart enough to think of that shit in the first place. If I'm right, he logged into your parents' portal and switched the phone numbers, so if anything ever happened, they'd call you instead of your mom."

I'm actually dumbfounded because it's genius coming from the perspective of a teenager, but it's so infuriating to be the one caught on the other end of it.

"That's brilliant, but I'm still mad at him. He hasn't talked to me since the fucking Puppy Bowl, and now I get a phone call that he's drunk at school and have to bail his ass out? Henry, what the fuck am I going to tell my parents?" I ask, and it dawns on me I'm going to have to talk to my parents. *Oh fuck. My parents.*

"Yeah. You are going to have to tell them something. Good thing we have some time left in this drive to figure out what we're going to say to them."

"We?"

I don't even care that I probably sound desperate right now. "Yeah, Mirabelle. *We.* You and I are a team."

I can't stop the smile forming on my face, even if I tried. "I think we make a pretty good team."

"I think so too," Henry says, squeezing my hand.

Honestly, knowing that Henry is by my side regardless of how this shit plays out, is enough for me to pull out my phone and press my mother's number, putting her on speakerphone. I might be a little insane, but at least I'm not chickening out.

His jaw unhinges, clearly not expecting that move. "What are you doing? I meant we still had time, not to call right this second—"

Henry's cut off because the phone only rings once before she answers. "Mirabelle? Is everything okay?" she asks immediately.

"Hi, Mom."

She takes a strangled breath, and it's nice to know I'm not the only nervous one, despite having an entirely different reason to be nervous. "I'm so happy you called. Bash said I needed to wait for you to reach out—that we needed to give you time, but I've missed you."

"I've missed you too," I reply, tears blurring my vision. I blink them back, wiping at my cheeks with the sleeve of my jacket. *Keep it together, Mirabelle. You can feel your feelings later.*

"I'm so sorry for how we reacted to your relationship with Henry. If he makes you happy, then I'm glad you're together. That's all we've ever wanted for you, Mira."

"I love you," I say, taking a shaky breath. "Mom, I need to tell you something."

"Please tell me you're not pregnant. There's only so many surprises I can take, but if you are, let me say congratulations," Mom says, and Henry sputters next to me, choking on air.

"I'm not pregnant."

She exhales louder than necessary. "What a relief. Do I need to find Dad for this?"

I look at Henry who nods, and I guess go big or go home. "Might be a good idea."

"Give me a minute."

That minute feels like the longest minute of my life. My stomach is twisting, and I think about how poorly this could go. "I shouldn't have called," I whisper to Henry, and he stares at me in shock.

"But you did," he whispers back, and I look out the window briefly as if it might contain a solution.

"I don't know what I was thinking. Why didn't you stop me?"

I think I might be sick.

"You keep telling me not to tell you what to do!"

"Well, how was I supposed to know you were going to actually listen that time!"

"Oh my god," Henry mutters under his breath, which is so not helpful.

"Mira? Are you still there?" Mom asks, and I actually consider rolling the window down to throw the phone out, but that's *insane*. I can't chuck my phone out of a moving car to avoid my problems.

"So, before I start, I'm pretty sure everyone is okay. Let me try to finish before interrupting, okay?" Fuck, I'm nervous, and I'm not even the one who will be in trouble. I wait a moment to see if they're going to say anything, but I guess they're staying silent. Henry rubs his thumb reassuringly on the back of my hand as I explain the situation.

"For fuck's sake. Love, what are we supposed to do with them?" I hear Dad ask in the background once I'm finished.

"I don't know, Bash." *I guess that makes three of us, but I'm going to keep that an internal thought.* "Thanks for calling, Mira. I just . . . I don't have words right now. You and JJ never pulled shit like this. Are you seriously driving back to pick him up?" Mom asks, and I'm curious about how Bailey has been acting toward them. I'd be willing to put money on them not knowing he quit soccer.

I didn't pull shit like this because I was training for the Olympics. And JJ is too much of a goody-two-shoes.

"Yeah, I figured it was the option that ended in the least amount of casualties."

"She's not wrong. I'm ready to strangle the kid," Dad mutters, and I'm glad at least some things never change, even if I haven't been around.

I guess it wasn't the worst thing in the world making this call.

Mom clears her throat, and I hold my breath instinctively. "I'm not sure if you've already left or not, but I know the season has started, and there's probably no chance in hell of this happening, but if Henry can come with you, I'd—*we'd* really like to talk to him. Only if he can swing it, or even if he wants to come, please will you let him know he's welcome?" Mom asks, and I steal a glance at Henry to see what he wants me to say.

I know I'm on the verge of tears because my mom is a lot of things, but hesitant is not one of them.

Henry doesn't move for a moment, and I know I shouldn't push, but the fact my parents are willing to get past their feelings to see me happy is everything.

"I'm driving the car. I heard everything, and I'd like that," Henry says, and I look away so he doesn't see the tears spilling down my cheeks.

Maybe I'm naive, but I didn't think it was possible to be this heartbroken while being so in love with someone at the same time.

CHAPTER TWENTY-ONE

Henry

I'M NOT SURPRISED TO SEE KAITLYN IN OUR PARENTS' living room, but I do a double take at the sight of both Walker brothers with short blond hair. Hell, I know they're identical, but with the same haircut, they actually look identical. The giveaway is only one of them is awake, while the other is asleep at the end of the couch.

I let go of Mirabelle's hand as Kaitlyn and Hunter's heads turn in our direction.

She cares so much about Bailey, and he doesn't have a fucking clue.

After that call with her parents, I didn't expect Mirabelle to say much. She didn't say anything for a while, but then she started explaining everything about Bailey since the fire. It suddenly made a lot more sense why we were going to pick Bailey up from school drunk.

Honestly? It hurts that this is the first I'm hearing about what's going on. I'm sure as shit going to focus on that so I don't conjure up the worst in my head for whatever happens with her parents when we get to the house.

I have a lot of questions for my sister, because I find it hard to believe she doesn't know why Bailey's acting out. She's mentioned he's been off, but I assumed it was a reaction to JJ going to school across the country and all the shit that's happened between Mirabelle and her parents.

"Henry!" Kaitlyn darts toward me, wrapping her arms around my shoulders. God, I can't believe how tall she is.

"Why aren't you in class, Kait?" I assumed Hunter was going to use the garage code to get in the house.

"Jerk, this is the part where you tell me how happy you are to see me." She groans, hitting my arm as Hunter approaches Mirabelle, pulling her to the edge of the living room.

"You're spending the whole weekend with me after your game Friday night," I say, ruffling her hair to annoy her. Kaitlyn rolls her eyes, swatting my hand away, but she can't resist smiling.

"Are you still coming to the game?" she asks, hope filling her tone, and I wouldn't miss it for the fucking world.

"Yes, but you should probably get some homework done if you're going to skip school."

"Seriously?" Kaitlyn asks, and I nod. "I hoped you'd take me with you."

I look back at Mirabelle, and she's still talking quietly to Hunter. I can't let her be the bad guy to Bailey again.

"Seriously. We'll talk later, okay?" I promise, stepping away to take one for the team by being the one to approach Bailey.

I'd like to dump water on his head to wake him, but instead, I push his shoulder. Bailey swings an arm without opening his eyes. "Leave me alone," he slurs.

"Henry, I can wake him up," Mirabelle adds behind me, but this doesn't need to fall on her shoulders.

"Bailey, get up," I say, keeping my voice level.

"No. I'm sleeping."

Now I don't feel bad about shoving him harder, and his

eyes flash open, anger and exhaust altering his youthful face. "We're leaving. Get up."

"Bailey, don't make this harder than it needs to be," Hunter says, and Bailey's scowl deepens when he catches sight of Mirabelle.

"Why is she here?" he spits out, wobbling as he sits up. "I don't want her here. Kaitlyn, I told you not to call her." Excuse me? I know he's not talking to my sister like that. Who the fuck is this kid?

"I didn't call Mira," Kaitlyn protests, and I bite my tongue.

"Then why the fuck is she here?"

Now I'm fucking over this. If I bite my tongue any harder, I'm going to bite it *off*. I grab his arm, pulling the lanky kid to his feet whether he likes it or not. I am so past polite. I look at Mirabelle who couldn't hide the devastation on her face if she tried, and it breaks my heart. I clear my throat, finding my sister is grabbing her backpack, following my directions. I'll check on her later, but school is important. It'll hopefully take her mind off this shit for a little bit.

Hunter and Mirabelle wordlessly follow Bailey and me to where Mirabelle's car sits in the driveway.

I have to remind myself that Bailey's a kid—*a stupid one*—but still a kid. I can't forget, or I'll consider knocking his teeth out for how he spoke to Kaitlyn and Mirabelle.

I open the back door of her car for him, shaking my head. "She's here because you're her brother, and she loves you. She's not the enemy. I don't know who is, but I can sure as shit tell you it's not Mirabelle."

"You don't know everything, Henry," he says roughly, climbing into the car. I shut the door behind him, turning to look at Mirabelle in disbelief as Hunter walks around to get in. Mirabelle drags a hand over her face, shaking her head.

I follow my instincts, closing the gap between us to pull

her into my arms. She sinks against me for a moment, and I'm at a loss. I feel slightly more grounded holding her, but I know we need to go. "I'm sorry. I shouldn't have shoved Bailey," I say, but I'm not sorry. I'm just hoping I didn't upset her more than the situation already did.

"Which time?" she asks, her voice muffled by my shirt.

Is this supposed to feel as natural as it does? I know I'm attracted to Mira, and I care about her, but what the hell does it mean if I breathe easier when I'm around her? If she makes me forget about all the pressure riding on my shoulders this season?

"I'm not sorry," I admit, shoving those thoughts away as Mirabelle snorts, pulling back.

"You shouldn't be, but I appreciate your help. I'm sure he would have put up a bigger fight if you weren't here," she says, and I open the door for her. "*Merci.*"[1] Mirabelle offers me the barest of smiles. I'm starting to have a whole new appreciation for the French language.

"*De rien.*"[2]

Bailey smells like he belongs in the basement of a fraternity house, but I'm hoping he doesn't get sick before we get back to their house.

I glance in the rearview mirror, noting that Hunter and Bailey could not be further apart in the backseat. Obviously, they're fighting about something, but whatever it is, it doesn't make sense for Bailey to be so upset with Mirabelle.

"How's soccer going, Bailey?" I ask, poking the bear. Bailey stays silent, but Mirabelle turns sharply to face me.

"What are you doing?" she asks, but I ignore her. This might be one of the dumbest things I've ever done, but Mirabelle isn't going to get answers if he remains silent.

---

1. Thank you.
2. You're welcome.

"I would think as a senior, you'd be getting plenty of playing time with how many scouts were at your games this summer. Have you started looking at schools?" I push further, and Hunter's looking at me questioningly too. "Bailey?"

"I don't know why you're asking me about this when I know *she* told you I quit the team," Bailey responds tightly.

"Why'd you quit? You're really good."

I mean it too. Bailey is really fucking good at soccer, and furthermore, he loves it. I remember Sebastian bragging about him last spring because Duke was looking into offering him a spot on their team, and they have one of the best programs in the country.

Mirabelle is shaking her head next to me, and I soften my voice. "B, we're all worried about you. If you talk to us, then maybe we can help."

"I don't want your help. You don't care about me. The only reason you're saying you care is because you're fucking my sister."

I clench my jaw so tightly I'd be shocked if I didn't crack a tooth. Mirabelle shifts in the passenger seat, and that's when I notice she's chewing on her nails again. I've noticed it's something she does when she's feeling out of control, and my patience is starting to run thin.

"Instead of ripping into Mira for doing nothing wrong, maybe you could say what you're actually pissed about."

Bailey's head moves in the mirror, his eyes rimmed in red finding mine. "Maybe she did do something wrong. Have you ever thought about that, Henry? Perfect fucking Mirabelle who could walk on water. How could any of us ever live up to her?" Bailey mocks.

Perfect fucking Mirabelle? Is that what he thinks about her?

I've watched her run at a higher capacity over the last few

days than any human should be capable of, but she does it with a smile. She doesn't complain about it; she is desperate to prove she belongs.

"B, come on. That's not true," Hunter pipes in, and now I'm wondering if I should have asked Mirabelle to drive so I could have sat in the back seat with Bailey.

"Whose side are you on?"

"Why do there have to be sides?" Hunter asks, and Bailey falls silent once more.

This time, for Mirabelle's sake, I let the conversation die completely. I turn the background music up higher, my heart aching at the sight of Mirabelle chewing her nails fucking bloody. I shouldn't have pushed him, but I hoped he'd give me something other than whatever the hell he's blaming her for.

I reach over to grab her hand in a smooth motion because I can't stand the sight of her hurting, even if it's self-inflicted, entwining her fingers with mine again to rest them on her thigh.

The faint squeeze she gives me eases the tightness in my chest, even though it should be climbing higher the closer we get to finally talking with her parents.

Thalia rushes to hug Mirabelle the second she steps out of the car while Sebastian hangs back on the front stairs. Bailey wavers, catching himself before he tips over after climbing out of the car.

"Bailey," Sebastian says sharply, and I know all too well how it can cut through to the bone, flaying you open from the inside out. "Go to your room. *Now.*"

Bailey scoffs as Hunter hangs his head, lingering by me. I'm not sure I'm the safest person to stand by when it comes to being here. Bailey brushes past his father, disappearing into the house, and I'm shocked he doesn't slam the front door behind him.

"Henry, why don't we go out back and talk." Sebastian's dark eyes feel as if they can see right through me as my confidence wanes. It's a statement, not a question up for debate.

"Okay," I agree calmly, and Thalia gives me a warm smile, so drastically different from the last few occasions we've been in the same vicinity. I wonder what caused the change of heart, but I'm not complaining if it means I'm no longer being accused of grooming Mirabelle.

Sebastian steps into the house, leaving the front door open for me to follow. I've been here so many times over the years, but I've never felt this much anxiety. Normally, I'd relax the moment I stepped through the door, but instead, my stomach is in knots. Is this what livestock feel like as they're lured into the slaughterhouse?

Owen isn't here to step in and keep Bash from killing me, but I'm hoping after what I heard in the car, murder isn't a possibility.

My hands are embarrassingly sweaty, and I wipe them on my pants as we step out onto the wraparound deck, overlooking the ocean. The salt air immediately hits me, and it feels like I'm home.

There's a reason my tattoo sleeve is centered around Poseidon and the ocean. I look out at the water, hearing the waves crash, and I understand that the only predictable thing is how unpredictable it can be. Maybe that's part of what draws me to Mirabelle.

She reminds me of the ocean with her natural beauty and unpredictability. I'd happily drown in her waves any day.

"I was wrong. I'm sorry," Sebastian starts, leaning on the railing. His shoulders sink as he glances at me, and I can tell he means it. For the first time ever, I don't see him as this legendary player I've been trying to live up to. I see Sebastian as another person who knows what it feels like to carry the weight of the world on his shoulders.

"Thank you," I say, taking the spot next to him.

"If you say nothing happened when she was . . . *a minor,*" he struggles to say it, and I don't dare interrupt. He looks back out over the water. "Then I believe you. I know I said a lot of things in the heat of the moment that I didn't mean, but this is hard for me to understand, Henry. I'm trying to, but I'm also being honest with you, and I'm asking you to give me the same respect."

God, I want to be honest. I should admit everything is fake between us, but even thinking that feels like another lie. I'm not sure what it is, but it's not fake.

"That's fair," I agree, following his gaze to the cluster of clouds brewing in the distance over the water.

"You're older than her, and it worries me. I know what kind of man you are and that she's an adult, but Mirabelle's my baby girl. I can't help wondering how many times I've left the two of you alone unsupervised over the years. It caught me off guard, and truthfully? I was hurt you didn't come to me yourself. That day at the field, I was out of line. I was on edge after the fire the night before, and then to learn from a press release that you and Mira were together . . . I let my emotions get the best of me."

"Bash, I swear to you, nothing has ever happened between us until after the Super Bowl. I'm sorry I didn't come to you first. I never intended to hurt anyone, but especially not you and Thalia. It all happened so quickly, and we were still trying to figure everything out when the pictures from the fire were posted."

Sebastian absently taps his fingers on the railing as he

inhales deeply. "Thank you for saying that. An apology doesn't excuse what I said, bu—"

"You were saying them out of love for Mirabelle. I get it. It's okay." I have never felt more guilty than I do in this moment.

"Thank you for being there for Mirabelle, in more ways than one, but especially today."

"Of course. She means a lot to me." I swallow the lump forming in my throat. He shouldn't be thanking me.

"I'm glad to hear that. She's a force to be reckoned with, but that doesn't mean she isn't breakable. Be careful with her love and trust, Mira doesn't give it easily. She's exactly like her mother in that regard, and if you care about Mirabelle like I think you do, don't let her be an almost in your life. You'll spend the rest of your life regretting it," he warns, knowingly. I feel like there's more to that than he's saying, but I'm not sure it's my place to ask. "I don't want to dwell on this anymore than we have to, so if you're willing, can we move past this?" Sebastian asks, and I nod, but his face doesn't relax. In fact, the tension radiating from him puts me on edge, and I thought we were supposed to be past the hard part of the conversation. "I need to ask you about something, and I need you to be honest with me. It's important."

Oh fuck, he knows. He knows the Panthers were going to trade me. All of this was for nothing. "Okay," I say, tightening my hands into fists to hide the shaking of how anxious this makes me. I don't want to disappoint him.

"Are you in contact with your biological mother?" he asks, and I'm not sure how Sebastian knows about the phone calls, but I'm so fucking relieved he doesn't know about my contract that I don't even care.

"I wouldn't call it being in contact. She calls once or twice a week, usually from a new number after I decline enough times, but I never answer. I did a couple of times a few years ago, but all she wanted was money, so I've been avoiding her calls since then. I tried changing my number a few times, but it doesn't matter. She keeps finding it, and it's not worth the hassle of changing my number every time."

"So you haven't seen her in person?"

I shake my head, failing to understand why this is so important. "No. I haven't seen her since I was a kid, but why are you asking?"

He scratches the back of his neck, and I have a bad feeling I'm missing some crucial piece of information here. "Don't worry about it, but if she continues calling, will you forward the numbers to me?"

What? What does she have to do with Sebastian? Do I even want to know? The questions linger on the tip of my tongue as he pats me on the back.

"You're playing well this season. Keep it up, and you might have a shot at a postseason run your first year starting." Sebastian smiles at me, and it's a refreshing change of pace from the hard looks I've been on the receiving end of for the last month and a half.

"You think?" I ask, accepting the change in conversation as the wind picks up.

"I do. I haven't missed a game. You held your own in Georgia when a lot of people would have let that crowd get to them," he says, and that means the fucking world to me. "How much is Owen fining you for missing today?"

"Seventeen grand," I admit, but there wasn't a shot in hell I was letting Mirabelle deal with today by herself. Owen told me his hands were tied because it would look like favoritism if he didn't.

He laughs, shaking his head. "He took it easy on you. Send me the invoice, I'll take care of it. My kid's the reason you left, so the least I can do is take care of it."

"Actually, I'd like to pay it myself. It was my choice to leave today, knowing I'd be fined. I wanted to be there for Mira."

Sebastian studies me for a moment, his face softening. "We should get back inside. There's a storm coming, and I think I have a kid to ground for life," he says, and the clouds look a lot closer than they did a few minutes ago.

CHAPTER TWENTY-TWO

Mirabelle

MOM'S LIGHT GREEN EYES ARE SHINING AS SHE looks at Hunter after he sets his backpack next to the door. "Who changed my phone number at the school to Mira's?" she demands, and I cringe, despite not being the one in trouble. Mom isn't yelling, but her tone isn't particularly pleasant either.

"I'm sorry," he says, hesitating to meet her gaze. That doesn't answer her question, and the frustrated exhale tells me Mom thinks the same thing.

"What is going on with you two?"

Hunter shakes his head, and my stomach drops. *He's not going to tell her.* Hunter promised me he was going to tell them everything when we go home. "Nothing," he says, confirming my thoughts.

"Bullshit. You can tell me now, or you can tell your father and I together. I can promise you I'm asking a lot nicer than he will." She puts her hands on her hips, waiting for him to make a decision. Unfortunately, he makes the decision to stay silent.

Mom laughs in disbelief, turning to look at me for answers now. "Do you know?" Mom asks, using a softer tone, and I look at Hunter, giving him one more opportunity to come clean.

His eyes widen in panic. "Mira, please *don't*," Hunter begs.

"You promised. I told you to tell them, or I would," I say. I love my brothers, but Bailey is clearly working through something. I can't keep this to myself. It's not fair, especially when today has only made it clear Bailey needs some form of help.

"Bailey quit soccer."

Mom's jaw hangs open in disbelief. "He—*what?*"

"I don't know why, or when he did it, but there's something going on with him."

"He's fine," Hunter tries to insist, shooting me a dirty look.

"No, he's not, Hunter. If you care about Bailey, then you'll tell Mom and Dad what's going on," I snap at him, fed up with whatever secret he's trying to keep for our brother.

"Bailey's right. Perfect fucking Mirabelle to save the day, like always. Just because you're all buddy-buddy with our parents again after choosing your boyfriend over our family, doesn't mean you can stick your nose into our business. You left, not us."

Hunter has played the peacekeeper between Bailey and me so often that I've forgotten his words can be sharp enough to go for the kill shot too. I didn't pick Henry over my family . . . *did I?*

"*Hunter.*" Mom gasps loudly, and I bite my inner cheek hard enough I can taste the blood on my tongue. "Give me your phone now, then you can bring all of your and Bailey's electronics to me, because if I have to get them, I'm going to break them into a million tiny pieces."

His face pales, and he ducks his head again, pulling his phone out of his pocket to hand it to Mom. "Yes, ma'am." He walks past without looking at me.

Mom sighs, pinching the bridge of her nose. "I don't even know what to say right now," she whispers, but I don't think she's talking to me. Behind her, hanging on the wall, is a picture of the six of us before Dad's last game. Our smiles are wide, and we look so damn happy. It's crazy how different things are now, not even a year later.

"I'm sorry. I should have told you sooner, but Hunter promised he would. I think Bailey needs help. I don't know what is going on, but he's not himself," I admit. Maybe I should have said something before now. Regardless of how things were between my parents and me, I should have told them about Bailey.

It's quiet upstairs, but Hunter returns with a basket holding all their things. He sets it on the floor in front of Mom, and I turn away, refusing to let him see how much his words impacted me.

Dad walks in from the kitchen with Henry behind him, and I feel tears prick my eyes when both of them look at me. Dad's mouth immediately twists into a frown, and I can't say anything, or I'll burst into tears. This is such a mess. I mean, what the fuck?

"Lia?" Dad asks.

Mom starts speaking in French, explaining everything to Dad. My eyes are glued to Henry as he walks toward me, but his expression turns feral as Mom repeats what Hunter said to me. My bottom lip quivers, and Henry immediately tugs me into his arms, holding me close.

"Are you fucking kidding me?" Henry practically growls, clearly having hit his breaking point for the day.

"Don't, it's not his fault," I say, unable to help myself from defending Hunter, even after he gutted me.

"No, I think I agree with Henry on this one. What the hell, Hunter?" Dad asks, and I twist to remain under Henry's arm, but Dad's face is unreadable when I look at it.

Hunter shifts his feet awkwardly, still staring at the floor.

I hold my breath, waiting to see if Hunter will look at me, but my heart drops when my phone starts ringing in my back pocket. The ringtone I programmed specifically for Stacey breaks the silence. *Seriously? She had to call at this exact moment?*

It's the worst timing ever, but a part of me is relieved to have a reason to escape the room.

"Sorry, it's my boss," I mumble, pulling the phone out of my pocket to retreat into the kitchen. I take a deep breath, clearing my throat to give myself a shot at sounding normal before answering. "Hi, Stacey," I greet, trying to sound as chipper as possible. I can feel Henry right behind me, his hand brushing over my lower back in reassurance. He didn't have to follow me, but I'm glad he did.

"Why does your voice sound like that?"

"Like what?"

"Like you're happy enough to be a Disney princess. I thought you had a family emergency, or at least that's what Henry told me after tearing into my office like a madman to beg me to let you leave for the day," she says, and my heart stutters in my chest.

He what?

"No, there is one. I'm just . . . this is my voice? I'm sorry, is there something you need me to do?" I ask, redirecting the conversation back to whatever reason she called for. I feel like she shouldn't be comparing my voice to anything, but I guess there are worse comparisons that could be made.

"I was calling to ask you to remind Henry he still needs to post online about your relationship. Please look it over before letting him post to make sure it's satisfactory," she says, and I can hear how quickly she's typing. She can multitask better than anyone I've ever met.

"I can do that," I say, and in the background I hear a door open, and someone's voice.

"Stacey, I couldn't get ahold of the photographer, and—" Miley's interrupted before she can finish. Stacey must have asked her to help get ahold of Jeremy, the photographer in charge of the next campaign that Henry is scheduled to be in for the team.

"Fine, I'll do it myself. Here's my dry-cleaning ticket, please go pick it up," Stacey says brusquely, and I cover my mouth to make sure a sound does not come out of my mouth. "Are you going to take it, or just stare at me?" *Holy shit. I would pay to see the look on Miley's face.*

The door shuts in the background, and at the same time, I hear Hunter's voice getting louder from the foyer.

"Mirabelle, can I expect you back in the office tomorrow? You're the only one who can apparently do their job correctly, and I need to know if I have to change what's on tomorrow's schedule," Stacey says, and I think this might actually be the best part of this shitty day.

"I'll be at work. Would you like me to call Jeremy and pass along a message?"

"No, I'll make the call myself," she says, and the typing resumes in the background.

"I'll be sure to remind Henry," I repeat, in case she didn't hear me the first time.

"Mirabelle?"

"Yes?"

"I hope everything is okay with your family. I'll see you in the morning." The line goes dead, and I pull the phone away from my ear surprised. Does Stacey actually like me?

"What?" Henry asks, sliding his hand up my back, and I'm not totally sure what just happened. *Henry begged her to let me leave for the day?*

"Um, Stacey wanted me to remind you that you haven't posted," I say, and Henry groans.

"Shit, I forgot," he says, pulling his phone out of his pocket, tapping the screen quickly. "Do you need to see it first before I post it?"

I hear my parents in the other room, and I'm so drained. I inhale slowly, twisting my hair back into a low bun. "Does it have any nudity in it?" I ask and Henry shakes his head, still looking down at the screen. "Are both of us in it?"

"No. Just you. Do you think that's okay?" he asks, looking at me unsure.

"I'm sure it's fine. Don't put any curse words in the caption, and it should be fine."

"Sugartits isn't a swear word, right?"

My eyes nearly bulge out of their sockets. "I'm sorry, what did you just say?"

"Should I not have posted that?" he asks, as if not understanding the gravity of the situation. *Stacey is going to take back every nice thing she might have said to me and murder me. Holy shit.* "Mira, I'm fucking with you. I know better than to call you Sugartits online."

I smack his arm as he laughs. "I can't believe you."

"I'm sorry, I wanted to try to make you laugh after everything today. Probably a bad idea," Henry says, sliding the phone back into his pocket, the ghost of a smile lingering on his face.

A second later, my phone vibrates with a thumbs-up from Stacey.

What exactly did he post? It's tempting to look, but I hear stomping on the stairs, transporting me back to reality.

I don't know if I can go back in there. I don't know if I have it in me to listen to Hunter and Bailey blame me for something I don't even know I did because neither of them will tell me. It feels like I'm proving them right by wanting to avoid the situation.

No, I can do this. I love my brothers, and I'd do anything for them, even if that means putting myself in the line of fire again.

"We don't have to go back in there," Henry says quietly, reading my mind.

"They're my brothers, Henry," I say as if it should explain everything.

"And you're their sister—not their punching bag."

I look at him sadly, picking at my cuticles again, the flicker of physical pain easier to feel than the emotional. "I'm not sure there's a difference."

CHAPTER TWENTY-THREE

Henry

"I'M PRETTY SURE SHE WANTS TO BE ALONE," WILSON says, catching me staring at Mirabelle again as she sits on the edge of the pool.

"Really? I had no idea," I say sarcastically, looking back at the book in my hands.

The other day was fucking brutal, and it's as if she's a ghost, simply going through the motions ever since. Mirabelle took everything the twins threw at her and still defended them whenever either her parents or I intervened.

She shut her eyes on the way back to Charlotte, but I'm not sure if she was actually sleeping or avoiding talking to me. I'm not sure I would have known what to say if she did want to talk.

Mirabelle's been waking up before me to go to work at an ungodly hour, driving separately. She got home an hour ago, walking straight past Wilson and me to the pool without a word, and hasn't moved since.

"Price, what happened with her family? She's been like this for two days now."

Stacey asked me the same thing earlier today, and I didn't know what to say.

I shut the book, setting it on the couch next to me. "I don't know," I answer, unable to resist looking back at Mirabelle like a moth drawn to a flame. I know she wants to be alone, but I'm not sure how long I'm supposed to let this continue. I know if Kaitlyn ever said anything like what Hunter and Bailey did, I'd be eviscerated.

"Maybe it's a good thing your birthday is next weekend. I think you both could use a night to relax," he says, and I'm honestly more excited for Kaitlyn to be here tomorrow than for an excuse to go out next weekend.

"Are you still cool with my sister coming tomorrow?"

"Price, it's your house," he reminds me, looking back at the playbook resting in his lap. "You don't need to ask me for permission, but if you plan on playing Yahtzee again, count me in."

"You hate Yahtzee," I point out, wondering if Mirabelle is starting to get cold out there. I don't want her to catch a cold.

Wilson chuckles, shaking his head. "I do, but I think it's hilarious watching your kid sister kick your ass at it. You win nearly every other game you two play, except for Yahtzee."

"I'm throwing it away before she gets here. You'll have to find your entertainment somewhere else."

"I could invite Quinn over and wait to see your head explode with jealousy as he fawns over Mirabelle. That sounds pretty fun."

White-hot rage spikes through me at the thought of watching my friend hit on Mirabelle. "I'm not jealous of Quinn."

"Sure you're not. You just announced to the whole team for fun that you were going to sit next to your girlfriend on the plane during the last away game. It totally wasn't you telling

Quinn to back off." Wilson snorts, and I flip him off, only succeeding at making him actually laugh this time.

"Aren't you supposed to be giving feedback on those plays tomorrow?"

"Isn't Mirabelle supposed to be your *fake* girlfriend?" Wilson counters, raising an eyebrow at me.

"She *is* my fake girlfriend," I say, but the words feel *wrong*.

"If you say so." He shrugs, letting this go far easier than I would have expected. "Then you shouldn't be bothered that Quinn's going to ask her out tomorrow, right?" Wilson challenges, calling my bluff.

The blood running through my veins turns to ice at the thought of Quinn asking Mirabelle out. Absolutely fucking not. Wilson laughs, finding this amusing. "Maybe you should go look in a mirror to see how believable it is that you aren't jealous of him."

"Fuck off, I'm not jealous."

I am jealous, and I'm done staring at Mirabelle as she deals with this on her own.

I stand up from the couch as Mirabelle slips under the water, disappearing from my sight. In the time it takes me to walk from the couch to the back door, she still doesn't come up. *What is she doing?* I push my sweatpants down, stepping out of them as I pull off my shirt, and then dive into the water.

Mirabelle resurfaces at the same time I do, wiping the water from of her face. "What are you doing?" she asks, her wet hair falling around her shoulders.

"I'm swimming in my pool," I say, simply because I don't have a better answer.

She tips her head back, exposing the smooth column of her neck to smooth her hair back from her face. "Right," Mirabelle murmurs, looking away from me.

Look at me please. Let me in.

"What are you doing?" I echo the question back to her,

hoping she'll give me some indication she's okay. Actually, that sounds stupid. Obviously, she's not okay if she's jumping into the pool fully clothed.

"You know, that's a great question. I wish I had an answer." Mirabelle seems as if she's in a daze as she trails her fingertips through the water, exhaling sharply. "I haven't called JJ back. He keeps calling, but I don't know what to say, so I haven't answered."

"When did you last talk to JJ?"

"I was on the phone with him when Bailey's school called me the other day. We were talking about . . . well, it doesn't matter what. I told him I'd call him back, and I didn't. Sister of the year, right?" she asks, her eyes shining as she finally looks at me. Mirabelle's face is a window to her battered soul, giving me a glimpse of what she's been hiding, and I'm utterly devastated as she wipes her cheeks hastily. *Fuck, she's crying. I'm not good with tears, but I'm even worse when it's Mirabelle crying.* "I'm sorry. I'm fine, I don't know why I'm crying."

"Actually, I'm shocked you don't cry more. You've had a lot going on. You don't need to apologize," I say, and she cracks a faint smile.

"Well, if I cried every time something went wrong in my life, I wouldn't get very much done."

"What's wrong with that? You're allowed to have feelings," I say, slowly wading closer with the hope I don't scare her into disappearing.

Instead, Mirabelle looks at me like I'm insane, which I most definitely am. I'm insane for trying to provoke her. "What's wrong with crying all the time? Are you seriously asking for an obvious answer? I know how much you love that word, Henry."

"What word?" I question, fully aware that I'm playing with fire to goad her into giving me a reaction.

The corners of Mirabelle's mouth tip downward as her

bloodshot eyes flicker with the first sign of life in two days. *Yes. More of that. Clearly, this is the right track.* "Obvious."

I feel like I'm missing something here, because I'm not sure why she thinks that. "Obvious? Why do you think I love that word?"

"Stop, you're distracting me," she says, her cheeks flushing as she attempts to turn away from me.

"I'm not trying to," I say, catching her wrist gently.

Mirabelle exhales, an exasperated laugh escaping her. It sounds like the most beautiful thing in the world to my ears. "It's so fucking ironic that you throw that word around when you wouldn't know 'obvious' if it hit you in the face. You said I obviously have feelings for Quinn, but I don't. It should be fucking obvious, but apparently, it's not. There are obvious reasons why I don't get to sit around crying every time something goes wrong in my life— because I'm highly aware of how privileged I am.

"Oh poor Mirabelle. Her brothers hate her because she's so goddamn perfect—they think it's okay to get drunk at school and blame her. Poor Mirabelle for having no friends at work—except her boss, who doesn't totally hate her, and her fake boyfriend—because they all think she's a nepo baby who sits around doing nothing.

"We should feel so fucking bad for poor Mirabelle, whose childhood home was nearly burned down, especially when her parents can simply call their best friend's son, a professional athlete, to ask if she can stay at his house with its amazing pool. Poor Mirabelle can't stop crying when there are people out there with real problems, who work all day to make ends meet, and still struggle to put enough food on the table for their families."

Shit, what the fuck was I thinking pushing her buttons? This was not a good idea. "Mira—"

"Do you want to know what I was doing when you

jumped into the pool?" she asks, the challenge lingering heavy like a finger on the trigger of a gun, waiting to fire. *I pushed too far.* "Ask me, Henry."

I swallow the lump in my throat, refusing to let go of her.

"What were you doing?" I ask hoarsely.

"I was screaming." She stares directly at me, tears welling up in her eyes again. "I went under the water where no one would be able to hear me, and I screamed until I couldn't breathe. I hoped it would make me feel better."

I'm out of my depth here, but I do know that this shit will drown her from the inside out if she doesn't deal with it. I wet my lips, buying myself time as Mirabelle watches my face closely. "Just because shitty things are happening in the world, it doesn't invalidate the shit you're going through."

"Why did you come out here?"

"Because I miss you. Because I've been staring at this shell of you since we drove back to Charlotte, and I'm fucking worried. Wilson's fucking worried, and even Stacey has noticed you're not yourself. I came out here because I'm tired of watching you punish yourself for something you didn't even do."

"But I did do it. I wasn't fucking there for Bailey when he clearly needed me to be, and now Hunter is pissed at me, and I didn't learn a goddamn thing from it because I'm fucking ignoring JJ too! He would have never let things get like this. I have ruin—"

I don't know how else to shut her up, but it's the only thing that comes to mind, so I cup Mirabelle's face in my hands, pressing my lips against hers. It's effective, stunning her into silence so I can make her listen to me. Pulling away, I wait to see if she's going to hit me, but Mirabelle blinks, opening her mouth, before deciding to shut it. I brush away the tears on her cheeks, forcing her to see how sincere I am, because I won't lie to her. "Then fix it. Call JJ back. You're human,

Mirabelle. You're allowed to make mistakes, but what happened with your brothers is not on you. I was there, and I heard every word of bullshit they spewed to place blame anywhere but on themselves. I know you love them, but it's not your fault. You're their sister, but you're not responsible for them because you're not their keeper."

Mirabelle leans against my bare chest as I wrap my arms around her. She shudders, and I hold on for dear life, hating how powerless I am to fix this for her.

I'm unable to resist pressing a kiss to the top of her head, and I know that if Mirabelle asked me, I'd do anything she wanted. She has me wrapped around her finger, and she doesn't even realize it.

"Henry?" she mumbles my name against my skin, and despite it being the absolute wrong moment, my heart beats faster in my chest. I'm sure she can feel it, but I don't think I care.

"Yeah?"

"Thank you."

I tighten my arms around her, the words nearly getting stuck in my throat, but I force them out regardless. "I've got you."

"She was crying and you kissed her?" Andrew asks, and I roll my eyes as I set my phone down to towel dry my hair. Stacey found time in my schedule today to make up for the day I took off earlier in the week, so I had to play model with a bunch of shit in my hair that took forever to wash out.

"Yeah."

Andrew's laugh filters through the line. "You're a fucking idiot."

"In more ways than one," I agree, but at least Mirabelle didn't hit me.

"Does it get worse than you kissing her while she cries?"

"Depends on who you ask," I mutter under my breath, grabbing a sweatshirt from Duke to wear tonight. With a hat, there's a chance I can fly under the radar, but if I show up wearing anything related to the Panthers, it's going to be a very long night.

"Oh shit. What?"

"Quinn asked out Mirabelle today." I'm not certain, but he definitely pulled her aside while I was in the training room getting my hamstrings stretched. The only thing that kept my mood in check was seeing Mirabelle more like herself than she had been in a few days, and we're hanging out with my sister tonight. I wasn't willing to ruin the first spark of life I'd seen in her over something I wasn't positive actually happened. I'm not sure if she should go to tonight's game since Hunter will obviously be there, and I'm not sure about Bailey's status for the night, but I can't promise I won't murder either of them if they upset her again. On the other hand, I don't have a death wish so I'm not going to tell Mirabelle what she can and can't do.

"Oh, I see," Andrew muses, and I wait for him to finish.

"What?" I finally ask when my annoying best friend decides not to say anything else.

"You like her."

It'd be impossible not to like her. Mirabelle's incredible. "I wouldn't spend time with her if I didn't like her," I answer, backtracking to my closet for my shoes.

"I'm not talking about liking her as a person. You're falling for her. That's why you're pissed off that Quinn made a move on her."

"It's fine if she wants to go on a date with him," I lie through my teeth, as my stomach twists at the thought of them together. Mirabelle is allowed to do whatever she wants. *Except I want her to do whatever with me.*

"Have you told her?"

No. I told Mirabelle to use me as practice for the lucky son of a bitch who actually gets to be with her because it causes me physical pain to see her hurting and upset. I haven't told anyone, and she hasn't brought it up again since I walked out of her room after coming in my pants like a fucking teenager. There's been enough shit going on, she doesn't need me to bug her about the list I told her to make. "There's nothing to tell."

"You're full of shit, but I guess you'll only have yourself to blame if she goes out with Quinn." Okay, I'm tired of hearing these lectures from Wilson, and now I'm getting them from Andrew?

"I'm officially uninviting you from my birthday," I say, stuffing my wallet in my back pocket, but I stop in my tracks when I see the paper on the floor in front of my door. "No fucking way," I swear under my breath, picking it up.

"What?" he asks curiously, and my jaw hits the floor.

"Nothing, I gotta go," I say, trying to wrap my brain around what's in front of me.

"Wait, you can't just—" I hang up, not feeling guilty in the slightest.

Mirabelle's to-do list:
Get better at blow jobs
Find my favorite position
Dirty talk
Car sex?
Skinny dipping
Phone sex
Bondage?
Mirror sex

Bonus points
Orgasm during oral sex
Orgasms in general
Sex in a public place

She actually put together a to-do list. This woman never ceases to surprise me.

A hundred different mental ideas run through my brain, and my pants grow tighter.

Andrew sends me a flurry of texts, but all I notice is the time. Fuck, we're going to be late if we don't leave now. I fold the list, putting it in my wallet as I adjust my pants, trying to think of anything to make my erection deflate.

Fuck, but the things on the list . . .

I grab my hat, setting it on my head as I make my way down the stairs.

"Mira? We gotta go if we're going to get there on time," I call out, unsure of what part of the house she's in. Wilson went with Crosby and Tyler for drinks, but he told me he would be back in time for game night.

"Sorry, I'm coming," she says, running down the stairs, her

footsteps loud enough to make it sound like there's a herd of elephants behind her. Mirabelle slides to a stop in front of me, her blonde hair pulled back into a messy braid, with pieces falling into her flushed face.

She's *beautiful*.

That fucking list is burning a hole in my pocket.

Blow jobs, mirror sex, all the different positions? I wonder if I could convince her to keep on the heels she loves so much. Oh fuck, my raging hard-on is back. I picked a bad night to wear sweatpants.

"Um, are we going?" she asks, bouncing on the balls of her feet, combing her hair back behind her ear. *Shit, she's wearing my sweatshirt too.*

I clear my throat, grabbing my hat to run my hand through my hair before putting it on backward. "Yeah, let's go," I say, and her cheeks flush bright red.

If I hadn't promised Kaitlyn I'd be there, I don't think we'd be going anywhere tonight.

I wonder if Mirabelle can read my thoughts because she ducks her head and escapes to the garage before I can do something stupid, like kiss her senseless.

I'm so fucked.

CHAPTER TWENTY-FOUR

Mirabelle

Holy fucking shit, I can't breathe.

I seriously think I'm going to suffocate in the car before we get to the game because Henry has stolen all the oxygen out of my lungs with how unbelievably hot he looks. It should seriously be illegal for Henry to look that damn good in a backward hat. Like seriously?

It might have even saved him from jumping into the pool with me yesterday if he had decided to rock that look sooner.

I'm not saying my heart wouldn't still be shattered in a thousand pieces over my brothers, but it would have been a nice little bandage to tape the pieces back together.

I feel dumb I gave Henry the list already because I would have added that I'd like to be fucked by him in that goddamn hat.

Honestly, it's been a great distraction from thinking about what else Hunter could say tonight that would pour salt on the already gaping wound in my chest. Bailey's definitely not going to be there, though, so I guess that saves me from one of them.

Henry shifts in his seat, his large hands holding the

steering wheel tightly, and I take a deep breath, forcing myself to look out the window. This is going to be the longest drive of my life. I should have waited to give the list to Henry, but I was afraid I'd chicken out.

So I slid it under the door, and hid in my room trying not to have a panic attack about the things I put on the list until Henry said it was time to go.

I'm assuming that by the way he stared at me before we left, he definitely saw it.

Henry clears his throat and turns down the radio. "So . . ."

I start fidgeting with my necklace. "So . . ."

"You put the sex list on a to-do list?"

"I thought it was funny," I defend myself, turning to look at him. He's chuckling, a small smile forming.

"It is funny," he agrees, and I relax a little in my seat. "Is there anything I should know?"

"What?" I ask, confused.

"You put question marks next to a few of the items," he continues, and my cheeks flush. If I want to do the things on the list with Henry, then I can suck it up and talk about them with him.

"Yes," I say, and Henry glances my direction. God, it's so not fair how hot he looks right now. I can barely think straight.

"Is there a reason you had question marks next to them?"

"Can you turn your hat the right way?" I blurt out, and a beautiful—*yet, infuriatingly knowing*—smile forms on his lips.

"Is it bothering you?"

"It's distracting."

Henry laughs quietly but makes no move to switch it. "I think the same thing when you wear those death traps to work."

Death traps? He likes my heels? It catches me off guard enough that I stammer out an answer to his question because talking about our sex list is somehow easier than asking more about how distracting my heels are. "Um, well, I wasn't sure about putting them on the list, so I thought I'd ask you about them to see if they were anything you were interested in? I mean, we don't have to do anything on that list if you don't want to do it," I explain quickly, and Henry reaches over to hold my hand.

My heart stutters in my chest as I look down at it, realizing the cuticle on my thumb is raw.

"Mira, I told you I'd do anything you wanted. I didn't see anything on the list that made me uncomfortable, but I wanted to ask about the question marks to make sure we're on the same page," he says calmly, and it's honestly a relief that he's being so nonchalant about this, because I feel like my lungs are going to collapse.

"So you're okay with everything on it?" I ask, needing to hear him say it clearly.

"I'm more than okay with everything on the list. I promise I'd tell you if I wasn't." Henry squeezes my hand reassuringly, and I feel a little better. "I'm looking forward to going three for three in the bonus points department, though," he teases, and my eyes bug out of my head. I only put the bonus points on there as a bucket list sort of thing. Like, hey, it's great if it happens, but no hard feelings if it doesn't? I didn't expect Henry to take this so seriously.

"You're talking a pretty big game," I choke out. Oh my god.

Henry brushes his lips over my knuckles, gently kissing the back of my hand. "I think we both know I can back it up after I helped you orgasm only by kissing you and playing with your nipple."

"Fine. If you can go three for three in the bonus points, I'll do something you want to do," I say, feeling the butterflies in my chest start to flutter.

"I like a challenge, but I don't need a prize. I'll already have you."

You already have me. Instead, I shake my head. "Whatever you say."

It's unfair that Henry gets to look the way he does, and say things like that. I'm going to throw away all his hats because I'm struggling to think straight.

"Do you want us to plan out when we're going to cross things off the list, or keep it spontaneous?" he asks, rubbing his thumb back and forth on my hand.

"I think spontaneous would be better, but I think it's important for both parties to be able to say no if they're not in the mood."

Henry nods, his face growing serious. "If it's not consensual, it's not happening. I promise you won't hurt my feelings if you tell me no at any point. I'd rather you enjoy yourself than agree just because you think I want you to. This is for you, not for me."

"Well, I want you to enjoy yourself too. If I wanted to practice with something inanimate, I'd just buy a dildo," I argue, and Henry chuckles.

"As much as I'd like to see that, I will definitely be enjoying myself. I don't want you to worry about that," Henry says, and I think someone needs to pinch me right now. There's no way this is my reality.

Is this what it's like to show someone every side of you and they still don't run? If I wasn't in love with Henry before, I'd surely be in love with him now.

Maybe I should be more concerned about the repercussions of all these decisions, but right now, I'm willing to accept everything will be fine.

The screen in Henry's car shows an incoming call from

Allison Price, and Henry's entire demeanor shifts as he blinks at it. He lets go of my hand to decline it, and I swallow all my questions, instead opting to pull out my phone to let my parents know we're on our way.

Growing up as a prodigy in the world of gymnastics, combined with my parents being who they are, I'm no stranger to people taking pictures of me and my family. Henry's attempt to be inconspicuous was a fail from the moment we got out of the car, even after he turned his hat around the right way to hide his face. However, I grossly underestimated how many pictures Henry and I would be asked to pose for with fans, both together and separately.

I've tried not to let it get to me, but it's made it difficult to watch the game. Thankfully, after Hunter threw his first touchdown, the attention shifted away from us.

The team we're playing is good, and unfortunately for us, our defense isn't as strong as our offense. We're only halfway through the first half, but it's becoming clear our offense is the only reason the team made it to this game.

Hunter has been holding out hope for Duke, but when I finally called JJ yesterday, he mentioned that Hunter received offers from UCLA and Clemson this week because he's one of the top recruits in his class. He and Bailey had a plan, before everything went to shit this fall for both of them to attend Duke together, but I have a feeling that's changed.

I turn to look at Henry, pulling his attention from the field. "Do you see how many recruiters are here?"

"I'm not surprised. JJ's killing it at Beaumont and is proof that you aren't the only Walker who got your father's athleticism. Hunter will have his pick of schools."

"He wanted to earn it on his talent, not on his name."

Henry leans forward in his seat, clasping his hands in front of him. "I know, but unfortunately, they're one and the same. Recruiting out of high school is a gamble because these players are untested against the pressures of playing for a college, but Hunter's different."

"He's holding out for Duke," I say, but I know Henry knows this. Sometimes I forget that Henry isn't just mine, he's close with my brothers too.

"They're here," he says, tilting his head to where I see a man wearing the colors of our alma mater, hovering on the end.

I squint, trying to make sure that's who I think it is. "Wait, isn't that—"

Henry nods slowly. "Coach Harris himself." Ian Harris was the head coach at Duke when Henry was there a couple years ago. I've had a couple conversations with him at fundraisers my family attends, since Dad is a notable alumnus who donates to the program.

"Did you call him?" I ask.

"No, but I told Hunter last year if he ever wanted me to put in a good word, I would. Hunt refused, and I respect his decision. It could be a good sign he came himself instead of sending an assistant coach. Harris came to my game the same day he offered me my spot," Henry says, and I had no idea Henry offered to do that for Hunter. This is the version of Henry I wish everyone else could see.

Hunter looks up at the stands, his blond hair slicked back with sweat, and he grins at me so widely I can't help but return it, despite the tears that spring into my eyes. *Shit, I can't remember the last time he smiled at me like that. It feels like everything will be okay.*

I'm glad we came.

I spot my mom near the fence at the front of the bleachers, her camera in hand, while Dad is hovering behind her with

Henry's parents. Dad greeted Henry warmly earlier, but I didn't miss the tension between Henry and his father.

"Are you going to talk to your parents tonight?" I ask after a couple more plays.

"Mom and I talk all the time," he answers, and I remember the last time I talked to Chris. Everything has been so crazy I forgot to mention to Henry how I told our dads about his biological mom calling. I wonder if Chris or my dad said anything to him about it?

"And your dad?" I prod, and Henry shrugs.

"He called after we got back from everything with the twins the other day, but I didn't call him back. It'll be fine, though."

"I'm sorry."

Henry looks at me, his hazel eyes swirling with confusion. "Why are you apologizing?"

"Because I shouldn't have brought this up. It's supposed to be a fun night."

He bumps my leg with his, a faint smile forming. "I am having fun. I'm with you, watching my little sister cheer under Friday night lights. How could I not be having fun?" he asks, and I relax a little.

"I'm excited to hang out with Kaitlyn tonight," I say, and his smile becomes more prominent.

"Yeah?"

I nod, turning my attention back to the field. "Yep. We'll have a great time." *Is it delusional of me to think that the longer we pretend to be a couple, the easier it will be for Henry to fall for me? Absolutely, but it's not stopping me from doing it.*

Henry has been doing everything he can to not bring attention to us, but that mindset disappears entirely once the cheerleaders begin their performance at halftime. He whistles so loudly that Kaitlyn looks up to see us, and I love watching her eyes light up as she smiles wider in our direction.

"She's amazing," he says, smiling proudly, and I can't help but smile too.

"Kaitlyn's amazing," I echo, agreeing with him as she performs flawlessly with the rest of her squad, and Henry resumes cheering loudly for her.

Dad approaches us up the stairs and it's honestly such a relief that we're not fighting anymore. "Price, you want to go talk to Harris with me?" he asks, and the fact he's making an effort with Henry nearly brings me to tears after the roller-coaster this week has been.

"Sure, as long as I don't have to hear you relive your glory days," Henry jests, and Dad scoffs.

"You're a starter for half a season and are already losing respect for your elders. I can't wait to hear what Harris has to say about this."

Henry looks at me, his face softer than it was a moment ago. "Are you good if I go?"

I blink in surprise. "You don't have to ask me for permission."

"Well, I don't want to leave you here with the wolves by yourself," he says, lowering his voice as he tilts his head in the direction of the teenage girls eyeing us like we're prey.

"They're teenage girls, not wolves," I remind him, but I'm absolutely hopeless and unable to resist smiling. "I'm going to go find my mom and Penelope," I add.

Henry's shoulders visibly relax, and he leans down to kiss my cheek, nearly sending my heart into a different rhythm. "Have fun." He winks, and Dad raises his eyebrows, but says nothing.

I take a moment to answer the text Emily sent me earlier to let her know I gave him the list, making my way down to where Mom and Penelope are standing.

"Hey, guys," I greet, pulling my braid over my shoulder.

"Enjoying the game?" Penelope asks, her eyes sparkling with joy.

"I am. Defense sucks, but Hunt's keeping it interesting."

Mom shakes her head in disbelief. "Aren't they awful? The least they could do is try to give the offense a moment to breathe before throwing them back out there, instead of letting the other team's offense score right away."

A parent walking past us glares, and Mom starts to lift her hand, but I push it down before she can flip them off. "Mom," I scold as Penelope laughs.

"Oh, Mirabelle. You should have let Lia flip her off. Her kid is the one who didn't block the wide receiver on that last play before halftime."

"Yeah, her kid sucks, and she has the nerve to look at me that way after buying his spot on the team? My kid is the only reason we're still in this game," Mom says, sticking her tongue out at the woman's back. Oh my god, my mother is a child. I don't have the brain capacity for this.

I'm glad to see her in better spirits than earlier in the week, but this seems a little petty. "*Mom*," I repeat, and she rolls her eyes.

"What?"

"I feel like as your child, I shouldn't have to tell you to be nice."

Mom pulls her hair back into a clip. "Then don't."

Penelope covers her mouth to smother her laughter as I gape at my mother. "How do you even know she bought his spot on the team?"

She points to the giant scoreboard. "Because Dean's mom told me they donated last year, and then he magically started getting playing time after it went up. Plus, the offensive coordinator told your dad."

Shit, maybe I should have gone with Henry.

I look over to where Henry had been, surprised to see him already returning as the announcer starts to speak over the intercom, announcing the second half of the game. I immediately spot the stony look on Henry's face, and worry blooms in my chest.

Henry pushes a smile on his face, but it's the fakest fucking thing I've ever seen. What the hell happened in that conversation?

"Why are you smiling like that?" Penelope asks him, and he forces a laugh.

"Mom, am I not allowed to smile?"

My mom looks at him skeptically now. "You don't normally smile, unless you're looking at my daughter when you think no one is watching, but that's not your smile. It's too wide."

Wait, what?

I look at her in surprise and Henry laughs. "This is a smile." He didn't deny that he smiles at me when he thinks no one is looking. Does Henry actually do that? Wait—this isn't the right time to get sidetracked by that.

"That's not your smile. I would know. Your smile is beautiful, but this one looks like someone is ripping out your fingernails while asking you to smile," I blurt out, and then I slap my hand over my mouth as Henry blinks, and his actual smile starts to appear. *Oh my fucking god.*

"You think my smile is beautiful?"

Maybe I don't want to die of embarrassment right now, because yeah, I do think it's beautiful.

The moments over when Mom snaps her fingers in front of my face, catching both of our attention again. "You two can flirt later. I'm still stuck on what happened before he came back over."

"It's nothing. The game is starting again, and we're going back to our seats because I'm over the twenty questions about my face," Henry says, grabbing my hand to pull me with him.

I have so many questions, but I'm afraid to open my mouth because I'm not sure what's going to come out of it.

I follow his lead, but when we get to the top of the bleachers, Henry turns around and kisses me out of nowhere. I open my mouth in surprise, and Henry greedily takes advantage of it. I instinctively hold onto his arm and the front of his jacket as Henry takes my breath away, but it doesn't last long. As quickly as it starts, he pulls away, tucking a piece of hair behind my ear. "I think your smile is beautiful too," he says softly, and I feel dazed by the intensity of my feelings for him.

I want more, but maybe that's the problem.

I'm always wanting more of Henry, and he's not mine to have.

CHAPTER TWENTY-FIVE

Mirabelle

"Yahtzee! I win," Kaitlyn shouts, throwing her arms triumphantly in the air, traces of glitter still on her cheeks from the game earlier tonight.

Henry frowns, staring at the score sheet in front of him. "No, there's no way."

Wilson grins, clapping his hands as I take a sip of my wine. "Little Price, thank you for making my absolute year right now."

"Shut the fuck up, Wilson," Henry says, still staring at the score sheet in disbelief.

Wilson bursts out laughing. "This is the best game night ever."

"How did you even find the Yahtzee?" Henry asks, and Kaitlyn sticks her tongue out at her brother. I think I agree with Wilson, this is the best game night ever. Every game night we've ever had on a family trip, Henry has dominated. I guess that's because we never played Yahtzee.

"Wilson asked me to bring the one from our parents' house. What happened to yours?" she explains and I laugh, leaning against the couch as Henry glares at Wilson.

"I had no idea you were such a sore loser," I muse, laughing quietly. He's like a little kid who can't have dessert before dinner.

"He hid it so he wouldn't lose. You're exactly right, Mira. Henry is a sore loser," Wilson says.

Henry stretches out, a playful glint in his eye. "I'm not a sore loser. If there were a gold medal for game nights, I would have one."

"Only one of us has a gold medal here, and it's not you," Kaitlyn chimes in and Henry rolls his eyes.

"I didn't say I had one, but that I would have one because I dominate at game night."

I lean over and pat his thigh. "Everything but Yahtzee, apparently."

Kaitlyn snorts, lying backward on the rug. "Mirabelle, have I ever told you how much I love you? Henry needs someone like you to help him relax a little."

"Wonder Woman would *really* help him relax," Wilson says, winking at me. *Oh shit.*

Henry's face is flaming red, and if looks could kill, Wilson would cease to exist. "I'm going to kill you."

"What does Wonder Woman have to do with Henry relaxing?" Kaitlyn asks, and then the dots connect in her head as I cover my mouth to stop laughing. "*Ew.* I didn't need to know that. Oh my god, gross."

"I was like fourteen," Henry exclaims, dragging his hands over his face. "Wilson, I'm literally going to make you sleep at your own house."

"That's cold, dude. At least you could offer to put me up in a hotel."

Kaitlyn pretends to gag, still not past it yet, and it isn't helping me laugh quietly. The last thing I want is for Henry's glare to turn on me because I'm technically the only reason Wilson knows about Wonder Woman.

"I am not putting you up in a hotel. If anything, you'll be lucky I don't hide your body in the walls of your house." Henry scoffs, tossing the scoresheet aside.

"I think I'm going to call it a night before anyone actually ends up murdered because Henry can't handle losing, or before I want to cut my ears off and burn them," Kaitlyn says, sitting up and pulling her dark hair back, wrinkling her nose.

"I can handle losing," Henry protests, and I drink the last of my wine.

"Whatever." Kaitlyn scoffs, and Wilson grabs his phone.

"I think I'm going to hit the hay too."

"Night, Kait. Love you," Henry says, momentarily forgetting his irritation at being bested by her.

"Love you too, bro," she says, smiling.

"I love all of you so much," Wilson says, and I laugh as I watch Henry flip him off in return.

And then it's only me and Henry.

I wonder if he's feeling half as nervous as I am, because I think I'm going to get the nervous shits.

A lot of things have happened recently that I never expected, but sleeping in Henry's room might be the icing on the cake. Actually, I think making a sex to-do list should be at the top of that list. Also, Henry kissing me out of nowhere earlier tonight to tell me he thinks my smile is beautiful, too?

It's like I'm in a goddamn romance book.

Actually, what if I bring a book to bed? Then it seems like I'm not expecting anything from that list to happen tonight, simply because we're supposed to sleep in the same room.

"Ready to go to bed?" Henry asks, scratching the back of his neck. Shit, now I don't want him to be nervous. I need confident Henry who told me to use him however I wanted.

Wait—I'm fucking confident too.

"Yeppers," I say, immediately cringing. Why did I say it like that?

I grab my empty glass, tempted to pour another drink before I go to Henry's room. Henry Freaking Price's room! I can't believe this.

Setting the glass in the sink, I take the initiative, looking at Henry over my shoulder to see if he's following.

Instead, he's looking at my ass.

Good. It's a good ass.

"Are you coming?"

Henry cracks a slanted smile, laughing shortly. "Yeah, I guess so."

I let out a shaky exhale after turning away, realizing what a phony I am. I falter in front of the door, but I push through and step into his room. I don't think I've been in his room long enough to look around. Sure, I've stood in the doorway, or I guess if I needed something, I'd walk in, ask for it, and then leave.

Not tonight, I guess.

I stand there awkwardly for a moment, and Henry grabs a pillow, dropping it on the floor next to the bed. "You can have the bed, I'll take the floor."

"No, you don't have to do that," I protest, kicking into action to pick up the pillow from the floor to put it back on the bed, only to grab a different one for myself. "It's your bed, Henry. I'm not going to kick you out of it—especially when you have a game this weekend. I'll sleep on the floor," I insist, and Henry shakes his head, moving to take the pillow from me.

"My house, my rules."

"You can take your rules and shove them up your ass," I say, plopping my amazing ass on the ground stubbornly. "You take the bed. I will take the floor."

Henry looks down at me, his face turning into one of amusement. "No."

"I'll get up if you tell me what happened at the football game with Duke," I bargain, and Henry frowns.

"No, I'm not telling you that."

"Then I guess I'm sleeping on the floor," I say, crossing my arms over my chest.

Henry drags a hand through his dark hair. "Mira, you're a woman, take the bed and let me take the floor."

I raise my eyebrows in surprise. "Oh, so you think because you're a man, you're superior to me?"

"That's not what I said," he argues, but I'm pretty sure that's exactly what he said. "I'm trying to do the right thing and give you the bed."

If I were standing up, I'd stomp my foot at that, so maybe it's a good thing I'm sitting on the floor.

"I don't need you to do the right thing. I need you to not be a sexist man and to tell me what happened tonight. Get in the goddamn fucking bed, Henry."

"Has anyone ever told you how bossy you are?" he asks, and I scowl up at him.

"*Va te faire foutre.*"[1]

"*Volontiers,*"[2] Henry replies.

"You're seriously not going to tell me what happened?" I ask again, hoping that he'll change his mind, but I'm definitely just distracting myself from Henry saying he'd gladly kiss my ass.

He looks up at the ceiling and sighs. "No, it's not any of our business."

I'm sorry, what?

"It involved Duke at my little brother's football game. Pretty sure that makes it my business." I stand up, staring at him. I kind of hate how much taller he is than me. Actually,

---

1. Kiss my ass.
2. Gladly.

now that I'm standing, I think stomping my foot is childish, but it would be effective for expressing how I feel at this moment.

"Mira . . ." Henry trails off, at least having the nerve to look guilty. "I'm sorry. I shouldn't have said that."

"You're right. You shouldn't have, but now you can be the stupid man on the floor. I'm taking the bed," I say, walking past him, only to realize I'm still wearing my outside clothes. I have a rule that clothes worn outside don't touch the bedsheets because the world is disgusting, but I didn't think to pack clothes. Ideally, I would shower too, but I'm not totally sure I trust myself not to jump Henry's bones.

"To sleep in the bed, you have to get in it," Henry adds, clearly choosing violence.

I roll my eyes, crossing my arms again. "I'm thinking."

"Outside clothes?" he guesses, and it's infuriating how well Henry knows me, yet at the same time, he's been so blind to how I feel about him.

"Yes," I grumble.

"The top drawer in my dresser has T-shirts and they'll probably fit you like a dress."

"Thank you," I admit, deciding I can forgo the shower tonight. I look over my shoulder to see him already lying on the floor, his tattoos peeking out from underneath the blanket he took from the bed.

As Henry scrolls on his phone, I change into the shirt and flip the light switch, before crawling into bed without further argument. I'm too tired to deal with Henry and my feelings.

Closing my eyes, a small part of me feels guilty Henry is sleeping on the floor. It *is* his bed, and there's plenty of room if we stay on our own sides.

Whatever. He's the one who won't tell me what happened tonight.

Hunter and I made some progress tonight. He was excited

about the win and even apologized for the shit he said to me earlier in the week. It was a huge weight off my shoulders, but it still doesn't fix anything with Bailey. I mean, what on earth is going on with him? Is it drugs? Actually, drugs would make sense. I didn't have it in me to ask Hunter if things had changed with Bailey because I was so fucking relieved he was talking to me, but would it be bad if it happened to come up at Sunday's game?

Oh shit, I should probably write down that I need to ask Mom if the arson investigators have turned up any new leads with the house. I'm not in any rush to move out of Henry's house, but it would be nice to know if they've found anythi—

"You are thinking so loudly I can't sleep," Henry interrupts my train of thought.

"How can thinking be loud if it's internal?" I question, giggling quietly.

"It just is, Mira. Go to sleep."

I roll in the bed, pulling the covers up to my chin. God, it all smells like Henry. "If you want to sleep in the bed, you can. There's plenty of room."

"I don't want to put you in an uncomfortable position. I'm fine down here," he replies carefully.

"Suit yourself. I'm making a pillow wall in case you decide you're sick of the floor. If you do come up, keep your hands to your own side of the bed." I use three pillows for extra measures, but I hope he says *fuck it* and throws them off the bed to hold me. *Please don't keep your hands to yourself.*

"Goodnight, Mirabelle," his deep voice rumbles. I close my eyes as I relax in Henry's bed, his crisp, comforting scent surrounding me.

"Night, Henry," I mumble back, sinking into a deep long sleep.

CHAPTER TWENTY-SIX

Henry

I WAKE UP WITH A HEAVY WEIGHT ON MY CHEST. THE scent of vanilla tickles my nose, and the early morning light peeks through the blinds covering my window. Rubbing my eyes, I clear away any lingering bleariness from my deep sleep. I honestly can't remember the last time I slept that well.

Mirabelle sighs, and I realize the heavy weight on me is her clinging to me like I'm a life buoy in the middle of the ocean. Her head is nestled into my chest, her blonde waves cascading everywhere as her fingers curl tightly into my shirt. Our legs are tangled together, but Mirabelle is lying on top of me, and I think this is pretty damn ironic considering she's the one who put up the pillow barrier in the middle of the bed.

She had already fallen asleep when I finally gave up on sleeping on the floor and climbed into my bed. If I didn't think the flash would wake her up, I'd have taken a picture of her fast asleep, hugging a pillow to her chest while curled into a ball.

Mirabelle looks so peaceful. I don't want to wake her, because I feel like she hasn't had many peaceful moments lately.

I couldn't tell her last night that Duke isn't going to offer Hunter a spot on their team—*ever*.

It's entirely a political thing.

Harris told us that he'd be doing Hunter a disservice by offering him a spot because the university has essentially said Hunter will never be allowed to see the field, as it risks the money Sebastian donates. It doesn't matter that Sebastian would never wield his money as a weapon to get his son playing time. In fact, he doesn't even need to. Hunter is already *that* good, with the potential for his talent to grow exponentially.

He'd rather see Hunter play for another team to reach his full potential, than ride the bench for four years.

I respect him for it, because that's not an easy choice to make, but I didn't want to add another burden to Mirabelle's shoulders. I know her, and she'd feel like it's her responsibility to fix things even when there's nothing that can be done. I should know better than anyone; it's what I would do too.

She scared the shit out of me earlier this week when she turned into a zombie, and I'm not sure if she's actually doing better now or pretending. I'd prefer not to add anything else to Mirabelle's plate if I can help it.

I only offered to sleep on the floor last night because I wanted to make it clear that just because she was sleeping in here tonight, it didn't mean I had any expectations of anything from that list happening. She's had such a rough week, and I didn't want to make Mirabelle feel pressured in any way.

It dawned on me last night Mira will eventually move back to her family's house once the remodel is done. That terrifies me for more than one reason, but the main one being, is it safe? The investigators determined that an accelerant was used, but they haven't found any evidence that could lead to who started the fire.

I've thought about asking Mirabelle if she's considered

rehiring the bodyguard she used after the Olympics a few years ago, but I'd prefer to keep my balls where they are. For some reason, I don't think she'd be crazy about that idea.

I like having her here. I know Wilson likes having her here, but would Mirabelle choose to stay if she had the option? Or will she want to go back to how things used to be before I made a shit show of my career to the point where she had to agree to fake date me so I wouldn't get traded?

Mirabelle nestles her head further into my chest, inhaling deeply. I stay deathly still, waiting to see if she's waking up. "*Henry,*" she mumbles, tightening her grip on my shirt.

Unable to resist, I brush a piece of hair out of her face, and her eyes blink open slowly. Mirabelle's lips quirk upward into a smile as she reaches up to brush her fingertips gently over my cheek and then my lips. I stay very, very still as a look of confusion washes over her. "Henry?" Mirabelle asks in confusion, her voice scratchy from sleep.

"Yeah?" I whisper.

She startles, bolting off me quickly, her knee driving straight into my groin in the process. There's a strangled cry and fucking stars dance across my vision as I roll over into a fetal position. *Oh my fucking god.* I think I'm going to be sick.

Motherfucker.

I can take getting sacked by linemen twice my size any day of the week, but this? This is fucking excruciating. Scratch that; I think I'm dying.

"Dude, I need you to stop making whatever those sounds are every time you move. Whatever freaky sex you had last night, I don't want to hear it," Kaitlyn says, grimacing as I adjust in my seat on the couch again.

Mirabelle's face flushes and she looks up at me apologetically from the book she's reading.

"Kait, there wasn't any freaky sex happening last night," I clarify, and she rolls her eyes.

"I don't believe you."

"I'm going for a run," Mirabelle squeaks, and I would ask her to stay, but I want to talk to Kaitlyn about Bailey. I'm not sure it's a conversation Mirabelle needs to be there for, even if it does involve her brother. I know my sister, and she'll be more willing to tell me what she knows if it's just the two of us.

Wilson went out to breakfast with his parents who are in town for the game tomorrow, so it'll leave the house empty for Kaitlyn and me.

"So if you didn't have freaky sex last night, why are you acting like you have the man flu?" she asks, tilting her head to the side after Mirabelle retreats upstairs.

Huh? I'm too old for this teenage slang. It changes every week. "What's the man flu?" I ask, momentarily sidetracked.

Kaitlyn laughs quietly, shaking her head condescendingly at me. Sometimes she makes me feel like I'm the younger sibling and not the other way around. "Man flu is when a simple cold knocks a man on his ass and he acts like he's dying, when a woman can still do everything like normal with a little pack of tissues."

"I do not act like a cold knocks me on my ass."

She crosses her arms over her chest. "Then what's wrong with you today?"

Mirabelle skips down the stairs, phone in hand. "I accidentally crushed his dick with my knee this morning. Sorry," she says, and I grimace at the painful reminder. My dick sure hasn't forgotten.

"Oh, so man flu."

Mirabelle chokes back a laugh and shakes her head. "I'll be

back in like a half hour. Maybe try an ice pack so my uncle doesn't murder me for being the reason you're walking bowlegged."

"I am not acting like I have man flu. Why don't I knee you in the nuts and see how you like it, Kait?" I ask, and she shakes her head as Mirabelle disappears out the front door, but not before I catch a glimpse of her sweet ass in her leggings. *Damn.*

"Well, that'd be crazy because I don't have nuts, and you shouldn't hurt women."

"I would never hurt a woman," I add seriously. It was a joke, but still, I need her to know that.

"I know," she says, smiling for real now.

I reach for my coffee mug, adjusting how I'm sitting again while trying not to wince because I don't have man flu. "So, I would normally segue into this better, but Mira's probably going to be back sooner than she said. Do you know what's going on with the twins?" I ask, and Kaitlyn immediately looks down at her lap.

"I don't know," she mumbles, and it's as convincing as a steaming pile of shit.

"Kait, please. If you know anything, I need you to tell me."

Kaitlyn sighs and turns the other way. "I don't know what you want me to say."

"I want you to be able to look me in the eyes and tell me whatever it is you know. Pretty damning that you can't look at me right now."

"Hunter is mad because Bailey won't tell him what's going on with him. I knew Bailey had quit soccer, but he wouldn't tell me a reason other than he didn't see the point anymore. He's been pretty upset since the fire, but every time I ask him what's wrong, Bailey shuts down." She shrugs her shoulders, stealing a glance at me.

Don't get upset with her. She's still a kid. "Why didn't you tell me he quit soccer?" Why do I get the feeling that's not everything she knows?

"Because I thought if I let B sort through his shit without involving you, or Mira, or our parents, it would all be fine. I didn't think he'd get drunk at school," she says, and I take a sip of my coffee, trying to process this rationally. I can't blame Kaitlyn for thinking that. Getting drunk at school is pretty extreme when it comes to teenage rebellion, but wishing she had told me then doesn't change anything now.

"I get that." Kaitlyn grabs a pillow and groans into it dramatically, and I raise my eyebrows in surprise. "You good?"

"Can I tell you something that you have to promise to keep a secret?" she asks, pulling the pillow down to peek at me.

"Does it involve anyone getting hurt?"

"I don't think so, but you can't tell Mira," she says, and damn, if that doesn't make me second-guess wanting to know.

"Kait, I want to make that promise, but if it involves Bailey, I don't know if I can," I say honestly, and I hate that I have to say it. It'd be so much easier if I could lie to her, but I can't.

"*IkissedBaileyorhekissedmebutweweredefinitelykissingandnowheisnottalkingtome,*" she rambles, and I'm not sure I caught any of that.

"Um, maybe I'm getting fucking old, but I need you to repeat that slower."

Her cheeks are flaming red, as if someone took an insane amount of makeup and painted them with it. Kaitlyn nods, hugging the pillow to her chest. "I kissed Bailey, or he kissed me. I'm not sure who started it, but we kissed the other night. I don't know what to do, Henry."

Okay, pushing aside the fact that hearing about my sister kissing a boy makes me want to shove nails into my ears, it entirely catches me off guard. I'm not sure what I thought she was going to say, but it definitely wasn't that.

"Can you say something?" Kaitlyn asks, and I shake my head.

"Need a minute," I say, getting up to take a second to think.

Kaitlyn and Bailey kissed?

She wants me to keep that a secret from Mirabelle? *Fuck*, Mirabelle is going to kill me if I don't tell her, but how do I share that when Kaitlyn told me in confidence?

Goddamn, this ice pack better help, or Owen is going to kill me. Who knew Mirabelle's knees were lethal? I certainly didn't, or I would have stayed on the fucking floor.

I snag the ice pack from the fridge and make my way back to the living room where Kaitlyn is texting on her phone. She immediately puts it away when she spots me, and looks like a kid caught with her hand in the cookie jar. "Are you mad?"

"I'm not mad. Mildly irritated you didn't tell me sooner, but I'm also trying to pretend you didn't tell me at all. I'm your older brother, and I know exactly how teenage boys think, and you picked a Walker boy?" I ask, leaving the rest unsaid. I know I've given her shit over the years about the twins, but I didn't think anything would happen.

"I feel like you can't judge me because you're literally dating the Walker girl," Kaitlyn turns it back around on me, and she has a fair point. Except Mirabelle and I aren't dating for real. Oh shit, I guess I can lie to my sister. The real question here should be: am I lying to my sister, or am I lying to myself?

"This isn't about me right now."

"Well, maybe it should be. I mean, maybe you can help me figure out what's going on. How did you feel the first time you kissed Mirabelle?"

How did I feel?

Like I had a thousand cameras shoved in my face and she made every single one of them disappear.

"Mira . . . she has a way of making me feel like I can't breathe," I say, scratching the back of my neck.

"That sounds scary," Kaitlyn says, and I think that's definitely the right way to describe it.

"Yeah. It is, but she also has a way of being the only person who can make me feel like I'm breathing as well. I'm not sure how that's supposed to help you figure out what's going on, because I don't even know what's going on," I say, moving the ice pack. I think it's helping, or at the very least, the idea of it's helping.

Kaitlyn looks at me like I'm stupid, probably because I am. At least I'm aware of it.

"You don't know what's going on?"

"Are you surprised?" I ask, laughing at my own expense.

"You're in love with her," she says, and my jaw unhinges. Kaitlyn laughs, shaking her head at me. "God, you are stupid."

"I'm not in love with her," I say, shaking my head. First, Andrew and now Kaitlyn? "We're supposed to be talking about Bailey, not me."

"I don't know anything else, so we might as well talk about you and Mirabelle."

"I love you, but we're not talking about my relationship with Mirabelle," I insist.

"You also love her."

I think Mirabelle had the right idea—maybe I need to go for a run too.

CHAPTER TWENTY-SEVEN

Mirabelle

I THOUGHT I WOULD HATE HAVING THE HOUSE TO myself, but it's kind of nice. If I wanted to snoop—which I don't—this would be a golden opportunity.

I had the chance to call Emily to fill her in on everything, but it's beginning to occur to me I can't spend all my time with Henry and his teammates because when they leave, who will I have here?

The Panthers are playing in the Thursday Night Football game this week, so they left yesterday for Colorado. I took full advantage of not having the guys here to check something off my list. I didn't need Henry to be present to skinny dip with me, and like he said, it's about me feeling more comfortable. It probably sounds dumb, but there was something so freeing about it. There's plenty of space between the houses next to Henry's, along with a tall privacy fence blocking the view. I almost chickened out, but it was an awful day at work, and I wanted to feel like I had accomplished something. So, I waited until the sun was setting and turned off the string lights over the pool before going for a swim.

It was definitely needed after dealing with Miley's snide

comments all day since Stacey traveled with the team, and I think I might need to start keeping a stress ball in my work bag for me to squeeze while I pretend it's her head. I don't think that will get me sent to HR, whereas anything I'm tempted to say definitely would.

The game is playing in the background as I scroll through Henry's social media pages, trying to find which posts have the highest engagement so we can continue boosting his presence with the younger demographic of fans.

His endorsements seem to do pretty well, but there's definitely a higher level of engagement on posts where he's shirtless. I can't blame anyone for liking those pictures, as the thought of printing and framing them has definitely run through my brain before. Of course, the real thing is so much better.

My favorite post appears to be everyone else's favorite as well, with over a million likes.

It's the one Henry posted to fulfill his deal with Stacey, and damn, he's good. He probably could have even captioned it *Sugartits*, and no one would have batted an eye. Henry must have taken the picture during the plane ride back from the last away game when I fell asleep on his shoulder. For being asleep, I honestly look pretty damn amazing.

The only part of Henry you can see is the shoulder I'm asleep on. I look peaceful with my hair falling slightly into my face, and you can see Henry's headphone poking through my hair. It's the exact kind of photo a girlfriend would hope her boyfriend would take of her, but it's the caption that sells it.

The only person I'd want to listen to audiobooks with.

I'm fine. Actually—I'm swooning, but it's fine. Everything is *just* fine.

My phone rings with a call from JJ and I answer, putting him on speakerphone. "Hey, JJ," I say, while typing up notes on a separate document for Stacey to look over.

"Are you watching this shit?" he asks, clearly not bothering with niceties today.

I look up at the television mounted on the wall, my jaw falling at the abysmal score. Now I understand his frustration. "When the fuck did that happen?" I ask, as the camera pans to my uncle, who is covering his mouth with a playbook as he says something into his headset.

"Refs blew a call that allowed the Blizzards to score, and then Henry couldn't find anyone open. Our defense fucking fell apart on their next chance, and Hill ran a forty-three-yard touchdown. We're better than this," JJ complains, and I groan.

"We're a lot better than this bullshit. I have it on, but I'm not paying attention. Stacey asked me to look at engagement on Henry's social media so that's where my focus was," I say, waiting to see if the camera will show Henry.

"Probably a good idea. Henry's ego is taking quite the hit tonight, I'm sure. He'll probably need you to kiss it better once he's back."

"Only if I'm lucky," I say, my heart skipping a beat at the sight of Henry commanding the field. I look down at the matching jersey I'm wearing with his name and number on it, and I have no doubt he'll be jealous I wore it when he wasn't here to see it. Maybe I'll send him a picture of me wearing it to make him jealous. He might think he's being sly, but Henry has dropped enough damn hints about wanting me to wear his jersey, he could have *obvious* tattooed on his forehead. *Now that'd be pretty damn ironic.* "Goddamn, he's hot."

"Yeah, yeah. I've only heard you say that a million times," JJ teases, before swearing at the refs for holding one of our receivers, resulting in Henry's pass being intercepted, and run in for another fucking touchdown.

"That's fucking bullshit," I yell at the screen, but Uncle Owen thankfully challenges the call before Henry can get himself into trouble yelling at the referees as they show Wilson and Tyler trying to be the voices of reason with Henry and Crosby. "Get your eyes checked."

"Mira, I hate to break it to you, but those are some very weak insults. Mom would be disappointed if she heard those," JJ says, and if this were a FaceTime call, I'd flip him off.

"I'm sorry? You're the one who called me," I say, scrolling on my computer again to pull up the statistics for a different post.

"Of course I called you. Everyone here is a fucking Cougars fan, so all of them went out to the bars for specials tonight."

"I'm sure the game is on at the bars. We have the prime-time slot tonight," I remind him, and JJ groans.

"It's raining?"

"That's a weak excuse," I say, and the replay shows there was offensive holding on the play, so not only do we get an automatic first down, we also get an extra ten yards from the Blizzards' penalty.

"I'm homesick, okay? I didn't feel like going out tonight because I'd rather watch our family's team play while talking to you," JJ admits, and I feel a little guilty for pushing his buttons.

"Aren't Mom and Dad coming to visit this weekend? At least that's what Hunter told me when I talked to him last night," I say, and JJ sighs. I feel bad I'm not going, but we're celebrating Henry's birthday this weekend, and Andrew is flying in tomorrow around the same time as Henry. I do know Dad already purchased tickets for the bowl game Beaumont qualified for, so we're all going to that.

"It's just Dad and Hunt coming now, unless they decide to leave Bailey with Chris and Penelope or with Uncle Owen and Aunt Blake. I told them they could bring him along, but they don't want it to feel like a reward for his recent behavior."

I rub my temples at the thought of my out-of-control

brother. "Dude, maybe a weekend with Chris is what Bailey needs. It's not going well at the house."

"I know," he says, exhaling quietly. "Are you having any luck with him?"

"Nope. I stopped at the house for a little bit last weekend after we drove Kaitlyn back, but he wouldn't open the bedroom door for me. I didn't feel right barging in either. I don't know how we'll get through to him, but I know invading his space is not the answer." Before Mom and Dad knew he had quit soccer, at least he was still kind of talking to everyone, even if he was a dick most of the time. They're making him go to therapy, and since they told him, he has started giving everyone the silent treatment.

"No, I agree. I don't know what the right thing to do is, but you're right about that."

"What do you think we missed that made him start acting like this?" It's the question I've been asking myself the last few months. I can't piece it together. Bailey says he doesn't need me and he wants me to leave him alone, but then he's mad and saying I haven't been there, which contradicts everything. He says I did something wrong, but he won't tell me what it is.

"Honestly? I have no clue. He was moody when I left for college, but he wasn't like this. Do you remember the last normal conversation you had?" JJ asks, and it's sad I have to think about what it could have been. It takes me longer than I'd like to admit.

"B called me after the fire. He was upset and asked if I was okay. That's the last time he was our little brother to me," I say. It breaks my damn heart to think about it.

"At least you can remember, I can't. Didn't think I'd have to remember the last time my brother was nice to me," he says, and I walk to the kitchen to pour myself a healthy glass of Chardonnay. I think this calls for wine.

The conversation finds a natural pause a few minutes later

as we watch Henry run in his own damn touchdown, and I jump up and down with excitement.

"God, I love your boyfriend sometimes, and right now is definitely one of those times," JJ says, sounding a lot happier than he did ten minutes ago.

"Fake boyfriend," I correct, but honestly, that line is so blurred right now I don't believe my own words.

"Bullshit. You guys are dating for real, but neither of you actually realize it. When are you going to grow a pair, and tell Henry that you have feelings for him?" JJ asks, changing the topic, but I'm distracted by a flash coming from the backyard. I grab my phone and glass of wine, walking to the window to look outside.

"I'll tell him."

"When?"

"Whenever I feel like it," I say, scanning the backyard another time, but I don't see anything.

I had to have imagined it, right?

I'm not sure if I imagined it or not, but now that I've let the anxiety in, I can't stop considering the possibility that the flash I saw could have been the arsonist. To make myself feel better, I'm sleeping in Henry's room tonight. I've also locked every single possible external door and window in the house, and I even double checked to make sure I set the security system.

I didn't tell JJ, but I did make him stay on the phone with me for the rest of the game before coming up here. I didn't tell him what was going on, because he probably would have made me go to our parents' house or a hotel, and I'm not hiding. I know I'm safe here, and I'm not letting anyone scare me away from my home. *I'm Mirabelle fucking Walker. I've got this.*

I sent Henry the picture of me wearing his jersey, and surprisingly, I haven't heard from him.

They ended up losing, but it wasn't for lack of trying. The game went into overtime and the Blizzards won with a field goal, but they fought hard.

See, now would be a totally great opportunity to steal a few more of Henry's shirts, but I'm slowly growing my collection, starting with the shirt he gave me after Quinn made me spill coffee on mine.

Maybe Henry isn't going to call me tonight. For all I know, I entirely misread all the hints he was dropping about wanting me to wear it.

I drop my phone on the comforter and flop on top of the bed just as my phone begins to ring. I roll over, my heart leaping when I see Henry's name on the screen.

"Good game, Price," I answer, trying to be smooth, but apparently I'm as smooth as a piece of sandpaper. Why would I bring up tonight's loss when I'm attempting to flirt with him? *God, I'm dumb.*

Henry at least has the decency to laugh. "It wasn't a good game, but always the optimist, Walker."

"Sorry," I say, laughing at my own expense.

"I'm disappointed you finally wore my jersey when I wasn't there to see it," he says, and I bite my lip to keep from screaming as I pump my fist into the air.

"I guess I'll have to make it up to you." My heart is doing flips in my chest.

"Wear it to the next game?" Henry asks, and I can hear the hope in his voice. It's fucking adorable.

"Maybe," I answer, trying to be coy. "I don't think I could wear the same outfit, though." *Oh shit, what am I doing?*

"Oh? Why's that?"

I play with the edge of the jersey, rolling the fabric between my fingers. "Because I'm *only* wearing your jersey."

Henry makes a choked sound, and damn, if it doesn't make me feel good. "Fuck, Mira," he swears.

"Where are you?" I ask, wondering how much further I can push this.

"I'm in my hotel room, wishing you were here," he answers, before turning it back around on me. "Where are you?"

"I'm in your bed, wishing you were here."

"Goddamn, I think you're trying to kill me. How the hell did I get so lucky to have a woman as pretty as you in my bed, wearing my last name?"

"Flattery will get you everywhere, Henry," I tease.

"I mean it, *mon cœur*. You're beautiful," he says.

"Thanks," I say, looking up at his ceiling.

"So is there a reason you're in my bed?" Henry asks, and maybe it's because we're on the phone and not in person, but I swear his voice gets a little deeper.

"I missed you." I sigh, putting on my big girl pants—*figuratively, of course*—and I set the ball in motion. "What would you do if you were here?" I ask, giving him the opportunity to shut this down, but I hope he doesn't.

"I'd take a moment to look at you, and then I'd kiss you."

"What would you do next?" I ask, my voice sounding breathy.

"I would pull you into my lap and tell you how incredible you look. I'd tell you enough times that you wouldn't have any choice but to believe me, Mira, and then I'd kiss you again, taking my time until we're both so thoroughly out of breath, we don't have a choice but to stop."

"Would you touch me?" I like where this is headed.

"*Mon cœur*, I wouldn't be able to keep my hands off you. I'd slide my hands under the jersey, because *fuck*, it took too damn long for you to wear it. I'd want to look at you in it as long as I could and memorize how you look when I play with your nipples, rolling them between my fingers the way you like as you grind against me," he says, and I squirm, the ache between my legs begging for more pressure.

Fuck, that all sounds perfect. I definitely agree, it took too damn long for me to wear it if this is the reaction I get.

"Henry, can I touch myself?" I ask, a whimper slipping from my lips as I play the scene in my head. Not even half a second later, the phone begins ringing with a FaceTime call.

I answer, relishing the look of desire and desperation on Henry's face. "There's no way in hell we're having phone sex, and I don't get to see you come in my jersey on my bed to my words, okay?" his voice rumbles, and this is better than I imagined.

"Do I get to see you come?" I ask, and the corner of his delicious mouth quirks up, clearly liking the idea as well.

"I'll let you see whatever you want, baby," he says, his voice rough as he sets up the phone to let me see him and the inked body I love.

I prop the phone up in the pillows to where he can see me on the bed, and Henry's core ripples as he takes his sweatpants off. Oh my god, he's brave for not wearing briefs. Holy shit, I'm not even sure where to look.

"This is what you do to me, Mira. I want you more than anything," he says, and I feel like I can't breathe.

Am I actually doing this? Are we really going to check something off the list?

"Take your underwear off. I want to see you," Henry instructs, fisting his cock as my mouth waters.

"I would if I had any on," I tease, trying to prevent my nerves from getting the better of me, and his full mouth curls into a smile.

"Fuck, Mira," he swears under his breath. "Show me how wet you are."

"Soaked," I answer, keeping my eyes glued to the screen as

I follow his directions. I refuse to look away from him as I dip two fingers into my core, and Henry moans, squeezing the head of his cock as I circle around my clit, my breath hitching.

"Show me," he says, and I hold them up for him to see. "Fuck, you're perfect," he says, his abs flexing again. "Use your other hand to play with your nipple. You make the sweetest sounds when I pinch them."

"Henry, you feel so good," I breathe out, pretending he's the one touching me instead of myself. I love his hands so damn much; it's a problem.

"That's it. Make yourself feel good, Mira," Henry says, watching me intensely, and I've never felt more in control of a moment with someone else than right now. "If I were there, I'd kiss you and slide another finger in you so I can feel you gasp. I fucking love it when you do that. I want to know every sound you make as I worship your body."

"Fuck," I swear, pumping another finger in my core, arching my back at the feeling. It'd feel better if they were Henry's, but it still feels pretty damn good. Who knew that phone sex could be so awesome?

"*Tu es incroyable,*"[1] he says, his eyes hooded as his hand quickens and I love watching him lose control as another low groan escapes from Henry's mouth. A lock of dark hair falls across his forehead, and I'd kill to brush it back, but that would also mean we'd be in the same bed right now.

"I want to taste you. Would you like that? Fucking my face?" I ask, lost in the moment enough that I don't feel self-conscious saying it. I don't feel silly voicing my wants and desires to him. Henry makes me feel safe, even when he's in a different part of the country.

Henry's jaw clenches tightly, and he stops moving his hand as he watches me. The head of his cock is an angry red

---

1. You are incredible.

color, and looks so hard it's painful. Why did he stop? He's breathing heavily, and I swear, next time I have the opportunity, I'm going to trace every line of his tattoo with my tongue. I'm honestly a little surprised I haven't done it already.

"I'd love that if it's something you want to do," Henry says roughly, and I nod quickly.

"Yeah. I'll add it to the list," I say and Henry laughs, giving me a real smile.

"Mira, it doesn't have to be on the list for us to do it," he says, but that sounds messy. That makes this feel too real, and as much as I want it to be, I can't forget that this is fake.

"There's something satisfying about checking something off a list," I defend, my body protests as I roll on my side to face him.

"We can add it to the list, but I didn't say you could stop touching yourself," Henry says, raising an eyebrow. "If I were there, I wouldn't stop until you were crying out my name so keep fucking my fingers, Mirabelle."

My name sounds like a sin coming from his mouth, and I love it, but I'm also feeling feisty myself. "But you stopped," I point out, and Henry laughs again, but it's strained.

"I stopped because hearing you ask me if I'd like fucking your face almost made me come, and I'm not coming until you do. Clearly you still don't believe me when I tell you the effect you have on me," he says, standing up to move closer to the camera so I can see properly.

There's a bead of pre-cum on the tip that Henry swipes with his thumb as he wraps his large hand around himself, jerking the thick length once. "I can't wait to feel you touch me, but the thought of you enjoying it is what makes me lose it. You make me want to lose it, not anyone else," Henry says, squeezing the head again.

"I want to see you lose control," I say, and Henry leans

back on the bed, his cock twitching as he drags his hand down it.

"Then show me how much you want to see it as you fuck your fingers pretending they're mine. I'm not coming until you do," he repeats, and I look away as a twinge of anxiety creeps in because what if I can't? I mean, what if last time was a fluke? I want to see Henry, but what if— *"Regarde-moi,"*[2] he says, interrupting my thoughts and I exhale softly, dragging my gaze back to him.

"Quoi?"[3]

"I don't want you to worry about me. I want you to focus on making yourself feel good, okay?" Henry says softly, reading my mind perfectly.

"Okay," I agree, lying back to let my hands return to their original positions.

"I've laid in that bed probably a hundred times thinking of you being in it," Henry admits, and I turn in surprise as my core throbs. "Fucking figures the first time you're coming in it is when I'm out of town," he says, trying to lighten the mood.

"A hundred times?" I ask, wondering if maybe there's a chance my hopes of Henry seeing me in a different light are working.

"Probably more." He tilts his head, his cheeks flushing. I relax a little, swirling my fingers over my clit causing a spark of pleasure to jolt through me. I bite my lip as I slip my fingers back in, curling them to hit the right spot. "That's it, *mon cœur.* Make yourself feel good."

Mon cœur. I want him to call me that forever.

"*You're* making me feel good," I correct, slowly climbing that hill again.

---

2. Look at me.
3. What?

"Are you still using two?" he asks, and I nod, pumping them again. "Let me see them."

I hold them out for him to see how slick they are with my arousal, and he grips himself, groaning. "Add another. Let me see how well you take them."

I push in a third, meeting little resistance from how turned on I am, and I turn my hips to give Henry a center view. "You feel so good." I moan, dropping my head back to let myself disappear into the pleasure.

"You're doing great. Pinch your nipple, baby. God, I can't wait to suck on them. I bet you'd like it if I'd bite them and kiss it better. I wonder what sound would come out of you then?"

My hips move on their own accord, chasing the high as I think of Henry doing those things. *"Henry."*

"That's it. Say my name. Tell me how much you like it when I make you feel good," Henry says, grunting and I turn slightly to see Henry jerking himself off again. "I'm close. Tell me when, Mirabelle."

"When, H-Henry," I gasp out, my climax sweeping over me, but I force my eyes to stay on Henry as his head drops back in raw ecstasy. Mini earthquakes tremor through my body as I watch Henry spill himself all over his abs, and I can't look away.

"Mira," he gasps out my name as my breathing hitches.

This might be the most erotic thing I've ever done.

Henry's throat bobs and he smiles tiredly at me through the screen. "I need a second before we talk about what you liked and didn't like, if that's okay?" he asks, reaching to grab a tissue from the bedside table to wipe himself off.

"I need to get cleaned up too," I say, forcing my jelly legs to hold me as I walk into the bathroom to clean up before returning to Henry's bed, this time crawling underneath the covers after flipping off the lights so the only illumination in the room is coming from the phone.

"You okay?" he asks, concern knitting his eyebrows as I hold the phone in my hands.

"I'm okay," I answer, but I'm not sure what to say.

"What did you like?"

It feels like a dumb question when the answer is all of it. I liked all of it. "Well, for one, I never thought I'd describe a dick as a work of art, but yours deserves to be in a museum or something. You're gorgeous," I whisper without thinking.

Henry, thankfully, doesn't call me a weirdo when it's probably what I deserve. "Thanks, but I'm a little attached to it, so I don't foresee it being in a museum anytime soon. Just remember that you're to blame when my ego hits new heights."

"I'm shocked your ego isn't sky-high already when you walk around with that in your pants," I tease, causing Henry to laugh. I think the fact that we can still laugh after phone sex is a testament to how natural a real relationship would be, but I'm aware I'm mildly delusional when it comes to Henry. "Is there normally that much talking during sex? I don't think Reid ever said anything other than 'suck it,' or 'stick it in your mouth,' but compared to what just happened, I'm not sure if my baseline is normal."

Henry shrugs, rolling onto his side to mirror my position in his bed as he grabs the phone. "Depends on the person, but that asshole could have at least been a little more creative. I think what I liked most was when you would say something so honest, you didn't second-guess it. Personally, I feel like during phone sex you have to be more vocal because the only way your partner can hear you is through your voice."

"That makes sense," I agree, making mental notes in my head. "Should I have talked more?"

"Mira, you did what felt right to you, and that's the only

thing that matters to me. I talked a little more than I normally would toward the middle because I could tell you were anxious after I said I wasn't going to come until you did, and it seemed to help you be more in the moment instead of in your head," Henry explains, and he's not wrong. "That's not a bad thing either, and I hope you don't take it that way."

"Are you sure?"

Henry's eyelids droop a little, but he blinks, forcing them open. "I'm positive. A good partner adapts to their partner's needs instead of forcing their own desires. I was just trying to adapt to you."

"Thank you," I say, as my heart turns to a puddle of mush.

"Anytime," he says, yawning. "I think you wore me out. I'm about to fall asleep," he says, his eyes falling shut out of exhaustion.

I think mine close too, but when I stir a few hours later, I see a low battery notification covering the still connected call between us. I plug my phone in, propping it up again so it's easier to pretend that the man I'm in love with is beside me.

CHAPTER TWENTY-EIGHT

Mirabelle

I FLOATED INTO WORK ON CLOUD NINE THIS morning, carrying a tray of coffees for everyone in an attempt to have a peaceful day. Yesterday was rough without Stacey here to supervise us, and Miley made everyone's day awful. I beat everyone in, but I'm also trying to get my shit done so I can leave earlier this afternoon.

I'm eager to see Henry, especially since his birthday is tomorrow, but I know after the team's flight lands, he'll probably spend the day resting.

I finished writing my reports on Henry's social media engagement before combing through social media to see if there are any fires I need to alert Stacey about after last night's loss, but I'm not seeing anything emergent. If anything, fans were commending Henry for his efforts on the field last night, and I took a screenshot of a few of them to send to him.

He deserves to know there are people out there rooting for him.

I'll never forget the look on his face when Stacey told him how close he was to being traded. It's part of the reason—aside from the obvious (*I still hate that word*)—that I was so quick to agree to this whole fake dating scheme. Henry looked devastated, and I understand why.

He spent all summer training with Uncle Owen and Dad, trying to show everyone he could fill the great Sebastian Walker's shoes.

Henry might not be happy about it, but he's done everything Stacey has asked of him.

Public perception is everything in this line of business. I understand how Henry felt, even though I was on the opposite end of the spectrum after the Olympics.

Growing up under the microscope with my dad's career being what it was, I learned to tune out a lot of what other people said. I was used to them watching me because of my last name, and most of the time, I could forget. I have a thick skin, but things were different after the Olympics.

I'll be forever grateful for my time competing and the opportunity I had to represent my country, but after reaching that pinnacle, I didn't even feel like a person anymore. I don't talk about it much because I'm past that point in my life, and I worked through it in therapy, but it doesn't change how I felt at the time. I had people all over the world on the internet talking about me as if I didn't have real feelings, thinking they had the right to comment on my body, my athleticism, and me as a person. Now for every negative comment like that, I have dozens of positive ones, but it's hard to focus on the positive when the negative screams so much louder.

I'll never forget when I was out shopping with my mom, and a stranger came up to me and started touching me as if she had a right to my body. It solidified my thoughts that I was a marionette doll, with strings for everyone else to pull.

My parents hired a bodyguard for me immediately after that, and Sam went everywhere with me for the next year until things died down. It was probably a bit extreme of a reaction, but it made me feel safe at a time when I needed it. Everyone aside from my parents, Uncle Owen, Aunt Blake, and JJ, thought Sam was there because my parents were being over-protective.

It's definitely the reason I lost my shit with that couple at the restaurant for putting their hands all over Henry, because they were treating him the same way I'd been treated.

Stepping down from elite gymnastics was the hardest choice I've ever had to make, but I wanted to feel like myself again. I wanted to love what I did, and the thought of going back to the Olympics for it all to start again was the reason for multiple panic attacks, but I didn't want to quit.

My PR team crafted a release stating that I wanted to focus on my education, and the coach at Duke welcomed me with open arms. Competing at Duke made me fall in love with the sport and with myself all over again. I know I have an ego the size of Texas, but I'd rather have that than feel like I'm not a real person again.

My biggest regret from dating Reid is how I let him make me feel like I wasn't good enough.

I roll my shoulders, shaking off the thoughts. *I'm Mirabelle fucking Walker. I've got this.*

My phone vibrates on my desk, and I smile automatically upon seeing Henry's name pop up. It's a screenshot of an audiobook, and another text follows it up.

HENRY

starting this one if you want to listen too

no pressure

MIRABELLE

I'd love to.

I purchase the audiobook as I pull one of my earbuds from my bag and cue it up.

Elias is the first one in the office, and if he's surprised to see me already here, he doesn't let it show. I'm usually one of the first people in this department here, but I'm often on the move, working from my laptop throughout the day as I shadow Henry. He tilts his head in acknowledgment, grabbing the coffee marked with an E. I've gathered he's not much of a morning person, but he sure knows how to plaster on a convincing smile when Stacey walks in.

Ginger walks in a few minutes later, smiling with relief at the coffee. "I think I love you," she says, and I smile back at her. I like Ginger the most out of my coworkers, and I think we'd actually have a shot at being friends if it weren't for Miley.

I'm convinced Miley might be Regina George resurrected.

Anytime Ginger is nice to me, Miley stares at her with this look that makes Ginger shrink, and I hate it. But I also know that if I fight Ginger's battles for her, Miley is never going to respect her. Elias has just decided it's easier to be on Miley's good side than to try to be my friend, which is fine by me.

My point is proven exactly right when Miley walks in, her smile more of a sneer as she bares her teeth at me and snags her coffee.

You can only control how you act, not how others react.

Yesterday was rough, and by the look on her face, today will be too.

Sometimes being the bigger person sucks, but giving her a reaction is letting Miley win. I ignore her and sip my coffee, trying to focus on the audiobook as a new email loads that Stacey cc'd me on with the details for the Panthers' upcoming charity gala next month. There's a separate email addressed only to me, explaining I'll be attending as a guest—and as Henry's date—along with a request to monitor any interviews given at the event since I'll be with him all night. I'm honestly a little surprised that she's asking instead of telling, but if I'm being entirely honest, Stacey is growing on me a lot and vice versa.

She's a little prickly at first, and I wasn't sure what to expect from having her as a mentor, but she's incredible at what she does if her effort to bump Henry's popularity is any indication. His jersey sales are growing in popularity, but my dad's is still our leading product.

I send off the analysis of Henry's social media engagement I put together last night when a forwarded email chain rolls in from Stacey, containing correspondence between her and Henry's agent with a list of companies that have reached out, wanting to partner with Henry.

Please look through these to see which ones would align best with our organization, and the image we are trying to create for Henry.

We'll speak later.

My eyes widen in surprise as I bump my knee against the bottom of my desk. "Shit," I mutter under my breath, rubbing it as if it will make the ache go away faster. My fingers dance over the small, indented scar on my knee that's identical to Henry's.

"Are you okay?" Ginger asks, peering up at me over her computer, and I pause the audiobook so I don't miss anything.

"I'm good, just clumsy," I say.

Miley looks at me, and it is so tempting to stick my tongue out at her, but it's not worth it. "What does Stacey have you doing?" she asks and I shrug. This feels like something that is way above my title as an intern, and if Stacey wanted everyone to know, she would have included them in her email.

"Work," I answer vaguely, unpausing the book, only to pause it again as she opens her mouth once more.

"What kind of work?" Miley continues, and Elias turns to look at her in annoyance.

"I'm trying to get my work done, and maybe you should do the same."

"I will after Mirabelle answers the question," Miley says, and Elias gives me a look.

Be the bigger person, Mirabelle. "An email," I say, plastering on a smile that I hope matches the same one Miley gave me earlier.

"Oh, perfect. Then when you're done with that very important email, maybe you can go pick up Stacey's dry cleaning." Is she serious? I'm not doing Miley's job for her.

"Miley, come on," Ginger says.

She's being rude, and I'm over it. My patience is already pretty damn thin after all of Miley's comments yesterday, and this is a moment when I hate that I inherited my parents' tempers. "No."

"No, what?" Miley tilts her head to the side, and I mimic the movement.

"No is a complete sentence. I'm sorry you don't get your work done within the time Stacey allots us, but that's not my problem. Stacey gave me things to get done before she gets back, and I agree with Elias. I'm trying to get my work done, and it sounds like you should stop worrying about what I'm doing so you can focus on yourself," I snap, honestly missing the days when all they asked about was my gold medal.

"You're able to get your work done because the three of us are busy running errands normal interns have to do, but I guess you're not normal, right?"

"Cry me a river, Miley." *Oh shit, I probably shouldn't have said that, but there's nothing I can do about it now. It's not like I hit her.*

Ginger laughs, slapping her hand over her mouth to smother the sound as Miley fixes her stare on her, before glaring at me again. "You're Sebastian Walker's daughter, and the head coach is your uncle. They were never going to make you do the grunt work. We're here while you get to go play with puppies and do interviews with your boyfriend."

I realize none of them know I'm pretending to date Henry because it's unofficially part of my job, but it hasn't been all sunshine and roses, even if last night it was jerseys and orgasms.

I weigh a quick pro and con list in my head. Pro: telling Miley off. Con: I still have to work with her.

"I can list off all my qualifications for this job *again*, but it's getting a little repetitive. Just like your bitching about how I'm not working as hard as you. If you have a problem with it, take it up with Stacey," I reply icily, over this bullshit.

Her jaw drops in surprise, but I have a feeling I'm going to end up working from home for the rest of the day. I log out of my computer, and grab my bag with my laptop, making sure that my fists are clenched so I don't walk out with my middle fingers up in the air.

I send Stacey an email on my phone as I walk out of the stadium, letting her know that I'll be working from home today, but if she needs me to come back to the office once the plane lands, I'll come back. I guess it's a good thing I came in early.

Fuck Miley and her stupid opinions.

CHAPTER TWENTY-NINE

Henry

ANDREW'S FLIGHT WAS DELAYED SO INSTEAD OF waiting at the airport for him, I decided to run home and shower first to wash off the feeling of flying. If I have enough time, I could probably take Mirabelle lunch. I'm learning she's not very good at remembering to eat when she's in the zone.

Opening the garage door, I'm surprised to see her car still here. Stacey didn't say anything about her working from home today, but I guess it's good I came here first.

I grab my bag from the trunk of my car, my stomach flipping a little at the thought of being in the same room as Mirabelle.

Last night on the phone might be the new fantasy I replay in my head, because holy fuck, she looked incredible. I was in a pretty awful mood after the game until I checked my phone, and the picture she sent of herself wearing my jersey blew my mind. I didn't call with the expectation of anything happening, but I'm sure as fuck not complaining. When Mirabelle asked for permission to touch herself in my bed, I think my brain stroked out for a moment.

I want to kill her ex-boyfriend for making her feel like she's not good enough, but I also want to thank the stupid son of a bitch for being the reason she looks at me like I hung the moon and the stars. It does something to me that I can't describe, but it's an addictive feeling.

I think for my birthday present I'm going to ask Mirabelle to wear my jersey—with pants—to the next game. That would be a dream come true. *Shit, I'm getting hard just thinking about it.*

I open the door, but the handle doesn't turn. *Why is this door locked?* We never lock the garage door. I pull my keys from my pocket, unlocking the handle, but the door still won't open. *Did Mirabelle flip the deadbolt too? What the hell is going on?*

It takes me a moment to find the right key, but I'm finally able to get in. Whoever thought of designing all the keys to be the same shape and color but for different locks deserves a special place in hell.

"Mira? Are you home?" I call out, setting my duffle bag next to the door, punching in the alarm code to disable the system. The house is silent, and it puts me a little on edge. A quiet Mirabelle is a sign of trouble, and I'm just hoping I'm not in deep shit with her.

Oh fuck. What if she locked the door to let me know she's mad at me for falling asleep on her last night? It was an accident, and I would think if she were upset, Mirabelle would have sent me a middle finger this morning instead of telling me she would start the book I sent her while she works?

She's in my room, sitting on the floor as she scrolls on her iPad with headphones on. I don't mind at all that she's in my room, but I feel like there's definitely an underlying reason for it that Mirabelle hasn't shared. She sets her iPad down to reach for her laptop when she finally spots me standing there.

"Henry, you scared the shit out of me." She laughs, pressing a hand to her chest as she takes her headphones out.

"Sorry," I apologize, because that wasn't my intention, but this sort of feels like déjà vu from a few months ago when I crashed her morning surf. That feels like a lifetime ago. So many things are different now, but I'm not sure I would change anything if it meant I wouldn't be with Mirabelle. Not that I'm *with* her, but I enjoy spending time with her like this. We've always been friends, but now I can't imagine going a day without talking to her.

Mirabelle tilts her head. "Are you?"

"Nope." I grin at her, moving to sit by her on the floor. "I didn't know you were working from home today?"

"It wasn't the plan," she admits.

"What happened?" I ask, and Mirabelle sighs, shrugging.

"Just more shit with Miley. It was either work from home, or get myself sent to HR."

Based on the little bit Mirabelle has shared with me, it sounds like nothing she does is going to be good enough for Miley. "That bad?" I ask, and Mirabelle drags her hands over her face, groaning.

"It could have been worse. I told her to cry me a river and to stop bitching about whether I'm doing my job, but that's the only time I swore," she defends herself, and I know I would have paid good money to see Mirabelle try to control her temper. "Stop smiling. I'm supposed to be a professional by not stooping to their level," she says, scolding me in a way that makes me want to lean over and kiss her senseless.

"You are a professional," I agree.

"Damn straight. Miley can fuck off," Mirabelle says, her eyes crinkling at the corners as she smiles.

"Or you could come run my PR team after your internship, but I'd understand if you want to quit to start sooner," I suggest.

"Are you serious?"

"Of course," I answer. "You're doing a great job. I think by the end of the season, people might actually start rooting for me." Stacey told me earlier things are looking a lot better for me, and I know Mirabelle's played a large role in that happening, even without pretending to be my girlfriend.

Her face lights up, and she grabs for her phone. "I saved these earlier to show you, but I think they already are," she says, handing it to me.

> *User59285483: price left everything on the field*
> *#myqb1*
> *cpfo0tball: henry price is my new fav player*
> *User82417: price is the next GOAT*

A lump forms in my throat, and I know it's just a few, but damn. It feels good to see that everything we're doing is working. It's . . . I can't even express how much it means to me that Mirabelle saved these so I could see them. "Thank you," I say, handing her phone back. Mirabelle's as pretty on the inside as she is on the outside. Like this is . . . I don't know. *I don't know what this is, but I think it scares the shit out of me.*

"Of course. I thought you would want to see them," she says, setting her phone down on the ground again.

I want to see you.

I return her smile, but before I can say anything, my phone starts to ring. *Mom calling.*

"Sorry, I should probably get this," I say, on the off chance that something is wrong. Penelope doesn't normally call during the day.

"Do you want me to go?" Mirabelle asks and I shake my head as I answer.

"Mom? Is everything okay?" I ask.

There's a cough, and a voice deeper than Penelope's catches me off guard. "Ah, actually, it's me. I didn't think you would answer if I called."

"Probably not. You haven't spoken more than a couple words to me in almost two months, Dad."

Mirabelle looks at me in surprise, and while I had a feeling this call was coming, I assumed Dad would call tomorrow on my birthday.

"I know. That's why I'm calling."

"And?" I ask, knowing I'm being a dick, but I'm hurt. I'm angry he didn't even try to come talk to me when I went to watch Kaitlyn cheer. I expected Thalia and Sebastian to be mad when we first announced our fake relationship, and I even understood why they were upset. It still hurt, but I understood. My dad, though? That one I didn't expect.

"I'm sorry, Henry."

"Okay," I say, trying to wrap my head around the fact he's apologizing because I know that's not easy for him to do. He's stubborn and proud, but I still love him.

"Okay," he replies, and I want to tell him how unfair it was for him to treat me the way he did, but is there even a point? I know Dad's a man of few words. I can vaguely hear whispering before my dad continues. "Can you forgive me?"

Did he even want to apologize, or is Mom making him? "Penelope wants to know, or you want to know?"

"Both," he confesses. "I understand if you're not ready, but son . . . I was wrong, and I shouldn't have said the things I did. I hope you can forgive me."

I drag a hand through my hair, and Mirabelle pushes her laptop away, resting a hand on my leg in silent support. "It's fine, Dad. I forgive you," I say, watching her closely, and while this doesn't make everything okay, it's a step in the right direction. I have to give him credit for that.

"Thank you, Henry," he says, clearing his throat. "So, um, how are you and Mirabelle?"

"We're good," I answer vaguely, because this just feels weird and unnatural.

"I'm not sure what you have planned for the weekend, but I hope you have a good time and that you're safe."

"Andrew's flight should actually be landing soon so I have to go pick him up at the airport. I think some of us are just going to hang out at a bar, nothing too crazy," I say, looking at my watch. *Shit, I still have to shower.* "Hey, Dad? I'm glad you called, but I have to get a few things done. Can I call you tomorrow?" I ask, leaving the ball in his court.

"Okay. Please give Mira my love and tell Andrew I said hello. I love you."

"Will do. Love you too."

"Wait, Henry?" he asks, catching me just before I hang up.

"Yeah?"

Dad hesitates for a moment, and it makes me a little nervous. "You're doing a great job with the team. Last night's game was tough, but you played well. I'm so proud of you."

My breath hitches as pride swells through me. "Thank you," I say, and he hangs up.

Did that just happen? I drag my hands over my face, rubbing my tired eyes. I should have slept on the plane instead of listening to my audiobook, but once Mirabelle said she was going to listen to it too, I knew I couldn't put it down.

"So, who do you think the serial killer is?" I ask Mirabelle, needing to talk about anything but my dad right now.

Mirabelle smiles, shaking her head. "Obviously it's the boyfriend."

"You think?" I ask, standing up.

"Obviously it's not the dad because he's in prison for the murders twenty years before. It makes sense if the boyfriend is the copycat because I think he started dating her to try to get a better insight into the dad's mind from the original killings," she explains, and I had the same theory.

"I thought so too," I say, walking toward my walk-in closet and bathroom on the other end of the room. "I'm going to hop in the shower quick, then I'm going back to get Andrew. Want to come with?"

"I would, but Stacey is going to call me soon to go over something she asked me to look into earlier. I'll be here when you get back, though. Unless Stacey asks me to do something else, I should be good to log off after our call."

"Okay," I say, grabbing clothes to change into.

I'm halfway through showering when I realize I never asked about the locked door. "Hey, Mira?" I call out, lathering my arms with soap. The lower half of the shower wall is tiled, extending up to my upper stomach before changing to glass paneling.

"What?" she calls back.

"Can you come here?"

"While you're in the shower?" she asks, her voice climbing in pitch like it does when she's flustered. I think it's cute because she already saw me naked last night, and Mirabelle didn't seem flustered when she wanted to watch me lose control.

Fuck, I can't think about last night right now.

Mirabelle walks in with her hands covering her eyes, and I can't help but smile. "Mira, you can't see anything unless you're wearing X-ray glasses," I tease and she pulls her hands down to glare at me.

"Yeah, well the parts of you that I can see are pretty damn distracting. Can't you put on like a shirt or something to cover up?" Mirabelle asks, her cheeks flaming as she waves her hand at my chest. "I mean, come on, Henry. It's unfair you're built like a Greek god. I feel like I need to write whoever your trainer is a thank you note."

"You want me to wear a shirt in the shower?" I ask, biting my lip to keep from grinning as Mirabelle covers her face again, groaning loudly. I think that's the best damn compliment I've ever received.

"Henry, just ask me whatever it is you want to ask me," she says, narrowing her eyes.

I choke back a laugh, stepping under the shower head to rinse off the soap. "Are you mad at me?" I ask, unsure of the best way to go about asking this. I probably should have thought more about that before asking her to come in here.

Mirabelle tilts her head in confusion. "No? Why do you think I'm mad at you?"

"You locked the handle and the deadbolt was flipped. Those are never normally locked, so I thought maybe you did it to passive aggressively let me know you were mad," I explain, wiping the water off my face before reaching for my conditioner.

And then her face pales, Mirabelle looking away quickly as if I can't already see it all over her face that something's wrong.

"Mirabelle, what happened?" I ask, trying not to let my brain run rampant, but the longer she stays silent, the more tense I become.

She hesitates, twisting her hands anxiously. "It's nothing, Henry. I thought there might have been someone in the backyard last night, but I'm pretty sure I imagined it. It just made me feel better to have everything locked up until you and Wilson were back. You know me, I have an overactive imagination," she jokes, trying to play it off as if this doesn't mean anything.

What the fuck?

"What?" I ask, the blood in my veins turning to ice. Mirabelle thought there was someone in the backyard while she was here by herself, and she said nothing about it? She's pretty sure she imagined it, but what if she didn't, and they broke in to hurt her? "Are you okay?"

I think I might be sick. God, the thought of someone hurting Mirabelle when I wasn't here to keep her safe makes me physically ill.

She's picking at her cuticles now, and I quickly dunk my head under the water to rinse out the conditioner, before grabbing my towel and wrapping it around my waist. Mirabelle tries to smile, but it doesn't reach her eyes. "It's fine. I'm pretty sure I imagined it. I looked, and there was nobody there." She shrugs, forcing a laugh.

"You thought there was someone there, *and you went to look?*"

"What is that supposed to mean?" Mirabelle asks, her eyes narrowing at me.

I thought I knew what fear felt like, but it's never felt like this for someone else. If there had been someone in the backyard, it would have been so easy for them to overpower her. "It means you're not supposed to go look if you think someone is trespassing. It means you're supposed to call someone, Mirabelle! Fuck, I know how strong you are, but you're also what? Five foot two at most? You're lucky if someone was actually there, they didn't—" My voice breaks, unable to voice it out loud.

"Who was I supposed to call? You? My uncle? Wilson? All of you were in Colorado, unless I dreamt the game I watched last night," Mirabelle exclaims, but her bottom lip is trembling. "I made sure the security alarm was set and everything was locked. There was no one there. It was fine, Henry."

"Mira, you call the police." I exhale sharply, holding my towel in one hand and dragging the other over the stubble on my jaw. She should have told me last night when I called her. I'm hurt she didn't, and I'm mad at myself for not knowing, despite the fact there was no way for me to know. "It's not *fine.* They never caught the person who set your family's house on fire, in case you forgot that."

Her jaw falls open, and I know I took it too far, but I need Mirabelle to take this seriously instead of trying to downplay it. "I'm very aware. For the record, I was on the phone with my brother when all of this happened. *Je ne suis pas une putain de gamine alors ne me traite pas comme tel.*[1]

She scoffs, turning on her heel to walk away. *Fuck! I'm not trying to fight with her, but I need her to listen to me.*

I grab my underwear and pants off the bathroom counter, quickly pulling them on so I'm not chasing after her with a towel wrapped around my waist. "Mirabelle," I call out and she ignores me, picking her things off the ground. "*Mon cœur,*" I say softer, and this time, Mirabelle stops.

She turns to look at me, her brown eyes glistening.

"*Tu n'es pas une enfant. Je suis désolé.*"[2] I mean it, too.

Mirabelle tilts her chin up. "You're acting like an asshole," she says. Her stubbornness, as infuriating as it is at times, is one of my favorite things about her.

"I am," I agree. I shouldn't have brought up her family's home.

"You're overreacting."

I scoff, shaking my head. "I'm not. This is serious," I say, slowly moving closer.

"Nothing happened."

"How do you know for sure there wasn't someone there?" I counter, and Mirabelle crosses her arms over her chest. "I'm not going to apologize for wanting you to be safe. You should have told me last night," I say, stopping in front of her. "I don't know what I would do if you weren't in my life. I'm sorry I made you feel like a child, but I'm not sorry for being upset about the possibility of someone hurting you while I wasn't here. I care about you, Mira. It would fucking wreck me if something happened to you."

Mirabelle's face crumples and she closes the gap between

---

1. I'm not a fucking child so don't treat me like one.
2. You're not a child. I'm sorry.

us to bury her face in my chest as I wrap my arms around her. Her tears hit my skin, striking me like daggers to the heart.

"You're being an asshole," she mumbles, and I run my fingers through her soft hair.

"I'm being an asshole."

"I care about you too," Mirabelle admits. "I'm glad you're back."

Yeah, me too.

CHAPTER THIRTY

Mirabelle

We went to a small local bar last night with Andrew and Wilson to play darts, and I wish we'd gone back there tonight instead of this trendy bar. It was easier to talk, and Henry was more relaxed. The guys on the team were excited they had a weekend off and Henry's birthday fell on Saturday night. Henry didn't want to kill the enthusiasm so he agreed we would all go out to celebrate.

Henry has his arm draped over the back of my chair as he and Wilson debate which past NFL team should have won the Super Bowl but didn't. I'm having fun people watching with my drink because I feel like I never get to see any of these guys outside of the stadium, and it's entertaining to watch them decide which girls to go up to.

Andrew nudges me with his elbow, his blue eyes dancing with amusement. "God, is this what you feel like living with them?" he asks, and I grin.

"Yes."

"I would think they spend enough time talking about football, they wouldn't want to do it at bars," he jokes, before nodding his head in Quinn's direction where he's chatting with a pretty girl. "Mackie has the right idea."

"You could go find a pretty girl to talk to," I say, and he gives me a perfectly slanted smile.

I know I'm in love with his best friend, but I'm also not blind. Andrew's nice to look at with his perfectly coiffed blond hair and striking eyes. Factoring in his height and charming smile, he's the total package if you're into blond men—which I'm not. I prefer dark hair and tattoos, but I can still appreciate Andrew's handsomeness. What is it about me that's doomed to spend all my time with men who look like they belong in a Calvin Klein advertisement? Actually, I wonder if Stacey would be on board with the guys on the team posing for a sexy calendar and donating the proceeds to charity?

I take a sip of my second vodka cranberry, feeling a happy buzz already.

"I'm already talking to a pretty girl."

Again, I can still be totally in love with Henry and be flattered that his hot best friend thinks I'm pretty. "You're sweet," I say, my cheeks flushing. Andrew leans closer to me to whisper in my ear, and my curiosity is piqued.

"I have a theory I want to test. Are you in?" he asks, leaning back with the same playful smile on his face.

I nod my head, interested to see where this is going to go, and Andrew stands up from his seat, drawing both Wilson and Henry's attention.

"Are you getting another round?" Henry asks and Andrew holds out his hand to me instead.

"Nope. I'm asking a pretty girl to dance with me. Mira, want to dance?" I blink in surprise at him, but he winks back at me. *What exactly is this theory of his?*

"Yeah, that definitely sounds more fun than debating the 1998 Cyclones and the 2007 Serpents," I say, standing up to slide out of my chair. Henry catches my wrist, stopping me.

"Que fais-tu?"[1] he asks, and I shrug, because I'm not sure what Andrew has up his sleeve.

"Je dance,"[2] I answer simply, leaning in to kiss his cheek. *"J'ai hâte de t'offrir ton cadeau."*[3]

"Qu'est-ce que c'est?"[4] Henry asks, raising his eyebrows, dropping my wrist.

"Viens me retrouver plus tard pour que je te le donne,"[5] I tease, winking at him. My plan is to bring the birthday boy to his knees figuratively, and be on mine literally. I guess that all depends on when—*or where*—he finds me.

I take Andrew's hand, letting him lead me to the dance floor, and I'm keenly aware of Henry watching every move we make. His crystal eyes are sparkling mischievously, and I wonder if I should be worried. "So do I get to know your theory?"

Andrew spins me, the unexpectedness of it causing me to laugh. "While you're beautiful, you're also off-limits in more than one way, but I'm trying to see how long it takes Henry to come over here and interrupt. I figured he'd have a better reaction to me asking you to dance than Mackie," he explains, and Andrew rotates us to where I can see Quinn watching us too. "Do you know how to salsa?"

"I was a gymnast, not a dancer. I can follow if you lead, but Andrew, we're literally in the middle of a trendy bar, and this is the wrong music," I point out as he positions me how he needs me. "How do you know how to salsa?"

"Honestly? My high school football coach made all of us sign up for dance classes, and salsa sounded a lot more fun than ballet. I ended up losing my virginity to my dance partner

---

1. What are you doing?
2. I'm dancing.
3. I'm excited to give you your present.
4. What is it?
5. Come find me later so I can give it to you.

after we won a competition," he says sheepishly, before slowly walking me through it.

"Don't look at our feet, but count in your head," Andrew instructs, moving us a little faster. "You're light on your feet."

"Had to be," I say, noting the faster we go, the easier it is to follow. "So what's your plan if he doesn't come over here and interrupt?"

"I think you seriously underestimate the effect you have on a room, Mirabelle," he says, pulling me closer as I relax and follow Andrew's lead.

I roll my eyes because that's ridiculous. "Okay, then explain your comment about Quinn. He's been talking to that girl all night," I point out, and Andrew twirls me, dipping me after.

"He has been talking to her, but he's been watching you all night. I would have put money on Mackie coming over to ask you to dance the second Henry got up to get you another drink. What did you tell him when he asked you out last week? I never did hear."

"How do you know about that?" I ask, my feet stumbling underneath me. I didn't even tell JJ about that, so how does Andrew know?

"Wilson told Henry about it," he says, and I had no idea Henry knew.

"He didn't say anything to me about it."

"Hence, my theory tonight." Andrew chuckles, but I can tell he's waiting for my answer.

"I told Quinn no." I wouldn't do that to Henry. My life would probably be a lot easier if I could.

He smiles again before looking to see who predictably appeared by our side. Henry has a smile painted on, but it sure doesn't reach his eyes. Oh fuck, I just thought we were going to mess with him, not piss him off on his birthday. "I was starting to wonder what was taking you so long," Andrew says. He's poking the bear—big time.

I choke on my laugh, shaking my head as Henry rolls his eyes. "Go find your own girlfriend, she's mine," Henry says, and instead of getting irritated he's going all caveman again after yesterday's argument, I feel like I'm the luckiest girl in the world.

"Thanks for the dance, Andrew," I say, leaning up to press my lips in a chaste kiss on Andrew's cheek.

He laughs, a booming sound from his chest. "I think I like you. I hope you're planning on sticking around," he says and I move closer to Henry, slipping my hand into the back pocket of his jeans.

"Not planning on going anywhere."

"Andrew, you can go somewhere else now. Literally anywhere but right here," Henry says and I'm trying not to read too much into this. He's jealous. I mean, I know he was jealous of Quinn, but to be jealous of his best friend? Maybe I'm just too far gone at this point, or Henry might actually have feelings for me. Is that insane to think?

I look up at Henry, beaming like a ray of fucking sunshine. "You're jealous," I tease, and Henry looks down at me, his eyes scanning my face before landing on my mouth.

"Damn straight I'm jealous," Henry grumbles, leaning down to kiss me. His hand slides up my neck to the curve of my jaw, the feeling of his touch forever imprinted on my soul. Henry brushes his thumb over my lower lip, and I hold my breath waiting to see what he does next. *I hope he kisses me.* "These are mine," he says, looking me in the eye so I can see how serious he is.

"Okay," I agree. I'd agree to anything Henry says right now. Actually, that's not much different from usual, but I feel a lot less argumentative.

"Mine to kiss, mine to touch, and mine to *fuck*."

Oh my god, thank you Andrew for testing your theory so I get to see this side of him. The expression on his face tells me this isn't Henry putting on an act for everyone else in the room. "Then I guess you better kiss me."

Henry doesn't need to be told twice, pressing his lips roughly to mine. This kiss is possessive and greedy, taking everything I have to give, and then more. I love him. I want more. Henry sucks my lower lip into his mouth and I moan quietly, feeling this kiss throughout my entire body. He pulls away, sliding his fingers through my hair. "You said something about a birthday present?" he asks, pressing another short kiss that isn't helping my brain function any better.

"Having a birthday party without the birthday boy makes this just a party," I say, trying to catch my breath.

"It's my birthday, and I'd rather be with you than talking to anyone here," Henry answers, and my heart explodes into fireworks inside my chest.

There's a wolf whistle near us and I turn to see Henry's teammate, Tyler, wagging his eyebrows at us. "Get a room, guys."

"That's the plan," Henry calls back, smirking at him, whereas Andrew gives me a thumbs up. *Don't read too much into this.*

"I think I like your friends," I add, following Henry back to the table.

"I think I like them better when they're not dancing with you."

I almost wish I'd had a third drink for extra courage before we left.

The tension in the air is thick as Henry tosses his keys onto the table by the door, and I swallow the lump in my throat.

But then he looks at me, and I forget all my anxiety about doing the right thing, saying the right thing, and whether *I* will be enough.

All of it disappears into thin air because Henry is looking at me like I'm the answer to his goddamn prayers.

We're a collision waiting to happen, staring at each other to see who is going to make the first move.

Keeping my eyes locked on Henry's, I move to undo the strap of my stiletto, but he shakes his head. "Keep them on, please," he says roughly.

"It's your birthday, whatever you want," I say, straightening.

I'm not sure who takes the first step, but the space between us shatters when we crash together. Henry's hands are all over me, refusing to leave a single part unmarked. My gold dress falls to the ground, leaving me in my white lace lingerie as I fumble with his shirt, trying to push it up so I can feel his skin pressed against mine in the best way.

"Unreal," Henry mumbles against my lips, as he grips my hip tightly.

"Take it off," I say, dragging my nails gently over the defined ridges of his abdomen. He's flawless. Henry's fucking perfect.

Henry pulls back and I hate the loss of his body against me, but the sight I'm rewarded with makes it a little more bearable. "So much better than through a screen," I say, chuckling as I step closer, resting my hands on him again. He inhales, placing his hands on my lower back to pull me flush against him again. I can feel how hard he is through his clothes, and I think this is better than I ever could have imagined.

"Way better," he agrees, his mouth turning upward as I run my hand over his chest decorated in ink before sliding both hands around the back of his neck.

"Happy birthday, Henry," I say, and his face softens.

"Thanks, *mon cœur*," Henry says, kissing me sweetly. It's slow, contradicting the rapid heart rate in my chest, but it feels right. It feels like we're getting to know each other differently than we have during any of the times we've kissed before. He pulls back, cupping my jaw, and I'm impressed by his control, because I'm ready to jump Henry's bones, or I guess, just one in particular.

His hazel eyes rove over my face, drinking me in like a fine wine, savoring every note. "Kiss me," I whisper, a quiet plea for more.

I can feel the calluses of his hand on my cheek, and my breathing is labored as I maintain some of the most intimate eye contact I've ever had. *"Je vais t'embrasser, mais je veux d'abord te regarder,"*[6] he says, and I melt. *Whatever he wants, that's what I agreed to.*

Henry presses his lips against my forehead, my temple, the tip of my nose. My eyes flutter shut, and he places featherlight kisses on both lids and along the curve of my jaw.

I twist my fingers into the dark hair at the nape of his neck, trying to hide how they're trembling with need, doing my best to hold still. My heart is betraying me, and I'd be shocked if Henry doesn't hear it.

And finally, fucking finally, I feel the ghost of his touch brush over my lips.

"Beautiful," Henry says, hovering. "Absolutely beautiful."

The next time our lips meet, his control snaps, kissing me. *Yes.* Controlled Henry is beyond hot, but unrestrained Henry? I'd let him do anything he wanted.

He slides his hands over my ass, smoothly lifting me as I hook my legs around his waist without skipping a beat, my heels digging into his back. I groan, opening my mouth to

---

6. I'll kiss you, but I want to look at you first.

Henry so his tongue strokes mine. *Oh my god.* Is this supposed to be as all-consuming as it feels? I pull away as he grips the back of my thighs, wanting to look at Henry.

Henry's pupils are dilated, his swollen lips glossy from kissing me, and I press my lips again to his cheek. "Let's go upstairs," I mumble, angling my head to kiss the sensitive skin of his throat.

"We don't have to do anything," he struggles to say, slowly moving toward the stairs. I give Henry a taste of his own medicine, nipping gently at the same spot.

God, is he stupid? I know we don't have to do anything, but I definitely want to.

"Henry?" I ask, dropping my head further down to kiss the beginnings of his tattoos on his shoulder.

He inhales raggedly, moving toward the stairs. "Yeah?"

"Shut up and let me give you your birthday present," I say, and Henry starts to take the steps two at a time. I smile, angling my head the right way to press my mouth against the spot where his jaw meets his neck.

We barely get his bedroom door shut behind us before Henry's lips are on mine, holding me against the door as he grinds his hips against my core in a way that makes my body sing for him.

Being with Henry feels like anything is possible. Everything feels like I'm falling in love all over again for the first time, and I can't get enough of it. It's extraordinary in the best way, and I don't know how anything less than forever could be enough.

He lowers me to the ground, bracing himself over me as we both breathe heavily. He cups my breast covered in detailed lace, his gaze filled with wonder. "Is this my present? You wearing this pretty little outfit for me?" he asks, his fingers toying with the underwire, and I smile. I considered wearing my old Wonder Woman costume, but after taking his fascination with my heels into consideration, I decided to save the outfit for the future in case I need to pull out the big guns as a bargaining chip.

"It's part of it," I admit, pressing a hand to his strong chest to move him backward. "Do you like it?"

"I fucking love it," he says, but I can practically see Henry's mind spinning until it explodes as I lower myself carefully to my knees.

I unbutton his jeans, never taking my eyes off his as I tug them down over his muscular thighs. God, he's a work of art. Every part of his body has been carefully honed for football, and it's a masterpiece. "Step," I instruct, taking the opportunity to be bold. As much as I enjoy Henry being in charge of these moments, I want to try this for the both of us. I want to make Henry feel as good as he makes me feel.

Henry lets me undress him, following every instruction until he stands in front of me in his birthday suit. His cock is fully erect, the head swollen and glistening with pre-cum as my mouth waters. *Holy shit, the camera didn't exaggerate his size the other night.* I grasp the base, pumping a few times as Henry bites his lower lip, watching me. It's hard, but the skin is soft as I drag my tongue along the vein underneath, a low groan rumbling from Henry as I close my mouth over the tip, swirling my tongue like it's my favorite flavor of lollipop.

I am so turned on having this control over Henry right now—even while I'm on my knees, it's electrifying.

"*Mirabelle,*" he hisses as I bob my head, taking him deeper into my mouth as my hand still wrapped around the length strokes in rhythm. It spurs me on further as my confidence grows, loving how the ecstasy on his face makes me feel. I suck until the need for air is greater than my desire to make Henry feel good, and I make use of the lubrication my spit provides as I take a moment to breathe.

"Does this feel good?"

Henry breathes out, a breathtaking grin forming. "Shit, *mon cœur* . . . anything you do feels good."

I feel the ache between my legs intensify, and I understand what Henry means when he says he enjoys making me feel good. "What do you like?" I ask, and Henry's jaw tightens.

"Spit in your hand—it'll help your hand move easier," he says, his eyes gleaming.

That'll be a first for me, but still, I do it, wrapping my hand around him again. *Henry's right; it is easier.* He wraps his hand around mine, tightening my grip before helping me get him off. I lean forward, capturing the sensitive head between my lips to suck as he inhales sharply. "Perfect. You're fucking perfect, Mira," Henry says, looking at me through half-lidded eyes, slowing our hands. I feel like I'm glowing from the inside out with the praise. "I wish you could see how pretty you look right now with your pretty lips wrapped around my cock looking like an angel in white."

I moan, rubbing my thighs together as I grab his thigh for stability so I don't collapse on the floor. I force more of him into my mouth than before, hitting the back of my throat, and his hips jerk, causing me to pull off, coughing.

"Shit, are you okay? I'm sorry," he apologizes as I blink back the tears that have formed in my eyes. Henry's touch is gentle, brushing my hair out of my face as I inhale a few ragged breaths.

"I'm fine. Sorry for choking," I say, feeling my cheeks warm with embarrassment.

Henry cups my face, shaking his head. "I don't care. Are you okay?"

I nod, smiling to reassure him. "I'm good. Actually, I have an idea . . ." I trail off, wondering how insane he's going to think I am for this. I resume stroking Henry, making sure I haven't made a complete disaster of this.

"What?"

"You said my lips were yours to fuck. I want you to fuck them," I say, forcing the words out of my mouth before I can second-guess myself. Henry's mouth falls open in disbelief.

"Are you sure?"

"Happy Birthday, Henry." I open my mouth, and Henry rests his hands on the back of my head, looking at me with so much tenderness, it makes my heart beat faster in my chest as he slowly enters my mouth. He's careful at first, trying to be gentle, but that's not what I want. I grip his thigh tightly, silently communicating as I look up at him that it's okay, as my other hand slips into my panties, feeling how drenched I am.

I'm prepared this time when he hits the back of my throat, moaning as I play with my clit. *This is incredible. Better than I thought it would be.* I close my mouth around him, moaning and Henry increases his pace, his fingers tightening in my hair. "Does it turn you on to have my cock in your mouth?" he asks, pushing and pulling my head to make himself feel good.

"You're taking it like such a good girl," Henry says through clenched teeth, his pace slowing to hold my head down, forcing past my gag reflex as my eyes water. He loosens his grip to massage my scalp, and I breathe in quickly through my nose as I hold the position. My jaw begins to ache, but I push it to the back of my mind as I squeeze his thigh, humming in ecstasy as I fuck myself with my fingers. "Are you okay to keep going?" he asks, and I moan my unintelligible response causing Henry to smile and wrap my hair around his fist.

There's control in relinquishing control.

"I wish you could see how fucking beautiful you look drooling all over my cock after asking so *nicely* if I'll fuck your sweet lips."

He's ruining me for anyone else, and he has no idea.

My fingers move faster, matching Henry's urgency as his hips jerk erratically while I chase my peak. I'm not sure if

Henry's still speaking or if I'm moaning that uncontrollably, but I don't dare close my eyes. I want to see everything.

"Mirabelle, I'm about to—" Henry tries to pull away, but instead, I pull him close to make him come in my mouth as his thighs shake under my touch before I let him go to fall apart myself. I come fast and hard, as Henry drops to the ground next to me, brushing my hair out of my face to press his lips to my forehead.

It feels almost perfect.

The only thing that would make this moment better, is if any of it were real.

CHAPTER THIRTY-ONE

Henry

I glance at the doors to the training room, waiting for Mirabelle to come storming through. I think she might actually try to kill me, but I don't think I care if it means she's safe.

I grunt in exertion as my muscles scream at me to listen while I bench press more weight than I probably should be doing midseason. Crosby eyes the weight skeptically. "Price, you sure you should be doing this much weight? I thought Coach said to go light today," he questions, helping me rack it as I sit up.

"He did, but it's fine. I'm done for the day, thanks for spotting me."

"No problem, man. Got your back any day," he says, passing me a towel that I throw over my shoulder. "Hey, isn't that your girl?" Crosby asks, pointing at the storming figure I have been expecting any minute for the last half hour. She had meetings all morning, and I knew she wouldn't have a chance to speak her mind until now.

"Yeah."

"She looks mad."

And then I see the shadow I hired indefinitely behind her. *Good*. Sam said Tom would be able to keep up with her.

"Mira's fine," I say, but now that I can see the rage on her face, I'm a little worried.

"Henry Joshua Price, please tell me you did not hire a guard to follow me around without talking to me first!" she shouts, causing some of the other guys to shake their heads at me while a few others who know her father turn away to laugh.

"No," I answer. "I hired ex-military."

I got in touch with Sam, the bodyguard her parents hired after the Olympics, to explain the situation with her parents' house and that she thought someone was in our backyard, to see if he thought I was overreacting. It made me feel better when he told me I'd done the right thing by reaching out to him, but he was currently working with pop star, Scarlett Ashford. He called in a favor to give me the name of a friend he had served with during his time in the Army who he thought might be a good fit. Sam also wished me luck, after warning me Mirabelle wouldn't be happy about this—as if I hadn't already considered that.

"You have no right," Mirabelle says, stopping to look down at me. Tom lingers a few feet away, dressed casually to avoid drawing attention to himself, but nice enough to still look like he belongs.

I rest my elbows on my knees, trying to keep from escalating the situation. "He's here to look out for you. There's no harm in it."

"*I—he—you—*" She scrambles to find the right words, and I think I've broken her. Mirabelle inhales, pressing her fingers to her temples before speaking a full sentence. "I'm so fucking mad at you."

I can't help it. I smile.

Mirabelle narrows her eyes at me. "Why are you smiling? This isn't funny."

"It kinda is. You look cute," I say, and Mira looks behind me at Crosby.

"Do you think this is funny?" she asks him, and I can only imagine the look on his face.

"Well, ma'am, I don't know the situation so I'm afraid I can't answer whether it's funny or not," he answers, sounding more professional than I've ever heard him. I turn back to him, raising my eyebrows.

"*Ma'am?* You're weak. You can go up against three-hundred-pound men charging at you, but she scares you?" I ask, the words slipping out of my mouth. Actually, maybe I shouldn't have just said that.

It feels like I have a gun trained at my head when I look at Mirabelle again, her expression has changed into one I can't read. "No, Henry, you're right. I'm not scary at all." She leans down to press her lips against my cheek, and it feels like a kiss of death. "He's fine for today, but get rid of him, Henry. *Je te verrai plus tard.*"[1]

I take it back.

I'm scared of her.

Mirabelle walks off, ignoring the bodyguard who is following behind her.

Crosby shakes his head at me, laughing. "You're a dead man fucking walking if you think she isn't scary."

I got a call from Sebastian earlier, saying that he and Thalia were coming into town this afternoon to meet with the builders at their house, and they want to see us after. We're

---

1. I'll see you later.

supposed to get dinner at Mira's favorite restaurant. I sent her a text earlier, but I never heard back. I haven't seen Mirabelle either since she came into the weight room to put the fear of God into me. She succeeded too. Wilson's car isn't in the driveway, so I guess he'll be spared the argument we're probably about to have. Lucky him.

Bracing myself for the wildfire that's surely going to incinerate me, I walk in the door, surprised not to hear a single sound from inside the calm house. That's not an encouraging sign.

All the lights are on, and I set my things next to the door, punching in the alarm code to disable it. My cleaners came today, so the place is spotless—coincidentally, great timing with the Walkers coming. The back door is open, and the string lights around the patio and pool area are on.

Maybe she's out there?

"Mirabelle?" I call out, fear starting to creep in. Where is Tom?

"I'm here, you don't need to yell," she says from behind me, and my jaw hits the floor. Her blonde hair falls in waves over her shoulders and down her back, over the jersey I immediately recognize as mine. Mirabelle's long legs are on display, and I'm not sure where to look. "Excuse me," Mirabelle says, tapping my arm for me to move. I think my jaw is broken because I'm incapable of picking it up off the floor.

She's a walking dream.

I stumble out of the doorway, letting her walk past me, my eyes lingering on my last name across her back. I have never craved anyone the way I crave Mirabelle. The night of my birthday has been stuck on a loop in my head, the image of Mirabelle choking herself on my cock as she stared up at me with trust shining in her eyes, wearing tiny lace scraps as she had her fingers buried in her panties. It was entirely worth the shit I caught from Wilson and Andrew for leaving some of our clothes in the hallway, but this image is definitely being added to that loop.

"Is that my jersey?" I choke out, knowing damn well it is.

She looks back at me as she nears the edge of the pool. "Sorry, you can have it back."

And then in one smooth motion, Mirabelle pulls off the jersey, dropping it in a pile on the ground as she dives into the heated pool, wearing nothing else.

"Fucking hell," I curse under my breath, nearly tripping over my own feet as I pull my own clothes off to eagerly join her.

The warm water feels amazing on my sore muscles, and I take a few purposeful strokes toward Mirabelle as she treads water in the deep end. She skirts away playfully, staying out of my reach. *She's going to be the death of me.* "Sorry, I'm swimming right now." Mirabelle smiles at me, and the dots connect in my head.

"Is this because I hired Tom?"

She disappears under the water, only to pop up further away from me in the shallower end of the pool. "Did you tell him not to come back tomorrow?"

A short, incredulous laugh escapes me. "No. He's for your own good." *Tom being with her gives me the peace of mind I need to know she's okay.*

"Oh? Then why didn't you talk to me about it before you did it?" she counters, and I move to where I'm within arms reach of touching her because I can't stay away. *Now that I know what it's like to be her person—to be the person Mirabelle Walker looks at like I'm the most amazing thing she's ever seen —I'm powerless to resist her.*

"Because you wouldn't have listened to me about why you need him."

Mirabelle raises an eyebrow. "You overstepped, Henry. You should have talked to me first."

I look at her knowingly. "Would you have said yes if I'd talked to you first?"

"I don't know, but at least I would have had a choice in the matter of who was going to be my shadow."

Women hurt my brain. So, if I'm following, she's not mad I hired Tom, it's that I didn't ask her?

"Tom's there to help keep an eye out for you. Mirabelle, you're a public figure, whether you like it or not, and I worry that something might happen. If you want me to look for someone else so you can help pick, then we can find someone else. My first call was to Sam so that you would have someone you were already comfortable with, but he wasn't available. Tom is who Sam recommended because he agreed you might be in danger, but if you want someone else, we'll get someone else."

She trails her fingers through the water, contemplating what I'm offering. "Tom is fine," she finally says, tilting her head.

I creep closer to her, resisting the urge to smile because maybe that means I'm not totally in the doghouse. "So you aren't mad?"

"I didn't say that," Mirabelle says, her dark eyes twinkling under the lights.

The rippling water is distorting the curves of her body that I'm desperate to hold.

"How can I make it better?" I ask, only a foot away from her now.

Mirabelle bites her bottom lip as she thinks about it, but all I can think about is biting that damn lip myself. I stop, mere inches separating us as a flush starts to creep up her neck. She can pretend to be unbothered all she wants, but her body betrays her every time. She reaches out, gingerly tracing the ink on my arm, and Mirabelle's touch burns, the feeling branded into my skin like another tattoo. I let her touch me, my cock painfully hard as I hold still, letting Mirabelle explore, dancing over the patterns leading to the back of my bicep. "What does this one mean? I've always wanted to know."

"The story of Icarus is a reminder of maintaining harmony between freedom and hubris, because if you fly too high to the sun, you can lose everything in the blink of an eye. I guess I probably should have kept that in mind while biding my time, or we wouldn't be in this fake relationship trying to revive my career."

The false truth lingers in the air as her eyes slide to meet mine, but neither of us corrects it.

Mirabelle leans forward, reaching up to rest her hands around my neck, silently communicating what she wants as she parts her lips. I lean down, taking the invitation to kiss her as Mirabelle pulls herself up to wrap her legs around my waist.

Fuck, yes.

Her hands roam over my shoulders, up into my hair, pulling on the short strands as I blindly move until I have her pinned against the side of the pool. The water sloshes between us as Mirabelle rolls her hips, grinding her core against my erection trapped between us.

I wrap my free hand around her wet hair, forcing her head back to expose her neck as a breathy moan fills the air around us. "Mirabelle," I whisper her beautiful name against her skin.

Her nails dig into my shoulders as I press my hips against hers, the slight sting of pain feeling like nothing compared to the utter agony I'm in, using every ounce of my strength to not drive into Mirabelle. I refuse to let our first time be in a pool. I want her spread out in front of me, a whimpering mess before I make love to her in a way that will make Mirabelle forget any man before me. "H-Henry, *fuck*." Mirabelle moans my name like a prayer, and I abandon the spot on her neck that makes her gasp to fuse our mouths together again.

She smiles against my lips, somehow reaching between us

to wrap her hand around my cock, applying pressure the same way I showed her the other night. Her thumb rubs over the sensitive head, causing me to bite down on her lip as my body jerks at the jolt of pleasure.

This woman drives me absolutely crazy.

I pull back, an apology already on the tip of my tongue as Mirabelle grins at me, pressing a hand to her mouth. "You bit me," Mirabelle says in disbelief. "Is it bleeding?"

Oh shit, her phobia of blood. I untangle my hand from her hair, gently moving her hand away to see a small split in her lip, but it's not bleeding. I exhale a shaky breath of relief. "No, it's not bleeding. I'm sorry, are you okay?" I ask, feeling a little embarrassed by how quickly I got lost in the moment.

Mirabelle laughs. "I'm fine, just surprised."

I smile, trying to recover by leaning down to press a sweet kiss to her lips, much different from the passionate ones.

"Do you trust me?" I ask, looking Mirabelle in the eyes. Her face lights up in curiosity, and she nods slowly.

"Of course I trust you."

"Will you sit up here for me?" I ask, patting the concrete on both sides of Mirabelle, and her cheeks immediately flush red under the glow of the lights.

"Henry, I'm naked."

I smile, highly aware of that detail. "I know. You were wearing my jersey before you took it off." I'm drunk off kissing her that I'm not thinking rationally, blinded by Mirabelle and the way she makes my heart race in my chest. "Do you trust me, *mon cœur*?" I repeat, desperate to taste her on my tongue.

Mirabelle's gaze is unwavering, despite the flush to her cheeks as she pushes herself up and onto the edge of the pool, exposing her beautiful curves to me. "Don't look at me like that," she says, a nervous laugh escaping from her mouth.

"Look at you like what?" I ask, resting my hand on her knee, rubbing my thumb back and forth reassuringly. There's a small indent and I press a kiss to the scar, causing her to smile.

"You know exactly what you're looking at me like."

I nudge her legs apart easily, stepping between them, causing Mirabelle to inhale a sharp breath. Kissing the insides of her thighs, I work my way up slowly, listening in case she asks me to stop.

I glance up at Mirabelle before I reach the point of no return, because once I get a taste of her, I'm not stopping until she comes on my face, crossing those bonus points off on her list. "Is this okay?" I ask, watching as she nods her head, biting her lip in anticipation. "I need to hear you say it, Mira."

"Yes, please."

My next move has Mirabelle twisting her hands in my hair, gasping in that way that tells me exactly how much she likes it when I drag my tongue up her core. I listen for the sounds she makes as I suck and lick greedily, discerning what Mirabelle likes and what she doesn't based on the way her legs start to shake and how tightly she grips my hair. I fucking love eating pussy, and the sounds she's making are as addicting as she tastes.

"Yes, fuck, *Henry*," she chants as I suck her bundle of nerves, holding my head closely as she moans.

I can tell Mirabelle's close based on the way she's starting to twist underneath me, her breathing labored. "Please, *more*," she says, and I hold her in place, gripping her shaking thighs tightly while I flick my tongue quickly over her clit as she cries out incoherently.

I continue eating Mirabelle out through her orgasm, feeling awfully pleased with myself when she shrieks, removing her hands from my head. "Oh my god!"

I lift my head up, licking my lips to look at my girl in confusion to see her hands are covering her chest, her eyes wide in horror. *What the hell is she looking at like that?* I turn and my heart fucking stops in my chest as she slides into the pool, going under the water before I can react. It's Wilson and her parents standing in the open French doors. *Oh fuck.* I forgot Mirabelle's parents were coming over, and I'm pretty sure they just saw me give their daughter an orgasm.

Wilson coughs to keep from laughing, quickly redirecting her horrified parents into the house.

I'm dead. They're actually going to murder me.

Mirabelle's head pokes up from the water, hiding behind me. "What are they doing here?" she whispers frantically, her face flushed.

"I, uh . . . *um* . . . talked to them earlier? Bash said they were in town this afternoon to meet with the builders and they want to take us to dinner after," I say, and she shoves my chest.

"You knew my parents were coming, and you didn't tell me? What the fuck, Henry?"

I splash water on my face. "I know, I'm sorry. I sent you a text, but I forgot all about it when I saw you in my jersey, and then my brain was obviously elsewhere."

"You never sent me a text. Holy shit, I can't go in there," Mirabelle says, shaking her head. "Henry, they saw you . . . you know!"

"Mira, we have to."

Her face twists into a glare. "No. *You* have to. Go get some towels."

"But I'm naked too," I protest, and the look she gives me is kinda scary. "I'll get some towels," I offer.

"Good idea."

Oh, I am such a dead man.

Whether it's by the hand of Sebastian, Thalia, or their daughter, I don't think I'm making it through this night unscathed.

CHAPTER THIRTY-TWO

Mirabelle

I should be celebrating I was able to have an orgasm during oral sex, but instead, I'm contemplating the best way to kill Henry fucking Price. I could strangle him, or maybe slowly poison him. Wait—I know. I'll drown him in the fucking pool.

I cannot believe he didn't tell me my parents were coming. I checked my phone, and I didn't have any texts from Henry about my parents. After Henry checked his, he realized he typed the message, but never sent it. I run a brush through my freshly blow-dried hair as I fix the collar of my turtleneck. There's a knock on the door, and Henry steps in with an anxious expression on his face. "Can you please come downstairs? It's really awkward with your parents."

I give him an unamused look, not feeling bad in the slightest. "At least they didn't see *you* having an orgasm. You should have thought about that before you didn't tell me they were coming. I'll be down in a few minutes."

"Can I hide up here with you until then? *Please?*" he asks, sitting on my bed.

"You're twenty-six, Henry. Sometimes we have to face the

consequences of our actions, and this is yours. You can't just leave them down there with Wilson."

I honestly don't have much left to do other than swipe some mascara on my eyelashes, but I'm enjoying seeing him squirm. I'm also dreading going downstairs with my parents.

However, this is his fault.

"*Mon cœur*," Henry says, trying to sweeten me with his pet name.

"Nope, you better go down there before they think we're continuing what you started in the pool."

"I'm pretty sure you started that."

My jaw drops. He's not wrong, but it wasn't my idea for me to sit on the edge of the pool. "No, I was going for a swim. Nobody said you had to join me. *Out*, Henry."

Henry looks like he wants to put up just a little bit more of a fight, but I think he knows he has no ground to stand on here. His shoulders drop, and he moves slowly toward the door like it's his death march.

Actually, it could very well be.

I look in the mirror, noting my lip is still swollen from when Henry bit me earlier. I touch it gently, grateful it isn't bleeding.

I stall as long as I can, but truthfully, I'm excited to see my parents. I'm just not thrilled they saw more than they should have.

I slip into my boots to head downstairs, wondering if this is how Henry felt.

I make eye contact with Henry first, noting his relief that I'm finally down here. Mom smiles at me, standing to hug me. "Hi, Mira."

I have a hard time making eye contact with my dad. I'm a little worried he's going to say something. Instead, he steps forward to hug me tightly, without saying anything at all. I let out a breath I didn't realize I was holding, relieved he didn't start yelling.

Honestly, I don't think I would blame them if either of my parents did start yelling. They're being supportive of what they believe is a relationship, but that doesn't mean they need to catch us in the act.

Dad pulls back, ruffling my hair with a smile. "Are you ready to go?"

"Yep. One car or two?" I ask, trying to act like my parents didn't just see me naked a half hour ago. Shit, no wonder Henry was trying to hide in my room. They're being nice, but I feel awkward as fuck.

Two cars would give Henry a short reprieve since he's been entertaining them or whatever he's been doing while I was getting ready.

"How about one car? It'll give us a chance to catch up," Mom suggests, looping her arm with Dad's.

Henry's eyes widen in my direction, and I stifle a laugh. He could be a little less obvious about how nervous he is.

"Perfect."

My parents sit in the front seat of their car, while Henry and I sit in the back. Henry taps his fingers rapidly on his knee, the only sign that he's nervous about any of this. I reach over, threading our hands together. He offers me a faint smile as my parents chat about the family trip to France we're taking for Christmas, where we'll also celebrate JJ's birthday.

I'm doing Thanksgiving in New York with Henry's family, as well as my aunt and uncle, since we'll be there for the Panthers game against the Stars.

Henry doesn't let go of my hand until we're seated at a table in the back of my favorite restaurant, and Mom orders a bottle of wine.

"So are you two attending the charity gala together?" Mom asks, her smile meeting her bright green eyes.

"Yes," Henry answers, resting his hand on my knee underneath the table.

Emily designed my dress herself. It's a sleeveless ivory A-line evening gown with fringe sequins and crystal embellishments, but my favorite part is the dramatic slit in the skirt that will show off my Louboutin heels. I'm excited to dress up, but I'm even more excited to see Henry in a tuxedo.

That is of course if he lives long enough to wear his tuxedo again.

"I think we're all sitting at the same table together if I'm remembering the seating chart correctly," I say, taking a sip of my glass of wine.

"Owen and Blake will be there too," Dad says, eyeing the glass in my hand, and I smile at him as he takes a sip of his own.

"I would assume he'd be there as the head coach of the team," I say, and Mom chuckles.

Dad sets his glass down as Henry takes a drink of his water. "I'm sure as your uncle, he'd also be willing to help me hide a body if I told him what we walked in on earlier."

My jaw drops as Henry chokes.

Mom gives him a look of annoyance. "Like you've never gotten yourself into trouble in a pool before. Leave them alone."

"Love, that was *so* long ago. Why do you have to bring it up?" he complains, and if I didn't want to plug my ears so I didn't have to hear another word of this conversation, I'd probably ask what Mom's talking about.

"I'm only saying at least they're together," she says amused while Henry continues coughing into his elbow to dislodge the water he's still choking on. I don't think my face will ever turn a different color than bright red again.

"This is not about *that*," Dad says. Actually, maybe I do want to ask a question. "I'm just—"

"Bash, this conversation can wait until we at least eat our appetizers," Mom interrupts, and I'm not sure Henry is even breathing. This is going to be the longest dinner of my life if Henry isn't going to say more than one word at a time.

I take a longer than appropriate drink of my wine, wishing the effects were immediate as Mom raises her eyebrows. I clear my throat, looking both my parents in the eyes. "Well, we might as well get whatever conversation Dad wants to have over with so we can move on from it. Dad, you guys saw me and Henry, and I'm sincerely sorry you saw that. Someone— *and by someone, I mean Henry*—forgot to tell me you guys were coming. I wish I could promise it's not going to happen again, but I think the only way I can guarantee that is if you give both of us a heads-up if you're coming to visit. Is that it?"

Henry gapes next to me, stunned by my bluntness.

"For fuck's sake, you are your mother's daughter," Dad says, dragging his hands over his face.

"And what exactly is that supposed to mean, Sebastian?" she asks, and I have to hand it to him, Dad's fast at thinking on his feet. I guess that's what two decades of marriage can teach you. He smiles at her, tucking a piece of her hair behind her ear.

"That she approaches awkward situations the exact same way you do, love: *straight forward.*"

My heart swells as I see my mother melt into my father's touch. "Nice save," she murmurs, and it's moments like this that are to blame for my brothers and me being hopeless romantics. Dad clears his throat, as if remembering we're in public.

"What I wanted to say was that I hope you are being . . . careful." He looks like he'd rather die than talk about this, and honestly, me too.

Mom rolls her eyes, shaking her head at him. "What Bash is trying to say, is please make sure you're using birth control. I don't think either of you are in a position where you're ready for a child, and there are means to prevent that, so use them. I'm too young to be a grandmother."

I manage a nod as Henry finally speaks, probably scarred from this entire evening. I'll be lucky if he ever dates me for real after tonight. "Yes, ma'am."

Mom smiles at both of us, and maybe there's a chance for us to have a normal evening. "Well now that we've gotten that out of the way, I want to hear everything."

"Maybe not everything," Dad mutters under his breath.

My parents left an hour ago, and I tried to lie down because I'm exhausted, but I kept tossing and turning, unable to get my mind to shut off.

I think I'm in way over my head with Henry, and I keep replaying everything that has happened between us.

He looks at me differently than he did a few months ago. He hired a fucking bodyguard for me after telling me how it would wreck him if something happened to me. It's that he literally calls me his heart instead of a generic pet name like babe or baby. Henry could have picked anything other than a French endearment, but that's what he went with.

The math isn't mathing anymore, but maybe I'm confusing the difference between lust and love.

I drag my hands over my face, throwing the covers off me. I snag a sweatshirt to pull over my shirt before quietly escaping my room. I don't feel like opening a new bottle of wine, so I snag one of Wilson's beers, popping the top off before going out to sit by the scene of tonight's crime.

Taking a swig of my beer, I sit down in one of the lounge chairs by the pool, curling my legs underneath me.

Maybe I'm just imagining everything, trying to see what I

want to see because I'm in love with Henry and want him to love me back more than anything.

I don't know what the hell I'm doing.

Maybe JJ's right. I need to grow a pair and just tell him. For all I know, he could feel the same and be afraid to tell me, but at the very least, I would finally have an answer.

I take a long drink of the beer, and it's gross, but better than nothing.

"There you are. What are you doing out here?" Henry's voice asks from behind me, causing my head to turn.

"Couldn't sleep, so I came out here to think. Were you looking for me?" I ask, feeling a little nauseous at the way my heart skips a beat.

"Yeah, I just . . ." Henry pauses, his cheeks flushing. "I don't know. What are you thinking about?" he asks, clearly deflecting.

"Something I probably need to talk to you about."

Am I finally doing this? Shit, maybe being blissfully ignorant is better than knowing.

His face shifts to one of concern as he takes a seat on the edge of the chaise. "What's up?"

I stall, taking another drink, the bitter taste getting better with every sip before setting it down on the ground. "Actually, never mind. It isn't important, Henry," I say, forcing a laugh to play it off, but he isn't buying it. *Shit, why did I open my mouth?*

"If it's something you think you need to talk to me about, then it is important. I'm listening," he says, offering me a smile that only further jumbles the words in my brain. The woodsy scent of his soap isn't helping me think rationally, either.

I stand up, needing to move and give myself a little space because I can't think straight around him. I shake my head, turning away because this is hard—*harder than I thought it would be.* I am so frustrated because, somehow, I can boldly speak my mind to everyone, except when it comes to Henry. I hate this because I'm not a coward, but what is it about admitting to Henry that I have feelings for him that fucking terrifies me? *Well, maybe it's because there might never be someone else I'll love the same way as Henry if he rejects me, and loving Henry is as natural for me as breathing oxygen.* I'm not ready to find out what it feels like to cut off my oxygen supply. I want to stay in the bubble.

"Thanks, but it's stupid, I promise. Please, just forget I said anything," I mumble, my mind racing as I try to think of a way out of this. It's better to exist in my fantasy world where I have a chance with Henry than to take away my dream of living happily ever after with him.

"Mirabelle."

But what if he returns my feelings? I can do it. I can be honest with him.

I turn around to face him, my heartbeat echoing in my ears. "Fine. I like you, okay?"

Henry's eyes widen in surprise, and he just fucking stares at me. *Please say something. Please say you like me too. Please say anything.* My heart drops as I stare back at him while he stays silent.

Oh my god. I've ruined everything.

"It's fine, Henry. It's just a stupid crush," I say, feeling the age difference between us for the first time. At least I didn't tell him that I love him.

"Mira . . ." he trails off, scratching the back of his neck. This isn't how I pictured this at all. "I don't . . ." Henry blinks, staring at me.

I can feel tears threatening to fall, and I blink rapidly, fighting them back. "I get it. You don't feel the same. Please forget I said anything."

Henry stands up, taking steps to close the distance between us. "Wait—" Henry reaches his hand out toward me, and I push it away as my feet twist under me, falling straight into the pool. It takes me a second to register that I've fallen in the pool, but once I do, I surface, sputtering to get rid of the water that went up my nose.

A hand rests on my shoulder, and I wipe the water out of my eyes, seeing Henry jumped in after me. I shrug away from his touch because, for the first time ever, I don't want it.

"Are you okay?"

Am I okay? No, I'm not fucking okay. "I'm fine, Henry. I don't want to be like everyone else in your life that wants something from you. Just go away, *please.*"

"Hey, don't do that. I know it's not like that with you, and I've never felt that way. We're friends, I know you."

I've. Never. Felt. That. Way.

My clothes are sopping wet as I pull myself out of the pool, and the words cut into my soul in a way I don't think I'll ever heal from. *Henry says we're friends, but are we?* My temper explodes, scattering the broken pieces of my heart. "Then what has it felt like to you? Because it didn't feel like we were friends when you went all caveman on your best friend while I was dancing with him the other night, or when you told me that my lips were yours to touch, to kiss, and to fuck? What about when you stood in my doorway, calling me *incandescent* while asking me to let you help me feel more confident during sex? What about the time you got up from your seat on the plane in front of your entire team so Quinn couldn't sit with me? Or when you look at me like I am everything to you? So tell me, Henry. What the fuck has it felt like to you?"

Henry shakes his head, staring up at me. "I don't know. I'm sorry."

That's all he's going to say right now? *I don't know? I'm sorry?* I bite the inside of my cheek hard, trying to reign in the hurricane of emotions swirling inside me. "I don't need you to apologize for not feeling the same."

I really thought . . .

A tear escapes, slipping down my cheek, but it blends in with the rest of my drowned rat look I'm rocking after my little trip to the pool.

Henry moves to climb out of the pool, combing his wet hair out of his face. "Mirabelle, that's not . . ."

"That's not what?" I ask, unable to keep the sharp edge out of my voice. He falls silent, water dripping from his clothes that cling to his body as he stops a few feet away from me. "Actually, please just forget I said anything at all. Like I said, it's not important."

"It is important, I just . . . I don't know," he repeats, and I think I hate those three words more than I hate the word obviously.

"I get it. You don't know. Why don't you let me know when you do know something."

I turn on my heel, stomping inside to retreat to my room, where I should have stayed in tonight, wondering how everything could have gone so wrong.

CHAPTER THIRTY-THREE

Henry

I FUCKED UP. I KNOW IT, AND I'VE SPENT THE LAST two weeks paying for it too. I'm impressed by how successful Mirabelle's been at avoiding me, taking full advantage of the team having last weekend off for our bye week to fly out and see JJ. She's ensured that anytime she's standing close enough for me to talk to her, there are enough people in the room that we can't speak freely without everyone knowing the truth about our relationship.

On the bright side, my image has never looked better.

Too bad I feel like an asshole.

I could have said anything other than "I don't know," but I froze. When I told Mirabelle it's never felt that way, I meant I've never felt she was using me to get something. I didn't mean that I've never felt that way toward her, because I have, and I do.

She caught me off guard, and I know I'm an idiot for not recognizing Mirabelle's feelings, as well as my own.

I've been denying my feelings for Mirabelle since the first time she kissed me, if not longer. She's everything I never let myself consider, because I think I knew that I'd rather live my entire life seeing her as a friend, than have to pretend I don't know what it's like to have those intimate moments with her.

To make matters worse, Quinn and Wilson have been bugging me about Mirabelle's mood, and I'm this close to snapping at them to mind their own damn business.

I hear the familiar click of Mirabelle's heels behind me. *"Allons-y."*[1]

I turn my phone off, forgetting about Stacey's email I was looking at, to follow her. I should be happy Mirabelle's my shadow again today, because it means I get to be near her, but I hate the spark missing in her. Mirabelle shines brightly in a room regardless of who is around her, but it's her spark that's infectious.

Tom is hovering a few feet away and I'm glad that as upset as Mirabelle is with me, she didn't fire him to prove a point.

"I didn't think you were going to be with me today," I say, trying to start a conversation.

"I didn't want to, but Stacey is busy. I'm going as your fake girlfriend, and I'm supposed to be gathering information about the profile we're doing to see how you'll do in a test demographic without being tied to me," she says, and my shoulders stiffen at the idea of Mirabelle and me not being an us. "Is it a problem I'm going with you?"

Mirabelle's dark eyes watch me, and I shake my head. "It's not a problem, Mira. We're friends," I say, trying to keep the peace.

She quickly turns away from me, without saying anything, and Tom shakes his head at me behind her, telling me what I already know. That probably wasn't the right thing to say, and I lengthen my strides to catch up to her.

Unfortunately, before I can try to fix it, Quinn walks around the corner, his face lighting up when she smiles at him.

---

1. Let's go.

"Hey, Mira. You busy making Henry look a lot better than he actually is?" he teases, but my jaw clenches as my girl laughs. I can't even get her to look at me for more than a few seconds, but she can laugh and smile at Quinn?

"Unfortunately, yes," she says, and I refuse to let anything come out of my mouth. I know I lost that right when Mirabelle told me about her feelings, and I said nothing back.

"Are we still on for tonight?" Quinn asks, and my blood boils underneath my skin.

"Sorry to break this up, but I have somewhere to be, which means Mira does too."

Quinn startles, caught off guard by the harshness of my tone and Mirabelle shoots me a glare. "Sorry, I didn't mean to make you late for anything," he says, and I know I'm being a territorial asshole, but I don't care.

I need to go for a run. One long enough that I'm able to clear my head and come up with a plan to tell Mirabelle I have feelings for her. I can't stand not being on speaking terms.

We walk away, and Mirabelle's mumbling under her breath, low enough that I can't hear her. She's probably wishing I would go to hell, but I'm already there. I sigh, shoving my hands into my pockets as I keep pace with her.

She looks incredible today. Her red blouse is tucked into a black pencil skirt, highlighting her narrow waist, and I can see a hint of lace if I angle my head the right way—

"Seriously, Henry?"

My feet stumble underneath me as I quickly swivel my head to look anywhere but at her chest. "Fuck," I swear, catching my balance.

"I think what you should be saying is, What the fuck? But don't worry, I'll say it for you since the only thing you can say is 'I don't know'. What the fuck, Henry?" she demands, resting her hands on her hips. Tom chuckles in the background, because I'm about to get my ass handed to me. "Are you going to say anything?"

"I don't know what to say," I reply. "They're just right there, and I didn't mean to look, but maybe I kinda did?"

"Je ne sais même pas quoi te dire! Tu es incroyable."[2]

"Que veux tu que je te dise? Tu as de superbes seins?"[3]

I can feel all the blood drain from my face. I need someone to put me out of my misery, because I keep fucking up with her.

"Tu sais qui d'autre pense la même chose? Quinn,"[4] she responds, and my blood roars. Her smile disappears as quickly as it appears. "You just proved my fucking point. You don't want me, but you don't want anyone else to have me either. I'm only good enough for the fake girlfriend position, right?" Mirabelle hisses, and I definitely deserve that.

"That's not it," I say, forcing the words out.

Her mouth flattens, and she crosses her arms over her chest. "Then what?" If I tell her now, Mirabelle will think I'm only saying it because of Quinn. She won't believe me. She shakes her head. "Let me guess, you don't fucking know."

I open my mouth to protest, but she's already walking in the other direction like she owns the place.

Mirabelle's at Quinn's apartment.

A very, *very* selfish part of me wants to text her to ask how it's going, but I'd be torturing myself. I'll find out how it went based on when she gets home. *If she comes home tonight.*

---

2. I don't know even know what to say to you right now! You're unbelievable.
3. What do you want me to say? You have great tits?
4. You know who else thinks the same thing? Quinn.

I hope she comes home tonight.

I continue watching replays from last week's game, jotting down notes to build on what the coaches and I talked about in our meeting today. I figured I might as well be productive while I wait for her.

My phone rings on the table next to me, and I pick it up on the off chance that it's Mirabelle calling. To my surprise, it is.

"Hello?" I say, immediately answering the phone, unsure if she meant to call me or not.

"God, I love your voice," Mirabelle says, but I can barely hear her over all the noise in the background. I almost drop the phone in surprise. *The only way this would make sense is if—*

"Are you drunk?"

Mirabelle sighs, and I'm praying Tom is with her. "Maybe just a bit," she admits, slurring her words enough to worry me.

"Do you have Tom or Quinn with you?" I ask, shutting my laptop as I grab my jacket.

"It did not go well with Quinn. I left before dinner was even over. So I came here, and had a couple drinks."

Thank fuck it didn't go well with Quinn, but where exactly is here? Why didn't Tom wait until she came home to leave? Actually, never mind. Mirabelle was probably persuasive enough to convince him she'd be fine.

"Where are you?" I ask, slipping into my sneakers, snagging my keys. "Hello? Mira?"

"Henry?"

"Where are you? I'm coming to get you."

"You are?"

Climbing into my car, I exhale, trying to keep my voice soft in the hope Mirabelle will be more inclined to tell me so I can get her out of there. "*Mon cœur*, I can't if I don't know where you are," I say while pulling out of the garage, driving toward the gated exit of my neighborhood. *God, what the hell happened at Quinn's?*

It takes her a moment to respond, kicking me into overdrive. "I like when you call me that, but it's confusing if you don't mean it."

"I mean it," I say, my voice thick in my throat.

"I'm at the new club downtown. Tower something," Mirabelle says, and hearing she's less than ten minutes away is definitely the best-case scenario here.

"I'll be there soon. Wait for me, okay?"

"I've been waiting, but you didn't want me," she slurs, and there's a crash as the call drops. Did she drop her phone, or hang up on me? Both options are a possibility, but neither makes me worry less.

I hate that Mirabelle thinks I didn't want her. I do. I want everything with her. I want to call her mine, and make sure she knows I mean it.

I pull up to the curb, pulling cash out of my wallet as I cut past the line, heading straight for the bouncer. I see it in his face that he recognizes me, wordlessly taking the cash after quickly opening the door. I scan the crowd, looking for the familiar blonde who drives me *oh so fucking crazy*. It'd be helpful if I knew what she was wearing.

A horrifying thought creeps into my mind that she's passed out somewhere in the building, and I might not be able to find her.

The flashing lights are warping my vision, making it hard for me to see, but I'm not leaving until I find Mirabelle. Finally, I spot her dancing with her hands above her head, her eyes shut as she's lost in the music. I push through the crowd until I'm behind her as Mirabelle turns, her eyes widening before she throws herself into my chest. I catch her, wrapping my arms around her instinctively.

"You came," Mirabelle says, smiling at me in a manner she

hasn't since I messed everything up. Fuck, I'll spend the rest of my life making sure she doesn't ever question again whether I'll show up.

"Of course I came."

"I'm so sorry I had dinner with Quinn. I thought I could make myself like him, but he wasn't you. I don't know how I'm ever supposed to want someone else, but I wish I wasn't like this," Mirabelle rambles, and I smooth her hair.

"It's okay," I try to reassure her as I spot someone out of the corner of my eye shining a light at us. Are you fucking serious?

Mirabelle doesn't notice, shaking her head. "It was so dumb, but it felt nice to be wanted, even if it wasn't by you. I'm trying, but maybe I'm not meant to find a love like my parents have."

Yeah, we're definitely continuing this conversation when she's sober so I can clear up all of this to make sure there's no mistaking how badly I want her.

"Mira, you're drunk. I think we should get you home, okay?"

She looks at me, stepping out of my touch as strobe lights momentarily blind me. I shield my eyes, seeing the look of hurt on her face makes me want to do nothing more than pull Mirabelle back into my arms and kiss her senselessly so I can fix whatever it is that I just said wrong, but I'm not going to do that when she's drunk.

"I don't want to leave. I'm having a great time, Henry."

I would consider believing Mirabelle if she wasn't wobbling where she stands, looking like she's on the verge of throwing up. "How much have you had?" I ask, hoping that Mirabelle will give in this one time.

Mirabelle's face goes white, and she takes a step back, but I don't think she's going to get very far.

I make a decision before Mirabelle disappears into the

crowd, pulling her back to me, lifting her like she weighs nothing. "No. We're leaving," I insist, making the choice for her before she gets sick in front of all these people with cameras on their phones.

"Put me down." She shrieks during an unfortunate lull in the music and if people weren't looking at us before, they are now. We only have a matter of moments before they figure out who we are, if they haven't already.

I put my mouth next to Mirabelle's ear, speaking clearly so she can hear how serious I am as I set her on her feet, but I don't remove my hands from her. "No. You are underage and drunk out of your mind. There is no reason for you to stay unless you're looking to be tomorrow's headline. I will put you down if you want to walk, or I can carry you." I doubt she could even walk out by herself, but at least I'm giving her the option.

She nods as I spot flashes from the pictures being taken around us.

"Fuck, we need to get out of here. Are you walking or am I carrying you?" I ask, moving us further away as more people turn our direction.

"Carry me please."

I'm going to have to call Stacey to give her a heads up about this. She's going to fucking kill me, and probably Mirabelle.

Mirabelle sways as I turn her, keeping my face angled downward. "I need you to jump a little, and wrap your legs around my waist." She's ungraceful, but I'm able to adjust her quickly, securing Mirabelle in a better position that allows us to move more easily through the crowd. Mirabelle tucks her face into my chest, letting her hair hide her face like a curtain.

"Please don't throw up on me," I say, making Mirabelle snort.

"I'm not going to throw up on you."

CHAPTER THIRTY-FOUR

Mirabelle

I WAKE UP WITH A LOUD POUNDING IN MY HEAD. I move slowly to pull the blankets tighter around myself. *What the hell happened last night?*

The pieces quickly come back to me: Quinn, the club, calling Henry, Henry carrying me in front of paparazzi, Henry telling me we'd talk tomorrow when I'm sober—which I guess would be today now—after I begged him to sleep in my bed. *Awesome.* Talk about a night of bad choices. I wouldn't blame Henry if he wanted nothing to do with me after last night. I'm embarrassed because I think I proved everyone who had concerns about my age right, because I now look like the sad, drunk girl who didn't get what she wanted and threw a fit.

I drag my hands over my face, tempted to smother myself with the pillow.

A creak in the floor catches my attention, and I sit up far too quickly for my head to handle the spinning. I fumble for the lamp next to me, the burst of light momentarily blinding me.

"Henry?" I ask, my head pounding. *He stayed?* "What are you doing?"

He sits on the edge of the bed next to me, a kind smile on his face. "Sorry, I didn't mean to scare you. I have to go to the stadium, but I didn't want to leave without saying goodbye." His hand unfolds to show me the piece of paper in his hand.

What?

My mouth feels like I've stuck a piece of cotton in it. "You stayed last night?" I ask, torturing myself because I shouldn't be trying to convince myself Henry has feelings for me.

"Yeah. You asked," he says as if it's as simple as that.

Fuck, that makes me want to kiss him silly, but apparently I have a penchant for breaking my own heart. I laugh, closing my eyes as I flop back onto the pillows. "No, you can't say things like that when it's just us. It fucks with my head, and it's not good for me."

"Mira—"

"I'm sorry for throwing myself at you, and drunk calling you last night, but I'd like to be left alone right now."

"I was happy it didn't go well with Quinn last night. I know that makes me an asshole, but I've been trying to talk to you for two weeks now. So no, I'm not going to leave you alone, even if that's selfish, because you're clearly hungover. I'm going to take advantage of you not being able to run and hide," Henry says, and I hold my breath, refusing to look at him. "I needed a minute to process everything, and you misunderstood what I meant when I said it wasn't like that between us. I know you don't want anything from me. I have never felt like you were with me because you would gain something from it. If anything, I'm the one gaining something, and I hate that because I don't want you to ever feel like I'm using you."

"Why didn't you just say that?" I ask, slowly moving to sit against the headboard.

"Because I was still figuring everything out in my head that I already knew in my heart, as fucking cliché as it sounds.

Mirabelle, I can't give you an answer as to when my feelings for you changed, but I haven't pretended anything with you for a while. I might have thought I was, but I wasn't," Henry says, and I think I'm having a stroke.

"But you told me you were helping me for the next man by using you to practice."

He exhales, nodding. "I did say that, but I think I was lying to both of us. At the risk of being called a caveman again, I hate the idea of you being with anyone else. I was an ass yesterday, but I didn't tell you about my feelings so you wouldn't think I was only saying it because of Quinn. I was trying—and failing—to do the right thing."

Oh.

Actually . . . that kind of makes sense. As irritating as it is, it does make sense.

"So what does this mean?" I ask, needing to hear Henry spell this out for me.

Henry's lips curve upward at the corners. "I'd like to be your real boyfriend, *mon cœur*. I don't want anything to be fake. Is that what you want?" he asks, nervousness slipping into his voice.

Oh my god. This is all I've ever wanted.

Not even the elephant stomping in my head could keep me from smiling. "I would love to be your real girlfriend, Henry."

He stands up, leaning over to press a kiss to my forehead, and I almost pinch myself. *Is this real, or am I still drunk?* "I'm sorry, I wish I could stay, but I do have to go. Let me know if you need anything today, okay?"

"Thanks, Henry," I say, mustering a smile, and he smooths my hair out of my face. Henry smiles at me again, and despite the fact my hangover is going to make today a day from hell, knowing I get to be one of the few people to see that smile makes me feel like I'm floating on cloud nine.

It's only when I'm leaving for work that I realize Henry still managed to leave the note on my nightstand without my noticing.

~

The only thing that got me through the shitshow that was today was knowing Henry wanted to have dinner tonight.

We spent most of the day trying to spin the comment section of the posts from last night to do damage control, but thankfully, it didn't seem to hurt Henry's image at all.

I'm just pissed because I gave Miley more ammunition to use against me, making me seem like I'm a spoiled brat. But I have a feeling this will all blow over in the next day or so when something more interesting happens.

Stacey pulled me aside, ripping me a new one for how irresponsible I had been last night. She was right to ask what I was thinking because with Henry being tied to me and my name, I could have undone everything we've worked so hard to fix. It was stupid and irresponsible, but I promised her it wouldn't happen again. At least she had the courtesy not to do it in front of Miley and the other interns.

My PR team reached out today, surprisingly not because of last night, but to let me know that with the Olympic Qualifiers coming up, my name has come up in more than a few articles. I would have rather they had called me to let me know anything else.

I told them to continue with the statement, I'll be attending to support my old teammates, but I will not be competing.

I think it's pointless to hope I'll be able to stay out of the headlines during the Olympics, but that's all I can do for the time being. I know I should be flattered everyone wants me to compete again, but I can't go back to being a puppet.

I exhale, trying not to drag any of this shit inside with me as Tom's truck pulls out of the driveway, pausing at the end to ensure I actually go into the house. *I can't blame Tom after last night.* I wave at him, opening the door as the aroma from the kitchen immediately hits me.

I can hear Wilson laughing over the music coming from that direction, and some of the weight on my shoulders from the day disappears. I slip out of my heels, leaving them next to the door as I make my way toward the kitchen.

Henry and I are together.

If that can happen after all these years, then I have to believe that anything is possible.

I hover in the doorway as Henry uses the spatula to sing off-key into as Wilson doubles over. Henry sways his hips as he gently flips the salmon in the pan. For someone who can't dance, he sure can swing his hips. I want to whistle, but I'm curious how long it will take for them to notice me.

"Since I helped you cook this, do I at least get to eat some of it before I'm supposed to hide in my room for your date night?" Wilson asks, checking the pot on the back burner.

"You don't have to hide in your room, just maybe don't be in the same area as us so it feels like a date," Henry suggests, and Wilson snorts.

"Yeah, I'm still going to hide in my room. You and Mira have an aversion to being naked together in your rooms, and I'd prefer not to walk in on you again."

Yeah, I think I'd prefer that too.

Henry shakes his head. "Sorry."

"Whatever. I'm glad you finally pulled your head out of your ass and admitted your feelings for her. Anyone with eyes could see how bad you have it for Mirabelle, you've basically already been together for a couple months now."

I clear my throat, not wanting to hear anything else unless it's directly from Henry. They turn my direction, and Wilson smiles, turning off the burner. "Hey, perfect timing. Henry is almost done with dinner," he says, and I look at Henry, and everything else from today feels easier to deal with.

I can't help that my feet rush forward of their own accord, and then I'm wrapping my arms around his torso. Henry's strong arms close around me, and I feel him chuckle. "Well, hi there," he says, his voice sends shivers down my spine.

"Hi," I squeak out, holding tightly to *my boyfriend. This doesn't even feel real. I wish someone could have told my younger self not to give up on love.*

"You guys are gross," Wilson says, and my laughter mingles with Henry's. "Get a room."

"This is my house. All the rooms are mine," Henry retorts as I pull away, my cheeks warming because I definitely just threw myself at him, but Henry pulls me back into his side, resting his hand on my hip as he presses a kiss to the side of my head. "Happy you're home. I put a bottle of wine in the fridge I thought you would like," he whispers against my hair, and I feel my breath catch.

Home.

"Me too," I say honestly, smiling before twisting away to grab the bottle and two glasses.

"Can I just say—"

Henry cuts Wilson off as he removes the pan from the hot burner. "No, you can't."

I chuckle, pouring two glasses and Wilson gapes at him. "You don't even know what I was going to say."

"I've heard you talk enough today. I want to hear about Mira's day," Henry says, dishing out a portion for Wilson. "Wilson, please go away," he says, holding out the plate to him.

"But—"

"Wilson."

Wilson groans, taking the plate, but he winks at me on his

way out of the kitchen. I love that Henry's friends fuck with him. Sometimes he's a little too serious for his own good, and he makes it too easy for them.

Henry pushes the sleeves of his sweater up, and I take a drink of my wine. *Down, girl. They're just forearms.*

"So how was your day?" he asks, and I know he's being sweet, but my day is kind of the last thing I want to talk about.

"I'd rather hear about yours if that's okay? Is there something I can help you with?" I ask, setting the glass down to help him.

"I'm wining and dining you. I want you to relax, so just sit pretty with your wine," Henry says, sending a warm smile in my direction. *Goodness, I still can't believe he smiles at me like that.* "My day was good. My hamstring was a little tight so Veronica, my favorite of our trainers, tried to make me scream when she used the massage gun on it. I'm not sure whether I hate ice baths or the massage gun more."

"Definitely the massage gun." I shake my head, still vividly remembering how it hurt more than it helped.

"You're probably right about that."

"This smells amazing. Thank you for making dinner," I say, my mouth watering as Henry carries our plates to the kitchen table. I follow with the glasses and the wine as he pulls my chair out for me. *"Henry."*

His bright eyes focus on me and I can see the golden tinge around the irises. "What? Let me be a good boyfriend and push in your chair."

I slide into the seat, allowing him to push it in, but I twist my head to look up at him. "Thank you."

"You deserve everything, *mon cœur*." Henry leans down to press his mouth briefly against mine, before pulling away. He is the only person who can take a bad day and turn it into one worth remembering.

I want everything, but only if it's with him.

CHAPTER THIRTY-FIVE

Mirabelle

I TOUCH UP MY MASCARA CAREFULLY IN THE MIRROR as I call Emily so she can see the finished ensemble.

Her dark eyes widen immediately upon answering. "Goddamn, you look *good*. I knew that dress was perfect for you. Where are you off to?" she asks, knowing full well where I'm headed, especially since she sent me the dress.

"A gala," I answer, giggling as I swish the sequined fringes and crystal embellishments. *I love this dress.* Emily knows me perfectly; she's like my fairy godmother.

"Oh, and where is your prince?" Emily teases with a knowing smile. Things have been going so well with Henry.

"Finishing getting ready himself." It's either that, or he's waiting downstairs with Andrew and Wilson. Andrew's flight arrived an hour ago for the gala since he's also on the board of tonight's charity. Henry and Andrew founded the nonprofit as a way to give back to the community, but until this season, Andrew was its face. After he was traded and Stacey found out Henry was the co-founder, rather than just a supporter as he wanted everyone to believe, she recommended the charity as the focus for the team's annual gala.

Andrew has to fly out early tomorrow, but he said he isn't going to miss it.

Emily grins, her dark eyes crinkling at the corners. "I wish you could film his reaction when he sees you, because if he doesn't consider dragging you into his room to skip the gala, I will have failed."

My cheeks flush, but secretly, I hope she's right. I want to have sex with him. I want to experience that level of intimacy with him.

"We're not skipping, but don't expect to hear from me afterward." I wink at her.

"Get it, girl. Make sure you tell the paparazzi just where you got your dress from."

I swish my hips, watching the tassels dance. "Of course. Bye bestie." I blow her a kiss as I hang up.

After slipping into a pair of Louboutin pumps, I tuck my phone into my clutch before stepping in front of the mirror again. *I look fucking incredible.* I smooth my palms down my dress before gathering some of the skirt in one hand to step out of my room, walking confidently down the stairs in my deathtrap heels.

Henry, Wilson, and Andrew are in the middle of a conversation, all dressed to the nines. Wilson is wearing a charcoal grey tuxedo that complements his dark skin, while Andrew is donned in navy that brings out the blue in his eyes. As attractive as they look, my eyes are only on Henry as his jaw unhinges slightly, taking me in.

Don't trip.

Whatever you do, don't trip.

I breathe a sigh of relief once I reach the bottom of the stairs, smiling brightly at them. "Are we ready to go?"

Henry is speechless, his full lips parted in shock. I take a second to appreciate the way his black tuxedo fits him, emphasizing his handsome features, which are already heart stopping.

Literally—I think I'm going to need a pacemaker to shock my heart into normal rhythm from how often he makes it skip a beat. His dark brown hair is tousled, and I resist the urge to run my fingers through the silky strands.

Andrew clears his throat, drawing my attention to him. "So, the town car has been here for a couple minutes now. Are we going to leave, or do you plan on staring at each other all night?"

Wilson laughs, patting him on the shoulder. "Dude, at least you don't have to live with them."

I turn to glare at Wilson as Henry coughs, clearing his throat. "Uh, guys, can you give us a sec? We'll be right out."

Andrew winks at him, smirking. "Sure you will."

I shift in place as they walk out the front door, and Henry drags a hand over his jaw. "I know I'm supposed to tell you how incredible you look, but that doesn't even begin to describe you right now. Mirabelle, you look . . ." Henry trails off, laughing under his breath as his eyes roam over my face and down my body. *"You look perfect."*

"I'm glad you like it." I step forward to straighten his bow tie. It doesn't need fixing, but I'm desperate to touch him.

His gaze slowly drags back up, and I nearly melt under the intensity of emotion in Henry's face. "I'm so fucking lucky to be the guy on your arm tonight, but as exquisite as you look in this dress, I can't help but think how much I want to see you out of it later." I bite my lip to hide how much I love the idea, but Henry lifts his hand to pull it free, running his thumb over my bottom lip ever so gently. *"Ne cachez pas votre sourire."*[1]

"We should go out there, or I might keep you all to myself," I whisper, forgetting why we have to go.

Henry exhales a shuddering breath, kissing the corner of

---

1. Don't hide your smile.

my mouth. "That thought is tempting, but our presence is required, and you deserve to be seen in this. *After you, mon cœur.*"

It's an effort to walk toward the door.

~

Henry hasn't left my side all night, except for his speech, and Wilson was glued to my side during it. This was Henry's compromise regarding Tom not attending tonight.

He and Andrew gave an amazing speech that had everyone opening their checkbooks, even before the silent auction started. Henry's arm is wrapped around my lower back as I lean into his side while we talk with Andrew and my uncle.

"How's Seattle working out?" Uncle Owen asks Andrew.

"I like it. The team's solid—solid enough we might even be seeing you in the Super Bowl."

"Hey, don't jinx it," Henry says, and I shake my head before sipping from the champagne flute in my hand. My entire body tenses when I realize Miley is approaching us, wearing a black gown to not draw attention to herself since she's working.

I'm aware if my parents weren't who they are, and I wasn't who I am, I'd be wearing the same thing.

Henry pulls me tighter to him, clearly feeling the change in my body language.

I force a smile, attempting to be polite. "Hi, Miley."

Her distaste for me has grown since I told her to take her issues with me up with Stacey—*which she clearly hasn't.*

"Mirabelle," she greets, and honestly, I thought she was smart enough to at least try to be nice in front of my uncle, Andrew, and Henry. *I think I give her too much credit.* Miley smiles at them before her eyes land on Henry, and she's about to find out just how sharp my nails are if she isn't careful.

"Henry, do you mind if I interview you about some of the work you've done with establishing this charity."

"Henry, will you hold my glass?" I ask, and he takes it without question as I slide my arm around his back, resting my hand on his chest possessively. "I thought Stacey had you working the front entrance to track who is in attendance?"

"She does, but I think it's none of your business since you're not working," Miley snaps.

"Which makes her a guest, and I've already completed my interviews for the night," Henry says, and Miley's eyes widen. She looks to my uncle as if expecting him to tell Henry he has to talk to her, but he immediately turns the other way. I'm not sure why she thought he would back her up, but whatever.

"But Stacey said—" Miley stammers to continue, and Henry chuckles.

"Stacey will be plenty satisfied with what I've said tonight, but I'm not sure she would appreciate hearing how one of her staff was treating a guest trying to enjoy their evening. Now if you'll excuse us, we were having a conversation."

Henry is officially the best boyfriend ever.

She straightens up, Miley's cheeks flaming red as she walks away. A small part of me feels bad, until I remember how horrible she is to me every single day. Still, I probably should have tried to pretend I didn't enjoy that as much as I did.

I smile up at Henry, and the corners of his mouth quirk upward in return. "Do you want to go dance?"

"What? Henry, there's no one else dancing." I glance around the room, but despite the classical music playing, no one is dancing. Henry sets my champagne on the tray of a passing waiter passing, unraveling himself from around me to lace our hands together.

"So? It makes you happy. I might not be able to salsa, but I can sway pretty romantically," he says, moving us toward an unoccupied area in the corner of the hall.

God, the way this man makes me feel has ruined me forever, and he doesn't have a clue.

Henry pulls me into him, and I loop my arms around the back of his neck as his hands fall to my hips. "I like you," I say honestly as we sway gently back and forth.

"Really?" he teases, his face filled with a quiet ease that speaks louder to me than any words could. "I had no idea."

If only he knew how true that was. Henry has no idea how long I've been pining for him.

His eyebrows furrow in confusion as I stay quiet. "Mira? I was just teasing you," he says softly.

"I know. I was just thinking."

"About?"

I could tell him the truth, but then I risk the chance that Henry will look at me like I'm a lunatic, or I can evade.

I choose option two, it's the one I'm best at when it comes to him. Now that I have Henry, I'm afraid to lose him.

"I'm thinking about how happy I am."

Before Henry can ask more questions, I distract him by pulling him down to kiss me. He kisses me back for a few moments, smiling against my mouth. Henry pulls back, resting his forehead against mine. It feels like he sees me—*the real me.*

"In case you haven't noticed because of what an idiot I've been, I really like you too." Roll the end credits.

All these moments with Henry have been precious gifts beyond my wildest dreams. Honestly, if he weren't standing in front of me, I'd think Henry was someone I had conjured up in a dream. I've always seen him for who he is, rather than how everyone else sees him.

Henry's a knight in shining armor, but he's mine.

"*Magnifique,*"[2] he says tenderly.

---

2. Beautiful.

I love you. The words are on the tip of my tongue, but it'd be insane to voice them when we've only officially been dating for a week.

"Toi aussi."[3]

There's a short cough to the side of us, and I turn to see my dad standing there.

"Mind if I cut in? Lia said she wanted some fresher arm candy," Dad jokes, and Henry wisely chooses to step back so they can trade places.

Dad spins me, and I laugh as I turn toward him. "You're much better at this than Henry," I joke, and Dad's smile lines are prominent. He and Mom have been so happy together; even when they're mad, they're still happy.

"So Owen just told us something interesting," he says, and I roll my eyes. Of course my uncle has already told them what happened with Miley. He's such a gossip.

"Miley is just . . ." I trail off as Dad shakes his head.

"He did tell us about her, but I'm more interested in why he said he was happy you and Henry were actually in a relationship now," he says, quiet enough that no one else near us can hear. My eyes widen as he sways us to the beat of the music. Uncle Owen told them? What the hell was he thinking?

"Dad, I-I'm sorry. It was fake, but we are actually in a relationship now," I admit quietly. I can't tell if he's mad or not. I try to look for Henry to see if Mom is ripping him a new one, but she's laughing and he's smiling?

"Except it wasn't ever fake for you. This thing with Henry."

I shake my head slowly. "No. It was never fake for me, but it was fake for him. I almost messed everything up, Dad. We're together now, but does it ever stop feeling like it could all slip

---

3. You too.

away so easily?" I ask, my voice no louder than a whisper as my bravado slips away.

His dark eyes, which match mine, soften. "Mirabelle, never in a million years could you mess things up with Henry as much as I fucked things up with your mother. And look where we are now? I'm still with the love of my life despite everyone who thought we were doomed from the start. I have a beautiful daughter who I love more than anything, and three sons who mean the world to me."

"What happened between you and Mom?" I ask, stuck on that part of his point because I've never heard anything other than my parents being happy together. They started dating in college after Mom's year abroad, and they've been together ever since.

"Maybe one day soon I'll tell you that story. I just want you to know if Henry is the one for you, there's nothing you could ever say or do that would mess things up permanently between the two of you. Live in the moment instead of worrying about the future, okay?" I feel my eyes well up with tears and Dad is quick to wipe away the one that falls. "Do you love him?"

"Are you going to kill Henry if I say yes?"

He laughs, shaking his head. "No, I'm not going to kill him."

"I've always loved him, Dad. It might have started as a stupid childhood crush, but I can't remember ever not loving Henry."

"If he hurts you, then I absolutely will kill him. It doesn't matter if he's my godson, you're my daughter. I love you, and there is nothing you could do that would ever change that. For what it's worth, I think he loves you too. Henry would be an idiot not to."

It's the way he says it that makes me believe him. I hug my father tightly.

"Don't tell your brothers, but you're my favorite. I know I'm not supposed to say that shit, but it's true," he whispers, and I pull away laughing.

"*Dad.*"

He holds his hands up in defeat. "I said nothing."

Mom and Henry stop next to us, and Mom's eyes widen. "Mirabelle, are you okay?"

"I'm perfect," I say, just as two guests walk up to us, and my parents are whisked away as that conversation runs through my head. Henry tilts my chin up, reading me.

"Were you crying?" he asks, his face shifting into concern.

I smile at him, hoping to reassure Henry as my dad's words echo through me. "They were happy tears."

"Are you sure?"

I reach up to cup his face, brushing my thumb over his cheek. "I promise," I say, and Henry relaxes, leaning down to kiss me softly.

I was wrong before. I won't ask for forever with Henry, but having the chance to grow old with him would be enough for me. I can only hope he wants the same thing.

He pulls away again, and the way Henry's looking at me, makes me believe every word he's said to me. It makes me believe I do deserve everything, that it would wreck him if something happened to me, and I am his heart. *It makes me believe if he doesn't love me yet, he will.*

And then Henry catches me by surprise, spinning me and causing the tassels on the dress to twirl around me. "Have I told you how good you look in that dress?" he says, holding me closely, like I'm the most precious thing in the world to him.

"Once or twice tonight," I say, my heart beating quickly in my chest. *"Mais n'oublie pas à quel point je serai belle sans. Je pense que je vais aussi garder les talons,*[4] I tease, and his eyes light up, his grip tightening.

"*Mirabelle, tu es un rêve devenu réalité.*"[5]

---

4. But don't forget how good I'll look without it on. I'm thinking I'll keep the heels on too.
5. Mirabelle, you are a dream come true.

CHAPTER THIRTY-SIX

Mirabelle

We took the town car for ourselves. Henry at least had the courtesy to tell Wilson and Andrew via text after we'd already left.

I'm slightly buzzed from the champagne I drank tonight, feeling more giggly and confident than usual, if that's even possible.

Henry tugs my dress up my thighs as I straddle his waist, kissing down the open collar of his neck as the tinted windows block us from everyone outside. The bowtie was pulled loose within seconds of us climbing into the car, and his jacket was discarded on the seat next to us. Honestly, I don't think I care at this point if the dress accidentally rips, but I would feel bad telling Emily.

I kiss Henry roughly, his calluses scraping deliciously over my thighs, and I can't wait to feel them everywhere. The thought causes me to press my lips harder against his, dragging my fingers through his hair.

I *need* to know what *everything* feels like with Henry.

Everything before now—*before Henry*—feels like practice for the big game, and I am so fucking ready for this.

He pulls my dress up again, and I break apart from him, my breathing ragged. "Careful, Emily will kill me if it's ripped," I warn, sitting up to help shimmy the fabric up over my hips.

"I'm not going to rip it," Henry says, his hair tousled sexily from running my hands through it for the last couple of minutes.

He runs his hands up the backs of my thighs, cupping my ass in his hands.

"You're not wearing any underwear?" he asks, his voice low, and I shake my head, undoing the buttons of his vest.

"No bra either." I shift, straddling his waist more freely.

Henry drops his head back against the window, looking at me in amazement. "You are something else."

"Or I just had high hopes for tonight . . ."

"Would it be presumptuous if I were to say the same?"

"How many things do you think we can check off that list?" I ask, ideas floating through my head, and the predatory gleam that forms in his eyes tells me Henry's on board. "You could tie me up and have me any way you want. I'm pretty flexible so it could be fun, or you could fuck me in front of a mirror so I can see how perfectly we fit together? I wouldn't mind practicing my blow job—" Henry silences me by clashing his lips against mine, devouring me with the hunger of a desperate man. Our noses bump as I try to keep up, his hands squeezing my hips, pulling me against him.

Fuck, I can feel how drenched I am.

Call me insane, but I love that Henry doesn't treat me like I'm made of glass.

My hands are shaking as I fumble with the buttons on his shirt, accidentally scattering a few of them as they pop off. I pull away, unable to stop myself from laughing and Henry's smile is wide. "I'm not allowed to rip your dress, but you can wreck my shirt?"

"Exactly," I say, as Henry combs his fingers through my hair, wrapping the long curls around his hand, tipping my head back to expose my neck to him. *"I want you."*

This time, his lips are featherlight as they kiss the rapid pulse in my neck, and I shift my hips, grinding against the bulge in his pants. "You have me," he says, scraping his teeth gently over the sensitive spot, removing the remaining hand on my waist to slide it up the side of my body to the strap of my dress. *Fuck.* I'm highly aware of every sensation, and a moan slips from my mouth as Henry alternates between sucking and biting at my skin. He chuckles against my collarbone as I shamelessly roll my hips, the seam of his zipper rubbing against my clit as I drag my hands over his powerful shoulders.

"So needy," he says, exposing my breast, flicking his tongue teasingly over my sensitive nipple. "You're fucking precious."

"Fuck." I gasp, feeling a sharp pinch as he pulls my hair harder, only heightening the pleasure by blowing cool air on my skin.

"Too much?" he asks, lifting his head to check on me. Henry releases his grip, massaging my scalp as my body craves more, and I have never felt more cherished.

"Is that all you got?" I challenge, trusting him more than I've ever trusted anyone.

"Not even close, *mon cœur*," Henry says, while his hand is trailing up my inner thigh.

He drags a finger over my slit, testing to see if I'm ready for him. "Goddamn, you're soaked." Henry locks eyes with me as he slowly pushes a finger in me, but it's not enough. I shift impatiently, and he adds a second, maintaining the agonizing pace as the nerves in my body threaten to skyrocket.

"Please," I whimper as he swirls his thumb over my clit,

pleasure shooting through every single nerve ending in my body.

"Please what?" Henry asks, and my breath hitches as I grab onto his shoulder and the ceiling for balance as I move, seeking more friction. *I'm getting close.*

The car hits a bump that forces Henry's fingers deeper into me, and I gasp at the feeling. *"More, please,"* I moan, and he smiles like the devil, curling his fingers and hitting the right spot that makes my legs quiver as I ride his hand, staring directly into his hazel eyes. He's watching me intensely, and I fucking love it.

"That's it, pretty girl. Make a mess on my hand. Tell me how much you like my fingers fucking your needy pussy."

Henry and his filthy mouth are definitely to blame for the praise kink I'm developing.

I don't care that the driver can likely hear what we're doing. I don't care about anything but the way Henry makes me feel, his thumb increasing the pressure on my bundle of nerves at the same time he adds a third finger, pushing me over the cliff.

Henry covers my mouth with his other hand, smothering the sound of my cry as my hips move erratically as he continues fingering me through my orgasm. "Fuck, you did so good. So fucking good," he whispers, kissing my forehead as I struggle to catch my breath, wiping his hand on his pant leg.

Henry kisses me sweetly, and at the same time, there's a knock on the partition.

Oh shit. The car isn't moving.

"Just a moment," Henry calls out, and I realize half his chest is exposed because I totally wrecked his shirt.

I slide off his lap, tugging my dress into place. Henry pulls his wallet out of the pocket of his jacket, passing it to me as I blink in surprise. "Henry, your shirt makes you look like you're on the cover of a Regency romance book. You need it more than me."

He looks down at himself, shaking his head as he shrugs. "I'm fine. Put the jacket on, Mira."

Another knock on the partition leaves no room for argument as I quickly slip into the jacket as Henry adjusts his pants, but it does nothing to hide his not-so-little problem. I grab a few buttons off the seats as Henry opens the door, offering me a hand to help me out.

He motions for me to go toward the house as he moves to talk to the driver, and I catch a glimpse of cash that Henry hands to him as I pull his jacket tightly around me. I'm not sure I even want to know how much Henry gave him, but I hope it's enough to keep him from selling the story of us getting freaky in the back of a town car.

Using the keys in the pocket of Henry's jacket, I unlock the front door, punching in the alarm code before hanging the jacket on the coat rack. *Wilson will never let us live it down if we leave clothes in the hallway again.*

The door opens again when I'm halfway up the stairs, and seeing how disheveled Henry looks already has my body screaming for him to touch me again.

Henry enters his bedroom seconds after me, his shirt hanging completely open now as he shuts the door behind him. The air feels charged with electricity as Henry watches me reach to pull down the zipper of my dress, letting it fall to the floor and slipping out of my heels.

Henry shrugs out of his shirt, and my breath catches as he walks toward me, undoing his belt.

"Where do you want me?" he asks, and I shake my head.

"I want you in charge."

His throat bobs as he stares at me like I'm one of the Seven Wonders of the World. "Get on the bed, Mirabelle."

I climb on the bed, watching Henry in awe as he

undresses, never breaking eye contact with me. He moves toward the bedside table, and I shake my head. "What if you didn't wear one?" I ask, my intrusive thoughts slipping out, and Henry's eyes widen in shock. *Oh shit.* "I mean, if you want to, we absolutely can use a condom. I got tested after Reid, and everything came back negative. I've just never gone without, and I have an IUD so I'm not trying to baby trap you, actually, I think I'll just stop talking now," I say, clamping my jaw shut, crossing my arms over my chest. *Bad idea, Mirabelle.*

Henry shakes his head as he sits on the bed next to me. "Mira, can I talk without you interrupting me?"

I nod, pulling my lower lip into my mouth to chew on it.

"You surprised me by suggesting it, and I don't think you asked so you could trap me by getting pregnant. I've never had sex without one, probably because I've never trusted someone enough to try it, but if you want to, then I'm okay with it. I like the idea of us having a first together."

"Yeah?" I ask, sitting up slowly.

"Yeah. Now come here and kiss me." Henry takes my hand, pulling me toward him, finally picking me up so I'm straddling his waist. "You'll tell me if you want to stop?" he asks, brushing my hair over my shoulders.

"I'll tell you, but I'm not going to want to stop."

Henry sighs, pulling me closer where I can feel his hard length against my thigh. "I know you said you want me in charge, but I need you to know that if you tell me to stop, I will."

"I know."

He tilts his head, kissing me sweetly, and I relax, losing myself in the moment. Henry's tongue dances against mine, and a small groan escapes from my mouth, causing his restraint to snap. Henry palms my breast with one hand, still sensitive from my orgasm in the car, and his other wraps around his cock, fisting it. I pull away, looking down between us to watch, sliding my own hand down to touch myself.

"Can I?" I ask, looking up at Henry.

"Later," he promises, kissing me. Henry lowers my back to the sheets, breaking our bruised lips apart. "Let me feel you," he mumbles, his fingers taking the place of my own. He starts with two, and I lift my hips up, silently asking for more, and he adds a third. "Fuck, you're so ready for me," he says, branding my skin as his mouth burns with unspoken promises.

I drag my nails over his back as he curls his fingers before withdrawing them torturously. *"Henry, j'ai besoin . . ."*[1]

"Je sais, mon cœur,"[2] he says, lifting his eyes to meet mine as he pulls one of my legs up to wrap around my waist, lining up our hips. I can feel Henry's body trembling against mine, and he slowly pushes in, moans filling the room from both of us.

Henry kisses me, my eyes falling shut in ecstasy as I hook my leg tightly around his waist, frantically trying to meet his thrusts. "Fuck me, *mon cœur,*" I whisper against his lips, my skin burning hot as pleasure threatens to burn me alive from the inside out.

He moans through gritted teeth as he hooks his hand under my other hip, bracing himself to thrust deeply.

I love you.

I rake my nails over his shoulders as the crescendo builds, and I lose myself in the feeling of Henry completing me.

I love you, Henry Price.

The words burn in my throat but I swallow them back as Henry threatens to consume me, my body singing underneath his.

My hand grasps for the sheets around me, and Henry

---

1. Henry, I need . . .
2. I know, my heart.

entwines his fingers with mine, his jaw clenching. I think I finally understand why they say eyes are the windows to the soul. Looking into Henry's, I see more than I'm able to understand, and I wonder what he can see in mine. *Probably the truth.*

I feel exposed, like my chest is cracked wide open for Henry to see. That while he calls me his heart . . . my heart beats *for* him. I'm not sure my heart will ever beat for anyone else.

His breathing turns ragged as Henry's hips start to move more erratically, rocking his pelvis against my clit, the stimulation enough to make my body shatter for him a second time. Henry follows, falling in step with me, my head spinning deliriously as I try to commit the sounds he's making to memory.

Except, the higher you rise, the harder you fall.

CHAPTER THIRTY-SEVEN

Henry

I KNOW I SHOULD BE PAYING ATTENTION, BUT I can't take my eyes off Mirabelle.

She's standing to the side next to Stacey as they oversee my postgame press conference. Tom is hovering at the back of the room, close enough to reach her in an instant if necessary, but not so close as to draw everyone's attention to himself.

Mirabelle finally threw me a bone and showed up at the stadium wearing the jersey I bought for her at the beginning of the season. It's probably a good thing I didn't know she was wearing it until after the game, I wouldn't have been able to focus if I had known.

She frowns, glancing up at me, and Owen kicks my leg under the table.

I blink, realizing there are a lot of eyes staring at me, and I'm not sure how long I've been staring at her. Clearing my throat, I lean into the microphone. "Can someone repeat the question?"

There's a chorus of laughter, and at least they find it amusing. A reporter raises her hand, drawing my attention to her. "I asked what adjustments were made during practices this week that contributed to today's win after last week's loss to the Cobras?" she asks, and I sip the water in front of me.

"I think it's all about showing up. We've got a terrific coaching staff that worked tirelessly to review footage from this season, running drills in practice that focused on weak spots in both the offense and defense behind that loss. The guys locked in this week, putting in the work off the field, and I think that showed today. The Wolves played a great game, but all the credit for those adjustments goes to Coach Lewis and his coaching staff," I answer, giving credit where it's due, hoping my answer was enough for Stacey not to throw me in the doghouse for getting distracted.

Stacey climbs the stairs, steps onto the platform, and the reporters groan, knowing the conference is over. "I'm afraid that's all the time we have today, but we hope to see you during our locker room access times this week," Stacey says, and I take the opportunity to get the fuck off this stage because I don't think I can go another minute without being within arm's reach of Mirabelle.

She smiles at me as if understanding I'm unable to fight the gravitational pull in her direction, desperate to be in her orbit. I'm not embarrassed in the slightest that I was caught staring at her.

Fuck it. "You played—" I cut Mirabelle off, cupping her face in my hands, pressing a searing kiss to her sweet lips that does little to quell the raging desire I feel for her. The roar of the room fades entirely into background noise, and I can focus on nothing but the fact that Mirabelle wearing my jersey today was as much her claiming me as it was me claiming her.

I still can't place the flavor of her lip balm, and it's driving me mad.

Kissing Mirabelle feels like the most natural thing in the world to me. *I wonder if it feels the same for her.* Despite it not being enough, I reluctantly pull away as her eyes flutter open to meet mine. The flashes of the cameras in my peripheral vision are bright, but nothing is as blinding as Mirabelle's smile.

She looks at me like I'm enough for her.

I'm the first to admit—*to myself*—that my issues with my biological mother are the reason I struggle in relationships. I worry I'm spending too much time focused on football to focus on them, or if they only want to be with me because of the benefits that come with being attached to me.

She's the gift that keeps on giving with her continuous calls, making it impossible for me to forget her.

"You ready to get out of here?" I ask, lacing her fingers with mine, pressing a kiss to the back of her hand.

Not soon enough, apparently. The room explodes with excited chatter, all directed at her.

"Mirabelle, did you know?"

"How are your parents taking it?"

"Why not Duke?"

"Will Hunter start at Oceanside?"

"Mirabelle!"

What the fuck just happened?

Owen takes over the press conference, his booming voice redirecting everyone's attention as Stacey ushers Mirabelle and me out of the room with Tom's help.

"Go home," Stacey instructs, and Mirabelle's grip on my hand tightens. I half-expect Mirabelle to offer to stay, but she nods.

"Thank you," Mirabelle says, and without responding, Stacey walks back the way we came. "Do you think our parents knew about Hunter?" she asks, glancing up at me.

"If they didn't, they do now." I knew Duke wasn't going to happen, but I never thought Hunter would commit to their rival school.

Mira pulls her phone out of her pocket, frowning as she

looks at the screen. "My parents said we're all meeting at your house. I guess Kaitlyn and Hunter left during the game to go there, but they're not answering their phones now."

At least, for once, we're not involved. I'll take the wins where I can get them, but the biggest win of all is knowing I have Mirabelle by my side. I'm crazy about her. I would have saved us both a lot of grief if I had been able to accept my feelings for her sooner.

I refuse to let go of her for longer than a few seconds on the drive back to my house as Tom follows behind us in Mirabelle's car. I need Mirabelle like a mermaid needs water to survive.

"I don't know if I've told you, but you're doing better with the press," Mirabelle says as I pull into my neighborhood.

"Because of you," I admit, stealing a glance at her. *Goddamn, she's so pretty.* I knew she'd look incredible wearing my jersey, but it's given me an idea for something I might like even better.

"No, Henry. It's because of you. You're finally letting everyone see who you are instead of refusing to speak with them at all. I'm proud of you," she says, squeezing my hand as a lump forms in my throat.

What I've learned since becoming a professional athlete is that most people only like the *idea* of me, but she likes *me*. I don't know what I did to deserve Mirabelle Walker's affection, but I'll do anything to keep it.

"Thank you," I say, my voice nearly caught in my throat.

I pull into the driveway, but as Tom switches vehicles to leave for the day, everyone else arrives.

"Maybe we should go in first, in case my parents are going to yell at Hunter," Mirabelle whispers. I wish I could try telling her she's wrong, but considering her parents' tempers, it's probably a good call.

"Do you really think they'll yell?" I ask, opening the front door.

"Who knows? It's Oceanside," she says, shrugging and I follow her through the doorway into the living room.

My jaw drops at the sight of Hunter and Kaitlyn making out on my couch, and it makes sense why they weren't answering their phones. Hunter's shirt is on the floor, and I'm ready to stare at the sun long enough for it to permanently burn my retinas.

"Oh my fucking god," Mirabelle swears, causing them to immediately separate.

"What? Are they not here?" Thalia asks from behind us while Hunter pulls his shirt back on, but there's no fixing their disheveled appearances.

"They're here, but I think what you should ask is what were they doing," Mirabelle muses, and I drag my hands over my face. I've been trying to wrap my head around Kaitlyn and Bailey, but now she's with Hunter? What the hell is going on?

"What were they doing?" Sebastian asks, and this is giving me serious PTSD from when they walked in on me and Mirabelle.

Hunter's cheeks are flaming red, and he scratches the back of his neck as he looks at Kaitlyn. "We're together."

Dad snorts, shaking his head. "Yeah, and I've been to the moon. What were you really doing? We've been trying to get ahold of you."

Kaitlyn looks at me, desperation shining on her face, and I know her well enough to understand that she wants to know if I'm going to say anything about Bailey.

Sebastian tilts his head before turning to my dad. "Chris, I don't think they're joking."

"We're not," Kaitlyn confirms.

"I'm living my dream. First, Mirabelle and Henry get together, and now Hunter and Kaitlyn? Lia, I totally called both of these relationships." My stepmom shrieks, and I'm lost. *How long has she hoped this would happen?*

Hunter grabs his phone off the coffee table, his eyes widening. "Why the fuck did you call me over a dozen . . . *oh*. That's why," he mumbles, continuing to scroll.

Mirabelle rests her hands on her hips. "Sorry, we'll circle back to this relationship, but why didn't you tell anyone about Oceanside?" she asks.

"I'm sorry. I swear, I was going to tell everyone after the game."

"You're still not answering the question," Thalia adds.

Hunter shrugs, putting his hands in his pockets. "Because I went with my gut. I knew if I asked everyone for their opinions, I wouldn't be able to decide. I like the coaches, and one of my old teammates who I trust plays there. I have a good feeling about this, but I didn't want to disappoint anyone."

"Hunter, you could've picked a community college if it made you happy, which is the only thing we care about. I'm proud of you for going with your gut. It's not easy to do," Sebastian says.

"So you're not mad I picked Oceanside?"

"I'm not mad," he affirms, and Hunter's shoulders relax.

Mirabelle turns to me, the initial shock gone from her face, whereas I'm afraid to open my mouth and risk saying the wrong thing. "We're not the only Walker-Price couple anymore."

I guess not, but this isn't the couple I expected.

Wilson went out with the team tonight, but after all the excitement earlier with Hunter, I'm glad for the quiet evening at home. Mirabelle is curled up on top of me, her head resting on my chest as we watch a movie, but my mind is a million miles away. I think hers is as well.

I'm running my fingers through her hair as she keeps a slight grip of my shirt in one hand, the other resting on my chest, our legs are tangled together under the blanket.

Unfortunately, my biological mother called while Mirabelle and I were swimming tonight after everyone else had left. Somehow, she still hasn't gotten the hint I have nothing to say or give to her.

I can't even count the number of voicemails I've deleted without listening to them. The number is that high. It's probably time to tell Sebastian she's still calling, but I'm not there yet.

"What are you thinking about?" Mirabelle asks softly, breaking the silence.

"Nothing important."

"I don't believe you." *I swear Mirabelle might know me better than I know myself.* She lifts her head up to look at me, her face knit with concern. "Is it still everything from earlier? I should have tried harder to get Stacey to back off—"

I smile down at her worried face, shaking my head. "It's not Stacey, or any of the shit she made me do today."

"Then what is it?"

I don't like talking about my mom. I mean, who enjoys admitting their mother willingly left them and only wants something to do with them because it's convenient for her? I can only assume the divorce was ugly because she's a taboo topic for my dad too.

"It's my mom, or I guess I should call her Allison. She hasn't exactly been much of a mother."

Mira's eyes soften, and I take that as my cue to continue.

"She won't stop calling. I'm afraid one of these days she's going to show up at my door or at a game, demanding to see me," I admit. "She wanted nothing to do with me before, but now I'm a professional athlete, I'm suddenly good enough for her?"

"Do you ever answer her calls?" she asks, chewing on her bottom lip. I lift my hand to brush her hair behind her ear.

"I used to, thinking it was a sign she . . ." I trail off, not wanting to admit that despite Penelope having treated me like her own, I still craved the approval of Allison. "I told her to stop calling me six months ago. She said she just wanted to talk. I-I hung up on her and changed my number."

Her nose scrunches up in confusion. "I thought you changed it because your phone number got leaked."

"I didn't want my dad to know she was calling me. It didn't stop her from finding my new one, though. I accidentally answered a call a few months ago, but I ended it as soon as I realized who it was."

"I might have accidentally told him and my dad that she was. I'm sorry, Henry," Mirabelle apologizes. "I didn't mean to, but I felt awful you were taking all this shit from everyone, and you didn't deserve it. You carry so much weight on your shoulders, and it wasn't fair for them to add to it with their accusations. My temper definitely got the better of me when I talked to your dad, and I shouldn't have said anything."

Well, I guess that answers my question about why Sebastian suspected we were in contact, but I don't understand when she would have had this conversation? "When did you talk to my dad?"

"The morning before the season opener. I didn't go to Uncle Owen's to talk to your dad, if that makes it any better? JJ and I were staging an intervention with Hunter about Bailey. Your parents were there too, and your dad tried talking me out of being with you. I just got so mad because no one ever listens to me or what I want. It just slipped out, and I didn't know how to tell you. I'm so sorry, Henry," Mirabelle rambles as she moves to sit up, attempting to pull away from me. I keep my arms wrapped around her, preventing her from moving.

I smile at her, trying to reassure her I'm not upset. "Hey, it's okay. I'm not mad." Mirabelle melts into me, exactly where I want her to stay. "How's Bailey?" I ask, trying to decide whether I should open that can of worms before I can talk to Kaitlyn.

"He's still ignoring my calls."

"Do you want to talk about it?"

"What's there to talk about? My brother hates me, and I don't even know what I did. Mom told me he hasn't said a word to anyone since I told my parents he quit soccer. JJ told me last week Bailey answered a FaceTime call, though. Bailey didn't say anything, so JJ said he rambled about his classes and teammates, but he still answered, so maybe there's hope."

Yeah, Bailey is definitely on my shit list. I hate that he's making her feel this way.

"I don't think you did anything, Mira. It's probably an extreme form of teen angst. He'll work through it, and things will go back to normal."

"Do you really believe that?" she asks, and the hope lingering in Mirabelle's question breaks my heart for her because I don't believe it. There's something going on with him, and until he learns to let someone in to help him work through whatever this is, I don't think things will go back to normal.

But I can't tell her that.

I crane my neck at an uncomfortable angle to press a short kiss to her forehead. "I do."

Her smile and the way it reaches her eyes make me feel a little better. *Lying doesn't always have to be a bad thing.*

Silence envelopes us as I hold the woman I . . . *as I hold Mirabelle.*

Everything will work out exactly the way it's supposed to.

CHAPTER THIRTY-EIGHT

Mirabelle

M Y JAW DROPS AS HENRY PUSHES MY PAWN OFF THE Sorry! game board and back at the starting place. "Sorry," he says, and Kaitlyn erupts into a fit of giggles as my jaw drops.

"Please tell me I imagined that," I say in disbelief, looking at all four of my pawns in the starting bubble.

Henry's eyes are bright as he coughs to hide his laughter. "I said sorry. This is the whole point of the game."

I purse my lips at him, crossing my arms over my chest. "No, the whole point of the game is to say sorry to everyone *except* your girlfriend. Penelope, can you believe this?" I ask, turning to face Penelope.

"I'm not getting in the middle of this. I'm trying to focus on my strategy."

Chris isn't playing, merely sitting next to Penelope on the loveseat in Henry's hotel suite, resting his hand on hers, squeezing it momentarily. He's a man of few words, something that has influenced Henry in some ways, but it's his actions that show how much he loves her.

I'm definitely reading too much into Henry's body language, but actions speak louder than words.

Like when he brushes my hair back when it falls in my face, holds my hand and presses a kiss to the back of it when I'm biting my nails, and pulls my bottom lip from my teeth so he can see my smile instead of letting me hide it. He does all of these little things, and maybe I just so desperately want him to love me back that I'm looking for it.

Penelope told me on the plane to New York yesterday our relationship reminds her of my parents' relationship.

It meant the world to me because all I've ever wanted was a great love like theirs. You can tell just by how they interact that they love each other.

I want that with Henry.

I don't think it's too much to ask for, right?

I turn back to Henry, sticking my tongue out at him immaturely. "I don't like you anymore."

It's infuriating he smiles in response, knowing how untrue it is.

Thankfully, the next time around the Sorry! board, I'm the one who ends up with the right card to bump one of his pawns back to his home base.

"It's on the other side of the board as yours, Mira. It would have made so much more sense to bump Kaitlyn's," he complains.

"You keep bumping mine, so it's only fair I get to bump yours." I smile triumphantly, and he just shakes his head at me as Kaitlyn laughs. "Sorry," I add, and Henry's lips turn upward in a smile, but he doesn't say anything.

"Just be glad Mom made me leave Yahtzee at home," Kaitlyn adds, and Henry rolls his eyes.

"I don't want to talk about that game," he mumbles, and I reach over to squeeze his hand reassuringly. Chris clears his throat, and I look at him to see if he's okay, but he's staring at our touching hands.

I guess he's not as okay with us as we thought.

The tension in the room rises, and I pull my hand back, playing it off like I wanted to put it up.

After the game, Henry's family is getting ready to head back to their suite, but his dad captures my attention. "Is it okay if I stay for a moment to talk to you?" Chris asks, and I hate how awkward this feels.

"Sure," I say, offering a slight smile. While things might be normal with Penelope and Kaitlyn, it's still tense with Chris. It's like he doesn't know what to do or say around me now, and I know he and Henry talked things out, but it doesn't seem like things have gotten better aside from them being able to exist in the same room together.

Henry hugs Penelope, turning in confusion before walking toward us. "Dad?" he asks, slipping his arm around my back to pull me protectively against him. *Oh god, this definitely isn't helping.*

"I want to talk to you both," Chris says.

"Of course," I say, not giving Henry the chance to try avoiding this conversation, because clearly it's long overdue. They can't keep going on the same way they have been. It's been less tense since the call on Henry's birthday, but it's nowhere near where their relationship used to be.

After sitting on the couch beside Henry, I rest my hand on his knee, trying to ease him, because acting standoffish isn't going to help us all move forward.

"I'm sorry," Chris says, his hands clasped in his lap. He doesn't look any less tense than Henry, and I don't think I'm wrong for being worried about how this is going to go. I almost wish Penelope had stayed behind with us to help mediate. "I'm sorry for all of it. Mirabelle, I should never have told you to break things off with Henry. Your age gap is concerning, but you're both consenting adults. I'm still trying to wrap my mind around this because I can see you're happy together, but I have to step back and let you make your own mistakes like I made mine." At his use of the word mistake, I flinch and fucking hate that I do. Chris's gaze softens, and I see the immediate apology on his face. It doesn't take away the sting of his words, though. "I didn't mean it that way—"

"No, you're just telling us that we're a mistake like you and my mother," Henry says, his words sucking all of the oxygen from the room in an instant.

Chris shakes his head, exhaling. "Love makes us blind. I love both of you, and I'm happy you're together. *I am.* At the same time, though, it doesn't erase the concerns I have."

"This doesn't feel like an apology. Chris, we're not a mistake," I say, trying to ease the tension, while standing up for myself.

"I'm sorry, Mirabelle. Can I speak to Henry for a moment alone?" he asks, and Henry scoffs in disbelief.

"No," Henry answers immediately. "Whatever you need to say in front of me can be said in front of Mirabelle."

"If that's how you want this to go, then fine. I'm not trying to compare Mirabelle to Allison, but the fact of the matter is that we never know the things people are capable of until we see them in unthinkable situations," Chris says, and while it feels like a blow to the stomach, I can also read between the lines to see this isn't actually about me.

"It's not my fault you married my mother and decided you didn't love her enough to try. She didn't just leave you, Dad. She left me too," Henry snaps, and all hell breaks loose. I stare at Henry, wide-eyed as he stands up, beginning to pace as Chris rises to his own feet.

"Is that what you think happened? I tried so fucking hard to save that marriage, but in the end, the only thing she wanted was money. She didn't want me, and I wish more than anything she had fought for you. I wanted us to have joint custody because I wanted Allison to be a part of your life, but she wasn't the person I had fallen in love with anymore. I spent *months* meeting with lawyers and going to court to gain custody of you. Allison changed when I chose to pursue my master's degree instead of entering the draft because I wasn't giving her the life she envisioned for herself."

Oh my god.

"Don't you get it? Mirabelle is the only one who doesn't give a flying fuck about my money! This situation isn't comparable at all, Dad, and that's exactly what you're doing. You're comparing Mirabelle to my mother, even though Mira has done nothing but be there for me. It's bullshit, and I won't let you disrespect her or our relationship," Henry shouts and I understand why he's so upset, but this isn't helping. We're going to get the police called on us because I'm sure everyone on this floor can hear them.

"Henry—"

Chris interrupts, speaking over me. "I'm trying to help you open your eyes so you aren't blindsided in case things go bad, which can happen despite doing everything to prevent that. Do you know who the two of you remind me of? Her parents, and there is no better lesson to learn than the one they had to, except it almost cost them everything in the process. Thalia and Sebastian nearly destroyed each other, and it tore them apart for years before they were able to overcome their shit to be together. You're acting like a fucking child, refusing to listen to anyone about the very real concerns we all have."

My brain stutters, trying to process everything. *What is he talking about? My parents have been together since Mom's year abroad in college? Destroying each other? They fight, but not to that extent.*

"You don't know anything about our relationship because you won't give it a chance. Do you even care that I'm happy with her? *How is my happiness a mistake?* If Thalia and Sebastian can accept and support us, then maybe the only person making mistakes is *you*," Henry says as I move in slow motion to get to him, hoping I can try to help him calm down before this gets worse. I'm not sure how it could get much worse.

I've never seen Henry lose his temper like this.

"Of course I care. Love isn't all sunshine and roses, Henry."

"I know that. I do." Henry shakes his head. "Maybe I'll answer one of the phone calls from my mother—"

My heart stops as Chris explodes, proving that this can get much worse than I thought just a second ago. "Allison is *not* your mother, so stop fucking calling her that. Penelope is the woman who helped raise you, earning that title. She wanted you. She loves you. Not the woman who was charged with child endangerment before she fucking kidnapped you to hold you for ransom to the Walkers. *Penelope is your mother.*"

My hands fly up to cover my mouth to prevent any sound from escaping. The silence in the room is deafening as Henry stares at his dad, all the color draining from his face.

"*What?*" he asks, his voice cracking.

Chris's face pales. "Henry, please just listen—"

Except, Henry backs away, bumping into the table before stumbling out. The click of the door shutting behind him causes Chris to fall to his knees. "*What have I done?*" I hear him whisper as his back begins to shake with silent sobs.

CHAPTER THIRTY-NINE

Mirabelle

Henry won't answer any of my calls or texts.

Penelope came into the room a few minutes too late, wanting to know what was taking Chris so long, but instead she found me frozen in horror on the couch and her husband crying on the floor. She pieced together what transpired based on Chris's state as he kept repeating the same sentence over and over again. Penelope explained everything as best she could.

Chris and Allison divorced just before Henry turned three. They had joint custody for almost a year, alternating weeks while custody was being decided, but after things went south in the divorce, my father hired a private investigator to look into Allie to see if there was anything that could help Chris win full custody. Allison would always ask Chris for money to take Henry out during her weeks, and Chris would hand over the money because he wanted his son to have fun with his mother. The private investigator discovered Allison was pocketing the money and leaving Henry unattended for hours on end while she went out with her friends. She was charged with child endangerment, and full custody was awarded to Chris.

Penelope lived in the same house as Chris and Henry, helping out in a pinch if Chris needed help with Henry, as he was starting his own accounting firm. It took off when my dad referred Chris to other players on the team, helping it quickly grow into one of the best practices in the Wilmington area.

When the divorce was finalized, the lawyers agreed Chris would only be required to pay alimony for two years, but when the payments stopped, Allison started calling Chris to ask for more money. He refused, telling her she wouldn't see a penny more. It sent Allison into a spiral, especially when she showed up at the house, and Penelope answered the door. They were still living together as roommates, but it was slowly turning into something more.

Henry had just started kindergarten when she showed up at his school to pick him up, and legally, the school couldn't withhold Henry from her as there was no restraining order in place and she was listed on all his paperwork as his biological mother.

She didn't call Chris, though. She called my parents, knowing—as Henry's godparents—just how much they loved him. Allison played them to her advantage, aware that they would do anything for Henry, so she threatened to take Henry and never come back unless they sent her five hundred thousand dollars. She promised if they sent her the money, she'd bring him back, and no one would hear from her again.

My parents paid the ransom without a second thought, and Allison brought Henry back unharmed that same night. Chris wanted to press charges, but my dad argued it was easier to let her keep the money. A restraining order was filed to prevent the same thing from happening again using the messages Allison had sent Chris asking for money, and they all agreed to never tell Henry.

None of them wanted Henry to find out because they thought it would be easier for him to think his mom abandoned him rather than to learn she had kidnapped him for ransom. Everyone thought they were protecting him.

It was the last time any of them saw or heard about her until I told Chris that Allison had been calling Henry. It explains a lot, actually.

I've been calling Henry for the last twenty minutes, hoping he'll answer the phone because he needs to hear the truth.

I don't know where he is, or where he would have gone. I'm not even sure Henry has shoes on. I know the truth won't make it hurt less, but it does explain a lot.

Chris was trying to warn Henry that the people we love can do inconceivable things, because I truly believe he loved Allison. Despite how it felt and hurt in the moment, he wasn't comparing me to her. Chris was trying to keep Henry safe in the only way he knew how.

Everything was fine an hour ago, and now, I'm not sure what's going to happen from here.

Fuck, I can't believe I let Henry leave without stopping him.

Moving toward the door, I slide into my shoes, trying to call Henry again. Penelope doesn't even realize I'm leaving, still trying to console Chris, and it feels like I'm intruding by being in the same room as them right now.

I understand why they didn't tell Henry in the first place, but seriously, what the fuck? If they could keep this a secret, what other ones are they all hiding?

I'm so far out of my depth. By sheer luck, I recall the room number my uncle gave me earlier and knock repeatedly until the door swings open, revealing Uncle Owen's murderous look.

"This better be a good fucking rea—*Mirabelle?*" His face softens when he looks at me, and the dam helping me hold it together breaks. Tears spill down my cheeks at a rapid rate, and his brown eyes widen in surprise. "Sweetheart, what's wrong? Where's Henry?" He opens the door wider, and I lurch forward to hug him as the look on Henry's face replays on a loop in my head.

"He's gone. I don't know where he went. You have to help me find him." I sob, holding onto his shirt.

"Mira, I can't understand you. I need you to calm down."

"Owen? What's going on?" I vaguely hear Aunt Blake ask as my uncle hugs me and shuts the door.

"I don't know, Blake."

Get it together. You can't help Henry if you're a blubbering mess. I pull away, hiccuping as I wipe my cheeks. It's no use, though. "Henry's gone. I-I don't know where he is. He won't answer his phone, and it was really bad," I ramble, and Aunt Blake pulls me further into their room.

"I thought you two were having dinner with Penelope and Chris tonight? What was really bad?" she asks, and my lower lip trembles.

"We did have dinner with them. Chris and Henry got into a fight after Penelope and Kaitlyn went to bed, and it all went so wrong so fast," I say, shaking my head, as more tears blur my vision. "Henry knows about what his mom did—how she kidnapped him and held him for ransom. He left, and I don't know where he is."

Hastily wiping the tears from my eyes, I see the worried look they exchange, and my heart sinks.

The official press release that went out this morning stated Henry had fallen ill with a twenty-four-hour stomach bug and would not be in attendance at the Thanksgiving game.

The actual reason was no one knew if he was actually going to show up today.

Henry did show up, but he was hungover as fuck, and anyone could tell he wasn't in the right state of mind to play. He was livid they wouldn't let him suit up, but his mood took a turn for the worse after the Panthers lost their small lead in the last few minutes of the game when the backup quarterback threw a pick-six, putting the Stars in the lead. The second that happened, I looked over at Henry in our private viewing room and could tell he was already blaming himself for the loss.

I tried talking to him, but he didn't want to talk about any of it: the game, his mom, or where he went last night. None of it.

Uncle Owen had my parents send their private jet to take us home immediately after the game.

Spending my Thanksgiving on a private jet with my hungover boyfriend staring silently out the window after his entire life blew up isn't exactly how I imagined spending my first holiday as Henry's girlfriend. I'm not sure anyone could have predicted this is how the trip would go.

I'm trying to read the book I brought, but I keep reading the same paragraph over and over again because I can't stop glancing in Henry's direction. He's been silent the entire plane ride, and I'm trying not to push, but avoiding this isn't going to make it go away. Henry's hair is sticking up from how many times he's run his hands through it, but at least he showered and changed clothes. Henry smelled like the back alley behind a dive bar when he showed up earlier.

I set my book down, getting up to sit in the seat next to him.

"Hey," I say, hoping Henry will look my way. *Except he doesn't.* He just continues staring out the window. "Why don't you take a nap?"

"I'm not tired," he answers. *On the bright side, at least Henry responded?*

"Okay."

I fidget with my hands as I sit there, unsure of what to do. Should I tell Henry what Penelope told me last night so he knows the full story? Do I continue sitting here or go back to the other side of the plane? I want to help him, but I don't know how.

"I don't want to talk, Mirabelle," he says, scratching his jaw.

"I wasn't saying anything."

He *finally* looks over at me, an unrecognizable look in his eyes, and I think I would rather Henry keep looking out the window than look at me like that again. "No, but I can hear you thinking."

I hear what he's saying, but what if by starting this conversation, Henry wants to talk about it? He's been perfectly fine ignoring me so far today, maybe this is a sign.

"I know you don't want to talk, but I think we need to," I say, trying to keep my tone steady.

"No, we don't." Okay, so maybe he actually doesn't want to talk about it.

Henry's guard is up, and I hate it, but I know better than to ask if he's okay because it's quite obvious he isn't. I wish I could take away all his pain and carry it myself, but he needs to know the truth.

I turn to face him completely. "No, Henry, we do. You left last night and never answered your phone. And then you showed up at the stadium today, expecting my uncle to put you on the field in the state you were in? We have to talk, because you're hurting."

"What exactly do you want to talk about? How I've always been just a check to cash for the woman who gave birth to me? How *everyone* in my life has been lying to me? My team lost today because I wasn't allowed on the field. Sorry, but no, I don't want to talk about any of it." *He's shutting down, and if anyone has a right to, it's Henry.*

Tread lightly. I feel my stomach twist, but if I didn't think the truth would help, I wouldn't be pushing for him to know. "I'm sorry she couldn't see the incredible person you have become. I don't think they were right to hide what she did, but they did it with the right intentions."

"Mirabelle," he warns, pulling away as I reach for his hand.

"Henry," I reply in the same tone, trying to mask how hurt I am from that small movement. "Do you have any idea how worried we were last night? Do you even care?"

It hits me like a ton of bricks why I don't recognize the look in his eyes. It's because they're empty. I've seen Henry at many different points in his life over the years, but I've never seen him empty. "I'm sorry. Is that what you want me to say?"

"I just want to talk, so you understand where they were coming from. It wasn't done maliciously. They were trying to protect you." I exhale, unsure of the right thing to do because I don't want to fight with Henry. "I want you to know that I'm here for you, whatever you need."

He looks out the window again, signaling the conversation is over.

I thought I had cried all my tears out last night, but I now feel the familiar sensation of tears threatening to slip past my barriers once more.

I love him.

I want to be there for him, but how can I if he won't let me?

I get up from my seat to retreat to my original one with my book, positioning myself so the tears beginning to fall can't be seen by Henry. I'm not sure why I bothered to turn, because he doesn't look away from the window once.

CHAPTER FORTY

Mirabelle

THE HOUSE IS EMPTY WHEN WE GET BACK. WILSON IS still in New York with the team, so we have the house to ourselves.

I'm mentally and physically drained from the last twenty-four hours.

"I'm going to go lie down. I didn't sleep much last night," I say, as I climb the stairs with my suitcase, heading to *my* room—not Henry's.

I don't bother looking behind me to see if he heard me because all I think he wants right now is a fight, and I refuse to give one to him.

I fall into a dreamless sleep almost instantly after curling up in *my* bed.

When I wake to the feeling of lips pressing against mine, it's dark outside, and the smell of whiskey is pungent. I'm groggy enough it takes me a moment to process Henry kissing me.

"Mirabelle," Henry slurs, breaking the kiss as he rests his head in the crook of my neck.

"Henry, are you drunk?" I ask, and he lifts his head.

"Kinda."

And then his lips are on mine again.

It's a drug I can't resist. I give into the feeling of being loved by Henry as his mouth coaxes a moan from mine. I hold onto his shoulders, getting lost in the moment as Henry moves to position himself over me. "Mirabelle, you're so . . . beautiful. I need you. Please." He struggles to get the words out and then everything that's always felt so right feels so wrong.

The bitter taste of whiskey is the only thing I can taste, and I immediately push Henry away so I can collect my thoughts.

"You're drunk," I say, sanity coming back to me.

"So what?"

"I'm not doing anything with you while you're drunk. You're not in the right state of mind," I say, moving further away from him on the bed.

"But I want you."

I feel something inside me break when I hear those four words. I know this isn't about me in any way, but this isn't Henry. "You couldn't even look at me earlier, but now that you're drunk, you want to fuck me?"

"Fine. We don't have to fuck," Henry says, as I turn the lamp on to look at him.

His eyes are unfocused and bloodshot; quite frankly, he looks terrible. I give myself a second to pause, trying not to react impulsively, but I'm not perfect. I'm hurt by how he treated me on the plane and by how it felt to have every single call rejected last night.

"Henry, I told you I'm here for you. Let me be here for you."

"And I told you I don't want to talk."

"I think if you know—"

Henry scoffs, and I don't recognize him. "Maybe Bailey is right. You're so caught up in your perfect fucking world that it's hard for you to understand my entire world is falling apart. My own mother didn't want me, and that's something you'll never be able to understand. I don't want to hear what you think. Life isn't always gold medals, Mirabelle. I was wrong to think you'd understand all I need right now is a little time to process my shit."

All the air rushes from my lungs with that well-placed blow. "I'm trying to give you time, but I don't think it's wrong to want to help you. I-I can't believe you'd even say my brother is right." This is wrong. I don't want to fight him. "I know you're going through a lot, but that doesn't give you the right to treat me like shit, when all I've ever done my entire life is love you. *I've spent years chasing after you, Henry.* I fucking love you, and I hate that I can't fix this for you, because it physically pains me to see you hurting. I can't do anything if you won't talk to me. Tell me you need time, and I'll give it to you. I'll give you anything you want."

Henry straightens. "You're right. You can't fix this, so stop trying." *That's what he got from that?*

"I love you, so respectfully, no. I'm not going to stop trying."

"Fine." He gets up, wobbling as he does. "Do whatever you want. *I don't care.*"

It feels like I'm breathing in shards of glass. "I will."

I grab my still packed suitcase, moving toward the door to carry it down the stairs quickly.

I'm not running away this time, but I am leaving to save us before we're broken beyond repair.

~

It's been two weeks since I left Henry's house in the middle of the night to start staying at my family's home again. The renovations from the fire were completed a couple of weeks ago, but there was never a reason to leave Henry's until now.

I've spent one hundred percent of my time doing my best to avoid him. I've grown more irritable by the day, glaring at my coworkers if they even look at me the wrong way. Not even Miley is willing to push my buttons.

We're not broken up, but we're not together either. It's a complicated game of chicken, with both of us waiting for the other to make a move.

I haven't been able to avoid him completely, considering being his shadow is part of my job. Our exchanges are quick, but they feel like well-placed shots to the heart when Henry looks at me with bags under his eyes and no hint of his beautiful smile to be found.

It takes everything in me not to help him, but he made it clear he doesn't want my help. This is something he wants to figure out on his own. Henry doesn't seem to be doing a great job, but that's not my problem at the moment. He wants space, so I'm giving it to him because I couldn't possibly understand what he's going through.

I told him I loved him, and he didn't bat an eyelash. He didn't even acknowledge I said it.

Instead, he said that he didn't care, and I was allowed to do whatever I want.

I haven't cried, though. It feels silly, but I'm proud of myself for that.

I do miss Henry, his smile, how I wake up with him holding me tightly to his chest—

I shake my head, pulling myself from my thoughts to resume responding to the email I received this morning from my old coach. She wants to know if I'm interested in a coaching position at the gym where I used to train, but am I ready to be a coach?

I look around the cubicles we all have, and I honestly

don't know if I would miss this job. I love being in the stadium and I love my work enough, but the environment in this department is toxic. It's not healthy for me, so maybe a change of scenery would be good for me.

My fingers fly across the keyboard, typing quickly to hit print before I can change my mind.

Holding the document in my hands is freeing.

Dear Mrs. Arnold,

Please accept this letter as my formal resignation from my position, effective two weeks from now. Thank you for all the valuable skills I've learned from you during my time here.

Sincerely,

Mirabelle Walker

A slow smile grows on my face, and I know that I'm doing the right thing. This isn't where I need to be right now.

My feet carry me swiftly to the glass paneling outside Stacey's office, and she motions for me to come in. I move to lay the paper on the desk in front of her, but Stacey snatches it out of the air to read it before I can.

"You're quitting?" she asks, her eyebrows raised in surprise.

"I am. I'll work the next two weeks, but no longer than that."

Stacey stares at the paper and then looks up at me, opening and closing her mouth a couple of times. I've rendered her speechless. I suppress my giggles, which are desperate to come out.

"Give me time to coordinate with the front office and Henry's team to figure out if they wish to replace you. After that, you're free to do as you please, Ms. Walker," she says, which is exactly what I expected. I knew Stacey would be disappointed, but I respect the hell out of her.

I nod, agreeing. "I would like to make a request . . . if that's okay?"

Again, I've surprised her. "You walk into my office to quit a job most people would kill for, and then you have the nerve to ask me for a favor?"

"It's not a favor, it's a request. You're free to say no, but I don't think you'll want to," I say, holding my ground as my stomach flutters with nerves. I hope she decides to listen to me, because this is something I need to do before I leave. I know I have the means if Stacey won't print it, then I can take it to someone else, but I'd prefer to give her this parting gift as a thank you.

Stacey leans back in her chair. "Okay. I'm listening."

CHAPTER FORTY-ONE

Henry

I HAVE NO IDEA WHAT THE FUCK I'M DOING. I'M barely keeping my shit together, but I still have to sit in this fucking meeting with my agent, Calvin, and my marketing strategist, Taylor, while they discuss next moves now that my reputation is better than ever. Supposedly, I'm not at risk of being traded anymore.

They're scheduling all of the commercials and sponsorship deals for the next six months, and I want to poke my eyes out with the stylus Calvin is using on his iPad.

I miss Mirabelle.

If I'm being honest, I don't even remember the last conversation I had with her. That whole night after I started drinking is fuzzy. The only thing I'm certain of is that Mirabelle grabbed her suitcase and left.

She's the fire in my life, and now that Mirabelle's gone, everything seems dark.

I'm sleepwalking while I'm awake to get through the day before I drown my sorrows in liquor until I fall asleep at night.

Wilson asked where Mirabelle was when the team returned from New York, and I didn't have an answer for him because I didn't know. The only question Tom has answered about Mirabelle—*despite me paying his salary*—is that she's staying at her family's house. The police still haven't fucking found who torched the house, but I know Bash and Thalia upped the security while it was being remodeled. He won't tell me anything else about how she's doing because I can "ask her myself".

The problem with that is I don't know what to say to Mirabelle when I'm with her.

I scowl at the table, tapping my fingers repeatedly on the surface, only half listening to the conversation until I hear her name.

"—matter with Mirabelle. I think we—" My head snaps up at the sound of her name, effectively cutting Calvin off at my quick movement.

"What about Mirabelle?" I ask, her name rolling off my tongue too easily.

He looks at me confused. "Henry, I called you last week and left you a voicemail about this."

See, I wouldn't know about any calls because Allison called me at the beginning of last week, and I threw my phone in the pool. It wouldn't turn on after I fished it out, and I refuse to get a new one.

It's somewhat helped my stress levels, knowing Allison can't get a hold of me.

The only reason I remembered this meeting is because Calvin retrieved me from the training room, where I was working off my hangover from last night. *I might be drunk every night, but I'm in the best shape of my life.*

"I broke my phone. Haven't had time to get a new one," I answer, still waiting for his explanation.

"I'll get a hold of your assistant to have her get one for you," he says, making a note on the tablet. "Mirabelle put in her resignation last week. Her last day is this Friday. Since she'll no longer be employed by the stadium, we have been coordinating with Stacey and have come to the conclusion that the best course of action is to issue a press release explaining the relationship has ended mutually to prevent any backlash against either of you," Calvin explains, but my brain is still stuck on his first sentence.

Mirabelle resigned?

"I . . ." I trail off, at a loss for words.

She's leaving, and didn't even tell me.

"What do you want to do?"

My fingers increase the pace at which they're tapping on the table. *This is for the best. It was only ever supposed to be temporary.* "Put out the press release that we ended on mutual terms," I murmur, the words almost getting stuck in my throat.

Neither of them think anything of it because Mirabelle and I never confirmed to anyone who believed it was fake that we were together. We allowed everyone to think whatever they wanted. It shouldn't have mattered to them whether we were together or not.

My head is throbbing, and I feel disgusting. They wouldn't let me shower before the meeting started so I have no doubt I reek of the alcohol seeping from my pores.

She's leaving.

"Do I need to be here?" I ask, cutting off Taylor.

She looks startled by my outburst. "I guess we've covered everything major."

I nod, pushing up from my chair. "Schedule me for whatever you want and add it to my calendar. I'll get a new phone sometime this week," I say, walking out of the room, hearing the door slam shut behind me.

I just can't bring myself to care anymore.

When I'm drunk, it blocks out all the terrible thoughts in my brain, including the conversation my dad had with me a couple days after we got back from New York. He forced me to listen as he told me everything, but it doesn't make it hurt less.

Sometimes the fictional version of what you believe to be the truth is better than the factual version.

A whole lot fucking better.

If anything, it fucking hurts more knowing I was only worth five hundred thousand dollars to her. That's the equivalent to my payoff for one game.

One game.

Clearly now that I'm worth more, she thinks she deserves a higher payout.

When I'm sober, this is what consumes my mind when I'm not thinking about Mirabelle.

I'm so lost in my thoughts that I don't see the person in front of me until the box of things she's carrying crashes to the floor.

"Watch where you're going," she snaps, immediately kneeling to pick up the things, and my eyes widen realizing it's Mirabelle. I immediately notice Tom's not with her, but it's not my place to ask. *She quit.*

"I'm sorry."

Her head immediately lifts up, and her mouth opens as she realizes it's me. "Are you?" she asks, refusing to break eye contact.

So I do.

I crouch down to help her pick up what I caused her to drop. "You're leaving?" I ask awkwardly, moving to grab her laptop charger at the same time as Mirabelle. She shies away from my touch, allowing me to put it back in the box.

"I'm leaving," she confirms, and my heart drops.

I drag my hand through my hair, not knowing the right thing to say, but is there a right thing? I torture myself by stealing a glance at her face, only to find Mirabelle already staring back at me.

Her blonde hair is pulled back, but strands are hanging in her face. I fight the urge to brush them behind her ear.

"Good luck," I say, standing up to walk away.

"Seriously?" Mirabelle calls after me once I'm halfway down the hallway, stopping me in my tracks, but I don't turn around to look at her. *"C'est tout ce que tu trouves à dire après tout ça?"*[1]

I hang my head and continue walking.

It's in the best interests of everyone.

I'm sitting on the edge of the pool, staring at the water in front of me as I finish my beer. It's my fourth one of the night, and my thoughts aren't nearly as loud as they were before.

I can push my parents' secrets to the back of my mind, but I can't forget the look on Mirabelle's face earlier.

She's fucking leaving.

"So this is what you're going to do every night? Drink yourself into a blind stupor and then spend the next morning throwing everything up from the night before?" Quinn asks, plopping down to sit next to me, offering me a water bottle.

"What are you doing here?" I ask, making no move to take the water from him.

"Wilson invited me over to try out the new *Madden* video game, and I thought I'd see if you wanted to join."

"Busy."

"Yeah, it *really* seems like you are." Quinn scoffs.

"Sorry, I'm not in the mood to pretend I'm fine. Every-

---

1. That's all you have to say after everything?

thing is a wreck," I mumble. *I'm sure if Andrew could see me now, he'd push my ass into the pool and tell me to sober up.*

"No, not everything. You had the girl, but you pushed her away. That's your own damn fault."

"I didn't push her away, she left," I retort, racking my brain again for another scrap to add to my memory of the conversation in her bedroom.

"If that's what you want to call it, but I can't imagine a scenario where Mira would ever leave you willingly. It was a dick move for me to ask her out, knowing I never stood a goddamn chance, Walker. I felt like a third wheel on a date in my own home because she spent the entire time talking about you with stars in her eyes."

Why can't he see that I don't want to talk? I don't want to do anything.

"I think the happiest I've seen you is when you're with Mirabelle," Quinn continues, and my jaw clenches. He's not wrong.

"Don't."

"*Don't what?* Point out what a fucking idiot you are by letting her leave?"

"She deserves better," I say, despite my stomach rolling at the thought of Mirabelle with someone else.

Quinn looks at me with clear disappointment. "Yeah, maybe she does."

CHAPTER FORTY-TWO

Henry

It's been radio silence from her since the article came out announcing we had gone our separate ways.

What a pretty way to say something so ugly.

Mirabelle and I are unofficially broken up since we never had a conversation where we explicitly said we were done; however, it's implied.

Owen and Blake welcomed me into their home for Christmas since my family and the Walkers were in France. I had a few days off in my schedule when I could have flown to meet them, but I chose to see Andrew instead. While I was there, photos of Mirabelle and Julien Dubois, a popular French actor, at a quaint bistro in Paris hit headlines. I stared at the pictures for hours, trying to dissect her smile directed at him, and what he could have possibly said to make her laugh so freely.

I asked Kaitlyn, and all she could tell me was Julien stopped by Thalia's gallery in Paris while Mirabelle was picking something up, and he asked her to go with him to the premiere of his movie. I couldn't bring myself to ask my sister any further questions about Mira during their trip because I'm a coward.

The pictures from the premiere gained more traction, and rumors started swirling that Mirabelle was moving on from our whirlwind relationship.

On the other hand, Greg loosened my leash, and while Stacey still accompanies me to everything, they didn't assign another intern.

I've become more of a recluse as I spend my nights drinking probably too much, but football is the only thing going right at the moment. We have one regular season game left before playoffs begin, and my approval rating among the Panthers' fan base is much higher than where I started last summer, which should feel like a relief.

Yet, it doesn't feel like I thought it would feel.

There's something missing—or rather, *someone*.

My jog slows to a walk as I barely make it to the bushes where I sometimes throw up any leftover alcohol from the night before. *I might need to buy a new plant for them if this trend continues.* I feel disgusting, but I continue on the last half mile to my house.

I spot the news vans parked on the road and the photographers on the sidewalk in front of my house before they see me, and I don't have the patience for this today. *What the fuck do they want?*

The second they catch sight of me, flashes start going off, and I regret having taken my shirt off on the last stretch.

"Henry—"

"What do you have to say about the photos of Mirabelle? What about the ones of the two of you?"

"Henry, over here!"

"Have you seen Mirabelle?"

I lift my hand up to block my eyes because I can't see a goddamn thing, and that's when loud honking causes enough of a distraction for me to push through. Wilson's pulled his car out of the garage, waving me in, and not a single person dares to step onto my property.

Wilson enters the house a minute after me, and I breathe heavily as I reach for my water bottle on the counter, swishing the taste of bile from my mouth. "What the fuck is going on?" I ask, and he shakes his head.

"See for yourself." Wilson unlocks his phone and hands it to me.

It's an article about Mirabelle and me, but I'm not sure how that warrants the insanity outside. There's a mature content label, and I look at him skeptically, but it's the grim expression on Wilson's dark features that spikes my anxiety. I scroll, skimming past the words detailing our relationship, but my heart stops fucking beating when I get to the pictures of Mirabelle naked in my backyard swimming, and more through the back windows, sitting on my couch in my jersey with a glass of wine in her hand. I feel nauseous, my blood boiling as scrolling further leads to more pictures of Mirabelle and I having sex in the pool. I turn the phone off, unable to look at the invasion of our privacy any longer. *What the actual fuck?*

Oh my god, she was right. The pictures of her in the house are from when we played the Denver Blizzards. Mirabelle said she thought someone was in the backyard so she went out to look, and this is proof there was someone.

I think I'm going to be sick.

I hired Tom to keep her safe, but I was the one who couldn't keep Mirabelle safe at the one place where I should have been able to.

"How the fuck did they get these pictures?" I seethe, looking up at Wilson.

"I checked the fence line. There's a few boards by the tree in the back that come loose to create a hole big enough for someone to squeeze through. Because of where they got in, I'm not sure the cameras will have captured who it was," he says, his voice shaking with anger. "I tried getting ahold of you, but you left your phone."

I barely carry my phone on me anymore.

What's the point?

"Can you call the security company to ask them to check the dates we were in Denver?"

"You think they came while we were out of town?" he asks, and I drag a hand over my face.

"Mira said she thought someone was in the backyard then. It's why I hired Tom for when I couldn't be with her," I explain briefly, heading upstairs to find my phone.

Fuck, I need to call Mirabelle. She's probably so far from okay, but I'm hoping she's with her family at the beach house. Kaitlyn let it slip in our conversation a few days ago, but she— *like everyone else*—clammed up when I tried to ask questions.

My phone is still plugged in, sitting on my nightstand where I left it earlier. The screen is lit by a steady stream of notifications, but one name stands out above all the others.

It only rings for half a second before the line clicks. "Is Mira okay?"

"Why the fuck haven't you answered your phone?" JJ snaps back at me, ignoring my question.

"I was out for a run, and I left my phone," I say, trying to keep my temper in check. "JJ, she's at the beach house, right?"

Please let her be at the beach house.

"No, she's not here. Why the fuck do you think I've been calling you? Mira drove back to Charlotte last night for a meeting this morning, and she won't answer anyone's calls. Please, can you check on her?" JJ didn't have to ask. I'm already halfway down the stairs again, swiping my keys off the hook by the door to the garage.

"I'm leaving now."

"We changed the code to the house: zero-eight-one-one."

The line beeps with another incoming call. I quickly decline it as I commit the code to memory, laying on the horn to scatter everyone blocking my driveway.

"I'll be there in a few," I promise, and there's yelling in the background on his end. "How are your parents taking it?" I ask, even though I already have a pretty good idea.

"Dad's been yelling at whoever he's on the phone with for a while now, trying to get the pictures taken down, but they're everywhere. Mom's on the phone with the lawyers, trying to send out cease and desists." JJ pauses and then scoffs in disbelief as Stacey calls again. "Are you fucking kidding me? What the fuck were you guys thinking?"

"JJ, we were on my property—"

"Yeah, that wasn't your best idea in the first place, but I'm talking about the audio recording that just dropped on social media of you two fucking in the backseat of a car."

"We weren't fucking," I say, as if that makes what we did any better. I paid the guy to stay quiet, but I never thought he could have recorded the audio. I should have used common fucking sense.

"Sure not what it sounds like, but whatever you say," JJ says, and I speed up. "Have Mira call me, please."

"Of course," I respond, just before JJ hangs up on me.

I'm not surprised to see an even bigger swarm of photographers hanging out on her street. Thank god Sebastian and Thalia had a security gate installed in front of the house during the renovation.

I honk in warning to tell everyone to get out of my way, and if they don't, *fuck it, I'll run them over. Nothing is going to stop me from getting to Mirabelle.*

They scatter like ants, choosing self-preservation as I pull up, entering the code. Looking at the house, you'd never know there had been a fire five months ago.

It's only when I step outside my car that I realize I'm still shirtless from my run because I didn't think to throw a shirt on. The photographers start yelling at me through the gate. I didn't consider the optics of showing up shirtless, but it's too late. I've already added fuel to the madness, and I can't do anything about it now.

I take a gamble that the garage code is the same as the beach house's, and thankfully, it is.

"Mirabelle? It's Henry," I call out, announcing myself after closing the door behind me. With everyone outside, I don't want her to think someone is breaking in.

I make it to the living room when she comes flying down the stairs behind me. Mirabelle slams into my chest, forcing my balance to waver as I wrap my arms around her. She sobs against me, her tears burning my skin as a lump forms in my throat.

"I'm here. I've got you. I'm not going anywhere, *mon cœur*," I say, holding Mirabelle tightly to me. Her knees buckle, and I catch her, carefully lowering us to the ground, cradling Mirabelle's shaking body in my arms. "I'm so fucking sorry," I whisper, pressing my lips to the top of her head.

"You're here. *You're really here*," she mumbles against my skin, and I stroke my hand over her hair repeatedly, tears pooling in my eyes as I silently promise I'm never going to leave her for as long as I live.

"*I'm here.*"

~

Mirabelle is curled up against my side on the couch where she fell asleep, completely exhausted.

We spoke with her parents and their lawyer, but there's nothing that can be done other than suing the shit out of the magazine that originally ran the photos, and hope they'll give up the photographer who took them. As for the audio recording that the town car driver posted, a cease and desist has already been filed, and the Walkers' lawyer is drafting a lawsuit for privacy violation. The original article and recording were taken down, but it doesn't matter. *They're already everywhere.*

I looked outside earlier, and there were even more people camped out than before, probably waiting for a shot of the two of us together. They're vultures.

I slip out from underneath Mirabelle to grab my phone from where I discarded it earlier on the kitchen counter. By the time I return the necessary calls, I'm drained, but I'm desperate for a shower.

I feel a little better after, but not by much. Borrowing clothes from Sebastian, I make my way toward the stairs to take a nap with Mirabelle when I see she left all the lights on in her room.

I flip the switches, and at the last second, I decide to shut the laptop sitting open on her bed. I wasn't trying to look at it, but when the screen lit up before I could shut it, I couldn't look away from the email to Stacey.

Stacey,

Here is the piece about Henry that I promised you. I hope you find it satisfactory. Please let me know if it requires any changes.

Best wishes,

Mirabelle Walker

Against my better judgment, I click the file Mirabelle attached to the email to see for myself if she wrote some kind of scathing article. Not that I wouldn't deserve it, I've been a total dick to her.

.   .   .

The Real Henry Price
By: Mirabelle Walker

Henry Price is many things. To all of you, he's the quarter-back for the Charlotte Blue Panthers, doing his best to help bring home another Super Bowl win. Henry probably looks like the kind of guy you dread your daughter will bring home: a brooding, dark-haired man with tattoos. While he does brood more than he probably should, when he smiles, it could light up the whole world.

I've had the privilege of knowing him my entire life, and yes, I do mean the <u>privilege</u>. Henry is one of a kind. You'll never meet a more loyal friend, a more supportive teammate, or a more dedicated player. He's the first person to offer you the shirt off his back, and let me tell you, the view isn't so bad either. Kidding! (Actually, I'm not, but for the sake of this article, we can pretend I am.)

Henry also carries the weight of the world on his shoulders, never settling for anything less than perfection. You're probably wondering what he could possibly be stressed about when he has everything?

He constantly worries about not being enough for everyone. That kind of pressure can be crippling, especially for a professional athlete. Henry puts his mental and physical health on the line every single day for this team. You praise him when the team succeeds, but the second he's human, it's time for the guillotine. It's harder than it looks to be the best when you're also competing against the best.

To me, Henry Price is a perfectly imperfect human being. He has good days and bad days. He's just like you, and like you, he enjoys having privacy despite being a public figure. Excelling at the highest level when it comes to throwing a football doesn't mean the private details of his life need to be made public for your entertainment.

I know that I'm biased when it comes to Henry. I've only spent half of my life loving him for who he is and not for who everyone expects him to be. He is an incredible person that we are lucky to exist at the same time as.

I have never met someone better fit to lead this team than Henry, and I think his teammates would agree with me. He has a way of making you believe you're capable of anything, and leaders like that are how teams thrive.

Have more grace and accept him for who he is, or find another team to root for because Henry Price isn't going anywhere.

My jaw hangs open.

She wrote this? After everything?

The floor creaks to my left, and I twist to see Mirabelle standing there, catching me red-handed. She offers me a timid smile, but her swollen eyes tear my heart apart. "Does it read too much like a love letter?"

"Did you mean what you wrote?" I ask, my voice thick with emotion.

"Every word."

I fucking love her. "Mirabelle, fuck . . . I'm so sorry," I say, cupping her face in my hands as her lower lip trembles.

"I don't want to talk about today anymore. It fucking sucks, but I'm *so* tired of crying. I want to forget this ever happened," she says, a broken laugh escaping her as a tear slips down her cheek. I quickly brush it away with my thumb, my heart pounding loudly in my chest.

"We don't have to talk about today," I agree. We'll figure the rest out later. *We're a team.*

"Henry, kiss me. Please," she whispers, and I don't need to be told twice, taking the opportunity I didn't think I'd have again.

CHAPTER FORTY-THREE

Mirabelle

Henry's lips on mine make everything from this fucking day fade into background noise. It doesn't feel like we've spent over a month apart, or how it's been radio silence since we ran into each other on my last day.

I convey all the hurt and anger I've felt by pressing my mouth harder against his much softer touch.

I don't want sweet and gentle.

I want rough and catastrophic.

Henry and I are an impending disaster waiting to happen. Or are we a disaster that's already happened?

I'm not sure, but we're already on a collision course that can't be stopped.

Is this a bad idea? *Probably. Actually, most definitely.* But I can't help myself. He's here. He already read the letter I poured my heart and soul into. What more do I have to lose?

I thread my hands through Henry's hair, pulling on it as he finally matches my urgency, pressing me against the wall. Nipping at his lower lip to get him to deepen the kiss further, Henry complies like he understands everything I need.

He understands everything except how much I need him

in my life. If he understood that, then Henry wouldn't have let me leave. He wouldn't have let me walk out the door without chasing after me. He wouldn't have been able to walk away from me in the stadium.

I love this man so much that it physically pains me to be apart from him, but loving him hurts too. I feel tears slipping down my cheeks and he tries to pull away from me, no doubt noticing that I'm crying.

I don't want to cry.

I'm so tired of crying.

I slip my hand down the front of Henry's shorts, wrapping my fingers around his hardening length. He thankfully stops trying to pull away from me, moaning into my mouth as I slowly begin to pump my hand.

Henry is threatening to devour me, but I refuse, fighting back to maintain control. He pulls away, dropping his head to kiss my neck as I increase my speed.

He presses his lips to my skin, and I want to feel his mouth everywhere on me. *How am I going to survive him?*

"Mon cœur," he says, his hips thrusting with my firm strokes. My heart is like broken glass held together with tape, but that pet name threatens to shatter it completely. Henry's amber eyes are hazy with lust as his hands clumsily move to the bottom of my shirt, and I let go, allowing him to pull it off me, his heated touch skimming over my torso and the curves of my breasts. He pulls off his own, and my breath hitches at the sight of his impressive body as Henry also removes his shorts.

"Tu es belle."[1]

"Merci,"[2] I whisper, unable to look away from his face, watching me in wonder.

Henry hooks his thumbs on the waistband of my under-

---

1. You are beautiful.
2. Thank you.

wear and shorts, pulling them down my body. He reaches behind my thighs, easily lifting me to move us to my bed. I push away my laptop, as Henry teases his fingers to see if I'm ready for him.

"Please," I say, my body arching into him as he pushes two fingers into me. I play with my nipple, biting my lip to hold back a whimper as Henry worships my body, dropping to his knees in front of me, his rough hands holding my thighs firmly apart.

When his mouth replaces his fingers, my eyes flutter shut as I'm unable to bite back the incoherent sounds falling from my mouth. My body is a language that Henry—*and Henry alone*—is fluent in. "Please, I need you," I beg, as his unshaven face scratches against my skin, causing sensory overload.

He kisses his way up my body. "I'm sorry," he says, and I shake my head as his body settles over mine.

"I told you I don't want to talk about today."

Henry kisses my neck delicately, lifting his eyes to meet mine. "I'm not talking about today," he says, and the most dangerous thing about Henry is his ability to make me hope. "Do you have any condoms?" he asks, his hand settling over mine on my breast to play with the sensitive peak.

"I haven't needed them," I say, offering a silent invitation. I recognize the predatory spark in his eyes when he realizes I haven't been with anyone. How could I? Henry is the only one who makes me feel alive. Despite everything, I don't want to be with anyone but Henry. I can't imagine it.

Henry wastes no time, hooking my legs around his trim waist, and thrusting deeply into me. "Fuck," he swears, pulling back painfully slow as he looks into my eyes. "I'm sorry I didn't stop you from leaving," Henry says, his hips slamming into mine hard enough I barely have a chance to process his words before he's pulling back again. "I'm sorry I didn't talk to you." *Repeat.* "I'm sorry I told you I didn't care." His eyes are shining with what I assume is . . . *regret.* "I care so fucking much, Mira." *Repeat.* "I'm sorry that you love me because I *don't* deserve it." Henry's hips thrust at an upward angle, hitting the right spot to make me gasp in pleasure as my heart bleeds out. "I'm so fucking sorry for all of it."

I know it's not healthy or remotely good for me in any way, but I've spent the last hour reading all the articles being published about me. I couldn't help but look at the comments either.

I waited for Henry to fall asleep—which didn't take long —before I slipped out of bed. It was too much for my heart to bear being held by him.

In all of his apologies, he never once said he loved me.

He finally acknowledged he heard me say I love him, but he also said he didn't deserve it. *It's my choice to decide who deserves my love.*

All of the solo shots of me swimming naked were from the weekend Henry was in Denver. The flash I convinced myself was a figment of my imagination while on the phone with JJ was real. Someone had been there taking pictures of me.

I shudder with disgust as my phone vibrates again, but for the first time today, I answer.

"Oh thank god, you *finally* answered. Are you okay? I can't believe the nerve of the fucking media for taking naked photos of you and then publishing them? It's like the world has gone fucking mad, Mira," Emily rambles, and I look back at the laptop screen.

"The world went mad a long time ago," I say.

"Are you okay?" she repeats.

"I feel kind of numb."

"I'm looking at flights right now."

"Em, you don't have to do that. Henry's with me. I'll be okay. A couple of nude photos never hurt anyone," I joke, but the reality of the matter is I am hurt. I feel violated in a way I never thought I would, even after how things spiraled after the Olympics.

"Henry's there?" she asks, her voice a pitch higher in surprise. Not that I blame her. I was a little surprised myself when I heard him come in earlier.

"Yep," I answer, not wanting to elaborate.

"Oh, I see."

I furrow my brow as I shut my computer. "You see what?"

"Are you getting back together?" Emily asks, causing me to rub my face.

"No."

We're not. I can't be with someone who doesn't believe they deserve my love. I know I was the one who walked away, but it was the right thing to do. I never imagined he wouldn't chase after me, but Henry's made it clear where his priorities lie, and they're not with me.

"Mirabelle, are you sure? You shouldn't make this decision now. There's a lot going on . . ." she trails off.

"Henry and I aren't getting back together. Today was a blip. It doesn't matter he showed up like a knight in shining armor, it doesn't change anything." No sooner are the words out of my mouth do I regret saying them. It didn't feel like a blip, but that's all it needs to be.

A throat clears behind me, and I turn quickly, nearly falling off the stool to see Henry standing there, staring at me.

"Uh, I gotta go, I'll call you later." I hang up before Emily can protest.

Henry folds his arms over his chest, a frown marring his handsome features. "So this isn't up for discussion?"

"What is *this*?" I counter.

"I want to be with you."

"I thought you didn't care." My tone is cruel, but they're his words.

He winces, and I'm glad they sting. "I was drunk, Mirabelle. Of course I care. I didn't remember that conversation until a few days after I ran into you at the stadium."

Ouch. "That was three and a half weeks ago, Henry. You had plenty of time to tell me you wanted to be with me, but instead you allowed Stacey to run an article saying *we had gone our separate ways.*" I can feel my temper starting to slip. "You didn't even have the decency to send me a text saying we were over."

"I didn't think you wanted to hear from me. I've been trying to figure everything out, and come to terms with what Allison did, but I miss you. I've missed you every single day, and I'm miserable without you. I've spent nearly every single night drunk off my ass, and it hasn't done a single goddamn thing to fix the part of me that is terrified of loving someone, and giving them that power over me. But being with you? You make me want *more.* You make me believe love can exist without strings attached. You make me want to confront my demons to be worthy of your love."

"I'm glad you want more for yourself, but you shouldn't do it for me. You need to do it for you," I insist, and Henry steps closer to me, taking my face in his hands.

"Mirabelle, I want to be the type of man you deserve, and I'm willing to spend every day proving I'll try to be him because I love you," he says, and it'd be so easy to give in to him. "I'm going to regret letting you walk away for the rest of my life, but I'm begging you to forgive me."

I want to believe him.

But it's because I love Henry, that I choose him, even when he won't.

"*No.*"

CHAPTER FORTY-FOUR

Mirabelle

THE WETSUIT CLINGING TO MY SKIN IS THE ONLY thing keeping me warm at this time of morning as the ocean laps at my legs straddling my surfboard. I got an early start today.

I spend nearly all my time out here now, entire days lost on the water as I stare into the distance, hoping if I stay out here long enough, I might find the answers to fix everything.

The rising sun reflects off the water as the salt air soothes the anxiety wreaking havoc in my mind.

Despite it being the middle of January, my cheeks and nose are sunburned from all the hours on my board.

I haven't left the beach house since returning from Charlotte. I've never been more thankful to have a private beach. It's my sanctuary from all the noise. Tom asked if I'd like him to stay on, but his family lives in Charlotte. I can't ask him to stay in Wilmington when I'm not leaving the house, so I told him I'd let him know if I needed his services in the future.

The ocean is glass today, leaving little possibility for any surfing, but I like sitting out here regardless.

My mother paddles up next to me, sitting up on her board.

"Good morning," she greets, and I offer her a faint smile in response. I trail my fingers through the water as she floats a few feet away.

My mind is plagued by memories of Henry. It's hard to find a memory he isn't a part of because I can't remember a time when I wasn't hopelessly in love with him.

"I told Dad last night I think one of these days you might turn into a mermaid with how much time you've been spending out here."

A short chuckle escapes me, and I shake my head at her. "I think it'd be fun to grow a tail."

"If it happens, make sure you let me know how, so I can join you." Mom winks, her green eyes taking on a sea-green color from the water around us.

"I wouldn't want to be a mermaid without you," I say, splashing her.

"C'est bon de te voir sourire."[1]

"I've been smiling."

Her smile is sad. *"Non tu ne faisais pas."*[2]

I look back out at the horizon, noting the seagulls crying out as they soar. "Henry asked me to take him back."

I've told her everything except for the conversation that took place before I asked Henry to leave that day. Honestly, I haven't said much of anything since the photos and that recording were released.

"And you said no," Mom infers, my silence only confirming it. "I know you're like your dad in most ways, but you're more like me than you know. The first time Dad

---

1. It's good to see you smile.
2. No. You haven't.

proposed to me, I didn't have an answer for him, and he left me."

I startle, nearly falling off my board in the process. "What do you mean he left you?"

"I mean, he left. He disappeared for a week, and I waited for him to come home. Bash . . . he didn't want to talk to me, so he told me to go, and I did. I went to Africa for six months, and his football career took off. He met another woman, fell in love with her, and then Mimi died. She told me to tell him I still loved him, and it was at her funeral I learned they were engaged."

"Dad was engaged to someone else?" I can't believe I've never heard any of this.

"Yeah, he was. I regretted not saying yes, every single day for almost four years," Mom confirms, and I blink, staring at her. *Oh my god, this is what Chris was talking about in New York.*

"I thought you have been together since college?"

She chuckles, shaking her head. "That's when we originally fell in love, but our story is a bit more complicated than that. To put it frankly, your sperm donor is a fucking idiot sometimes."

"Gross, don't call Dad that." I wrinkle my nose in disgust, but my curiosity is dying to know the truth. "So what happened?"

Mom smiles, wistfully staring at the horizon. "It's a long story."

"I seriously have nothing but time, Mom."

She wasn't lying, it is a long story. Parts of it make me laugh, whereas other parts cause my jaw to literally drop in shock, and I shed more than a few tears as Mom explains just how much more there is to their story than I ever thought possible.

"I can't believe you never said anything . . . that's just . . . wow."

"It all turned out the way it was meant to, but it took us a lot of heartbreak to get here, so your father and I decided we would tell you all if there were ever a reason to. Maybe we're wrong for that, but this felt like a pretty good reason so you know it's okay to not have everything figured out instantly."

"But if I wait too long to figure it out, then I risk losing him forever. I don't want Henry to be an almost in my life," I say, understanding what Mom's getting at.

"You're my daughter, and I love you no matter what. Please don't forget who you're named after," she says, reaching across the space between us to squeeze my hand, tears shining in her eyes.

"I haven't."

"I wish you could have met Mimi. She always seemed to know the right thing to say," Mom says, and I smile at her.

"You do a pretty good job, Mom."

Bailey is sitting on his phone while Hunter's eyes are glued to the television along with our parents, watching Duke compete in the College Football Championship game. I'm reading my book, but I keep looking over at my parents sitting together on the couch. Dad has his arm wrapped around Mom's shoulders, and normally I'd think it's embarrassing, but now I don't feel anything but happy for them. I never in a million years would have guessed that Dad was engaged to someone else. It's just so weird to think of him with someone other than Mom.

There's a fresh bouquet of flowers that was waiting for Mom when we came in from surfing. Dad's drilled it into us our entire lives that flowers are special and shouldn't be used only as an apology. Flowers are meant for the most ordinary of days and for doing small things for the person you care about to make them happy.

My name coming through the speakers draws my attention to the television.

"—andal with Mirabelle Walker. It seems to have made him more popular with the ladies, if you can believe it. I've even heard rumors Calvin Klein has reached out to him about a sponsorship. I'm fairly certain the kids are calling that big dick energy," one of the male sports announcers says to the circle of others sitting around the table.

All of the men laugh as the one woman at the table looks disgusted.

"Have you seen the videos of women waiting outside the stadium with signs for him? I've never seen anything like it. It makes me think about hiring someone to leak naked pictures of me," another says, and Hunter moves to mute the speakers, but I shake my head.

"Leave it, Hunter. It's fine."

He looks uneasy, but sets the remote down.

"This is a classic case where the man is praised and the woman is shamed, despite both of them having their privacy violated," the female announcer interrupts.

She's not wrong. I've been called every derogatory name in the book, and new ones are even being created to describe me.

"I'm not shaming her, but I am wondering why she never pursued a modeling career—" one of the men starts to say, but Hunter mutes the sound before he can finish his sentence.

I turn to look at him, and he stares right back at me. "I'm not listening to them talk about you that way."

"The same way everyone else is talking about me? This isn't going away, so we might as well stop avoiding it." I fight the urge to go back out to the water. I need to return to the land of the living at some point. The longer I hide out, the harder it's going to be.

"Mirabelle, he's not avoiding it. Hunter did the right thing. You don't need to listen to that shit," Dad says firmly, leaving no room for argument.

"Dad—"

"No, Mira. I don't want to listen to it either, unless you want me to end up in jail."

Hunter offers me a reassuring smile. "I would like to point out how wrong he was, though. If any of us is going to pursue a modeling career, everyone knows it'll be JJ."

It's the exact wrong thing to say, which is why it does such a perfect job of diffusing the tension.

The room erupts into laughter and Dad shakes his head at us. "How the hell did I get stuck with kids that are so much like Owen?"

CHAPTER FORTY-FIVE

Mirabelle

THE ROAR OF THE STADIUM IS LOUD AROUND ME. I'M not surprised, considering how at the beginning of the season, everyone thought Henry would never be able to lead us to the playoffs.

Tom is sitting by the door of the private room where we're watching the game, but you can still hear everything going on outside.

My family is in their box, and I'm going to try joining them later, but I need to work up to it. I'm already nervous about the conversation I need to have with Henry after the game, and there's only so much I can handle at a time.

Oh fuck. I think I'm going to be sick.

I twist the bouquet of flowers I brought in my hands as a peace offering, and I hope he accepts them. Honestly, I wouldn't be able to blame him if he didn't.

"Mirabelle, you're going to destroy those flowers before you can give them to him if you keep twirling them," Tom says, and I groan, setting them down on the table.

"Sorry, you're right," I mumble, taking a seat in the chair as I watch the screen on the wall broadcasting the game, waiting for a glimpse of Henry. "Do you think it's dumb I got him flowers?" I ask, peeking in Tom's direction.

"Henry won't think it's dumb if it means something special to you."

"Are you sure?" My leg won't stop bouncing, and Tom raises his eyebrows at me.

"I'm sure."

I exhale, refocusing on the screen.

The talk with my mom was exactly what I needed to hear, and I weighed the pros and cons of being with Henry, and being without him. The pros of being with him outweighed every single con I could come up with.

I want to be with Henry, even if he doesn't believe he's deserving of my love. I've never wanted to be with anyone else.

My phone vibrates in my pocket, and I pull it out, extremely confused why Uncle Owen is calling me, when the Panthers are supposed to be walking onto the field shortly. I answer, holding it up to my ear. "Hello?"

"Did you come today with your family, or did you stay at the house?" he asks urgently, and Tom is looking at me with concern.

"I'm here in a private room with Tom. What's going on?"

"I need you in the locker room as quickly as you can get here," Uncle Owen says.

"The locker room? Why?" I ask, but the line drops. "He hung up," I say, looking at Tom confused.

"Who is asking you to go to the locker room?" Tom asks, handing me the hat we used to get me into the stadium without drawing everyone's attention to me. I'm wearing the jersey Henry gave me earlier in the season, along with jeans and sneakers, so at least I'll blend in.

"My uncle," I say, pulling the hat low to hide my face, leaving the rest of my things in the room.

Tom leads the way, getting us there without anyone seeing,

and I slip into the locker room. Every single player looks at me, and I feel my face flush bright red under the attention. I breathe a sigh of relief when Wilson walks toward me, a warm smile on his familiar face, but I'm distracted by the arguing in the background.

"You have no idea how happy I am to see you," Wilson says, grabbing my hand to pull me along.

"Why am I here?" I ask, trying to keep up with his long strides.

"I already told you I'm not going out there unless it's wearing this jersey," Henry says firmly, not seeing me because his back is to me. *What's wrong with his jersey?*

"Price, I'm sympathetic to the big romantic gesture you're trying to do for my niece, but unless you've legally changed your last name to Walker, the league isn't going to let you wear that jersey. All you're going to do is rack up fines, and I can't play you without the whole team facing penalties," my uncle argues, and I realize instead of *Price* in block letters on the back of Henry's jersey, it reads *Walker* with his number below it.

Oh. That's why I'm here.

"Then I'm not going out there."

Oh my god. I know I'm hallucinating. Henry did not have an official jersey made with my last name on it.

"It's a fucking playoff game. Your teammates did nothing to deserve their quarterback—" My uncle falters, finally noticing me. "Thank god. Maybe you can talk some sense into him. He won't listen to me." Uncle Owen scoffs, throwing his hands up in the air.

When Henry turns around to look at me, it feels like the world has stopped spinning and time stands still.

His eyes widen as he blinks, rubbing them as if he can't believe I'm actually here.

"Hi." I offer a short wave, and I immediately feel my

cheeks burn from mortification. *Waving? I seriously couldn't think of anything better?*

"Mirabelle?"

Oh god, I messed up thinking I was doing the right thing by pushing Henry away.

"How are you here?" he asks, and I shrug.

"Haven't you heard my dad used to be someone important here, or something?" I joke, and an impatient look from my uncle tells me I need to hurry this up. *Got it. This isn't our romantic reunion yet.* I wipe my sweaty palms on my thighs. "You're wearing the wrong jersey," I say, and Henry shakes his head.

"I'm not."

It's the intensity of his gaze that tells me he means it. "Henry, they're not going to let you play. This game is more important than the last name on your jersey," I say, and he drags a hand through his dark hair.

"Is it?" he questions, rendering me fucking speechless.

I've missed him more than words could ever try to explain.

"I-I can't be the reason you're not on the field with your team today. I would never forgive myself, so if you won't do it for them, do it for me," I say, and Henry looks as torn as I feel. Uncle Owen stops his pacing as an official comes up to him, and it's now or never.

"I'd like to make it clear I'm only doing this for you," he says, pulling off the jersey, and I can't resist smiling as the whole locker room erupts into cheers when Henry pulls the proper one over his gear.

"Thank fuck, get your asses out to the tunnel before we're fucking late," Uncle Owen yells, and the locker room explodes into chaos.

I turn to disappear the way I came, when my hand is caught, stopping me. "Can I see you after the game?" Henry asks, and I hate the uncertainty in the question. I put that fear in him, but we're stronger together than we are apart.

"Only if you win," I say, knowing he needs a challenge, and he grins.

"You can count on it," Henry promises, stepping away to follow the team, but before he disappears from view, he glances back to see if I'm still standing there.

I'm not going anywhere.

~

"Is it true you almost didn't play today because you refused to take off a jersey with your number and the last name Walker?" Erin Marshall, a rising sideline reporter, asks Henry in the postgame interview playing on the television in the private room.

"Yeah, it is," Henry confirms as if it's an everyday occurrence for him.

"Why would you risk it during playoffs?" she asks, and Tom nudges me.

"You could be down there with him. It looks like quite the celebration after the win they just pulled off," Tom suggests.

"I'm good here," I say, listening for his answer.

Henry smiles, and it's the one usually reserved for me. I'm a little jealous about sharing it with everyone, but his next sentence makes up for it. "Because I'm going to marry Mirabelle Walker, and being loved by her is worth risking everything."

Shut the fucking front door.

"Did he really—"

"I told you not to be worried about the flowers," Tom says, and I'm wondering if I'm stuck inside a fever dream.

It feels like forever before Henry steps through the door and Tom exits.

A sense of calm washes over me, all my anxiety finally disappearing now that I'm in the same room as Henry. "I know it's my fault we're not together right now, because I stupidly told you no when you asked me to forgive you. I thought it was the right thing to do, but I think it caused us both a lot of unnecessary pain," I say, twisting the bouquet of flowers in my hands.

"Mirabelle—" Henry begins, moving closer to me.

"I'm not finished," I interrupt, offering him the wild-flowers I picked out. He looks at them, confused, and I take that as my cue to continue. "My dad has always bought flowers for my mom. I asked him once why he did it, and he told me the fact he *wanted* to buy them was how he knew she was *the one*. He said remembering to do the small things for someone shows how important they truly are to you. I know it might be weird for me to be the one giving you flowers, but I want to remember to do the small things for you because I love you."

Please take the flowers, Henry.

Henry's fingers brush over mine as he takes them from me, sparking electrical shocks through my body. "I don't think anyone has ever gotten me flowers before," he says, making me wonder if this is how Dad feels when buying them for Mom.

"I know roses are standard, but I thought they were a little cliché, so—"

"*Je les aime et toi,*"[1] he states, staring directly into my soul.

"*Vraiment?*"[2] I whisper, and Henry sets the flowers down carefully.

Henry pulls me into his arms, and I instantly wrap mine around his strong torso, pressing my face into his chest. "*Vrai-*

---

1. I love them and you.
2. Really?

ment,[3] he confirms, holding me tight. I'm certain there's no better feeling than having Henry's arms wrapped around me.

I feel lighter than I have in weeks. Henry rests his chin on the top of my head, and I breathe deeply.

I feel like I'm home.

"Can it be my turn to talk?" Henry asks after a few minutes, and I look up at him.

"Of course."

I pull away, but Henry intertwines our fingers, pulling me into his lap after he sits in one of the chairs at the table. His brow furrows as he thinks of the right words to say, and I squeeze his hand reassuringly to let him know I'm not going anywhere.

He exhales slowly, shaking his head, turning away.

I use my free hand to turn his face to me. "Henry, what is it?"

"I saw Allison at the last game. She showed up right before kickoff, demanding to be let in," he says. I can't help the little gasp that escapes, because this explains why he looked miserable during that game. "I always knew it could happen, but I never thought she'd actually show up."

"I'm sorry."

"I'm not. You were right when you said I needed to face my demons. I was planning on going to see her after that game before postseason began, but she saved me a trip."

Oh Henry.

My heart melts for him, this incredible man.

"I had them put her in a private room—actually, I think it could have been this one for all I know—until after the game. Allison made excuses, saying she's doing better and wants to be a part of my life again. That's what all the phone calls have been about."

---

3. Really.

"What did you say?" I ask.

"I wrote her a check on the spot for five hundred thousand and asked her to pick: me or the money," he says, running his thumb back and forth over the back of my hand. "She picked the money, which I expected, but I told her to never call me again, and if she did, I'd file a restraining order before the phone call was over."

"This might be a dumb question, but are you okay?"

He chuckles, lifting our intertwined hands up to press a kiss to my knuckles. "Believe it or not, yeah . . . I'm okay. I thought I had this void in me because my birth mother didn't love me enough to stay, but the truth is, I have a mother who picked me—who *chose* to love me, regardless of biology."

Tears spring to my eyes because that might be the sweetest thing I've ever heard him say. "I'm so happy for you."

"The only thing I had left to do was convince you that we belong together, but I guess you came to that conclusion all on your own. I even made a list," Henry says, and I laugh, wiping my eye as a tear escapes.

"You made a list?"

He smiles warmly, lighting up the whole room. "I did. I know how much you like checking things off, and everything on it seems inevitable for us, but it could be fun to check them off together."

"Can I see it?" I ask, and my head explodes when he pulls it out of his back pocket, handing it to me.

Henry's to-do list:
Convince Mirabelle to forgive me
Move in together
Propose
Take her last name

Adopt a dog
Kids?
Learn to salsa

<u>Bonus points</u>
Grow old together
Make a new list together

My vision floods with tears, and I didn't think it was possible to feel this understood. Henry wipes my cheeks gently with his thumb. "*Mon cœur*, don't cry."

"*Don't cry?* You can't write all this and expect me to not cry," I say, sniffling as I try to regain control over my emotions. "Is there a pen in here?"

"Do you have one in your bag?" he asks, reaching for it, and thankfully, there is.

I pull the cap off and check the first thing off the list. *He's right, I do like to check things off.*

"I love you," I say, smiling widely at the man I've loved my entire life.

"I love you too," he echoes, leaning forward to kiss me, making the whole world fade away.

Epilogue

MIRABELLE

I DRAG MY SURFBOARD ONTO THE SAND, ABSOLUTELY exhausted from the last hour I've spent with Henry, shredding some of the best waves we've ever had at this beach. It's too bad JJ's in Florida for spring break with his friends from college. My parents are in France, and Hunter is in Mexico with Kaitlyn, Chris, and Penelope.

Bailey stayed here with me, not out of choice, but basically because Mom and Dad said they weren't going to reward his behavior with international trips.

It's been seven months, and he's still barely speaking to any of us.

I look back at the water just in time to see Henry fall off his board. He pokes his head up from under the surface and climbs back on the board before paddling in.

"You fell again," I tease, sitting down in the sand once he's close enough to hear me over the crashing waves.

"You fell too," Henry retorts, setting his board next to mine, and I laugh.

"Yeah, but I only fell once, and that was the fourth time you've fallen."

He shakes his head like a dog, plopping down next to me on the beach. "Yes, you're right. I fell four times," Henry admits, looking over at me with a dopey smile on his face.

"You fell four times, but I still love you," I say, smiling, and his somehow shines brighter. I lean over to kiss him briefly on the lips, deliriously happy to be here with Henry.

"Je t'aime aussi."[1]

I move to sit between his legs, leaning against Henry's chest as we watch the large waves roll in.

"I could get used to this," I say, and Henry presses a short kiss to the side of my head.

"Me too. It's a nice change of pace from the craziness during season," he admits.

"Definitely," I agree, exhaling. Thankfully, things have started to die down in the media, but I'm still trying to figure out my path forward. All I know for sure is I can do anything with Henry by my side. "Do you think we should invite Bailey to surf with us?"

"If you want to, but I'm not sure he'll say yes."

I've tried repeatedly to talk to Bailey, but I haven't been able to get through to him. I don't know how to help. My little brother is a shell of who he used to be. It makes me sad.

I hear Henry sniff behind me, and I turn around to look at him confused. "Are you smelling me? That's kinda weird, babe."

There's a flicker of amusement on his face, but he shakes his head. "No, I'm not smelling you. Do you smell smoke?"

I inhale the familiar smell of salt that fills my lungs, but Henry's right. I do smell smoke. *No, no, no.* Bailey's in the house. Fear instantly floods my body at the thought of my brother getting trapped, and Henry and I not being able to do a damn thing about it.

---

1. I love you too.

I leap to my feet, Henry just a mere second behind me as we run, slipping every few feet on the loose sand to get to the house.

My heart fucking stops at the sight of a blazing fire in the brush, dangerously close to the house, with Bailey standing in front of it.

"Bailey, what the hell are you doing?" I yell, grabbing his arm to pull him back before the flames can burn him. "Henry, call 911!" I shout over my shoulder as Henry dashes up the deck stairs to get one of our phones we left inside.

His emerald eyes are rimmed with red as they slowly focus on me. "*Nothing.* I'm doing nothing," Bailey slurs, speaking to me for the first time in months. My brain stutters, feeling like it's working overtime to understand the situation.

"Are you drunk?" I ask, my brain racing to piece everything together.

I look closer at the fire, this time noting all the soccer apparel in the thick of it, but lying on top is the framed photo of our entire family at Dad's last game, the glass shattered.

"Did you light this?" I ask, staring at my younger brother in horror, spotting the box of matches in his hand.

"Get away from there before the wind shifts. The fire department is on their way," Henry calls out, and I can't breathe. "Mira?"

"Did you light this fire?" I repeat my question, but I don't think I want an answer. Bailey wobbles, yanking his arm from my grip.

"You don't understand, Mirabelle!"

"What don't I understand? For fuck's sake, Bailey, how can I when you haven't said anything? We can't keep going around in circles like this!"

"Everyone is a fucking liar, and I can't stand it! You left and lied about Henry. You don't care about us anymore, you only care about him! Mom and Dad have been lying our entire lives, and Hunter lied about Kaitlyn! The only one of us who isn't a fucking liar is JJ," Bailey seethes, and I take a step back from him.

I wanted him to talk, and he's finally talking.

"What exactly are Mom and Dad lying about?" I ask, my entire body frozen.

"Dad was engaged to someone else, and then he cheated on her with Mom. He left her, refusing to help her with anything. He is horrible and walks around acting like he's the king of the fucking world. I hate him, I hate Mom, and I hate this fucking family."

Henry wraps a protective arm around my waist, tugging me away from the heat of the flames. "I'm not sure where you got any of that information, but it's not true. That's not what happened with Mom and Dad, but even if it were, that doesn't give you an excuse to burn all your soccer gear! What if the house catches on fire? What am I supposed to tell our parents?"

It's only then that the truth hits me.

"You're the arsonist." I exhale as Henry's grip on me tightens.

"It was me, and I'd do it again. Maybe it all deserves to burn," Bailey confirms, his face painted with hatred as the sirens of fire trucks are audible in the background.

Acknowledgments

It feels surreal for my third book to be out in the wild, but luckily, I've been surrounded by a wonderful support system that has helped this book become what it is.

To my parents, thank you, but in the nicest way possible, I hope you never read this book.

Nicole, thank you for your endless support and being the voice of reason when my brain overthinks absolutely everything. Thank you for always answering the phone and reading the hundreds of drafts I sent your way. You're the best friend someone could ask for, and I've never been more thankful for a game of sand volleyball in my life.

Grandma Sandi, thank you for giving me a safe place to work on this book when the rest of the world was so loud I couldn't put more than two words together at a time. Not only did you have a book written in your house, your name will live in it forever now! The Farm will forever be my favorite place in the world to escape to.

Bryce, Suzanne, and Scott, I feel so incredibly lucky to have you in my life. Thank you for shouting about my books from the rooftops, supporting me, and making sure I know I'm always welcome.

Paisley, I can't begin to tell you how grateful I am for you. Thank you for believing in me, and for being the best cheerleader an author could ask for. My heart is so happy for your family, and I can't wait to see what we do in the future together!

To Amanda and Kennedy, it only feels right to group you

together in this, because in my mind, you're a package deal. I'm not sure I have the right words to describe what your friendship has meant to me over the last year since our paths crossed. Thank you for being my sounding boards, my confidants, and for reminding me why I love to write on the days when I struggled the most. You're incredible hype women who never fail to put a smile on my face, and I truly can't thank you both enough. This book wouldn't be what it is without your support, but most of all, thank you for loving my characters enough to wait for the last few chapters to be written one at a time. My sincerest apologies for that initial jump scare!

Aurélie, a million thank yous for sharing your wonderful knowledge of the French language with me to add that extra special layer to Henry and Mirabelle's relationship! I am so grateful for your help and support.

To Hannah, thank you for helping *Chasing After You* become the best version of itself. You are an absolute rock star, and I'm eagerly awaiting our next project together! Your attention to detail was incredible while helping preserve my voice in my writing. I appreciate you more than you can ever know, and I have to say I'm right there with you when it comes to loving Henry!!!! #TeamHenry

My ARC readers, thank you from the bottom of my heart for giving my book a chance, and for shouting from the rooftops about Henry and Mirabelle. I am so appreciative of the time you spent reading and creating a review.

To Bonnie, thank you for helping me proof the final manuscript! You did an incredible job with polishing everything to help me wrap it neatly into a bow!

Thank you to the amazing team at Books and Moods for creating my incredibly jaw dropping cover. I could not dream of a better face for my book, and I don't think I'll ever get over how beautiful this cover is.

Lastly, my heart is so full of love from everyone who has

given my book a chance. This wouldn't be possible without you.

Before You, the second installment of the Reckless Love series, is out now, and I can't wait for you to find out if JJ finds his love from France.

Bonus Chapter

HENRIETTA & THE LESSON

MIRABELLE

I miss you.

I press send on my text to Henry just as my alarm goes off, reminding me my class starts in five minutes.

He's currently at the Panther's training camp, staying in the dorms of the college it's at every year. I visited the first week, but I had to get back to teach my classes, and he needed to focus on getting ready for this upcoming season.

Henry calls every night to check in, but last night was the first time he fell asleep before calling. He called me back this morning, but I was already at pilates with Wilson's boyfriend, Jason, and our friend, Erin, so I missed it. I'm trying not to be upset with him, because logically, I know it's not his fault he fell asleep, but I *miss* Henry. *It feels like a part of me is missing when he's gone.*

Erin was the reporter who asked Henry after the playoff game a year and a half ago about the jersey he wanted to take the field wearing, and Henry gave his now infamous declaration of his plans to marry me. She reached out to me a few weeks afterward on social media to ask me if I knew what he was planning that day, and we've been friends ever since.

Jason and Wilson started seeing each other last summer after Wilson participated in a celebrity softball game to raise awareness for pediatric leukemia. Jason's a left wing for the Carolina Dolphins, and we've grown close since they started dating. He's a really great guy, and told us this morning he wants to ask Wilson to move in with him.

Since last fall, I've been teaching beginner classes at the same gym I trained at growing up, and I've loved every second of it. It's been nice to have something to focus on, because those first few months after Bailey ran away, I tried everything I could think of to track him down. I spiraled further after Bailey called JJ five weeks after leaving to ask us to stop looking for him, and the guilts threatened to consume me. My parents filed a missing persons report, but because it was a week and a half before Bailey turned eighteen, the police looked, but when nothing came of it, we were told we'd be notified if his description matched any unidentified persons descriptions found.

Bailey has so far checked in almost every six to eight weeks, but only with JJ, and the calls are just long enough to tell JJ he's okay before hanging up.

It took months before I started feeling like myself again, but I'm convinced the guilt I feel has become part of my new normal. I miss my little brother so much it physically causes me pain, but I haven't lost hope he'll come back.

I sigh, pulling my long blonde hair back into a braid, trying to ignore the sadness threatening to overwhelm me today. Some days are worse than others, and I have a feeling today might be one of those days. Seeing my friends this morning helped some, but at least Henry will be back next week.

I climb out of my car, heading inside the gym to put my

things away, the atmosphere is already helping to calm my fraying nerves. Being here helps more than I ever imagined because I do my best to put aside my personal feelings for the kids in my class to give them the best experience possible. It's what they deserve.

Greeting some of the parents in the sitting area by the bathrooms, but when I walk into the gymnasium, my heart feels lighter to see some of my girls already practicing their cartwheels. They started learning how to do them last week, and every single one of them chose to cartwheel to their parents at the end of class, instead of walking to them.

"Hi, my sweet friends. Are we ready for class?" I ask, happy to see all three girls smiling.

"Yes! Can I tell you something?" Amanda asks, running up to tug on my hand. Her dark hair is braided back in twin braids, far neater than mine.

"Sure," I say, smiling at her as she threads our fingers together to pull me to the spring floor where we have our classes. Margot is quick to take my other hand, and Piper skips in front of us.

"I was showing Mommy what you taught us last week, but I accidentally broke the light," Amanda says, and I know it's not funny, but I've definitely broken my fair share of lamps before.

"And where are we supposed to do gymnastics?" I ask, and Piper turns around to walk backward.

"Outside or at the gym!"

God, it's hard to be upset when I'm with them. "Why?" I ask, causing Margot to laugh.

"Cause you don't want us to get hurt or in trouble for breaking things, Miss Mira."

"But what if we don't break anything because we're super careful?" Amanda asks, and I swing our hands.

"Well, that's why they're called accidents, but I don't want to see any of you get hurt, so lets stick to the rules," I advise as we approach the group of students laughing and running around the spring floor, excited chatter bouncing off the walls.

I wasn't expecting teaching gymnastics to children would bring me the joy I deserve to have in my life, but I'm grateful it does.

"Good morning! Everyone please line up so we can get started with our roll call," I call out, listening for the sounds of my kids running across the padded floors as I pull up the roster for today's class on my tablet. It doesn't change often—usually because my classes are full—due to them being free, especially compared to the rates of the other instructors who teach at this gym. I pay a monthly fee out of my pocket to rent the space for my classes each week. What good is it to have all this money if I don't use some for things like this?

I go down the list, each of the girls instructed to shout out their favorite color this week to account for who is here. There's an extra name at the end, and my brain pauses because it's a name I haven't seen before: *Henrietta*.

"Brown."

My head snaps up instinctively to see the owner of the voice, who is definitely not a six-year-old girl named Henrietta. Instead, I see my boyfriend for the first time in weeks, and I can't decide if I want to cry tears of joy or laugh until I can't breathe.

There's something about seeing your six foot two boyfriend, showcasing his tattooed muscles in a skintight tank top and pants exactly like the ones worn by male gymnasts in competitions. Henry still manages to pull it off, even if he looks a little ridiculous at the same time. When he makes up his mind, he's committed.

"Hi, Henrietta," I say, while my class erupts into giggles. This must have been what they were all laughing about on the way in.

Henry offers me a breathtaking smile, and my heart stops in my chest. *God, I'm so in love with him.*

Blair, one of the older girls in this class, raises her hand, attracting my attention. "Yes, Blair?" I ask, fighting the urge to stare at Henry.

"Is he your husband?" she asks, her smile wide. I can't help, but chuckle because that seems to be an inside joke between us. Despite his declaration in the interview with Erin, Henry and I are still not engaged, but he sure thinks it's funny to drop hints all the time. My favorite time was at the Panther's annual gala last November, when he knelt down on the red carpet outside the art museum, and then tied his shoe while smiling at me. Those pictures are still circulating everywhere.

Before I can answer, Henry is raising his own hand.

"Yes, Henrietta." I bite back my laugh at the name, and his hazel eyes refuse to leave mine.

"Blair, while I might not be her husband *yet*, I plan to be soon if she'll have me," he says, and I have to cover my mouth with my hand to hide my smile. *"N'ose pas cacher ton beau sourire maintenant que je suis là pour le voir en personne. Je ne te fais pas de demande en mariage aujourd'hui, mais je le ferai bientôt, je te le promets."*[1]

"What does that mean? When?" Blair asks, being as nosy as I want to be right now. I do listen to Henry, though, dropping my hand to smile at him.

He shrugs as if this isn't a huge deal at all. "Before the end of the year, but I think we should focus on what Miss Walker plans to teach us today."

Their enthusiasm brings my mind back to what I had planned for today—*the splits.*

---

1. Don't you dare hide your beautiful smile now that I'm here to see it in person. I'm not proposing to you today, but it will be soon, I promise.

Oh, this should be interesting.

"Now, I know last week many of you were excited to learn how to do a cartwheel, but I figured we would go with a skill this week that doesn't put your parents' furniture at risk. We're going to practice our splits, but first, we need to do lots of stretching so no one gets hurt today."

I resist the urge to laugh when Henry's face pales as I walk the girls through our stretching routine, adding more than normal. *He'll be fine.*

I'm helping Sienna correct her form so she doesn't pull a muscle when I hear a thump to my left. Henry's now sprawled on the ground next to a laughing Amanda and Piper. I move toward the chaotic pair, too busy laughing to see me coming.

"No, that's not how you do a cartwheel. You're supposed to hold your arms out like this, and then kind of just fall over," Amanda says, demonstrating a perfect example. She might have broken her mom's lamp, but you can tell she's practiced.

"I think I got the falling over part down," Henry jokes, sitting up.

"Yes, you do," I agree, smiling so hard my face hurts. "Are you okay?"

"Would you believe me if I said I fell to get your attention?"

"You know, I think I might. Too bad that fall won't end with us having matching scars," I point out, my fingers twitching as I resist the urge to wrap myself around him and never let go. Definitely not the time and place, though. *Keep it together, Mira.*

"Mira! Look, I did it!" Kennedy cheers from behind me, and I turn to see her right split executed flawlessly.

"Great job, that's awesome," I say, moving towards where Sienna is still trying to get the hang of it next to her. "You're so close, and I bet if you keep practicing, you'll get the hang of it," I say, ruffling Sienna's hair before offering Kennedy a high five.

The girls beam at me, but I notice their gaze shifts to look over my shoulder. The gentle grazing touch that dances along my lower back a moment later is familiar and *so wanted*, but not right now. I'm barely managing to keep my hands to myself.

"Miss Walker, I'm afraid I can't get the hang of my splits," Henry murmurs in my ear, sending goosebumps over every inch of my body. Phone calls are nothing compared to the real thing, and I've missed him so much.

"Or your cartwheel, Henrietta," I tease, tilting my head up to look at him. "That's okay. You can't be good at everything."

"Touché."

"Keep working on your cartwheel with the three musketeers over there," I instruct because I'm not going to be able to focus with him next to me. These girls deserve my full attention.

Henry salutes playfully. "Yes, Miss Walker."

I raise my eyebrows at him in disbelief, and he mouths *I love you,* making sure to follow it with a wink that sends the butterflies in my stomach fluttering.

I lean against the headboard of our bed, waiting for him to walk out of the bathroom in only a towel. This is one of my favorite things to do, and every time is as amazing as the time before.

With steam floating around him, Henry looks as if he's walked straight out of my dreams.

"Mon cœur, you're staring," his voice rumbles, and I grin, sitting on top of my hands. *I can last longer than a few*

minutes before jumping him. I'm actually a little surprised I didn't get into the shower with him.

"Duh. Have you seen yourself?"

Henry shakes his head, sending tiny droplets of water flying everywhere from his damp hair. "Unlike you, I don't spend nearly as much time in front of the mirror staring at myself."

"That's okay, I'll look enough for the both of us."

"I know you will, Mira. Were you wanting to stay in tonight or go out?" he asks, glancing at me in the mirror above his dresser while opening one of the drawers. I can tell from the faint shadows under his eyes he's tired, and if I'm honest, I don't want to share him with anyone tonight.

"Stay in. I was thinking I could make you dinner, go for a swim in the lake after, and maybe end the night, making out a bit while pretending to watch a movie?"

"That sounds perfect to me," Henry says, offering me a grateful smile.

Henry and I started looking for houses right around the time Wilson and Jason started seeing each other. We had paparazzi parked outside on the street constantly, and our neighbors were as sick of it as we were. Wilson offered to buy Henry's old house once we found this place, and while Henry has a longer commute to the stadium, the privacy we have is worth it. We're in a gated community with a security guard monitoring the front gate 24/7, and our house backs up to the lake. It's about as close as we can get to the ocean without driving three hours to visit either of our families.

"I bought a new book the other day, and I was thinking we could read it together, but if you're already in the middle of a different one, I'd be okay just sitting next to you," I say, watching as Henry rifles through his clothes. I'm secretly hoping he doesn't put much on.

"We can read the one you picked out. I finished mine on the drive earlier."

"You know it's a good thing you came back, because I was a little upset with you this morning. I feel like we've barely talked this week," I admit as Henry pulls out briefs and a pair of sweatpants, but I notice he doesn't grab a shirt.

"I didn't want to let it slip I was planning to come see you if I couldn't make it happen. I wasn't even sure until this morning, but I am sorry I fell asleep last night. Owen put us through the wringer yesterday, and then there was team bonding last night that wiped me out. I woke up with my phone on my chest, and your phone number dialed."

"I get it, it's fine. I'm sorry, I'm not trying to make you feel bad. It makes sense because you are terrible at keeping secrets," I say, and Henry laughs.

"Only from you, baby. You're the only one who can read me like an open book, but I'm more than happy to make it up to you," he says, and I lean forward, eager for my favorite part of his shower routine to happen. Henry drops his towel to the floor, giving me the perfect view of his toned ass as he steps into his briefs. *Henry's perfect.*

"I can think of one secret you've kept from me," I say, bringing up the topic we've been skirting around the last year and a half. Henry made it clear a proposal would happen, but I have no idea when. I've been getting my nails done every couple weeks just in case, though.

"Oh?" he asks, looking at me over his shoulder.

"You told my class you're going to propose this year."

Henry pulls up his sweatpants, the grey material contrasting nicely with the tan he's developed from being at training camp. "You lasted longer than I thought you would before bringing that up," Henry says, taking a seat next to me.

"You left your towel on the ground," I point out, my nerves

about this conversation getting the better of me. Despite every-thing with Bailey, things have been going so well between us. It doesn't make sense to be nervous, but I'd rather not get my hopes up for another moment like the one on the red carpet.

The corner of his mouth quirks up. "Do you really care about the towel, or are you deflecting?"

"I don't want to say the wrong thing and scare you," I admit slowly.

"I'm the one who told your entire class today I'm going to propose soon. We own a house together. There's a video clip with millions of views, watching me tell Erin I'm going to marry you. Between the two of us, I think I have the worse track record of saying the wrong thing."

"You haven't said anything wrong, Henry."

"Ask me why I said my favorite color today is brown."

What? Why on earth is he talking about that right now?

"Why is your favorite color brown?"

Henry's face softens as he gazes at me, his hand lifting to cup my cheek. *One touch, and I feel like I've been struck by a hundred lightning bolts.* "Because it's the color of your eyes. People think the only colors worth noticing are the more exotic ones like blue and green, but I love that yours are brown. I've never seen them the same shade twice, and it makes me want to memorize the hue every time I get lost in your eyes. In the sunlight, they appear golden, but when you're angry, they turn a molten bronze color. Sometimes, I swear I can see a ring of green near your iris, but it only ever happens when you're wearing green. *Brown is my favorite color because of you.*"

"*Henry.*" My voice is thick, and the next thing I know, Henry's pulling me into his lap to hold me. I wrap myself tightly around him, pressing a kiss to the bare skin on his collarbone. He smells like his body wash, and I'm not ashamed to admit I've used it once or twice in the last few weeks.

"Fuck, being away from you for that long almost killed me. I just need to hold you for a couple minutes," Henry whispers, pressing his nose into my hair and inhaling deeply. "I don't think I can do it again, *mon cœur*. You're the last thing I think about before falling asleep, the only one I dream about, and the first thing I think of in the morning. I think about you all the goddamn time, and I can't imagine ever feeling this way for anyone else. Love has never felt this way for me before, and you make me feel worthy of it. You are a part of me, whether you like it or not, Mirabelle Walker."

It's reassuring to know I'm not the only one who suffered during this. "I am so in love with you."

"I feel like there's worse problems to have," he jokes, laughing quietly, and in his arms, I feel like I can take a deep breath for the first time since leaving Henry at training camp.

"Right? Could you imagine having to eventually change your last name from Walker to Price? It's a tragedy," I say, wanting to see his smile.

"You better take that back," he warns.

"Never." I grin at him, acting as if I'm about to climb from his lap. To my delight, Henry flips me flat on my back, easily pinning me down with his body. *Yes.*

"Take it back, Mirabelle."

"What are you going to do about it?" I taunt, and Henry retaliates by dancing his fingers over my sides. Squealing, I try to get out from under Henry as he tickles me relentlessly.

"I c-can't breathe—" I choke out through fits of laughter. "Henry!"

"Do you give up?" Henry asks, stopping to lean in like he's going to kiss me. *Please.*

"Being Mirabelle Price doesn't sound so bad," I admit, my heart quickening in my chest at our position.

"Lucky for you, the to-do list I made has me taking your

last name. We have to follow the list to cross it off," Henry reminds me, and I brush a lock of his dark hair back into place.

"That might be the sexiest thing you've ever said to me."

"I can think of a few better things, but I guess it tracks with how much you like lists."

I do love a good list. My attention drifts to his full lips. "Do you know how much I missed you?" I ask, and Henry's eyes gleam.

Leaning down to capture my lips in a gentle kiss, Henry wordlessly tells me he does know, and it really doesn't get better than this.

I lose track of where I end and where Henry begins, accepting the reality that on the deepest level, we're connected, our souls intertwined on a cosmic level by threads of fate that will never be severed.